Praise for Beverly Swerling's Saga

City of Promise

A Novel of New York's Gilded Age

BEVERLY SWERLING

SIMON & SCHUSTER PAPERBACKS

New York London Toronto Sydney New Delhi

Simon & Schuster Paperbacks
A Division of Simon & Schuster, Inc.
1230 Avenue of the Americas
New York, NY 10020

First Simon & Schuster trade paperback edition August 2012

SIMON & SCHUSTER PAPERBACKS and colophon are registered trademarks of Simon & Schuster, Inc.

Map by Jason Snyder; based on map "The City of New York," Will L. Taylor, chief draughtsman (New York: Galt & Hoy, 1879. Library of Congress, Geography and Map Division). Accessed at hdl.loc.gov/loc.gmd/g3804n.pm005990.

For information about special discounts for bulk purchases, please contact Simon & Schuster Special Sales at 1-866-506-1949 or business@simonandschuster.com.

The Simon & Schuster Speakers Bureau can bring authors to your live event. For more information or to book an event, contact the Simon & Schuster Speakers Bureau at 1-866-248-3049 or visit our website at www.simonspeakers.com.

Designed by Jaime Putorti

Manufactured in the United States of America

10 9 8 7 6 5 4 3 2 1

The Library of Congress has cataloged the hardcover edition as follows:

Swerling, Beverly.
        City of promise : a novel of New York's Gilded Age / Beverly Swerling.
        p. cm.
        Sequel to: City of God.
        1. New York (N.Y.)—History—1865–1898—Fiction. 2. Manhattan (New York, N.Y.)—Fiction. I. Title.
        PS3619.W47C66 2011
        813'.6—dc22   2011010782

ISBN: 978-1-4391-3694-2
ISBN: 978-1-4391-3696-6 (pbk)
ISBN: 978-1-4391-5670-4 (ebook)

For Bill as always.

And for Michael, our forever darling boy, RIP.

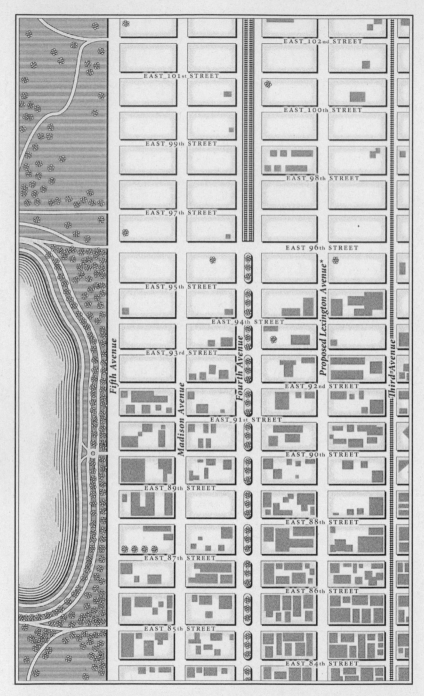

EAST_102nd_STREET

EAST_101st_STREET

EAST_100th_STREET

EAST_99th_STREET

EAST_98th_STREET

EAST_97th_STREET

EAST_96th_STREET

EAST_95th_STREET

EAST_94th_STREET

EAST_93rd_STREET

EAST_92nd_STREET

EAST_91st_STREET

EAST_90th_STREET

EAST_89th_STREET

EAST_88th_STREET

EAST_87th_STREET

EAST_86th_STREET

EAST_85th_STREET

EAST_84th_STREET

Fifth Avenue

Madison Avenue

Fourth Avenue

*Proposed Lexington Avenue**

Third Avenue

*Until the late 1880s, when it was widened to accommodate the subway, Lexington Avenue was a dirt track above Forty-Seventh Street.

City of Promise

Prologue

November 25, 1864

SUCH A CITY. Tumbling, raucous, never-to-be-forgotten New York.

Royal Lee detested it. He hated the town with almost as much passion as he had loved his wife and his babies and Birchfield, the South Carolina plantation that had been in his family since 1770.

All gone now. Raped, murdered, pillaged. Dead.

The Southerners met at the intersection of Prince Street and Broadway. Northeast corner, Royal had told them. Look for Niblo's Pleasure Garden. When they came together they were simply four fashionable gentlemen dressed in pale, slim trousers and black tight-waisted, knee-length coats and shiny black top hats. Royal, however, wore his grays underneath. The uniform added some bulk, hid how the war had ground him down, made him less than he was before. Inside and out.

The hustle and the hawking—newsboys, vendors of everything from pies to parrots—were as he remembered. So too the crowds. Everyone rushed from place to place; on foot or carried by horses and carriages and by omnibuses, known as horsecars, that could take thirty people behind a team of four. The traffic all seemed to go in every direction at the same time, everyone fighting for priority. It was always the same in this town. But these days New York was more than a crowded city; she was the financial engine that fueled Mr. Lincoln's war.

Royal and his companions kept their Southern tongues in their mouths and walked with the swagger and confidence bred into their class, as if they had every right to be where they were. Consequently, no one paid them any mind. A year before that would not have been the case. Merely looking as they did—like gentlemen—would have been enough to cause howling mobs to scream for their blood. In July of '63 New Yorkers had sacked their city; turning on themselves, eating their own flesh and gnawing their own bone. To Royal and the other Confederates the reason was obvious: a military draft from which a man could exempt himself if he had three hundred dollars was guaranteed to produce volcanic resistance. How, the South wondered, could the warmongering Union men, who claimed the right to hold those who would peaceably go, not understand so obvious a truth? Royal knew the answer. Because this was the world that had spawned them. Great masses of people and buildings, all crammed together breathing each other's stink, and nowhere a horizon to rest a man's eyes, or a whiff of green country to soothe his heart. That was their accustomed reality. Men who lived in such conditions were certain to develop a perverted understanding.

Cities such as New York were a Northern abomination. They invited the world's rabble to labor in their mills and factories and shops, then packed them into festering slums where violence was a contagion more virulent then lice, and they were left to make their own rules and govern themselves without the civilizing influence of their betters. Then the Union fools wondered at the consequences. It was, Royal knew, in the nature of rats to form packs and hunt prey. No plantation owner in the entire Confederacy would allow such conditions to prevail in his slave quarters, much less his villages and towns.

That moral superiority had not saved the Confederacy. This War of Northern Aggression was all but lost now. Everything the South held dearest, its entire way of life, was coming to an end. Mr. Lincoln's election to a second term had insured the war would continue until the Confederates were made to heel.

It was well known that the South had no good choices, and that desperate men do desperate things. Royal was aware of the surveillance of the pickets of the Seventh Regiment—once the 23rd Militia and under either name the city's military elite—who were posted at every intersection. The Union troops did not, however, eye the four with wariness. Apparently they perceived no threat from well-dressed men who wore their privilege with casual and accustomed ease.

Royal and his companions were officers of the Confederacy who had volunteered to do the most dangerous job in the military. They had become sappers, the men sent to harvest hell. Packages of Greek Fire, a mixture of phosphorus and bisulfide of carbon that ignited on contact with the air, were packed into their shiny boots and hidden in the sleeves of their fashionable jackets and stuffed beneath their fine linen shirts.

On the corner of Broadway and Ann Street, near P. T. Barnum's American Museum, the sappers parted company. Each carried in his head a list of targets. Royal's knowledge of the town where his wife had been born and raised, where her family still lived, had been particularly useful. He'd mapped out all the major hotels: the Astor House, the St. Nicholas, the Metropolitan, and nine others. He'd specified as well that they should aim to burn as many docks as they could manage, all fronting the Hudson River. Not, he assured himself, because the shipping business of his Devrey in-laws was concentrated on the East River shore. In his experience, he told the others, there was always a good wind blowing on the Hudson side. It would carry the flames up the island and finish the job the draft riots had started. With luck and the help of a just God they would burn New York City to the ground.

Every man for himself, they said. Meet up again across the border in Canada, they said. Royal looked away and murmured something that could be taken for assent.

Would he be doing this if Ceci and his babies were still alive? Royal Lee did not ask himself the question because he did not know the answer.

Book One

1864–1874

1

THE LAD RAN pell-mell into his office soon after dawn. Zac had slept in his clothes in a makeshift bed in the Devrey Building that housed his shipping business, nothing unusual in that these days. War changed a man's habits. "It's him, sir! I'm sure it's him!" Frankie struggled in the grip of the bigger and older man who had tried to stop his headlong rush.

Zac held up his hand and spoke first to the man, one of his clerks who did double duty as a night watchman. "I know the boy. It's all right, let him go."

The man took a step back. Frankie shook himself free, like a puppy let off the leash. He was, however, no puppy. Zac had long since spotted the boy's rapacious talents and nurtured them. "Who exactly? And why should I care?"

"It's the reb what you sent me to see those times 'bout a year ago. He's the one they caught. Got him down by City Hall now. Got a stake fixed and everything. Gonna burn him the way he done the town. Thought you'd want to know.'"

Jesus God Almighty.

Zac stood up and pushed past the boy and started running. Through the counting room that occupied the ground floor of the grand white marble building that represented two hundred years of the wealth of nations brought to New York under Devrey sail, and of late, Devrey steam; out to the street, ignoring Frankie chasing after him with hand held out for the coins that were his due for bringing word. He paused only long enough to unhitch the nearest horse. Not his, but that didn't matter. Not the empty-handed urchin either, though he felt bad about that. Never mind. He'd deal with such things later. They could be fixed with money. If his brother-in-law, who was also his oldest friend, was burned alive by a rampaging mob, that was a thing as admitted no possibility of repair.

The heavens opened while Zac whipped the horse down Broadway, weaving his way between the carriages and the horsecars that moved like sludge, trapped in their own conflicting wakes. Even after such a night as it had been. Even with a riotous crowd baying in the streets. Even with the acrid stench of dozens of major fires still hanging in the air—beaten out mostly in the nick of time, though word was the damage would cost millions—even so. Nothing could tame the New York City traffic.

Worse when the weather turned bad. Always.

Finally, City Hall Park, and Zac hatless and coatless, and uncaring that the cold of the November dawn was made worse by slashing rain. The downpour was a mercy of sorts. Meant they couldn't burn him. Not that a rope was any less effective. Either way, he'd been too late and Royal was dead, the loss permanent and irreparable.

The tips of his brother-in-law's boots were level with his eyes. Motionless now. By Zac's calculations it was some minutes since the rope around Royal Lee's neck had snapped taut. Enough time for the tall body clad in Confederate gray to stop swinging.

God damn this war to everlasting hell.

The rain was letting up some, but Zac was already soaked to the skin.

His glance was pulled from the toes of his dead brother-in-law's boots to a much younger man standing some twenty feet away. Drawn in that direction perhaps because the other man was looking at him. Recognition came all at once, with no doubt, though it had been three years. "Joshua?" Zac spoke aloud, though his half brother was surely too far away to hear.

The pair began maneuvering their way toward each other—Josh, it seemed to Zac, carried by the throng, half stumbling as the two narrowed the space between them.

How thin Josh was. The planes of his face seemed only bone covered by skin, nothing substantial enough to be named flesh. Taller than the boy he'd been when, barely sixteen—headstrong, foolish, and determined—he enlisted in the First Mounted Rifles without asking leave of his parents or anyone else. Uncaring that men of their class were officers, or stayed home to tend the business that paid for war. Joshua Turner went his own way, and even back then the family knew there was no coming between him and what he wanted. Eighteen now. And alive. Thank God Almighty.

"Josh!" The space separating them, filled as it was with strangers, narrowed enough for Zac to know he could be heard. "Josh! It's you, isn't it? God be praised. It's you."

"It's me, Zac."

They were near enough to touch. Zac reached out his hand. A woman abruptly shoved her way between them, ignoring both and looking up at the dangling corpse. She moved in and began hauling on Royal's left boot. The gesture set off a swirl of similar scavenging. The brothers hesitated for a moment, each knowing there was no hope of stopping this next desecration. They moved aside.

"I didn't get here in time," Josh said.

"Nor did I," Zac said. "But I suspect there was nothing we could have done."

"If I'd been in time, I might have been able to get him away," Josh insisted. "Spirited him out of here."

Zac's thought as he had thundered south along the Manhattan streets was to use the authority of Devrey Shipping to demand imprisonment, and a judge, and a proper trial. No doubt an insane hope in the face of hatred fed by years of carnage. As absurd as Joshua thinking he could have contrived a secret escape through the city's narrow alleys and close-packed doorways. Zac shook his head. "Unlikely."

He opened his mouth to say more, but shock stopped the words. The crowd had fallen sufficiently away for him to see his brother whole. Joshua had marched off to war on two strong legs. He'd come home walking with a stick, and only air below his right knee.

It was in 1845 that Dr. Nicholas Turner built Sunshine Hill for Carolina Devrey, the love of his life and pregnant with his child, though she was not his wife. In those days what was officially Seventy-First Street and First Avenue was still much as old Peter Minuit had found it some two hundred and fifty years before, when he weaseled Manhattan from the Canarsie Indians: steep hills and rushing streams and heavily wooded glades and glens, and bobcats still to be found prowling the cliffs above the East River. These days over half of the city's population of nearly a million lived north of Fourteenth Street, and stretched itself as far as the small Fifties. Carolina and Nick had long been married. Respectable enough, so before the war, in his Princeton years, Carolina's eldest son did not hesitate to bring home his friend Royal Lee from Virginia.

"A slaveholder, Zac," Carolina, whose abolitionist sympathies were well known, had said with distaste.

"Do not," Nick cautioned her, "bring into our home the discontent that rules everywhere outside it. All Zac's friends should be welcome here."

That Royal might be smitten by Ceci as soon as he saw her was something none of them anticipated. When Ceci wanted to marry him, her mother and her stepfather let their feelings be known, but reconciled themselves to what they couldn't change.

Life had taught Carolina to be grateful for whatever blessings came her way. That night, when Zac brought home her second son minus one of his legs and the story of Royal Lee's hanging, Carolina wrapped her arms around both her boys and did not forget to count her blessings, though her heart ached with her daughter's sadness. Southerner Royal may have been, and entirely wrong on the matter of Negroes, but Ceci had loved him and borne him three children.

They must bring Ceci and her babies home to Sunshine Hill, Carolina told Nick later that night. Get them right away from Virginia and here to New York where they could be looked after.

Nick's mind was more on the need to look after Josh's rough wound—done, Nick was sure, by no proper surgeon—and see it healed clean. And on afterward, on how they could insure a future for Josh that would not be diminished by the loss of a leg. It wasn't that Nick didn't love his stepdaughter, only that just now she was outside the range of his ability to be of use. He refrained from pointing out that they had not heard from Ceci in many months. Instead he said, "I can't see how we could bring her here, my dear. Not until after the war."

"I shall speak to Zac," Carolina said. "He has kept some lines of communication open, I know. Zac may find a way."

The notion was never put to the test. Royal's letter arrived a week later. It was addressed to Zachary, his dear brother-in-law and friend as Royal called him. Sent from Canada by a Confederate comrade. "One of the sappers who was with him, I'd wager," Zac said, speaking to the entire family gathered in the library at his behest, looking at him now, waiting.

"You think Royal really did help to set those fires?" Nick's way always to believe the best of everyone. His private explanation for Royal's presence in the city was something to do with Zac. Carolina was right about Zac having kept some channels open. He and Royal had,

Nick knew, occasionally met secretly, looking to lay groundwork for reconciliation at war's end. "I can't believe Royal would—"

"He did it." Zac's tone was without emotion but allowed for no disagreement. "And he meant the city to burn to the ground."

"And himself to die in the bargain," Josh added. "Otherwise he'd never have worn his grays under those civilian clothes."

"Perhaps for the shame of it," Carolina murmured. "Not for pride."

"Neither," Josh said, moving closer to her side. "I think Royal had taken as much as he could, and didn't care much about the consequences."

Carolina drew a sharp inward breath. Her mind was leaping ahead the way it inevitably did. (Too clever for her own good. For any woman's good. She'd heard that plenty of times.)

Josh took her hand. She gave up the foolish hope that she was wrong. "General Sherman," she whispered. "I thought . . . According to the newspapers his route didn't go through southern Virginia. Not through Clarksville or anywhere near Birchfield."

"There were others," Josh said quietly. "Rogue bands of blues who went off marauding on their own."

Nick felt the anger rising in him, the bitterness. "I told them. All those shortsighted Washington men, the generals. Even Mr. Lincoln himself. You can't involve civilian populations without unleashing the worst inside any man, particularly in wartime." Sherman's march, he'd said, the policy of scorched earth, would give them all tacit leave to wreak havoc. No one listened. It was Dr. Turner's celebrated medical skills the government prized, not his opinions on how to make war.

Zac unfolded the letter and cleared his throat. Josh waited, knowing what was coming because he'd been told. Zac had gone to Josh with the dreadful news first. There were twelve years between the brothers but that moment they'd shared standing beneath Royal's corpse had made them conspirators of a sort, contriving to make it easier on the others. No matter now.

Nonetheless, the others seemed to know without being actually told. Even young Simon who was sitting at his mother's feet, leaning against her knees. He was letting her stroke his hair; content for once to be her baby, though he was fourteen. And sixteen-year-old Goldie, perched on the arm of Papa's chair with her embroidery hoop in her hand. She had not taken a stitch in many minutes.

"My dear brother-in-law and friend," Zac read. "Much as I hope for the success of our mission to burn New York to the ground, I also pray God that you and yours will somehow survive whatever turmoil we unleash. Not, I assure you, because it gives me any kind of perverse pleasure to tell you the terrible news that I have lost my darling wife and my precious three babies to the bayonets of Union soldiers . . ."

2

IT WAS THE quality in her coming out through the needle. Each time Auntie Eileen inspected a piece of Mollie's newly finished embroidery that's what she said. "And," she inevitably added, "I know quality when I see it." Usually by then Eileen Brannigan would have spread the bit of lawn or cambric over her knee in order to inspect the tiny stitches that blossomed into an exquisitely formed flower or bird.

On this occasion, with a log fire crackling brightly in her private sitting room and a winter snowstorm whitening the early December world beyond her windows, it wasn't needlework Eileen was inspecting. She had her hand beneath her niece's chin, tipping Mollie's face to the gaslight so she could see it more clearly. "I know quality," she said, studying the blue eyes surrounded by tangled dark lashes, and the cheeks that didn't need pinching to be stained pink. "You're not a great beauty, Mollie my love," this while she pushed back a black curl escaped from the ribbon that tied the rest into place. "Your face is a bit too thin and sharp, and the rest of you is far too straight and angled to gain a man's instant approval. You take some time to appreciate, no denying that. But for any as have eyes to see, the quality in you jumps straight out. She did that much for you, did Brigid Brannigan, for all her foolish willingness to have a bit of fun with never a thought for what would happen next."

This assessment of her origins was a story Mollie had heard repeatedly. Auntie Eileen had for a brief time been married to Brian Brannigan, the brother of Mollie's mother. Just long enough, Eileen said, to cross with Brian and Brigid from the Old Country to the New. And for Eileen to be the one who buried them both within a year of stepping onto the pier at Castle Garden.

Brian was taken by the yellowing fever, and his sister by the fever that all too often followed childbirth. Leaving on their own Eileen and the month-old infant Brigid had insisted on naming Mollie, though Eileen would have preferred something a bit more elegant and a bit less Irish. "I could have changed it since you were so young," Eileen always said, "but it did not seem right. She loved you, Mollie, empty-headed though she was. Poor little fool fell into it on the boat. Put paid to all the grand plans to find her a husband in New York once we got ourselves settled. Though from the way you cooked up there's never been a doubt in my mind that she spread her legs for one of the gentry. Someone from the first-class cabins on the upper decks most likely. Not," she invariably added, "that Brigid shared my ability to discern quality. She was simply, on that occasion, lucky."

Mollie thought it a strange kind of luck, but she never said so. As for her own good fortune, Mollie reckoned it had little to do with her nameless father. It was the fact that Eileen Brannigan had assumed responsibility for the child who was a niece by marriage, not even her own flesh and blood, that first kept Mollie alive, then spared her the horror of growing up in some depraved Five Points rat-infested hovel with the rest of the drunken, brawling, dirt-poor Irish who poured into the city looking for a dream and finding a nightmare.

Eileen released her hold on her niece's chin. "Put a fresh log on the fire, Mollie, while I pour us another cup of tea. Then we'll get down to business."

The pleats of the pink petticoat that showed beneath Mollie's rose-colored taffeta day dress made a soft rustling sound when she moved, and when she added the log her aunt had requested the fire roared up and filled the room with the rich scent of applewood. Eileen Brannigan would burn nothing cheaper. "Applewood," she said, "is quality. And for all everyone's busy switching to heat provided by a coal furnace in the cellar, such a thing will never bring the comfort of a fire."

Which was not to say that Eileen Brannigan was profligate. She paid rigorous attention to every penny spent or earned, and relied on her niece to record both. The girl's ability to do quick and perfect mathematics, frequently in her head, had been manifest by the time she was eleven. Eileen promptly put her niece in charge of the financial records. Good bookkeeping, she said, was the very foundation of good business. One reason, Eileen maintained, she owned this elegant three-story brownstone on the corner of University Place and Eleventh Street.

Which, by cleverness and will, and what she called her instinct for quality, she had turned into the best whorehouse in the city.

Eileen never bothered to say parlor house, much less brothel. Quality, according to her, had no need to hide behind euphemisms. Her competition—in as far as she conceded she had any—was simply not in the same league. There were other houses in respectable residential areas, a great many of them, and many that like Mrs. Brannigan's catered to the finest sorts of gentleman. The so-called Seven Sisters on West Twenty-Fifth Street—threaded between fashionable houses like jewels in a necklace—sent engraved invitations to famous men whose arrival in the city was announced in the press. Their callers were required to wear evening dress, and the ladies who received them were gowned and bejeweled as grandly as any woman in the city. Eileen aspired to nothing so formal. Ostentatious, she called it. What set Brannigan's apart was that it was truly a home from home.

The most influential and the wealthiest men of New York City came to Mrs. Brannigan's not simply because they required a place to put their peckers. Though Lord knows such men needed a bit of relief from the cares that weighed so heavily these days, what with the war raging and fortunes to be made if one danced to the right tune. The high-stakes game such men played demanded at the very least relief from the weight between their legs and the burdens on their backs. Eileen was the first to say so. And given that their wives were frequently confined for many months awaiting the birth of a child, or sequestered for many more after the ordeal ended, likely as not they couldn't get what they needed at home. They could, however, find it on pretty much any city block, and for a tenth the price Eileen Brannigan charged. Even houses deemed expensive, where they offered a variety of experiences—small boys, or women in multicolored assortments, or everything done up to make you believe you were in an Oriental seraglio—even such places as those didn't command Eileen's prices.

The fantasy Eileen Brannigan catered to was the one in a man's most hidden heart: That a woman who looked and sounded and acted like the demure and chaste creature he thought he'd married would, once they were in the bedroom, behave as the willing, even lusty, companion of his most secret imagining. Such a woman was not only capable of making a man believe himself to be a god, she showed herself worthy to make the judgment. That was a pleasure so heady, supplying it meant Eileen Brannigan could name her price and get it.

Add to that the one-client-per-evening rule that prevailed at Brannigan's, and the house became as desirable for the women who worked there as for the men who patronized it. Eileen blessed the day she had thought up the scheme and found the courage to try it. But however successful, it was not a solution to the problem that faced her just then, with the applewood fire burning brightly and her niece sitting with her sewing on her lap, waiting to hear what her aunt had to say.

"Your birthday is next week, Mollie. You will be eighteen."

"I know." While threading a needle and rolling the end into a knot between her thumb and forefinger.

"You are," Eileen said, "approaching twenty. And twenty is spinsterhood. I do not believe, dear child, that is what you want."

"It's not." A home of her own and babies were what Mollie wanted. Meaning she had to have a husband. Faithful, mind you. Not someone who'd go running off to Brannigan's or a lesser establishment at the first opportunity. But definitely a husband. "I wish," Mollie said, "to be married. But only to the right sort of man."

"Well," Eileen said, "given the circumstances, that is not a simple thing to find. You must face facts, Mollie. You are a bastard and you've been raised in a whorehouse. It was never going to be easy."

Mollie kept her eyes on her needlework, but her heart rose and sank, then rose again. It didn't seem likely her aunt would have raised the subject if she didn't have a prospect in mind. On the other hand, they had circled the topic any number of times in the past year. The issue was never resolved and the dream of herself as a bride and eventually a mother seemed unlikely to be fulfilled.

"I've had an offer," Eileen said. "The question is whether you will entertain the idea."

Mollie had been about to take a stitch. She stopped with the needle hovering in midair.

"Max Merkel," Eileen said.

A few seconds went by. Mollie did not speak.

"He's considerably older than we might have wished," Eileen conceded. "But his breweries are very successful. And—"

"Mr. Merkel became a widower last year, didn't he?" Mollie was not particularly interested in her suitor's breweries. She had a vague notion he had two, possibly three, but that he could afford to visit Brannigan's as often as twice a week said everything necessary about his financial status. "And his wife had been ill for a long time before that. That's correct, isn't it?"

"On death's door for at least five years," Eileen said eagerly. She'd been afraid Merkel's age and his unfashionable black beard and his paunch would put Mollie off. As it was the girl was only raising her usual objection—that she could not see any point in marrying a man who had already proved himself incapable of fidelity. "Possibly six or seven years," Eileen added. "No man could be expected to live like a monk for all that time, could he?"

Mollie had lapsed back into silence. After a few moments she began to sew.

"Well?" Eileen demanded.

"I will talk to him."

The meeting—only herself and Mr. Merkel, Mollie insisted—took place on a Sunday night. Since Brannigan's was always closed on the Sabbath the downstairs reception rooms were empty, but Mollie refused to discuss Max Merkel's suit in the rooms where he met his whores. Since it was winter, the postage-stamp garden behind the house was out of the question. Needless to say, her bedroom under the rafters was the least suitable place of all. Eileen's private sitting room was the only venue possible.

"Very nice in here," Merkel said, cocking his head to examine the ornate plaster ceiling, and take in the flocked, cream-colored wallpaper. "A lady's private chamber. Very nice."

"Where do you live, Mr. Merkel?"

"Please, call me Max. And across the river I live, in Brooklyn. Near my first brewery. Which I opened when I came from Munich. Thirty years ago now. I may call you Mollie?"

"Yes, if you like." If he'd opened a brewery thirty years ago he had to be closer to fifty than forty as they'd first thought. "Do you have children, Max?"

"Two. Nine and eleven. With their auntie they live. In Boston. For some years now. When my wife became ill her sister took them. They are settled. I am not right away thinking of bringing them home. A new wife first is necessary."

Well, no bones made about that. Not that she minded. As long as she could have babies of her own she'd be happy enough to mother two others. It wasn't, after all, unlike what Auntie Eileen had done for her, though she suspected not getting stepchildren in their infancy would make things more difficult. "Yes," she said, "of course."

Mollie was in her aunt's usual place, sitting in an armchair upholstered in crewelwork Mollie had done some years earlier, apples and pears and lots of green leaves. Merkel was on the green-and-white-striped sofa near the fireplace. He patted the place beside him. "Come, Mollie. Sit next to me. Let us get to know each other a little better."

It was a reasonable request. Mollie got up and sat beside him, though she positioned herself at the opposite end of the sofa and hung on to the arm, rather as if she thought he might try to yank her closer. Merkel chose an entirely different maneuver. He scrambled across the cushions and came to rest with his thick thigh a scant inch away from the voluminous skirt of the dark red frock she had chosen for the occasion.

Max Merkel smelled of beer, but not as strongly as she had feared. She could get used to it, she told herself. And when he leaned over and kissed her cheek she determined she could learn to tolerate the scratchiness of his beard and his mutton-chop sideburns.

The kiss was over very quickly. "You are blushing," he said when he drew back. "So, in a place like this you grow up and you can still blush. That is good."

"As you say, Mr. Merkel, I grew up here. I do not work here."

Merkel roared with laughter. "Spunk," he said. "I like that in a woman. So, Mollie, shall we be engaged?"

She wasn't entirely ready. However much she wanted to be. "I am prepared to consider it, Mr. Merkel. That's all I can say at this time."

Mollie spent the next two days thinking not of Max Merkel but of wedding finery. White had become fashionable for brides since Queen Victoria chose white satin when she married Prince Albert in 1840.

But white, Mollie thought, did not flatter her. Blush pink perhaps, or even a slightly darker shade. And she could embroider the skirt with roses and pick out their edges in tiny seed pearls. Not real of course, such extravagance was the prerogative of the daughters of millionaires being married from Fifth Avenue mansions.

As for what might happen after the wedding—not in the bedroom, she could hardly avoid knowing all there was to know about that— but in the day-by-day life as the wife of a Brooklyn brewer more than twice her age . . . Mollie could not imagine that it would be anything but rather dull and boring. Never mind that, she told herself. Concentrate on the babies. There were sure to be babies. Because, in the normal way of things, it took considerable effort to prevent them.

She had heard her aunt's instructions on numerous occasions. They involved inserting various herbal potions before and flushing with warm water after. There were screened areas in each bedroom, and behind the screens basins and pitchers of water and a small tub to squat over while one performed the ablutions. "I've made it as easy as I can," Eileen informed her ladies. "Now it's up to you to take advantage." Each woman knew that if she was not scrupulously careful it was the end of working at Brannigan's.

Mollie was never home when one of them was screaming herself clean of a bastard. On the days such events were scheduled Auntie Eileen inevitably sent Mollie off to shop or do whatever else might amuse her. Though afterward Mollie would know which it had been, because a week later the woman would be gone. "I don't put one of mine on the street because she was stupid enough or unlucky enough to get in the family way," Eileen Brannigan always said. "And I will pay to have her done with it, if that's what she wants. But after that, she no longer shines. She has lost the special something, the quality. And it's the quality makes a man of stature put down sixty dollars for an evening's pleasure. I know quality. That's why they come to me. The women and the men alike."

The women came as well because Eileen's rules concerning pregnancy were, for all their strictness, a protection of sorts. These days, with every abortionist in the city hounded by such things as Mr. Comstock's Society for the Suppression of Vice, it was not a simple matter to arrange the procedure. But Eileen Brannigan always managed. And the abortionists she brought in were competent. Mostly women exercising a skill that had been passed down through generations. Other medical needs were the province of men, proper doctors. Eileen had tamed a few of those to her needs as well.

It went without saying that the women at Mrs. Brannigan's would not give a man the French disease. "A bath once every three days," Eileen insisted. "And in the morning when your client leaves, you must wash between your legs with carbolic soap. And do the same every evening before the gentlemen arrive." But just to be sure, Eileen had a doctor come once a month and inspect each and every employee for signs of infection.

Mollie wasn't entirely sure what the doctor did because she had never been in the room when he did it; but the physician's visits to the house had been a regular part of Mollie's life for as long as she could remember. She was, however, surprised when three days after Max Merkel's visit her aunt interrupted her reverie about seed pearls and embroidered roses to say that Dr. Steinfeldt would be arriving shortly.

"Is someone ill?" Dr. Steinfeldt lived some ways to the east, in the neighborhood below Fourteenth Street known as Kleindeutschland, and his regular visits to University Place were scheduled for Thursday afternoons, not Wednesday.

"No. He is coming to see you."

"Me? Heavens, why? I'm perfectly healthy." Mollie reached up to pinch her cheeks, thinking perhaps the winter cold had drained them of color. "Really, Auntie Eileen, I feel quite well."

"I know."

"Then why—"

"Mr. Merkel has requested it."

Mollie's mouth opened, but it took a few moments before she said,

"He wants me checked over. Like . . . Like a man buying a horse. That's what you're saying, isn't it?"

"No," Eileen spoke so softly it was hard for Mollie to hear her words. "Not exactly. Mr. Merkel wishes to be assured that you are . . ."

The very fact that she couldn't say the words told Mollie what they were. She had heard the phrase *virgo intacta* from one of the women who, before coming to work for Eileen Brannigan, had been a student at the Female Medical College in Philadelphia. The woman had decided she could not bear the aromas of that profession, and wished for reasons of her own not to return to her parental home, so she had knocked one afternoon on the door of the house on University Place and assured Auntie Eileen she need have no qualms about employing her. "I'm not *virgo intacta*," she had said. "My virtue is already compromised. You need have no qualms about that."

Mr. Merkel apparently did have qualms. "He thinks," Mollie said, "that I'm . . . compromised."

"Only that you might be," Eileen said, adding quickly, "It's not entirely surprising, Mollie. I mean given all this." She waved a hand to indicate their entire small and exceptional world.

"But I told him. I said I lived here but I didn't work here."

"I told him as well. Of course I did, but he—"

"Mr. Merkel does not believe us," Mollie said. "That's what it comes down to. He wants to be my husband, entrust me with the care of his children, but he believes both you and me to be flat-out liars."

"Yes," Eileen agreed, knowing from the look on her niece's face that Merkel's suit had been decided, and not in his favor. "I suppose that's not putting too fine a point on it."

"Tell him," Mollie said, "not to trouble himself. The matter is no longer his concern." Then, reaching for a piece of her aunt's thick-as-cream Tiffany stationery, "Never mind, I shall tell him myself."

It was one of those moments when Eileen Brannigan was most proud of herself for having mustered the influence required to enroll the girl in Miss Lucy Green's fashionable Fifth Avenue school, despite the objections of the headmistress to having among her students a child living in a whorehouse. Miss Green's had not simply taught Mollie to read and write; the school had put the final polish on her. Mollie was a lady.

Eileen wanted a husband for her niece; her plan had never been to offer the girl as an unpaid housekeeper and captive whore. And Mollie was right: Max Merkel had shown himself nowhere near good enough.

Eileen had small plump hands, and a love for jewelry that made her wear a ring on six of her ten fingers, and five of them fair-size diamonds (which like her writing paper always came from Tiffany's). A month after what Mollie had come to think of as "the Merkel affair," she was watching her aunt's bejeweled fingers smooth a square of gossamer on which Mollie had embroidered—freehand, making it up as she went along—a swan riding the crest of a wave. As usual, though the fabric was exceedingly sheer, there was nowhere a pucker or a stitch out of line. "It's exquisite, Mollie," Eileen said. "But what's it for?"

"I'm not sure. Can Mrs. Mullaney make a wrapper around it?"

Mrs. Mullaney was the new dressmaker. She came once a week to Brannigan's since Rosie O'Toole, who was Auntie Eileen's good friend, went off to become manageress of the new fitting and alterations department at Macy's dry goods store at Sixth Avenue and Eighth Street.

Eileen had no difficulty finding a replacement to come once a week with finished gowns for some of the ladies, and bolts of fabric to drape around others in a revolving chain of lucrative custom. The women sometimes complained at the expense, but Eileen would brook no other arrangement. She had the final say on each and every frock, and no interest in the current trend toward ready-to-wear. Why should she when her way of doing things was a source of additional profit?

Rosie O'Toole had paid Eileen Brannigan ten cents on every dollar the Brannigan's ladies paid her. When she hired Mrs. Mullaney, Eileen set her commission at twelve. "An essential change," Eileen had told her niece. "The war," she'd added with a sigh.

Mollie wasn't sure how the cost of keeping the South in the Union added to her aunt's expenses and justified raised rates. Indeed, exactly the opposite seemed to be the case. A thing Mollie knew because she always read the newspapers the gentlemen left behind. Hatty Ellis, who had been Brannigan's cook from the day the house opened, never threw them on the kitchen fire until after Mollie looked at them. She therefore understood that though New York had come reluctant to the battle—not good for the economy, the men of the city said—once war was handed to her, the city made the most of it.

New York business was booming, and it was inevitable that good business among the wealthiest and most influential men of the city meant better business at Brannigan's. Now, more than ever, Eileen ruled all things beneath her roof and no detail was too small to escape her notice.

The women were allowed only certain scents—Hungary Water and Jameson's Attar of Roses were approved, but not Trezise's Tincture of Devon Violets—and cabbage was banished from the kitchen because the odor lingered after it was cooked. Gowns must never be black—too mournful or too sophisticated depending on the cut—and jewelry kept to a minimum since the men were to think they had come to their own home, not a salon, when they visited Mrs. Brannigan's. Never a bonnet for the same reason, though a fancy comb was sometimes permitted. No professional musicians ever, though on occasion one of the women might play a piano selection. With such attention to minutiae, no question but what Eileen's writ ran to the destiny of each piece of needlework done by her niece.

"Not a wrapper, no," Eileen pronounced, setting aside the gossamer swan. "I shall have a frame made and hang it in my room. Above my bed, with all the other most prized examples of your artistry."

Mollie did not object. Eileen had long since proven herself devoted to her niece's well-being.

The childbed fever that carried off Brigid Brannigan when Mollie was a month old had dried up her milk a few days after the child was born. It was Eileen who took the starving infant to Sadie Jones. Sadie

was the most fashionable wet nurse in the city; her tits were her fortune. She did not take them out of her dress for free. So, Sadie asked,
how was a greenie like Eileen Brannigan, widowed and lumbered with
a newborn not even her own, planning to pay for the use of them?
"With your twat I expect," she said before Eileen could answer. "Like
most of the rest of your kind. It's what you Irish are good at. But you'll
have to wear your cunny out if you mean it to support you and this
mite both." Dandling the baby on her knee all the while. And Mollie,
as Auntie Eileen told the story, screaming with hunger but not being
given a look or a nip at those famous tits.

"I will keep my legs crossed and my purse open, you can be sure
of that," Eileen reported saying. "Now give that poor child suck or I'll
tell everyone in the city you tried and failed and your day is past. Not
a drop left and here's the starving babe to prove it."

Not just the words undid Sadie's wrapper in Eileen's version of the
tale. "I put a solid gold five-dollar coin in her hand at the same time.
And she took one of those massive pappes out of her gown and you
latched on and drank as if you were perishing with hunger, as indeed
you were. Poor little love."

For years Mollie wondered where the gold coin came from, since
to hear Auntie Eileen's stories they were poor as church mice that initial year in New York when first her husband and then her sister-in-
law died and Mollie was born.

The older she got the more Mollie puzzled over that small mystery,
along with wondering how, by the time she was five, her aunt had been
able to buy a house and go into the business that afterward supported
them so well. "Tell me the Sadie Jones story, please, Auntie Eileen,"
Mollie would frequently say. Her aunt always obliged, but each time
the tale ended with the wet nurse capitulating and Mollie being saved
from a hungry death. The gold coin was never explained, and on the
few occasions Mollie tried to probe, Eileen always looked like thunder
and abruptly changed the subject.

She didn't hear the rest of the story until the winter she was twelve, when Hatty climbed up to Mollie's attic bedroom before dawn and shook her awake. "You come with me, Miss Mollie. Your auntie needs you." Hatty brought a still groggy Mollie to stand beside Eileen's bed and pulled the quilts aside. "You hop right in there, Miss Mollie. And snuggle up."

"It's not her concern, Hatty. There's no cause for Mollie to—"

"Just you hush. And you hang on to that girl so you remember what you've done, and what's important in this world and what is not. Now I'm going to make you both some breakfast, and I expect you to be your spit-and-damn-'em regular self when I bring it."

At first "hang on" was all Eileen did, wrapping her arms around Mollie and pulling her close, keeping her cheek pressed to Mollie's hair, but eventually humming a little song under her breath. And soon enough their toes were toasting near the fire Hatty had made in the sitting room, and they were eating eggs and bacon and Hatty's cornmeal mush, rich with butter and cream, and Eileen was indeed her spit-and-damn-'em regular self.

That was such a remarkable transformation that when her aunt said, "Time to tell you about that five-dollar gold coin, Mollie my love," Mollie wasn't entirely surprised to find the old mystery linked to whatever had so troubled her aunt that morning.

"I was an Armagh O'Halloran before I married Brian Brannigan," Eileen said. "And that was the start of it."

Armagh, Mollie knew, was a place in Ireland. And O'Halloran was Auntie Eileen's maiden name. She nibbled a piece of bacon and waited for the rest of the story.

"Armagh," Eileen said, "is in Ulster, and it's where St. Patrick began preaching Christianity to the heathen Irish as they were then. It's also where the O'Hallorans developed their art. And mind you, Mollie, dipping is an art. At least the way the O'Hallorans do it."

"Dipping?"

"Dipping," Eileen repeated. "And it doesn't seem possible to be raised in this house and be as much an innocent as you are. I'm not sure I've done you any favors, Mollie. Well, time you learned. Dip-ping," she said again, "especially if you're an Armagh O'Halloran, is removing a person's property without their ever knowing you've done it. Not a hint or a whisper. Never. Done to perfection, or not done by an O'Halloran from Armagh."

"Picking pockets," Mollie said, eyes wide as the reality became clear. "That's what you mean. Like Oliver Twist in Mr. Dickens's book."

"Not like Oliver Twist at all," Eileen corrected, nodding toward the shelves that housed the books and magazines that fed her niece's imagination. "I learned the art from my parents, and they from theirs, and we didn't live in any filthy hovel I promise you. We had a grand house in Armagh and went to Dublin or even London for a few weeks every season, and dipped enough to keep us until the next excursion. It was a fine life. But then I met your Uncle Brian, who could dip a bit as well, but never as artfully as I, and we decided to leave the old ways behind and come to New York and make our fortune here. With his little sister, of course, since Brian was Brigid's only relative and he couldn't leave her behind." Eileen leaned over and poured them both another cup of tea. "And you know all that happened after that."

"I suppose I do now," Mollie said thoughtfully. "That's how you got the gold coin, isn't it? The one you gave Sadie Jones so she'd let me nurse. You dipped it."

"I did."

Mollie was beginning to recognize the power of the key she'd been given. "And because you're an O'Halloran, you dipped enough to buy this house and start the business."

Eileen nodded. "I did," she admitted a second time. "But things are seldom as easy as they might be, Mollie. However careful one tries to be about remaining in the good graces of those who matter most."

A certain stiffness came over Auntie Eileen then. It was the closest she ever came to tears, that way of setting her chin and her shoulders. She took an exquisitely monogrammed handkerchief—embroidered by Mollie two Christmases past—from the pocket of her woolen wrapper and dabbed at her eyes and her cheeks. As if she had been crying, though she had not. "Never forget," she said, repeating a rule she had pronounced numerous times before, "the authorities must be dealt with. No different in New York than in Dublin or Armagh or even London. I grew up knowing that. I have never begrudged Boss Tweed's people their fair share, Mollie. You know that."

She did know it. Seven hundred dollars went to Tammany Hall each month and was entered in the ledger under the heading of charity. "Auntie Eileen, are you saying Boss Tweed should have—"

Eileen raised her hand to forestall the question. "I am a realistic woman, Mollie. I believe in looking after those who can look after you. Don't be greedy and in the normal way of things you will be permitted to go peacefully about your business." Eileen was now furiously patting her cheeks with the embroidered handkerchief. "But Theodore Paisley," her voice began to spiral upward though she did not, of course, shout since shouting was forbidden at Brannigan's, "is not in the normal way of things. He's a Protestant Ulsterman from a long line of them in Belfast. As is the horrid Mr. E. L. Godkin. Apparently Boss Tweed can control neither of them."

The ledgers Mollie kept did not identify the clients by name, only by number, but the women tended to titter about this and that over their late morning breakfasts around the table in Hatty's kitchen. Over the years Mollie had heard various names bandied about, but neither of those her aunt just mentioned. "Is Mr. Paisley a client, Auntie Eileen?"

"That wretch?" Something between a shout and a whisper, though not normal speech. "Never!"

"Mr. Godkin then?"

"No." The whisper prevailed. "More's the pity," Eileen said. "I would have some influence if he were a client. Mr. Godkin is recently become the editor of a magazine called *The Nation*. In which he means to advocate for what he calls the correct ordering of society. *Laissez-faire* must not be threatened. That's French, Mollie. It means business must do as it likes with no government interference. No tariffs on goods.

No unions to make rules about how long a man may work in any day, or how many days in any week. And according to Mr. Godkin, no one should be permitted to vote except educated gentlemen who have been to college."

Auntie Eileen frequently expressed exactly those points of view. "I thought you agreed with all that."

"To a point, of course I do." Eileen was once more dabbing her cheeks with the handkerchief. "How else can men become wealthy enough to indulge such luxuries as we provide here? But in a correctly ordered society, Mollie, spite would not be permitted to overrule common sense."

"Spite of what sort, Auntie Eileen?"

"The sort that carries a grudge for years and years." Eileen paused and drew a long breath. "The latest issue of Mr. Godkin's magazine," she said in a voice that sounded again as sad and as desperate as it had when Hatty first brought Mollie to her aunt's bed, "contains an article by the wretched Theodore Paisley. In it he tells all New York about the special skills of the O'Hallorans of Armagh, and identifies me as one of them. As if that were not enough, he talks in detail about our house and says flat out it is located at number fifty-three University Place."

Mollie started to say something, but Eileen waved her words away. "You'll have to hear the rest of it, dear child, since it's your future Teddy Paisley's ruined along with mine. Every gentleman who comes to Brannigan's, he says, should be careful to leave his valuables elsewhere, or expect 'the light-fingered Eileen O'Halloran as was' to relieve him of them."

Eileen lost her battle to keep the no-shouting rule. "Light-fingered!" she wailed. "My name and address right there in print for anyone to see. Think of it, Mollie." Her voice had once more become a hushed whisper. "Eight years work to make this the finest whorehouse in New York and raise you in a respectable manner, and for seven of them I haven't dipped once, though God knows I've been tempted. Now I'm called light-fingered in a magazine read by exactly the sort of men we cater to here at Brannigan's. We are ruined. I shall fight back of course, but Teddy Paisley has dealt us what I fear may be a mortal wound, may his soul rot in hell."

Not, as it turned out, quite so mortal as all that. Boss Tweed's influence was sufficient to get a guarantee from Mr. Godkin that he would publish no further articles written by his old comrade Mr. Paisley. Friendship was one thing, having every stick of furniture in his office repeatedly busted and broken by Tammany hoodlums was quite another. As for the scandal, it slowed business at Brannigan's for a few months, but gradually the impression faded and the clients returned.

Things to do with commerce were long since back to normal on that day when Eileen Brannigan held in her bejeweled fingers the latest proof of her eighteen-year-old niece's skill with a needle, and announced that the gossamer swan would be framed and hung above her bed. Still, Mollie had been a bit down in the mouth since the Merkel affair, and the question of her future remained unresolved. At least from Mollie's point of view.

Eileen had reached two conclusions.

"First," she said, "I am raising the price of an evening at Brannigan's to seventy dollars. The war of course. And each of the ladies will be paid twenty dollars for her night's engagement rather than eighteen. Always be fair in business, Mollie. It's the best way."

Mollie nodded at the admonition she had heard numbers of times before, meanwhile doing the calculation with practiced ease. "That should be a monthly increase of forty dollars a night," she said. "So presuming the same six-day schedule that will mean . . . an additional twelve thousand five hundred twenty dollars a year."

"Exactly," Eileen said, because while she couldn't do mental arithmetic with the speed of her niece, she had already worked out the numbers using paper and pencil. "And I am going to put it all toward your dowry."

"You've found someone? Perhaps a bit younger than Mr. Merkel and—"

"Not exactly. And I believe we have exhausted our resources here at Brannigan's. But that doesn't change the fact that since I am opposed to your being a spinster and you're too lean and too clever to be a whore, you must be a wife." Then, leaning forward and cupping her niece's chin with a gentle hand, "That is still what you want, isn't it, Mollie? I do not wish to force you into marriage."

"It is, Auntie Eileen. I want to be a wife and mother, but—"

"Then," Eileen said firmly, "we must find you the right sort of husband, and you have to want him, not just me. We are agreed on those basic terms, are we not?"

Mollie nodded.

"Excellent. It's settled. I am sending you away."

"Away?"

"Not very far. You will live in a boardinghouse for ladies on Twenty-Third Street. And I have secured employment for you. Not, however, as Mollie Brannigan. We must purge the association if we are to improve your chances. You shall be Greek."

"Greek!"

"Exactly. Mollie Popandropolos. It is a Greek name. I read it in a magazine."

"But how—"

"For heaven's sake, Mollie, people from every corner of the world arrive in New York to find their fortune. Why not a young Greek girl? One with a substantial dowry who is in need of a husband, but not about to settle for someone less than equal to her in quality."

"Popandropolos." Mollie tried out the strange word, then repeated it. "Popandropolos. I suppose I could be. But I still don't see where I'm going to find a suitor of the sort—"

"You haven't been listening to me, Mollie. I have found you a job in a place where everyone in New York turns up sooner or later. You are going to work at Macy's."

3

THANK GOD FOR the ladies who shopped. They were the drivers of progress.

It was because of them the merchants who made their fortunes in retail took advantage of the latest marvels in construction and stretched their marble and cast-iron palaces wider than had been possible with buildings made of brick. Such advances allowed the aisles of their emporiums to be wide enough for feminine underskirts and overskirts, and all the silk and satin bustled behind. And to make room for all the choices the ladies demanded, the men piled floor on top of floor, these days as high as seven or eight stories; a thing made practical because of Mr. Otis and his steam-driven elevators. Still more important, it was the ladies who pulled the town up the island.

The women of New York were no longer content to live above their husband's businesses in the pattern handed down from Dutch New Amsterdam two hundred years before. Their menfolk indulged them, since there was much to be gained by separating domestic life from commerce. Besides, good use could be made of the space available

once residential life moved uptown and enterprise took over the space
left behind. Traders and bankers and manufacturers profited by having ready access to each other. Even Cornelius Vanderbilt, who made
a hub for his four railroads in the impressive Grand Central Depot uptown on Forty-Second Street and Fourth Avenue, oversaw his empire
from a downtown office.

By that peculiarly cold spring of 1871, six years after Lee surren-
dered at Appomattox, New York City was humming and thrumming
its way to ever-greater profits, and the saloon and the spittoon ruled
below Canal Street. The hitching post as well. The old streets on the
southern tip of Manhattan were so narrow that carriages and horsecars were almost always hopelessly snarled, and there wasn't a hope
of adding the streetcars of the horse railway that ran along metal rails
embedded in the middle of the road. Given such a Babel of traffic,
many of the men preferred horseback, since getting about quickly was
an advantage in the making of money. Never mind that further uptown a car drawn by four horses could move thirty-five men, each
paying a nickel fare, or that the ratio of one beast per man exponen-
tially increased the amount of manure on the streets.

The ladies were not so forgiving. Surely Mr. Constable and Mr. Best
and Messrs. Lord and Taylor understood that no woman wanted to
drag her skirts and her dainty laced-up boots through all that when
she went to shop.

Rowland H. Macy quickly spotted the trend. He moved north,
from Eighth to Fourteenth Street on Sixth Avenue, and soon B. Alt-
man's, Best & Co., and Stern Brothers marched past him and established themselves between Union Square and Twenty-Third Street. The
avenue—a broad thoroughfare well served by the streetcars threading
the cobbles on their narrow tracks and the free-ranging horsecars either side—overtook Broadway as the spine of retail. It didn't take long
for the stretch to be known as the Ladies' Mile. Macy did not object
to company; he knew neighbors in the same line of business meant
high traffic, and that meant more custom. It only mattered that the

ladies tried his store first for whatever they wanted. Furnishings, furs, household goods, kitchen utensils, books—all could be had at Macy's. Departments, he called these separate areas of commerce within his always growing emporium. Other retailers developed different lines, but eventually they too were no longer dry goods stores but department stores. By the time that happened Macy was preparing to best them yet again.

It was common sense, Macy said, that a woman would prefer another women to attend her, particularly now that clothing bought off the rack was taking over the garment trade. All New York was aghast when he made his cousin Margaret Getchell general manager of his store, and instructed her to hire females for the selling floor. "What has happened to the morality of the ladies that they would consider taking from a man the means to support his family," thundered an editorial in Mr. Godkin's *Nation*. The women—who mostly had neither husband nor father to support them and must work or starve—paid him no mind.

Macy's clerks wore a blue-gray uniform purchased from the store and paid for by a deduction from their twenty-two-dollar weekly wage (fifteen for women). They were forbidden to talk except to their customers, and they regularly worked a twelve-hour day, longer during sales or at Christmas when the store opened at nine and closed an hour before midnight. Employees were required to be at their posts by six a.m. to set out the stock, and remain on duty an hour after closing to put it away. Men who finished these eighteen-hour stints frequently stretched out on the counters to get a few hours sleep before the next day began. Propriety demanded that the women trudge home.

Nonetheless, Mrs. Getchell, who demanded refined speech and superior comportment, had ten female applicants for every opening. Working at Macy's was a cut above being a domestic, the store was cleaner and pleasanter than a sweatshop, and above all, Macy's was respectable. Eileen Brannigan always said it was because respectable

employment for a woman was so hard to come by that the city was so
well-supplied with whores.

Mollie Popandropolos, as she was known at Macy's, first saw Josh
Turner when he was standing in the doorway of the small work space
that was entirely her domain.

She was unused to visitors in the little room tucked into a corner of
the third floor. Her hours were less draconian than those of the salesclerks—Mollie started at eight and finished at six—and in the normal
way of things she went round the floors as soon as she arrived, picking
up the bits of specially ordered embroidery and lacework and the like,
then carried them back to her workshop. Finished things were neatly
labeled and put in a basket by the door to be picked up by a stock boy,
who came after hours when no customers were about. It was rare that
anyone disturbed Mollie during the working day. And certainly not a
man, his bulk all but filling the open door, hat under his arm so she
could see his tousled red hair. "Hello, I take it you're Mrs. Popandropolos. They told me I'd find you here, hidden deep within the Macy's
maze. I'm Josh Turner."

"Oh yes, Mr. J. Turner." She recognized the name and her glance
went immediately to his right leg. You couldn't see a thing different.
At least while he was standing still as he was now. The trouser hung
perfectly straight, despite covering a thin, strapped-on wooden peg
rather than a full-muscled, flesh-and-blood leg.

Josh saw the direction of her stare. "Works perfectly," he said. "Lining the leg with buckram does the job. I hated having the fabric flap-
ping about as it did. I wanted to come and say thank you before this,
but they never told me where you were. Until today when I finally got
the gentleman who supplies my cravats to 'fess up. You're Macy's big
secret, Mrs. Popandropolos. They must be afraid one of their rivals
will entice you away."

"It's Miss Popandropolos," Mollie said. "And I'm very pleased that my solution works for you, Mr. Turner." It had been simple enough once the tailor explained the problem. She was surprised he hadn't thought of it himself. As it was he had not, and ever since each pair of trousers Mr. Turner purchased was sent to her to have buckram hand-sewn into the right leg below the knee. Four pairs these last two years. And she'd finished a fifth yesterday. It had taken longer than usual for her to get to the job because so many ladies were getting their finery together for the Easter Parade in a few weeks. "I'm sorry you had to wait for the gray gabardines, Mr. Turner. I finished them yesterday. They're sure to be delivered today."

It was a secure promise. Wagons blazoned with the name R. H. Macy's and driven by men wearing the same blue-gray uniform as the salesclerks traversed the city every day but Sunday. "New York-ers want everything in a flaming hurry," Mr. Macy said. "And Macy's never disappoints."

Joshua waved aside the matter of his new trousers. "I didn't come for that. Only to say thank you, as I said. You took some finding." He nodded toward the sprawling selling floor behind him.

Mollie had a sudden vision of what he'd walked through to arrive at her little room: shelves and racks and counters full of ladies' cloth-ing. Just outside her door were a selection of ladies' lace-trimmed pan-taloons, and immediately beyond that row after row of crinolines and petticoats. Her cheeks colored simply by virtue of the mental image. She set her embroidery aside and went straight to him, boldly taking his left arm since he held a walking stick as well as his hat under his right. "Do let me show you the quickest way out, Mr. Turner. It is a bit of a maze, just as you said."

"I believe, Miss Popandropolos," Josh said, his grin widening, "you're giving me what is known as the bum's rush."

"Never, Mr. Turner. Macy's values your custom far too much for that. I only wish to be helpful." They were past the crinolines by then, and while Mollie was aware of the stares of a few of the women, most were too busy with their shopping to notice.

Josh paid no attention whatever to the women around them. His attention was absorbed by the one who had attached herself to him in such a determined manner, and managed seemingly without effort to match her gait to his. The top of her dark head came somewhere below his earlobe, and she had a pleasant voice and an accent that seemed naturally cultured, not one of those exaggerated attempts to overlay an immigrant brogue or a shopgirl's slur. He particularly liked that she turned her face up to his when she spoke, with no trace of practiced artifice in the gesture.

A delightful face he realized, amazed at himself he hadn't more quickly noticed the large dark blue eyes, or the dimples on either side of her mouth when she smiled. She wasn't the sort of beauty who knocked you over first thing, but a beauty nonetheless. "Listen," he said, "it really is Miss Popandropolos, not Mrs.? That's not some Macy type of tomfoolery for his lady clerks?"

"I am mistress of special sewing, Mr. Turner. Not a salesclerk. And yes, it really is Miss Popandropolos." Now he knew she was a spinster. Well, so be it. The way things had turned out didn't suit Auntie Eileen—Mollie living these last four years in a ladies' boardinghouse and working for her living with still no husband in sight—but now that she'd accepted the fact that she was never to have children of her own, Mollie had found much to like in being independent. Of course it might not be as nice if she had to manage entirely on the seventeen dollars a week Macy's paid her (the male tailors earned twenty-four), but Auntie Eileen still paid her thirty dollars a month to keep her books, a job Mollie did on Tuesday evenings. All together, things had turned out better than Mollie expected. Including the task of getting Mr. Joshua Turner through the ladies' intimates department without causing an uproar. Perhaps it was because of the stick and his walk having a slight jerk to it that they were spared open stares. These days everyone assumed such a condition to indicate a soldier injured in the war and turned respectfully away.

In minutes they were at the bank of elevators in the third-floor vestibule. "Here we are, Mr. Turner. Thank you for coming to see me. It was most gracious."

"You hated it," he said. "Will Mrs. Getchell give you the rough of her tongue because of me? She manages the store, doesn't she? I'm told she's a harridan."

"Mrs. Getchell believes as we all do, Mr. Turner, that the customer is always correct. So if you wished to see me, Macy's is happy to oblige."

Those were the same words he quoted back to her three days after his first visit, on the Thursday afternoon when he again appeared at the door of her sewing room. "The customer's always correct you said. So I've come to bring you these," holding out a bunch of dark purple violets surrounded by hand-cut paper lace and tied with a pink ribbon, "and you must say, 'Yes, of course, Joshua. I will be happy to go coaching with you Sunday afternoon.' I've just purchased three new pairs of trousers, so I'm the customer and I insist."

"Thank you for the posy. It's charming. But I can't . . ." It was not his improbable arrival that tied her tongue. It was the sight of Auntie Eileen's best friend, Rosie O'Toole, looming over his shoulder. Mollie had no doubt that in a matter of hours Mrs. O'Toole and Eileen Brannigan would be sitting together over a cup of tea, and that Auntie Eileen would be aware that Mollie at last had a suitor. Then, when it didn't work out as Mollie was quite sure it would not—why should the likes of Mr. J. Turner be seriously interested in a woman well past marrying age?—her aunt would be disappointed, and say Mollie had become too independent. "Thank you again," she said. "The violets are lovely. But I'm afraid this Sunday is out of the question." Behind him Rosie O'Toole's face turned dark with disapproval.

"Why? Are you spoken for?" Joshua demanded.

"No, but—"

"I'll be happy to ask permission of your father or guardian. I'm perfectly respectable, you know."

Behind him Rosie O'Toole was nodding her head in vigorous agreement.

"I barely know you, Mr. Turner."

"Not so," he said, sounding very grave, "you've had your hand up my trouser leg for three years."

Most females would have blushed. Or been outraged at his familiarity. Mollie giggled. She couldn't help herself. And when he hoisted that trouser, displayed his peg, and said, "Nothing improper of course, since that leg's made of wood," she was undone.

"You take it so well," she said, his courage suddenly making her insides feel as soft as warm butter. "It must be very difficult. Do you never want to complain?"

"Not much point in it. Now tell me where you live and I'll collect you at two on Sunday afternoon."

Mollie hesitated. Nothing would come of it. Auntie Eileen would be disappointed yet again. Rosie O'Toole took a step closer and loudly cleared her throat. Joshua Turner, Mollie noted, did not appear startled. Instead he gave the definite impression he was aware of being watched and was unfazed. It struck Mollie all at once that this was not a usual sort of man. "Miss Hamilton's," she said, "Eight East Twenty-Third Street."

"Miss Hamilton's," Joshua repeated. "I'm honored, Miss Mollie Popandropolos. And I very much look forward to seeing you on Sunday."

Good thing, Mollie thought, she wasn't a regular churchgoer. The absence of devotions allowed her to spend three hours Sunday morning deciding what to wear. It was a bit warmer, fortunately. And the sun was shining. She settled on her blue-and-white-striped dress, because she particularly liked the way the flounced skirt bustled behind her—she wore a padded underbustle to emphasize the effect—and made her waist look really tiny, and she could wear over it a blue short cape trimmed with ruched red velvet. The dress had a matching parasol besides, and when she twirled in front of the mirror Mollie decided the effect to be quite charming.

The outfit wasn't new, but since she'd never been coaching before, or indeed anywhere with Mr. Turner, that hardly mattered. Anyway, her bonnet was new. It was white straw trimmed with blue feathers and she'd bought it at Macy's two weeks earlier. It had been marked down to a dollar seventy-five from two, and with her employee's discount— something only Macy's offered—had cost a dollar and sixty-one cents. Good value, Mollie decided as she surveyed the full effect. And in the afternoon, based on the expression on Mr. Turner's face when he saw her, Mollie was pleased with her choices.

He drove a small straw-bodied phaeton, open to the elements and pulled by a single bay. "Glad you brought a parasol," he said when he handed her up with as much ease as might a man with both legs. "Perhaps someday I'll be rich and proper and take you coaching in an elegant black brougham."

"I shouldn't like that half so well, Mr. Turner. After all, one wouldn't be able to see as much from inside a brougham."

"Or be seen," he agreed, giving her another look Mollie thought to be approving. "Which after all is the point. And you must call me Joshua. Josh if you prefer."

"I must, must I?"

"Absolutely."

"Why is that?"

He took a moment to reply. "I can't really say, except that it would please me enormously."

"Then Josh it will be."

"And may I call you Mollie? Miss Popandropolos is a bit of a mouthful."

"Mollie is acceptable."

Josh grinned and snapped the reins and clucked the horses into action.

Fifth Avenue's procession of luxurious mansions had begun marching north from Ninth Street in the 1850s. These days, when he turned the phaeton onto Fifth at Twenty-Third and headed uptown, Josh and Mollie were in the thick of that opulent parade. "That house over there," he nodded to his left, "is said to have a picture gallery and a private theater, as well as a library and a ballroom. And solid gold banisters throughout."

"Must be terribly difficult to keep them free of fingerprints."

He laughed. "Fair enough. What about that one then?" with a nod to his right. "Has its own third-floor chapel with stained glass windows. Plus marble staircases, ebony paneling, and plaster cherubs in the bathing rooms. I'm told there are four of those."

"Cherubs or bathing rooms?"

"You are impertinent. In a charming way. Bathing rooms I suppose. Men of the type who own such places buy their statuary by the dozen. Or at least their wives do. I take it you are not impressed."

"Well I am, sort of. But . . ." But she had seen too much of what the men who built these castles got up to in the time they didn't spend making money. And all the newspapers had reported the time Mrs. Singer ran into the street from the mansion her husband's sewing machines built, screaming she'd been beaten enough for one day. "I don't think grand houses necessarily make people happy."

"A noble sentiment. Am I to take it that's the sort of thing young ladies are taught in Greece? Popandropolos is a Greek name, is it not?"

"It is, but I'm afraid I know nothing about the country." Paying close attention to the need to adjust the hem of her dress. "I was born here in New York."

"Of Greek parents, I take it."

"That's right." This time it was her parasol that required adjusting.

"Has anyone ever said you look particularly Irish?"

"No," Mollie answered, turning to him at last and speaking in her firmest tone of voice, "never."

He shot her a quick and piercing look she wasn't quite sure how to interpret, but all he said was, "End of the handsome houses. At least for now."

They had reached the crest of Murray Hill at Thirty-Seventh Street.

From there on the brownstone palaces gave way to mostly open fields. Because the paved avenues and cross streets of the grid had been built a bit above grade level to make construction easier, the undeveloped countryside fell off to either side. Driving along Fifth above the Thirties it seemed they looked down into a different world. There was a good deal of rubble left over from laying out the roads, interrupted by an occasional tumbledown shack or a sprawling dwelling that housed hundreds. Rookeries everyone called them, huge barracks-like structures where landlords crammed in as many of the working poor as could pay a few dollars' rent. And everywhere half-dressed urchins who frequently stopped playing long enough to stare after the phaeton until it was out of sight. Then, at Fifty-First Street, the desolation gave way to a half-built pseudo gothic pile that since 1858 had been promising to become the Roman Catholic Cathedral of St. Patrick.

"Do you think," Mollie asked, "the city will ever come up this far? Perhaps when the Catholic Church is finished. Will all the grand mansions march up to meet it?"

"I suppose they will, but that's not what interests me. I'm in real estate as it happens, and I can assure you, what this town needs is not more grand mansions. What's required is a way to shelter the middle classes who make New York run. There has to be something between a shack, or a rookery for the poorest of the poor, and a castle on Fifth Avenue."

"But there is," Mollie said. "Block after block of ordinary brownstones without any nonsense like gold banisters. And more being built everyday."

"True enough, but one house per family is not going to solve the problem for the future. We're an island, don't forget, and there's only so much filling along our shores we can do. Land is the one thing New York City can't manufacture."

"And do you have a solution to this problem?"

"I have ideas, Mollie. Or I should say, one idea with numerous variations."

She started to ask what exactly the idea was, but they had reached Fifty-Ninth Street and were entering Central Park. Joshua immediately became occupied with making his way into a close-packed string of vehicles, while for her part Mollie was lost in wonder.

Stately broughams and elegant coaches and racy landaus were making their way along a winding thoroughfare lined with trees just beginning to green. There were few coachmen. Almost everyone drove themselves, that being part of the afternoon's pleasure. A number of the gentlemen took great trouble to show off their skill at handling teams of two or even four, and bettering their rivals as they did so. This involved a lot of side-by-side maneuvering on a roadway planned for single-file traffic in each direction, and you could hear the drivers taunting one another as they managed to bob and weave their way to the front of one carriage, only to be confronted by half a dozen more.

Josh was soon in the heart of that competition, obviously enjoying the challenge of taking on grander carriages and frequently beating them. He'd gotten to his feet—he was remarkably steady despite the peg—and though he held a whip as did the other drivers, he seemed only to crack it in the air, and to control his horse with nothing but the reins. His hat fell off as he worked the phaeton around a particularly challenging curve, and the sunlight shone on his red hair. He looked, Mollie thought, like someone from the books she'd read as a young girl: a hero from the days of old, his head circled with laurel.

Strollers, meanwhile, were thick on the ground either side, and all the women, riding or walking, wore brightly colored dresses, while the men sported cutaway coats and top hats. "Quite a sight, isn't it?" Josh asked with another of his broad grins. "Welcome to coaching, Mollie. Now tilt your parasol so everyone can see your gorgeous feathered bonnet. And don't forget to smile at the gawkers. You're exactly what they've come out to see."

❦

There were countless boardinghouses in New York City. Rooming houses they were called, and the great majority accepted only single men. A few were willing to accommodate entire families in one or perhaps two bedrooms, though they were obliged to take their meals with other residents in the communal dining room. Most of these establishments occupied brownstones that had been deserted by the fashionable in the rush uptown. Never mind that every house built in the city after 1840 was equipped with running water, indoor plumbing, gas lighting, and central heating; if it was below Tenth Street it was no longer a place where a family with even modest social pretensions chose to live, and it was promptly sold and turned into a dwelling for the masses who could afford better than a rookery or a slightly less-crowded tenement, but not a whole house.

Edith Hamilton's rooming house on Twenty-Third Street was an exception only in that it was reserved for those relatively few single ladies who did not live with their families. Mollie sometimes amused herself by thinking of the ways in which her present situation was like living at her aunt's. Here as at Brannigan's, six single women lived under another woman's care and constant observation, but nothing on God's green earth was more proper than Miss Hamilton's Residence for Ladies.

Room and board cost fifteen dollars a week (not an inconsiderable amount considering that the poor souls in the rookeries paid a few pennies a night and those in the tenements fifteen dollars a month). Meals at Miss Hamilton's were served at precise hours: breakfast at half past six and a light supper at seven-thirty. On Sundays there was as well a midday meal at one. Among the house's amenities was a single bathing room with a large porcelain tub and big brass taps. Each lady was assigned a weekly half hour in which to use the facility. Apart from that she had a washstand with a large bowl in her room, and permission to fill a pitcher with hot water twice daily. The bedrooms were austere in their appointments, the greatest luxury apart from the washstand being that every room was provided with a Bible.

And while it went without saying that no males were permitted above stairs, the women were also forbidden to visit each other's bedrooms. Visiting, according to Edith Hamilton, was a thing meant to be done when one was fully and appropriately clothed.

A ground-floor sitting room was provided for the purpose of social intercourse. Moreover, though at twenty-two Mollie was the youngest of the residents, not even the eldest, a seventy-year-old who had been a governess, was permitted to entertain a gentleman caller without Miss Hamilton acting as chaperone. That was true when the former governess's elderly brother came to see her, and definitely true on the two occasions when Joshua Turner, having cornered Mollie in her workroom and more or less invited himself, showed up for Sunday afternoon tea.

On the occasion of the second visit Josh put up with Edith Hamilton's restrictive oversight for no more than ten minutes, then stood up, crossed to Mollie—Miss Hamilton had arranged them in two chairs with the tea table between—and took her hand. "It is far too nice an afternoon to be cooped up in here, Miss Popandropolos. We are going for a walk." With that he pulled her up, nodded toward the chaperone, and practically pushed himself and Mollie out the front door.

He made straight for Madison Square Park across the street, and steered them toward the Twenty-Sixth Street end, though he stopped as soon as they were well inside the leafy fastness. "The old biddy won't see us here, even if she's peeking through the lace curtains. Now," gesturing at two benches with his stick, "sun or shade?"

"Sun," Mollie said, choosing the bench bathed in the soft light of the waning April afternoon. "Or we can stroll if you prefer." Then, her glance dropping to his peg leg, "I mean because you said . . ."

"I know what you meant. Don't fuss. I never take offense. Anyway, I promise I can stride along at a fairly fast clip if I've a mind to. But just now I suggested a walk to get us out from under the harridan's beady gaze. I want to talk, Mollie. I love talking to you. Why don't you want to talk to me?"

"But I do, Josh. Why would you think otherwise?"

"Stop it," he said. "Stop playacting. It's the very thing I liked about you from the first. That you're genuine, at least mostly. But ever since we went coaching you've treated me like something with a bad smell you don't want too close. Please tell me why that is, and what I have to do to get back to where we were. Where I thought we were," he amended.

A crossroads and Mollie recognized it as such. "What did you mean . . . mostly genuine?"

"Popandropolos," he said immediately, "is poppycock. A made-up name if ever I heard one. You're Irish, though I have no idea why you prefer not to say so. I know the Irish aren't held in high regard, but no one's likely to mistake you for a Five Points doxy, Mollie Whoever. So why the masquerade? And, more important, why have you decided not to like me?"

"I do like you. I think you are charming and fun to be with. And very, very courageous."

"Then why— Good Lord . . . Mollie, are you married after all? To some blighter who's gone off and left you to fend for yourself? Someone named Popandropolos, perhaps?"

"No, nothing like that. I am not married, Josh. I give you my solemn word I'm not."

"Fair enough. I accept it. But that still leaves the question of why you've been holding me at arm's length for a month."

Across from them a small girl with pink ribbons in her hair was rolling a hoop along the grass, and an even smaller boy was toddling into his father's open arms. "Because," Mollie said, "I am twenty-two and grown accustomed to being a spinster, and I don't wish my peace to be disturbed by dreams that can't come true."

The sheer brutal honesty of it left him without a response for several long seconds. Then, finally, recognizing that he was wading into waters much deeper than he'd first intended to brave, "Why can't your dreams come true, Mollie? How can you make that assumption without giving them a chance?"

She shook her head. "Some things have to be concluded on the body of evidence."

"Spoken like a lawyer," he said. "Was your father a lawyer, Mollie Whoever?"

"I don't believe so."

Josh cocked his head and studied her. "But you don't know for sure. I think I begin to see some shape to this story. Are you a little bastard, sweet Mollie? Or should I say bastardess? Is that the big secret, the shame consigning you to spinsterhood?" And when she didn't answer, "If so, you should know I'm exactly that. A bastard."

"You're not! Your father is the famous Dr. Nicholas Turner, and your mother was Carolina Devrey of the shipping Devreys."

"Ah! I see you like me well enough to have done some investigating. I'm delighted. And it's all true as far as it goes. But apparently you did not probe far enough into the dark and dreadful past. My mother and father weren't married when I was born. And I was a six-year-old page at their wedding, that's how brazen they were about it."

Mollie waved his words away. "It's an old story, Josh. No one cares about it anymore."

"True enough. No one does. And whatever your story may be, no one—or at least no one named Joshua Turner—cares about it, either."

The sun was beginning to disappear behind a row of stately linden trees and the air was quickly cooling. Above their heads a number of small birds flitted among the wooden houses erected for them when the park was established in 1847, each labeled in now-fading lettering as Custom House or Exchange. There was even one called Macy's— because some wit had commented, in New York even the birds had to be occupied with business.

A breeze ruffled Mollie's hair and Josh realized he hadn't given her an opportunity to take a wrap when he dragged her out of the house. He put his arm along the bench behind her shoulders. "Are you too cold to stay here a short time longer?"

"No."

"Good, because I want to tell you another story. One that's far more to my discredit than my parents' romantic disregard for social custom."

"Josh, there's no need—"

"Yes," he interrupted. "There is. If we're to even consider going forward together a bit, seeing where it takes us, there's every need in the world. I'm not the war hero you think me to be, Mollie. I did not lose my leg in some stirring battle. I was mustered into the First New York Mounted Rifles in August of '62 because since I was four I could sit a horse better than most. Apart from that I was sixteen and knew nothing about anything, except that I wanted to fight to preserve the Union and free the slaves. My mother, after all, was an active abolitionist and my father shared her views, though he was less vocal about them. But neither of them knew I meant to volunteer until after I'd done it."

"Is that why they let you go through with it? Because they were abolitionists?"

"I think it was that they knew they couldn't stop me unless they pretty much tied me to a bedpost. I'm accustomed to getting my way, Mollie. Be warned."

This last with a brush of her cheek with the head of his stick, gold and shaped like a horse's head. She had asked him about it earlier and he'd said it had been in his family for years. That was a big part of her conviction that this could never be more than an escapade, her certitude that Josh Turner would soon lose interest. And her reason for keeping Josh's attentions secret from Auntie Eileen, who would only be disappointed once again. For all the scandal concerning his parents, both the Turners and the Devreys were old New York families with deep New York roots. It was one thing to have thought she might marry the likes of Max Merkel; it was quite another to imagine herself acceptable to the Turners. "There's nothing dishonorable in being stubborn," she said.

"Ah, yes. The rest of the story. As I said, I was mustered in during August and saw my first action on a Virginia battlefield in September. Zuni, a small and largely inconsequential fracas over a railroad bridge.

Except not so inconsequential for me. I was taken prisoner in the first ten minutes. Never got off a shot."

Paralyzed by the horses snorting and whinnying and frequently squealing with terrible pain, and the booming artillery firing from the hill behind, and the blood. All of it so much more terrifying than anything he could have conceived. And no way he could explain that to a woman. Not sitting here in a city park with sunset approaching and the sound of children's laughter barely faded. "I don't know why the reb who captured me didn't kill me." *Sweet Jesus Christ, you're barely off the tit, lad. With his bayonet an inch from finality.* "But he did not. He grabbed the reins of my horse instead and pulled me out of it, and next thing I was in a particular outpost of hell called Belle Isle Prison camp. An island in the middle of the James, with fierce rapids either side so any attempt to escape was suicidal. No barracks. Just a few shacks and some tattered tents. No food to speak of. Little medical care."

Mollie reached out her hand and lay it on his thigh. The one that had only air below the knee. Dusk now and they were mostly alone. No one to notice the remarkable forwardness of the gesture, or to see Josh cover her hand with his.

"I thank you for your commiserations, sweet Mollie. But I fared a good deal better than most. I started out young and healthy, and I survived off my own fat at Belle Isle for two years and four weeks. Then a high-ranking someone or other happened by who chanced to work out I was Ceci Devrey Lee's half brother, and hauled me off to my sister's plantation. Birchfield it was called, in the heart of the southern Virginia lakes. Well away from the fighting, or so we thought. I spent six months being nursed by my sister and her slaves and when, after being cosseted in this particularly luxurious enemy lap, I was once again well, I did not go looking for my regiment. I headed for north and home."

"Small wonder," Mollie said.

"Patently illegal," Josh replied. "I'd signed up for three years and there were four months left to run. And I'd never so much as wagged my finger at a Confederate soldier."

"It wasn't your fault," she insisted. "No one could say it was." And when he didn't reply, "What about your leg?"

"Oh yes, my leg. I lost it during the trek homeward. To a bear trap on a Maryland farm. The farmer's wife saved my life by hacking the gangrenous part off with a kitchen knife. She'd never heard of the sulfuric ether my father is so famous for using during his painless surgery, nor what he calls germs, but at least I convinced her to wash the knife in carbolic before she started."

Mollie let a few seconds go by. "What about your sister?" she said finally. "How have she and her plantation managed after the war. Without slaves, I mean."

Josh's face stiffened. Rather, Mollie thought, the way Auntie Eileen's did when she was crying without shedding any tears. "Birchfield was burned to the ground by Union renegades around the time General Sherman was torching pretty much everything between Atlanta and Savannah. That barbarism freed the Union conscience, it seems. Some men found they quite liked the old raping and looting and pillaging sort of warfare. They fed off that damnable march and went rogue. Apparently my darling sister and her three children, none of whom had ever done any harm to anyone, were bayoneted where they stood. After that my brother-in-law came north to avenge their killing by burning New York to the ground. He wound up hanging from a tree in City Hall Park."

"That," Mollie spoke very slowly, "is a truly dreadful story."

"Yes, it is. But it can't be changed, Mollie, and I'm alive and grateful for it. Now, since in this world there's no telling how long that's to be . . . Will you see me again, Mollie? Without our needing to be watched every second by that Hamilton creature?"

"Yes, Josh. I will. But I can't say what's to happen beyond that."

"Fair enough, neither can I. But I'm a gambling man, Mollie. And I'm prepared to let my winnings lie, and wait for the next card to be turned."

4

"MORE TEA, ROSIE?"

"No, thank you, Eileen. But perhaps a bit more sherry wine . . ."

"An excellent idea." Eileen lifted the decanter and topped up first Rosie O'Toole's glass and then her own. "Your good health, my dear."

"And yours, Eileen."

She wasn't using her Waterford, not for the woman who had once earned her living by dressing Eileen's ladies, and they drank her second-best Amontillado. But Eileen had told Hatty to bake the chocolate-topped cake known as a Boston cream pie, which she knew to be Rosie's favorite. Indeed, they had devoured fully half the cake between them. Replete now they sipped their sherry silently for some seconds, then Eileen said, "I take it things are going well at the store."

"Things generally go quite well at Macy's. Mrs. Getchell will have them no other way."

"I take it my niece still meets with her approval."

"My dear Eileen, how could Mollie not meet with anyone's approval? Such a charming and polite lady is bound to be liked."

Eileen noted the use of the word "lady" rather than "girl." Twenty-two and unmarried, it was to be expected. "I remain enormously grateful to you for recommending her for the job, Rosie."

"Mollie's talents are much appreciated. By the customers as much as the staff," Rosie added, not quite looking at Eileen as she spoke. Choosing instead to pick up a stray crumb of Boston cream pie on the end of a delicately moistened finger.

Eileen's every sense was instantly alert. "Perhaps another slice of cake, Rosie. It's your day off after all. You should indulge just a wee bit."

"Well, perhaps only the tiniest sliver. Hatty is such a fine cook."

"Indeed, she is." Eileen cut a substantial wedge of the remaining cake and put it on the other woman's plate. "We're all gifted in something, don't you think? Just like Mollie. Gifted with a needle." Having brought the subject back to her niece, Eileen waited.

Rosie lifted a forkful of cake to her mouth, chewed, swallowed, then washed the delicacy down with a sip of sherry and sat back. "I shouldn't perhaps tell tales out of school as it were . . ."

"Of course you should," Eileen said. "As long as you tell them only to me. I am Mollie's only living relative, after all."

"Yes, you are. And I know you have her best interests at heart, always." Rosie leaned forward.

"Always," Eileen said, leaning forward in turn, so their heads almost met across the table.

"I believe," Rosie allowed herself a single delicious sigh of pleasure, "dear Mollie has a suitor."

There followed a full report on Joshua Turner, during which both women admitted to remembering the old scandal attached to his birth, and decided it mattered not at all since it was so long ago. "He's come to the store to see her at least four times," Rosie said. "And I think they have walked out together a few times apart from that."

"Are you sure?" Eileen demanded.

"I am rather sure," Rosie said with a smile. And related the details of the time Mr. Turner had invited Mollie coaching—*I happened to be there, my dear, and of course I silently encouraged her*—and another occasion when she overheard him say something about their taking tea together. "I take it Mollie hasn't mentioned any of this?" The dressmaker had finished telling everything she knew about Joshua Turner and Eileen's niece, and clearly taken pleasure in being the one who, on this occasion, knew things.

Eileen had trapped herself with her eagerness to find out what Rosie had clearly come to tell her. She had no choice but to admit she was not in Mollie's confidence. "Not yet," she said. "But I'm sure she shall."

"Oh yes," Rosie agreed. "She will. Undoubtedly. And of course I shan't mention any of this to her."

"Or another living soul," Eileen said with a slight sharpness to her tone.

"Of course not, my dear. No one . . . I would never do that."

She would not, Eileen knew. There was, for one thing, just that hint of employer and employee that remained as a minor undercurrent in their friendship. Eileen was always in a slightly superior role. For another, Rosie quite enjoyed being friends with someone who, whatever her reputation might be, could provide Sunday tea with excellent sherry and delicious Boston cream pie. Eileen's onetime dressmaker would keep her mouth shut. Her niece's reluctance to confide that Mr. Joshua Turner was wooing her was a bit more difficult to understand. He was, after all, the very sort of gentleman Mollie had been sent to Macy's to find.

Five minutes after Rosie left, Eileen, thankful that it was Sunday and she did not have a houseful of men grunting and groaning and sighing with pleasure in every room of the place, unlaced her girdle and set it aside. She put on a silk wrapper and curled up on her bed, happily scratching every bit of reddened, welted flesh. And the explanation came to her. Mollie wasn't sure of him. She had not mentioned Joshua Turner because she did not believe he would propose marriage. *She's resigned herself to being a spinster,* Eileen whispered aloud.

"She's Miss Popandropolos, the lady who sews, and she's found a certain comfort in the role." Mollie, Eileen realized, didn't want to disappoint her aunt. More important, she didn't want to disappoint herself. Well, something would have to be done about that.

Odd, Josh thought, his confiding his story to a girl he'd seen fewer than half a dozen times. The only other people who knew were his father and Zac. Though it was likely the outlines of the tale—the bit about his not having lost the leg in battle—would be apparent to the man he was on his way to meet.

His destination was the bar of the Grand Union Hotel, across from Vanderbilt's newly completed Grand Central Depot. The hotel marked the finish of Lexington Avenue, that bastard child inserted in the 1830s between Third and Fourth Avenues from Gramercy Park to Forty-Second Street, and the end point of polite society's northern reach. Beyond Grand Central hundreds of trains rattled and racketed along Fourth Avenue; so many of them these days that the professors of Columbia University at Forty-Ninth Street claimed they couldn't hear their own lectures. The Common Council was trying to get Vanderbilt to sink a tunnel and bring his trains in and out of the town belowground. Possibly some property opportunities if he did it, Josh thought, particularly in the wasteland of the East Fifties and Sixties, but so far there was no deal.

He got to the hotel a few minutes before seven. The lobby was a swirling mass of men in evening dress and women in softly swishing satin and silk, their talk punctuated with laughter and the air around them a heady mix of scents. The smell of success, he thought. Replaced in the gentlemen's saloon—the Coach and Four it was called at the Grand Union—by cigar smoke and scotch whiskey, the smell of money.

Trenton Clifford was waiting for him, seated by himself at a small table off to the side of the long mirrored bar. Far enough from any of the gaslights so he was in the shadows. Josh spotted him quickly none-theless. Clifford's walrus mustache and his full head of pale blond hair caught what light there was around him, for one thing. For another, few men had planted themselves so indelibly in his memory.

He made his way to the table and stood silently beside it. Clifford looked up, but didn't rise. Just watched him. "Captain," Josh said fi-nally. He could not bring himself to wish the other man a good eve-ning, and he did not extend his hand.

Clifford made a gesture as if to offer his, then thought better of it and nodded toward the chair across from his. "Sit down, Josh. And it's Mr. Clifford these days. Or Trent if you prefer. War's over, son. Let it go."

"It's not the war I remember so vividly."

Dwindled corpses the poet Walt Whitman called the men he saw released from Belle Isle when peace came. Tobacco-colored and stooped like gnomes, in Whitman's words. Some days—the hottest of them usually, so the prisoners couldn't resist—they were encour-aged to swim in the river. Inevitably some got too close to the rapids. That's what the rebel guards were waiting for. "There's another trying to escape!" one of them would yell. And they picked them off like clay pigeons, one after the other. Target practice. Captain Clifford was camp commandant. Josh remembered him standing on the bank one afternoon with a brand-new Colt revolver. Shooting one after another and calling the tally aloud. "Six hits," Clifford said as he walked away. "Didn't jam once. I declare this to be a fine sidearm, gentlemen. Best the North has to offer."

"Your note said imperative." Josh still wasn't sure why he'd come. Maybe because if he had not he'd have thought himself still cowering.

"Imperative to you. Interesting for me." Clifford signaled toward the bar. "What are you drinking?"

"Scotch," Josh said, and put his own silver-dollar coin in the wait-er's hand when it arrived.

Clifford smiled at the gesture, then sat back, looking not at Josh but at the cigar whose end he was trimming with a gold cutter. "You always were what my old mammy would have called a long pisser, Joshua Turner. Prepared to aim your stream whether or not you've got anything to back it up. But big ideas. Always."

Josh tossed back the whiskey, then stood up to go.

"Sit down," Clifford said, some of the old authority creeping into his voice. "You've come this far through curiosity. Probably as much about yourself as about me. Might as well hear me out, don't you think?"

Josh sat down.

"How'd you lose the leg? You had a matched pair at Belle Isle. And the way I hear it, you didn't spend any time on the battlefield after that sister of yours cleaned you up and turned you loose."

"Lost the leg in a bear trap. And who told you all that?"

Clifford shrugged. "I hear things. That's what I do, Josh. I listen. Made my fortune."

"Here in New York? A ways out of your element, aren't you? For a Southern gentleman."

"I take it that's meant to disparage all Southern gentlemen by association. Don't bother trying to insult me, Joshua Turner. Rolls right off my back." Clifford paused to light the cigar, holding the match an inch or so away from the end and inhaling the flame toward it, puffing greedily when the tobacco caught. "Excellent cigars," he said when a wide plume of gray smoke rose above his head. "Excellent everything is available in this city. Sex, food, shelter, whatever a man desires can be had. Only thing at issue is the cost. That's what's left, Joshua. The things money will buy. The North destroyed my way of life to protect its own. Only game left to play is the Northerner's game. And a man like me, I'm bound to play something."

"Is that what you brought me here to say?"

Clifford held up two fingers in the direction of the bar. "You were a clever young 'un, Josh Turner, and you're a clever man. Doesn't surprise me. And you are also well enough established in this town to make those brains count for— Take your hand out of your pocket, damn you." The refills had arrived and Clifford interrupted himself long enough to insist on paying for them. "Drinking whiskey I buy doesn't make us friends. And friendship's not what I have in mind."

"I'm still waiting to know what is."

"I hear you've an idea to make gentlemen live stacked on shelves under a common roof. Like bags of flour. You think they'll go for it?"

"Where in hell's name did you hear such a thing?"

"Are we back to that? You're never going to know my sources, son. Not if we sit here for twenty years. Now, tell me why you think gentlemen this side of the ocean will agree to live in French flats."

The way Josh saw it, either he answered the question or he got up and walked out. And if he intended the latter, he'd not have come in the first place. "Middling sorts of gentlemen," he said. "And they'll agree because pretty soon they're not going to have any choice. There's not enough room on this island for the numbers of people who want to live here. It's that simple."

"Keep 'em out then. Make the place more exclusive. What's wrong with that?"

"They're needed, these engineers and accountants and senior clerks. Business can't run without them. New York's all about business."

Clifford nodded, but raised another objection. "Brooklyn," he said. "Queens. The Bronx even. What about them?"

"Nothing about them. Some will move there. Many already have. But it's inconvenient. Brooklyn in particular's a devilish journey. The ferry's unreliable in any kind of harsh weather."

"There's the bridge," Clifford said. "Going to change everything. Don't you agree?"

"Might do if it ever gets built." The granite tower on the Brooklyn side was complete, rising an improbable two hundred seventy-two feet above the high water mark, but the one on the Manhattan side—at Dover Street and the river—was a much slower effort. John Roebling, the engineer who designed the bridge, was dead of tetanus after crushing his toes against a piling. His son had taken over, then succumbed to some mysterious on-the-job illness he was chasing round the globe trying to cure. "Just now," Josh said, "that's looking less than likely. Queens is no easier to get to and it's a wasteland beside. As for the Bronx . . ." Josh shrugged, "all those places have one major drawback. They're not New York City."

"Very well. But that fellow Hunt, the architect as put up those flats over on Eighteenth Street, he's beat you to it, wouldn't you say?"

"I would not. Richard Hunt's used a hundred feet of frontage to make twenty apartments on four floors. Not much advantage there."

"I went over and had a look this afternoon," Clifford said. "It's five stories."

"Top floor's only accessible after four flight of stairs. Too many for most people. The fifth-floor units have skylights. They're let to artists for studios. The whole venture's interesting, but not economically sound. Not here in the city."

"The way I hear it, Hunt's going up eight stories over on Twenty-Seventh Street."

Josh nodded. "Better location. And this time his client's Paran Stevens, who owns a fair parcel of city land to start out with. Hunt's been assigned the entire block between Fifth and Broadway, and he's going to install at least four of Otis's steam elevators. But it's a far cry from what I have in mind. Stevens's building is to have eighteen suites, each almost as big as a house, with ballrooms and butler's pantries and dressing rooms. Communal servants quarters as well. Upstairs in the attic. Under, of course, a properly fashionable mansard roof."

"You don't approve?"

"I don't think it answers the problem. If business is to thrive we need to shelter more people of the ordinary sort. As I said, we don't have much land on Manhattan Island. We have unlimited air. The solution's to go higher."

Clifford's blond head was wreathed in cigar smoke. Josh could barely make out his nod. "Problem becomes that the higher you go, the more of those damned cast-iron pillars you need to hold everything up, and the closer together they have to be. Thicker walls as well. Pretty soon your construction materials are eating up your living space. That's so, isn't it, young Mr. Turner?"

Josh had given away as much of his thought on the subject as he intended. "Maybe," he said. "Maybe not."

Another nod. This time Clifford reached into his breast pocket and pulled out a card and pushed it across the table. "Talk to this man. When you and he figure something out, let me know. I'll back you."

A cold day in Hell, Josh thought. But he pocketed the card.

"I hate it," Josh said, "that I can only see you on Sundays."

Mollie laughed. "I'm a new sort of woman who works for my living, and you have to take me as you find me. You haven't told me where we're going."

"You'll see." He kept a loose hold on the reins and the bay was pulling the phaeton along Third Avenue, but Josh was obviously in no sort of hurry. "Tell me then, do you believe in all this carry-on about ladies' rights, that they should become doctors and lawyers and such? Even vote. Who'll look after the children and the households if they do all those things? Presuming they still marry and have families. And what will happen to the human race if they do not?"

She was of a mind to quote her aunt about the correlation between decent jobs and indecent whores. Mollie thought better of it. "Well and good," she said, "if all women have a man to look after them. What about those who do not?"

"My mother," Josh said with a hoot of laughter, "would approve of you, Mollie as-calls-herself-Popandropolos. She's a follower of Miss Anthony, along with all her other unconventionalities. Will you come with me to Sunshine Hill someday soon? I'd like my parents to meet you."

She fussed a moment with one of the rows of pleated ruching that circled the skirt of her pale green dress, letting her fingers slide over the soft cotton dimity made practical by the warm weather of late May. It was hard to imagine herself as someone a gentleman would want his parents to meet. Even if years ago they had themselves been a source of scandal. *Tell us about your family, my dear. Where were you raised?* "Josh, I told you, I don't wish to—"

"—to pursue dreams that cannot be realized," he finished for her. "But you refuse to tell me why they are out of reach."

Mollie pursed her lips and stared straight ahead.

"Very well," he said. "We won't talk about it now. Anyway, this is what I've brought you to see." Josh tugged on the reins and brought the phaeton to a halt on the corner of Eighteenth Street and Third Avenue, across the street from the French flats he'd discussed with Trenton Clifford. "What do you think of that?"

"The building?" They hadn't spoken much of his business interests in the three months they had known each other, but she remembered him saying he earned a living in property. "Do you perhaps own it, Josh?"

Another of his bursts of laughter. "Small chance, Mollie. Nothing so grand. At least not yet."

"I thought that might be why you've brought me here."

"I wasn't laughing at you, Mollie. Only thinking that the idea is both too large and too small." He gestured with his stick, drawing it in a straight crossways line to indicate the entire facade. "That frontage," he said, "represents four of New York City's approved twenty-five-foot-wide lots. In this city, that's a goodly amount of space. And the building goes up five stories." The stick made a perpendicular line in the air. "The top floor is studio space. The other floors are divided into living units—French flats as they're called—for four families."

"Rather as if," Mollie said as she worked out the geometry, "each family was confined to nothing more than the parlor floor of a brownstone."

"You sound disparaging, but that part is exactly as it should be,

Mollie. I don't want to bother your head with figures, but the average man of New York—neither poor nor rich—the sort doing what the newspapers call white-collar work, he earns two thousand dollars a year. These days an ordinary brownstone, not a mansion, mind, sells for a minimum of ten thousand. And that's in the least desirable parts of the city. It can be as much as eighty thousand in a truly fashionable neighborhood."

"And you're saying," she said, "that on a weekly wage which averages thirty-eight dollars and forty-six cents, this white-collar worker is never going to afford even a ten-thousand dollar house."

Josh cocked his head and studied her. "That was quick. Two thousand divided by fifty-two. Without a pencil at that."

Mollie blushed. "I find numbers easy. It's rather like a parlor trick. I didn't mean to show off."

"Well, parlor trick or not, you are exactly right. The men we're talking about can't afford to buy a whole New York house for their families, however modest the house may be. So they stuff their wives and children into rooming houses and hotels and leave them behind when they go off to their jobs. And since we have more and more of these types of workers, and the city needs still more if business is to continue to grow, we are soon to run out of places to put them."

Mollie didn't reply because a woman was coming toward them with an air of purpose. She wore a prim black dress and an old-fashioned black bonnet. Rather like a governess or a nanny, Mollie thought.

"I see," Josh said, "that we're about to encounter the controversial *concierge*. Having modeled his building of flats on those in Paris, Mr. Hunt saw fit to adopt as well their idea of a nosy old biddy to sit by the door and mind everyone's business."

The woman approached with a rolled-up newspaper clutched in her hand, as if it were a weapon for beating them off. "Were you folks wanting something from one of my families? If so, I expect you're out of luck. They's most of 'em out on a fine day like this."

"And you," Josh said, "no doubt know which ones and exactly where they've gone."

"It's my job. I'm a convenience. Says so right in here." She unrolled the paper with a flourish and waved it under their noses.

"Excuse me," Mollie said, snatching at the paper, "may I see that?" Seconds later she gave the woman back her paper and turned to Josh. "Please take me home at once."

The phaeton was at Miss Hamilton's door in fifteen minutes. Mollie had not said a word on the journey and Josh had not probed, but when he reined in he did not immediately get down and come around to help her out of the carriage. "Please tell me what's happened and how I can help."

"Thank you, that is very kind. But it's a private matter."

"Not very private if it's splashed all over the front page of the Herald."

A fair point and she knew it. Besides, his help would be useful. It would mean his knowing all her secrets, but at the moment that didn't seem important. "I need to go to the Tombs," she said. "As quickly as possible."

"Well," taking up the slack in the reins as he spoke, "I wish you'd told me that first thing. We've just gone five blocks in the wrong direction."

"I needed to get money to hire a cab or—"

"Post bail for someone, I imagine," he interrupted. "Never mind, I'll sort it."

Properly it was the New York Halls of Justice and House of Detention, but everyone called it the Tombs. Put up in 1838, the massive building was set atop what had been the old Collect Pond, these days surrounded by Centre Street and Leonard Street and Franklin. The hulking, windowless structure was meant to resemble an Egyptian mausoleum, and constructed of stone set on wooden caissons to keep it from sinking into the swampy ground. The tactic was only marginally effective. The Tombs were a dank misery below and an unsanitary hellhole above.

Even Eileen Brannigan found it difficult to keep her look of quality after a night in such a place. Her cheeks were sunken, her eyes red-rimmed, and half her hair had escaped from the twist at the nape of her neck. Her dress was torn and soiled, and worst of all, her wrists were shackled in front of her.

The guard who brought her to Josh and Mollie kept a tight grip on her arm nonetheless, jerking her through the milling crowd in the busy hall at a pace just below a trot. "Here she is then. Mind your belongings, folks. Seems this here's the most notorious pickpocket in all New York."

"Auntie Eileen!" Mollie couldn't get her arms around Eileen for a proper hug, but she managed to press her cheek against her aunt's. "What's happened?" And to the guard, "Let her go. You're hurting her. She's not a criminal."

"Yes, she is. Caught red-handed," the guard said. "In Union Square."

"Let her go." Josh slipped a bill into the man's hand. "And take off those handcuffs." Another bill disappeared into the guard's outstretched paw.

"But I know you wouldn't do any such thing." Mollie was staring incredulously at her aunt.

"Of course I wouldn't." Josh's last bribe had freed her and Eileen was busy chafing the circulation back into her wrists and arms.

"Red-handed," the guard repeated. "Copper found the gent's purse in her fancy pocket, just like he said it would be. Though must say, it don't look so fancy now." Eileen frequently held what was called a chatelaine pocket, a purse that could either be held or clipped to her frock. That's where the black velvet pocket she'd had with her the previous day was now, hanging limp and torn and clearly empty from the nipped waist of her bedraggled dress. Ransacked no doubt by the police for whatever money she'd carried with her, and by the other prisoners for her Hungary Water and smelling salts and no doubt exquisitely embroidered handkerchief.

Josh put his hand on the other man's chest, shoving him firmly away. "I think it's time you gave us a bit of privacy. I'm sure I've bought at least ten minutes' worth."

Mollie waited until the guard had removed himself to another part of the room. Then, "Where is Mr. Duggan, Auntie Eileen? Why isn't he here?" Jeremy Duggan was Eileen's attorney.

"Apparently he doesn't know. I'm sure he'd have come immediately if he did."

Mollie bit back the obvious response, that since the arrest of the ". . . notorious owner of Brannigan's brothel" was on the front page of the *Herald*, and probably every other newspaper in the town, it was hard to believe the lawyer didn't know. "Never mind. We'll deal with Mr. Duggan later. Now we must get you out of here. This is Mr. Joshua Turner who has kindly agreed to help us."

Josh tipped his hat. "Delighted." He had to work to suppress a broad grin. That Mollie was the niece of the woman who ran the most exclusive whorehouse in the city explained a great deal. And all of it to his satisfaction. The mistress of a bordello was a lot easier to deal with than an irate Greek husband. "Has bail been set, Mrs. Brannigan?"

"I have not yet seen a judge, Mr. Turner. I'm told they were too busy for me yesterday, and that this being Sunday, they are all at their devotions."

"Surely Mr. Tweed won't allow this to continue, Auntie Eileen . . ." Mollie found intolerable the thought of her aunt remaining in this dreadful place. As for Josh, whatever he might think of Tammany, that would hardly be the most shocking revelation of the afternoon.

"I am informed," Eileen said, "that Mr. Tweed is away in Saratoga."

"Someone," Josh said, "appears to have taken trouble to let you know exactly how difficult your circumstances are. Sounds like what I think is called a put-up job, Mrs. Brannigan."

"It does, Mr. Turner. Very cleverly put up. But—"

Her words were interrupted by the return of the guard. Followed closely by another man. "Here now, you can go," the guard said. "Seems like this gentleman's a lawyer and it's all arranged."

The lawyer was not, however, Jeremy Duggan but a stranger. "Compliments of Boss Tweed," he said. "And I'm instructed to tell you he's sorry he only today heard of this terrible miscarriage of justice."

"If Auntie Eileen had picked the man's pocket," Mollie said, "he wouldn't have known a thing about it."

She and Josh and her aunt were in Eileen's sitting room. Hatty had fixed an early supper of creamed finnan haddie on toast, and fed them before the fire, and though Mollie had only one glass, her aunt and Joshua between them finished off a bottle of French wine, a Graves from 1863 which Eileen pronounced of the highest quality. It was time for truth telling. "Auntie Eileen," Mollie said, "is an Armagh O'Halloran. They are famous for their skill at dipping."

"Entirely so," Eileen said. "You must have some brandy to settle your digestion, Mr. Turner." She poured a snifter from the decanter at her elbow, then another. "I shall join you. Just this once. Since it has been such a difficult day. My niece never takes brandy."

"I notice," Josh said, "that Miss Popandropolos is modest in all her habits."

"Don't tease, Josh," Mollie said. "It's Mollie Brannigan. As you now know."

"My fault she deceived you," Eileen said. She'd been racking her brain for a scheme that would let her influence Joshua Turner's courtship of Mollie and now the opportunity had been handed to her. Never a cloud but what there's a silver lining, as her mam would have said in the old country. "I'm the one who insisted Mollie use a false name when she went to work at Macy's. I didn't want her tarred with my brush. All for nothing as it turns out." Eileen raised her snifter in Josh's direction. "Your health, Mr. Turner. And I drink it happily, though Teddy Paisley's had the best of me this time."

"I thought he must be the one to have done this," Mollie said. "But how could he have known where you'd be?"

Eileen held up her hands. Every one of her rings—stripped from her hands by the police when she was first arrested—had been returned to her before they left the Tombs. Entirely unexpected, and a courtesy Eileen attributed to the intercession of Boss Tweed. "The grand opening of Tiffany's new store in Union Square . . . I was bound to show up."

"All right, I see that," Mollie said, "but how did Paisley manage to get his purse into your pocket?"

"Not himself. I'd have spotted him instantly. Clearly he had someone inside the store. And I obliged the villain by not clipping the pocket to my dress but carrying it in my hand. And when I put it down to try on a brooch . . ." Eileen shrugged. "Teddy's waited all these years. I'm sure he made provision for every eventuality."

Josh let the matter of some old grudge slide. None of his business and he really didn't care. "Why do you say this Paisley's had the best of you, Mrs. Brannigan? You obviously have, as they say, friends in high places."

"Indeed I do. And I am assured Boss Tweed will see to it that the charges are dropped. But . . ." She got up and walked to the window. "Come over here, Mr. Turner."

Josh did as he was bid. Eileen pushed aside a length of emerald green velvet, exposing the lace curtain beneath. "Look at that," she said.

There was a crowd of perhaps two dozen men on the street below. All circling Eileen Brannigan's front door. "Do not mistake these creatures for importunate clients begging us to open our doors, Mr. Turner. They are reporters," Eileen said.

"So many," Josh said, "that no client, however importunate, to use your word, can get near the place."

"Yes, though that doesn't matter tonight. The house is always closed on the Sabbath. But the clients won't come tomorrow night either. This is the second time Teddy Paisley has managed to have my heritage become an item of interest to the New York press. Other houses could sustain such an onslaught, Mr. Turner. Not Brannigan's. It's entirely contrary to the spirit of the place."

"A man's home from home," Josh said. "With a companion that might be his wife, if his wife was as beautiful and intelligent—"

"—and willing as well as skilled in the bedroom," Eileen finished for him. "Exactly. So we're done."

Mollie had come to stand beside them. "It's dreadful, Auntie Eileen. What shall you do?"

"Oh, I shall find other ways to keep myself occupied. No fear of that. But what, my darling Mollie, shall we do about you? That's the question."

"Me? I don't understand . . ."

"My niece," Eileen said, aiming her remarks at Joshua Turner, "is astonishingly capable and talented and I think lovely, as long as one does not have a taste for the flamboyant. But, Mr. Turner, sometimes— to use an expression from the old country—she's as thick as two short planks. Mollie," turning to her, "the reporters for the gutter press hang about the Tombs like the water rats they are. You were no doubt seen when you arrived and carefully observed when you left with me. By tomorrow you will be a featured part of the story of my disgrace. You as well, Mr. Turner, though I doubt it will be as problematic for you as for my niece. It's only women who are seen as the villains in matters such as these. The men are their victims, led astray by their natural instincts."

"No problem at all for me," Josh said. "As you rightly point out. But will Mollie not be perceived simply as a loyal and loving niece coming to her aunt's aid in a time of trouble?"

"Yes, Auntie Eileen. That might—"

Eileen made a sound somewhere between laughter and a derisive snort. "Not a chance, Mollie. Mrs. Getchell will be done with you. No scandal of any sort, that's what's allowed her to keep on hiring women at the store despite public disapproval. Rosie O'Toole will speak for you I'm sure, but it won't make a penny's worth of difference. Macy's will no longer have a job for you, my dear, and I daresay Miss Hamilton will want shot of you as well. You can, of course, come back and live with me. But then it's spinsterhood for sure and certain. Unless—"

"Auntie Eileen!"

Eileen paid no attention to her outburst. "Unless you would like to marry her, Mr. Turner."

"I would, Mrs. Brannigan. I most assuredly would."

"Stop it! Both of you. How can you think I—"

"Hush, Mollie. This is a negotiation and I am far more experienced than you in such matters."

"Joshua, I will not—"

"Listen to your aunt, Mollie. Hush." This with a small and surreptitious pat on her bottom.

Eileen pretended not to notice. "Shall we go back to the fire, Mr. Turner? And will you have a touch more brandy?"

Josh and Eileen returned to their seats. Mollie stayed where she was, unsure if she was more astounded by the conversation or that extraordinarily intimate touch.

Josh held out his snifter. Eileen splashed in a generous portion of dark gold brandy. Josh murmured his thanks.

"Now," Eileen said, "you must tell me how you propose to support my niece if this marriage takes place."

"I manage property, Mrs. Brannigan."

"Your own?"

"Much of it, yes, though some belongs to my parents. During the war when prices were depressed my father purchased six lots on Sixty-Third Street between Third and Fourth Avenues. We intend to build on them and sell the houses."

"And do you," Eileen asked, "have Croton water and gas lines as far north as East Sixty-Third Street?"

"We have. The city put them in when they paved the streets and avenues."

"Then given running water and light, housing so far uptown is a possibility. And building it an undertaking that requires clever management," Eileen said. "But who will want to live so far from the town?"

"No one yet," Josh admitted. "Nor on the property my mother purchased in the downturn. It's even further north. Truly in the uncivilized wilds."

"Ah yes, the remarkable Mrs. Devrey Turner," Eileen said.

Mollie had figured out hours ago that Eileen knew all about Josh. She had no doubt that was down to Rosie O'Toole, but it was too late now to fret about that. She took a few steps toward the fire. "Auntie Eileen—"

"Do come and sit down, Mollie. And do please hush."

"Yes, Mollie," Josh said. "Please hush."

He was twinkling at her.

Mollie sat down.

"Where, Mr. Turner, is your very clever mother's property?"

"She owns, Mrs. Brannigan, all the lots from Eighty-Seventh to Ninety-Fifth Street along the east side of Fourth Avenue."

"A shanty town," Eileen said. "Even less likely to appeal to people looking for housing than your father's property in the East Sixties."

"I agree with you," Josh said. "But that will not always be the case."

Eileen nodded. "Possibly so. But for now you are a gentleman bearing the legacy of a very unfortunate wartime injury, who claims to be 'managing' property in a part of town where no respectable person would consider being seen. Please tell me how this equips you to provide a living for my niece."

"My family was extremely kind when I returned from the war, Mrs. Brannigan. Admittedly, calling me manager of their property was more a promise for the future than a source of present income, but my brother's company made me a loan that enabled me to begin acquiring property of my own. Mostly brownstones deserted by the gentry. They are now rooming houses. Like your Miss Hamilton's," with a nod to Mollie. "The rents provide me a decent income. And the loan from Devrey's has been paid back."

"But," Eileen said, "your rooming houses are an asset with little room for expansion. One can charge only so much rent for any room. Even in New York City. What about the future, Mr. Turner?"

"I have plans, Mrs. Brannigan."

"Do tell, Mr. Turner."

"We are running out of housing room on our island. I am going to change that by building flats." He turned to Mollie. "That's why I took you to Eighteenth Street. I wanted to explain—"

"French flats," Eileen said. "That's what you plan to build? On the lots belonging to your mother and father?"

Josh shook his head. "The French flats are like my idea, but they are not my model. Nor is the new place Hunt's building over on Broadway. And while I'm not quite sure exactly where I'm going to build, I expect at least my mother's lots to be many decades away from being suitable for what I have in mind. And it will still be some years before the city catches up to our holdings in the East Sixties. Where, however, is a more easily solved problem than how." He leaned forward and began moving the remains of their supper about the table to illustrate his point. "I can pile these plates and cups and saucers on each other easily at first." He made a stack of a cup topped with a dish and then a wineglass, then picked up another dish and held it above the glass's rim. "But if I try to go too high it will all fall down." He replaced the plate on the table, avoiding any jeopardy to Eileen's crockery.

Mollie was so intrigued by the discussion she forgot the humiliating reason for it: that she was being haggled over like a piece of merchandise at a Macy's sale. (Not, of course, that Macy's permitted haggling, fixed prices having been the engine that fueled the remarkable rise of all the department stores of the Ladies' Mile.) "But," she said, "that's because you chose to put a narrow cup at the base of your stack. If you built it on a dish or a soup bowl, it could go higher."

"In principle, yes. A broader base allows you to build a higher structure. But to achieve such a thing in a building rather than a tower of dishes, you have to keep making the walls thicker. Granite is an improvement on bricks. That's why we can do so much more with newer granite and cast-iron buildings. But a wider and therefore stronger granite base dramatically cuts down on usable space within the building, particularly on the lower floors which command the highest prices."

"And do you have a solution for this conundrum, Mr. Turner?"

"Not yet," he admitted, "but I'm working on it." Ebenezer Tickle it said on the card Trent Clifford had given him. It was in his breast pocket now. Picking up the card along with his money clip and his keys and his pocket handkerchief had become a regular part of Josh's morning routine. Ebenezer Tickle. At an address on Dey Street downtown. *Figure out how to do it and I'll back you.* A man who had stood on a riverbank shooting at desperate, unarmed men as if they were clay pigeons. "It's not a simple matter, Mrs. Brannigan. I don't wish to lie to you. Not simple at all. But I intend to solve it."

"Am I correct, Mr. Turner, in thinking that the solution is likely to involve a considerable sum of money?"

"That's part of it, yes."

"My niece," Eileen said, "comes with a hundred-thousand-dollar dowry."

"No! Auntie Eileen, you've gone too far. I won't have it."

"The rate increase," Eileen said, addressing her niece but acting as if she hadn't heard a word of Mollie's protest, "over four years brought it to sixty-something. I'm rounding up."

"Rounding!—you are practically doubling. Auntie Eileen, this is just like the Merkel affair. I told you then, I am not a horse to be bargained for at an auction."

Josh reached for her hand. "I have no idea who Merkel is, but you can't think I believe you to be a horse or anything else to be bargained for. Surely you've known for months I want to marry you. I don't think there's another woman anywhere to whom I could speak with such frankness, let alone one so adorable and—" He broke off, as if remembering that he and Mollie were not alone, and looked at her aunt. "Thank you, Mrs. Brannigan, but I don't require a dowry. Only Mollie's answer." Then, turning to her once more, "Will you marry me, Mollie Brannigan?"

Eileen held up her hand. "Wait a moment before you answer, Mollie. Mr. Turner, that is a very gallant statement, and I can on occasion be as charmed by romance as any woman, but it's not good business to turn down an offer of one hundred thousand dollars. The pair of you will have a desperate time of it in future if you're no more sensible than that. On that evidence I would strongly advise you to refuse, Mollie."

"I didn't say I wouldn't take the money, Mrs. Brannigan." Josh still held Mollie's hand. "Only that I would not accept it as a dowry. Mollie is beyond price, you and I both realize that, and I'm bound to add that however large a sum a hundred thousand sounds, it won't be enough for what I have in mind. It will certainly help, however. And I'd be pleased to know that when the time is right I can count on you investing that sum in my endeavors."

"At a favorable rate of interest, no doubt," Eileen said.

"Very favorable. And perhaps delayed for a period. So let's say an interest-free loan during construction,"—Eileen started to respond, but Josh wasn't finished—"and to remain interest-free for the first three years after completion."

"A loan of a hundred thousand dollars," Eileen said. "Unsecured, no doubt."

Josh nodded.

"And interest-free for a period of years."

"Exactly," Josh said.

Eileen smiled. "Done, Mr. Turner. At least from my perspective."

"Then it's up to Mollie." He had kept hold of her hand. Now at last he turned back to her. "What about it? Will you marry me, sweet Mollie Brannigan?"

So here it was.

After all the years, after she had schooled herself to accept spinsterhood as her fate, a man had appeared who wanted to marry her. And not just any man. Someone who frequently made her laugh, who made her heart beat faster each time she saw him, a man whose touch was making her feel quite warm in ways to which she was entirely unaccustomed. Mollie gathered herself, waited a few seconds, aware of how momentous her next words must be. Then, finally and firmly, said, "Yes, Joshua Turner, I will."

5

EBENEZER TICKLE WAS a dwarf.

Josh had seen General Tom Thumb in Barnum's museum; barely three feet tall and dressed up like Napoleon, or Cupid, or the commander of a Highland regiment. Unlike Thumb, Tickle was not a miniaturized man as he might be conceived by someone making a drawing. The man facing Josh had an ordinary-size head and torso, with powerful though short arms, a barrel chest, and hams like oaks. It was the shortness of his legs that dictated his height.

The address on Dey Street had turned out to be a small room cut out of a corner of a coal cellar. With the door shut the only light came from an old-fashioned whale-oil lamp that cast flickering shadows on the raw brick walls and the sparse furnishings. There was a cot, a small table, and two wooden chairs. Josh sat on one and Tickle on the other—both legs stuck out straight in front of him—smoking a corncob pipe. The pungent smell of his tobacco hung over the place like a pall. "'Bout these flats of yours, Mr. Turner. There's no question what's needed."

"It's a question to me, Mr. Tickle."

"Steel," Tickle said.

Josh brought his eyebrows together over the bridge of his nose. "Steel?"

"Yup." Tickle was tamping more tobacco into his pipe meanwhile. "You want to build a building as goes up a fair number of floors and doesn't have to give up half its space to bloody great stone walls and tree trunk beams, you need steel. Plenty as know that. I ain't telling you anything worth much on the open market."

"Sounds as if you're describing an ancient castle, not a modern building, Mr. Tickle. Not too many tree trunk beams around these days. We use cast iron."

"Ain't safe above seven, maybe eight floors," Tickle said. "Least-ways, not safe enough. Not unless you put a bloody great iron pillar every ten or so feet. Sometimes not even then."

"True," Josh said. There had been half a dozen bridge collapses over the last quarter century. And any number of building cave-ins. A few years back someone got the idea of building an elevated railway along Greenwich Street. Take the Babel of traffic up over everyone's heads. Except on the first attempt the iron framework hadn't proved strong enough for the task and they had to build it a second time. "I take it steel is stronger than cast iron."

Tickle had just taken a long pull on his pipe and his snort made smoke pour out of his nose and mouth. "Ten times as strong. Maybe twenty." He reached over and opened the drawer of the table and pro-duced a piece of metal. It was gunmetal gray in color, some six inches long and four inches wide and an inch thick. "Steel," Tickle said. "Stron-gest building material in the world. And the thinnest. Make yourself a framework of that, clothe it up with brick or granite outside and plaster in. You can pile on as many stories as suits your fancy. Steel framing it's called. Everyone's known about it for maybe two hundred years."

"Then why," Josh asked, "has it not been done?"

This time Tickle took a few moments before he answered, using the pause to scrape the embers out of the bowl of his pipe and begin the process of refilling it with fresh tobacco. "You a scientific sort of man, Mr. Turner?" he asked finally.

"Not really, no."

"Well then, I'll try to tell it simple. Iron for casting, pig iron, it's got more 'n two percent carbon mixed in. Steel's got less. You make steel by taking most of the carbon out of iron. Find a way to do it without taking all the time and trouble it used to took, you got yourself something special."

"Am I to assume, Mr. Tickle, that you're a man who knows his way around the foundry floor?"

Tickle nodded. "Foreman over at Novelty," he said. "They say the little people got a calling for the foundry trade. You probably heard that."

Josh allowed as he had, and that he knew of Novelty Iron Works.

"Besides me, nine of my kind works there. Mind you, that's ten out of two thousand, and I'm the only one as is a foreman. I can't say for sure it's a calling, Mr. Turner, but I can tell you working iron's as hard a job as a man can do, whatever his height." Tickle clamped his pipe in his teeth and drew back the shirt sleeve of first one arm then the other. Both were knotted with muscles and crisscrossed with the reddened welts of burn scars. "Thing I do know, it's a ways better than being a dressed-up doll in Barnum's freak show."

Josh didn't comment on that. "I seem to remember," he said instead, "that Novelty was the last of the ironworks to be unionized."

"That's so. Happened a few years back during the war. Before my time that was, but the North needed iron if they was going to win. Foundry workers had some cards to play and they played 'em."

"And you, Mr. Tickle, are you a member of the Iron and Metal Workers League?"

"I am. Proud of it as well."

"Yet you're not with your brothers today," Josh said. "It's my understanding they're marching down Broadway as we speak. Demanding an eight-hour workday. Do you not believe in their cause?"

"I do, Mr. Turner. But they can march to hell and back and it won't make a difference. They're not going to get the same day's pay for two hours' less work. Not if every laboring man in the city joins together to demand it. The bosses say the eight-hour-day's Communism, say it'll put an end to any kind of economic progress here in America. Mayor's in thick with the bosses. Says he's never going to let no eight-hour-day Communism come over here. His Honor's going to send in the police with their clubs. A man like me, I don't figure to do very well in that sort of thing."

Josh could not argue with that truth and he did not try. "We were discussing steel, Mr. Tickle."

"So we were, Mr. Turner. It's stronger, thinner, a hell's sight easier to work with. Nothing new in that, like I said. Thing is, it's never been easy to make steel. Open hearth mostly, though I heard tell of other ways over in Europe. Way we do it here, furnace needs to be a hundred tons at least. Furnace that size eats fuel faster 'n a dog eats his dinner. Takes a huge amount of charcoal. You'd have to cut down every tree between here and China to get as much as you'd need to make any sizeable amount of steel that way. Course," cocking his oversize head and examining his visitor, "there's some easier methods nowadays."

"And what methods are those, Mr. Tickle?"

"Depends who you ask. The way it's mostly told, man named Bessemer over in England invented a process to force out the carbon with a blast of air. You still has to melt the iron and that takes a fair bit of fuel, but you can use coal you dig out of the ground. Don't need charcoal made from wood. And air's free, Mr. Turner. Means the whole thing becomes a sight more practical than it was before."

Limited land here in New York, but unlimited air. That's what he'd told Trent Clifford. "Then I don't see the problem, Mr. Tickle."

"Like I said, Bessemer holds the patent. Won't say how his process is done unless you put your hand in your pocket and pay him for a license. Ain't too many else as knows how to do it apart from him. A few, but not too many."

Josh's eyes were starting to tear in the smoky atmosphere, but he didn't wipe them. Narrowed them instead. And sat back and considered

Ebenezer Tickle with great attention. "I think you're going to tell me you know how Bessemer's process works. Am I correct, Mr. Tickle?"

"You are, Mr. Turner." Tickle jumped off his chair and headed for the door in the back wall. He walked with the waddling stride common to men made as he was, but he got where he was going soon enough. The rear door opened on a trash-strewn square of space hardly big enough to turn around in, but it admitted a wave of relatively fresh, warm June air, and that helped some with the tobacco fumes.

The dwarf returned to his visitor and hoisted himself back into the chair beside the table. The maneuver was performed too quickly for Josh to see exactly how it was done. He's learned ways to cope with his situation, Josh thought. As have I.

"Better?" Tickle asked, gesturing toward the open door. And when Josh nodded, "I was talking about Mr. Bessemer over in England and his patent . . . Weren't his idea to start out with."

"It was yours? Is that what you're saying?"

"Nope." Tickle shook his head. "Never said that. Never would. Man named William Kelly. Came from Pittsburgh, Pennsylvania, but did his steelmaking in Eddyville, Kentucky. West part, right where I was born. Kelly's the one thought up using air to blow the carbon out of iron and figured how to do it. Got himself a patent and everything."

"Let me guess. You worked for Kelly when he was in Kentucky."

"Him and his brother," Tickle said. "Right from the first day."

"Is this Kelly likely to be less parsimonious with the rights to his kind of steelmaking?"

"Doesn't have 'em. Not anymore. Good people, the Kelly brothers, but foolish about business. Went bankrupt. Sold their patent to Bessemer. Who says he had anyways invented the same thing over across the ocean." Tickle shrugged. "Don't matter now. You want to know how to blow carbon out of pig iron using something that looks like this . . ." Tickle pulled another treasure out of the drawer of the desk, a drawing of a kind of furnace, an elongated oval on legs, "you got to pay Bessemer."

"Unless," Josh said, "you already know how to do it."

Trickle smiled.

The appeal of embroidered roses outlined with faux pearls had faded. Fashion had changed, and the years on the Ladies' Mile had refined Mollie's taste. Something a bit simpler she thought. Depending for its charm on cut and fabric.

Given that she was no longer a working woman but once more living with Auntie Eileen, Mollie had plenty of time to consider the matter of her wedding dress. She was aided in those deliberations by her aunt and Rosie O'Toole, who came frequently to discuss the matter. It was Rosie who produced a copy of *Harper's Bazaar* for the first week in June. The magazine had three pages of illustrations of the latest bridal fashions from France. "Something like this would be lovely on you." Rosie pointed to a dress described as being ". . . of fine white Swiss muslin, trimmed with pleated ruffles of the same, and folds and bows of white silk."

Eileen particularly approved of the silk ribbons around the waist—Mollie's was barely seventeen inches when she was laced into a good tight corset—and of the frock's modest V-neck accented with a wide bertha collar. "You're not going to bubble up over a plunging décolletage no matter how much push-up the corset applies," she said. "So this would definitely suit you." Her niece's deficiencies of bosom had been one of Eileen's minor worries these many years.

"Worn with," Mollie leaned over the copy of *Harper's Bazaar*—published every Saturday, ten cents a copy or four dollars a year in advance—and read aloud, "a long blond veil held in place with a wreath of orange blossoms, with long sprays falling over the back."

"Mrs. Jackson can make that veil and headpiece for you in no time," Rosie said. Mrs. Jackson was Macy's head milliner.

"Will Mollie need to visit the store?" Eileen asked. As she'd predicted, Mrs. Getchell had fired Mollie the day after a sketch of her niece appeared in *Frank Leslie's Illustrated Newspaper,* and Mollie was identified as having gone to the Tombs to help arrange the release of the notorious Mrs. Brannigan.

"That hardly matters, Auntie Eileen. I'm let go from my job, not banished from shopping at Macy's."

"No one," Rosie said, "is banished from shopping at Macy's. The old man would be apoplectic if Getchell suggested such a thing. But I shall make your wedding gown on my own time, Mollie darling. I'll copy this one exactly and start as soon as you get the material. No charge for my labor, of course." Leaning over to pinch the younger woman's cheek. "Made your first party dress when you were four. This one will be my present on the occasion of your marriage."

"Very kind," Eileen said. "But don't go thinking Mollie will name her firstborn after you if it's a girl. The first daughter's going to be Eileen, isn't she?"

What if she was too old to get pregnant? Spinsters who somehow managed to find a husband late in life seldom became mothers.

"Late in life as in their forties," Eileen said on the single occasion when she and her niece discussed the subject. "Women marrying elderly widowers who want a housekeeper without having to pay a wage. Nothing to do with you, Mollie."

"But you always said I'd be a spinster after twenty."

"Seen as such. Not actually dried up and past your prime. For heaven's sake, Mollie. Use the brains God gave you. You're twenty-two. How many women stop having babies at that age? Most go on adding to their broods until they're over thirty. Otherwise Brannigan's might not have been such a success." This last with a sigh for things that had been and were now lost.

A number of things, however, remained as once they were. Eileen, for example, still refused to say anything more about Teddy Paisley and his grudge. A spurned lover, Mollie thought. Probably someone she'd tossed aside to marry Brian Brannigan. Though Mr. Paisley had certainly taken it hard if he was seeking vengeance after all these years. As for Eileen's keeping her own counsel in the matter, that was less of a surprise than her continued refusal to have anything but open fires and to burn only the finest applewood. Mollie suggested it might be sensible to consider installing a coal furnace, which would prove cheaper in the long run. "It could be put in over the summer when no heat's needed, Auntie Eileen. And centrally heating the whole house involves so much less effort and mess it's bound to pay for itself in no time. You won't need a maid living in. Just one to come and clean a few days a week perhaps. Hatty can see to things between times."

"I can't abide heat from radiators. They dry out the air and that's bad for the complexion. I shall economize, of course. Just not in that way."

Her aunt had negotiated a lower monthly payment to Tammany Hall; Mollie noted it when she did the books. And certainly the payments to the butcher and the grocer and such like were less with six fewer mouths to feed. But other than the fact that the clients were gone along with the whores, little changed in Eileen Brannigan's life. Tiffany's even delivered the sapphire bracelet she'd ordered on the fateful visit to the grand opening of their Union Square store. "I've already paid for it," Eileen said, waving away her niece's offer to take the piece back to the jeweler. "And it's a lovely bracelet, don't you agree?"

"It's beautiful, Auntie Eileen. I just thought . . ."

"I know what you thought, dear child. But you needn't think it. Nor worry about the expense of your wedding. And don't look like that. I'm not considering a return to dipping. All those years, Mollie. All those remarkable men coming here over and over . . . I had no lack of investment advice, and I was not shy about taking it. Now, have you decided about where this marriage is to take place?"

It was a worrying question. Both the O'Hallorans and the Brannigans were Catholics, but neither family had ever taken the matter as seriously as some among the Irish. Mollie had inherited no religious fervor. Nonetheless, Josh suggested she might like to be married in St. Ann's Catholic Church over on Eighth Street. "All the same to me," he said, "as long as you're my wife at the end of it."

The pastor was not so sanguine. Mollie went to see him and produced her certificate of baptism, but it seemed there were more documents required and she had none of them. Proof of First Holy Communion for one, and Confirmation for another. And a note from some religious authority attesting to her regular attendance at Holy Mass. "And since you insist on marrying a non-Catholic," the priest said, "we can't of course allow the ceremony to take place in the church itself. Unless your husband-to-be would like to convert. Have you suggested that, Miss Brannigan?"

Mollie didn't mind the thought of catching up on the rituals she'd missed, but she refused to tell Josh he wasn't considered good enough as he was. So a Catholic church was apparently not an option.

Sunshine Hill, the remote home of Josh's parents, was. Carolina Turner made the suggestion when Josh brought Mollie to meet his parents. "Nick and I were married in the rose garden on that bluff over there," she said, pointing to a spot on a cliff overlooking the East River. "If you and Josh would like to have your wedding in the same spot it would be our pleasure."

Two days later Carolina took to her bed with what Dr. Turner pronounced a weakness of the heart, something he explained that likely had been coming on for many years and had nothing to do with Josh's upcoming marriage. The notion of a wedding at Sunshine Hill, however, had to be dropped.

"There's always City Hall," Josh said cheerfully. "Or any Protestant church as takes your fancy."

Mollie could not imagine arriving in City Hall wearing her lovely blush-pink, ruffled-and-bowed wedding dress, and her veil trimmed with orange blossoms. But she didn't think it likely any Protestant church would welcome Eileen Brannigan's now infamous niece as the bride, or Auntie Eileen herself as an honored guest.

"You're not allowing for the influence of my brother Zac," Josh said. "Would Grace Church over on Broadway do?"

Which is how it happened that on the third day of August in the year of Our Lord 1871, Mollie Brannigan became Mrs. Joshua Turner in perhaps the most fashionable Episcopalian church in New York.

They went directly from the ceremony and reception to what was to be their first home together, Zachary Devrey's spacious, if no longer fashionable, brownstone on Grand Street. Zac had kept the house because it was easy walking distance to what everyone called the Devrey Building on Broadway and Canal, a marble palace celebrating the accomplishments of better than two centuries of the city's mightiest merchant fleet. These days, after the fearsome pounding American commercial shipping took in the war, Zac spent much time in England, seeking new alliances, and ways to win back lost business. He was off to Liverpool immediately after the wedding for what promised to be an extended stay. "Have the house, Josh, for as long as you need. I travel so much the place gets little use. When I'm home I've everything I require at the Devrey Building. I won't be in the least inconvenienced."

"Your brother never married?" Mollie asked as Josh closed the front door behind them.

"Never. There was talk of his having met a woman he cared for in England years ago, but she was promised to someone with a title and a fortune, and he was apparently the underbidder."

He was behind her, helping her out of the dove gray capelet that was part of the elegant traveling costume she'd changed into after the wedding. She felt a touch on her neck as he spoke and thought at first it was his hand, then became aware of the warmth of his breath and judged the gentle caress to have been delivered with his mouth. An opinion confirmed when he dropped his hands to her waist and turned her toward him and kissed her. He'd done so a number of times in the two months since they became betrothed. But not like this. This kiss was not in any way restrained. It asked something of her, rather than merely making a promise, like those before. Mollie sensed the question, but had no idea of the reply. She stiffened.

Josh lifted his head. "Kiss me back," he said. "You did for a moment once a few weeks ago. In your aunt's sitting room," he added.

She did not need reminding. She had on that occasion been nearly overcome with her feelings for him and gone limp in his arms. Only the sound of Auntie Eileen returning with the picture she'd gone to fetch—a sketch of Mollie at age five—had brought her back to her proper senses. But such senses were no longer appropriate; she was Mrs. Joshua Turner and her husband had rights and she duties. But it was not duty making bubbles seem to rise from her toes, as if she'd downed an entire bottle of champagne and it was fizzing inside her. Mollie turned her head to look over her shoulder. "The servants . . ."

"There are none. Zac has a woman who comes to clean a few days each week, but she's not here now. You will have to see about a cook, but not tonight, my sweet Mollie. Tonight we're entirely alone. Please kiss me the way you did."

She did not need to summon limpness in any conscious way. The bubbles bursting inside took care of it. And when she felt the demands his lips were making, hers opened almost of their own accord. "So soft," Josh said when he at last lifted his head. He traced her mouth with his finger, taking its measure as if it was a gateway to all the rest of her. Not just her body, Mollie realized. Her new husband was seeking that interior she had revealed to no one. Her secret self. It was a demand she had not expected, at least not consciously, and she trembled.

"Look," he said, aware that for all the extraordinary truths of her background, and her being, at least in years, not a girl but a woman, he was making her afraid, which was certainly not his intention, "as I said, there's no cook, but I believe some provisions have been laid in. Are you hungry? We can probably find some supper."

"I'm not in the least hungry," Mollie said. "But if you are . . ."

Josh shook his head.

"Then," she said, "perhaps we should go upstairs. At least," not able to prevent a fierce blush, "I presume the—" She could not make herself say bedroom, though that was what she meant, and having just promised before God to love, honor, and obey Joshua Turner, he was her master and she belonged in his bedroom whenever he wished her to be there. But he hadn't made the suggestion, she had. She blushed a second time, more fiercely than before.

"Yes," Josh said. "We should go upstairs."

She had become so accustomed to his injury she barely thought about it. Now she was acutely aware of the tapping of his wooden leg, and the asymmetric sound he made climbing behind her up the stairs to their bridal bed. Did he sleep with the peg? And how was it involved in this activity, which after all was neither passive nor, she imagined, particularly restful?

Mollie paused at the top of the stairs, not knowing which way to go. "Right," Josh said, passing in front of her to lead the way. "In here." He opened the door to a large bedchamber overlooking the street. The bed, a four-poster with tied-back, dark, and heavy velvet curtains, dominated the room. Her cases, she saw, had already been brought upstairs, delivered no doubt during the interval of what they called the wedding breakfast, though it had been an elaborate luncheon served at three in the afternoon in the elegant Metropolitan Hotel on Broadway and Prince Street. "I'll leave you for a moment, shall I?" Josh said.

Mollie nodded and he started to go, then turned back to her. "Look . . . It's been a mad sort of day for you. All the excitement . . . I can sleep down the hall if you like. We've plenty of time, Mollie."

"No, Josh." All those years and all those men who came to Brannigan's because their wives were unavailable. She meant to begin as she would go on, not establish a pattern of behavior that would drive him to seek elsewhere for what she did not give. "Allow me fifteen minutes, then come to sleep in here."

"Right," he said and let himself out, closing the door softly behind him.

One of her cases was on the folding luggage stand and Mollie remembered it as the one in which she'd packed the elaborate satin nightdress she had embroidered with the roses she'd abandoned for her wedding dress. Sure enough, it was folded carefully on the top. Mollie lost no time in stripping off her gray traveling frock, and her corset, and finally her chemise and pantaloons. Then, standing in the altogether as the Brannigan's women called it, she changed her mind. She left the exquisite nightdress where it was and climbed into the bed as naked as a newborn babe.

At the last minute, when she could hear the tap of his peg signaling Josh's return, she remembered that her hair was still up and she quickly pulled out the pins and put them on the night stand and shook her head so her curls tumbled free, and scooted back under the sheets just as he opened the door.

"All right?" he inquired.

"Entirely all right."

Some of the remaining daylight of the August evening seeped through the bedroom curtains. Enough for her to see his face as, having obtained her permission, he came further into the room. He looked grave, and somehow older. Purposeful she thought. Prepared to do his duty. Suddenly she wanted to giggle, though of course she did no such thing.

She had been imagining him in a nightshirt. Maybe even an old fashioned nightcap, though that seemed unlikely. The picture had not attracted her and she was glad instead to see that he still wore his shirt and trousers, though he'd removed his stock and the morning coat that marked him a fashionable groom. His shoe and stocking as well. The foot below his good left leg was bare. The blunt tip of his peg showed next to it. He pulled the shirt over his head and dropped it on a small chair beside the door, then crossed to the bed and sat on it with his back to her. "I know," he said, "that it's supposed to be the bride who is shy and embarrassed on her wedding night, but you must admit I have more reason than most men to share the feeling."

She nodded, then remembered he wasn't looking at her and said, "I understand that. But you shouldn't be so. Not with me. I could not admire you more if you still had both your legs."

He didn't turn to face her and his voice was very low when he said, "You really mean that, don't you?"

"I really do. I love the way you've allowed yourself no bitterness over your loss, the way you never complain, and always cope. And I know you count no man your better because he has both his legs when you have one."

He didn't answer, only sat still for a few moments, and Mollie feared she may have said too much. *A wise woman always allows the man to control the conversation, Mollie.* Then, when he moved, she was sure she sensed greater sureness in his movements, and a greater ease with her.

Josh loosed the buttons of his trousers, and stood up long enough to drop them and quickly afterward his cotton undersuit, and suddenly she was looking at his superbly muscled naked back. And the taut, very white flesh of his equally uncovered buttocks. There was a leather strap around his waist and she realized it was part of the harness for his wooden leg, but she wasn't staring at that. She'd been raised in a whorehouse, to use Auntie Eileen's blunt language, and she'd never before seen, even from the back, a naked man.

Another of those blushes she didn't seem able to control. Never mind that he couldn't see her. He knew what she was seeing. She heard his peg drop to the floor with a soft thud. Well, that was one question answered.

Then he was beside her under the sheet and lightweight summer coverlet. His hand touched her waist first, then slid down her hip a few inches, before traveling upward over her midriff. "Well, well," he murmured. "I don't have to struggle to find you." He leaned over and kissed her forehead. "I like that very much, my darling Mollie. Very, very much."

Suddenly she was astonished at her own forwardness, and embarrassed by it, though she had not been until this moment. "You must think me shameless not to have worn a nightdress. I made one, but—"

"But you guessed what would please me more," he finished for her. "And I think you are my Mollie the magnificent." Then his mouth was on hers again and there were no more words.

So what had she learned, being raised as she'd been? The mechanics were, of course, entirely familiar to her. She knew what he had and what she had and what fit where. Even all about how long the thrusts were supposed to last and what it was supposed to mean if they went on for a shorter or longer than average time. Talk of such things had been all around her when she sat at Hatty's kitchen table and heard the morning-after chatter of the women with whom she lived. But no one had ever mentioned what she was feeling now. A great wave of delight welled up and filled her. It was not a physical satisfaction of the sort that came from some pleasurable sensation such as sinking into a hot bath, or loosening a corset after a long day and scratching where it itched. It was instead more pure and more intense and considerably more profound; a sense of rightness and belonging, and even . . . however strange, a joyful power. She had something to give him that Joshua Turner wanted very much, and in the giving of it she was made at last completely alive.

For his part, Josh could feel the blood rushing in his veins and the thudding of his heart, and knew he wanted to roll on top of her and drive himself toward that explosive moment of gratification his body demanded. But he held back.

His first time had been as a boy of fourteen, in the back kitchen at Sunshine Hill. The woman who came once a week to do the laundry had asked him to come and help her move a large kettle of hot water to one of the copper tubs in the yard, but he never got as far as the stove before she'd pushed him up against the wall and had her hand down the front of his trousers and one of her enormous breasts squashed against his face. Later he'd seen her laughing with the cook and the old man who looked after the stables. He figured he'd been a dare of some sort. Never mind. He was glad to have that mystery solved.

There had been any number of whores since, but to the best of his knowledge, he'd never been with a virgin. Least of all one he cared for as deeply as he cared for this creature who had shown herself so different from the first moment she'd taken his arm and guided him through the twists and turns of Macy's department of ladies' lingerie.

When he was paying for the privilege he didn't give a damn what a woman might think of his mutilation. With Mollie the thought that she might be repulsed had been on his mind from the moment she agreed to marry him. Earlier even. It was why he hadn't broached the subject until Eileen Brannigan forced the issue. But he sensed no withdrawal in Mollie, no disgusted retreat because he was not whole. She'd come naked to his bed in a gesture of remarkable generosity, and she trembled in his arms in a manner that spoke more of anticipation than fear. He loved her for both.

Josh rolled himself above her, supporting himself on arms grown enormously strong with the need always to balance his incomplete lower half, and held himself at the ready long enough to look into her face. She did not have her eyes closed in the feigned ecstasy of commercial intimacy. Instead she was looking at him and he read in her glance both surrender and demand. "Now?" he asked.

"Now, Joshua."

He met a moment of intense resistance, and saw her wince, but while he might have found enough self-discipline to hold back a bit because of it, she made it clear there was no need. Mollie rose to meet him and moved in rhythm with each thrust and he sensed her opening herself with an astonishing abandon that had he not just encountered the proof of her innocence might have caused him to wonder. Not just instinct, he realized anew. The rightness of it all. Whatever they might be apart, together they were perfect and it seemed they both knew it.

6

EBENEZER TICKLE MADE his way through Washington Square, and turned into the narrow passage, the mews, that ran between the fine houses on the north of the park and the stables behind them. There were a few steps at the far end. They were hewn from natural stone and moss-covered and cool and damp, even now in the August heat, when the setting sun was a fiery ball in an orange sky. The steps ended below ground level at a stone outcropping and appeared to go nowhere.

Tickle knew better. He drew level with the descent, slowed his pace, and glanced over his shoulder. The passage was empty. He clambered down the stairs to a strip of ground ankle deep in windblown trash, including a few yellowed leaves which hinted at the autumn to come, and waded through the debris to a narrow opening between it and the foundation of the adjacent building. Tickle slipped through the gap and disappeared. Anyone standing at the top of the stairs would have thought he'd been magicked into the ether.

By the time he entered the cellar known as Mama Jack's Cave, he was in the midst of a noisy cacophony of talk and music—eight-foot-tall Black Tonio wailing on his trumpet, and bearded Sally banging on the piano—and, according to a legless woman who called herself Zarina and claimed to be a gypsy gifted with second sight, the moaning and bleating and wailing of the ghosts of those who had frequented this spot in colonial days when so-called bawdy houses hid themselves in the woods. Places for folks who, like the people who came to Mama Jack's, would not be comfortable in an ordinary taproom or tavern. Freaks as some called them. Ghost freaks as well as the real ones of the present day. Their spirits occupied the shadows beyond sight.

A pair of sisters joined at the hip, until in an infamous act of desperation they cut themselves apart with a butcher's knife and bled to death.

A man with a spiny growth like a unicorn's horn protruding from his forehead.

A woman with a black growth the size of a man's fist clinging to her jaw.

The legless and armless and blind, and people whose faces were eaten away by the pox, as well as mere fugitives from so-called justice.

Dwarves.

These creatures of the past hovered just out of sight some said, but this night there were at least half a dozen little people in various parts of the large cave—really more of a cellar dug out centuries before for some long-forgotten purpose—who were alive and breathing. Tickle headed for two who sat at a low table on stools made to suit their height, each with a tankard of ale. "I've news of a sort," he said by way of greeting. "Some good and some as is not."

George Higgins, the dwarf to Tickle's right, said, "I'll have the bad first."

"Aye, save the good for an ending." The second speaker was Israel McCoy. He was built the same as they, but McCoy didn't come from the western lakes of Kentucky like Ebenezer and George. Israel had been born in Daniel Boone country, the Appalachian hills on the border between Kentucky and West Virginia, and he spoke with the slight burr of the descendants of the lowland Scots who had populated the area. There were fewer little people among the mountain-men, but dwarves were not unknown in Appalachia, where every kind of human condition showed up except good fortune and wealth.

"Seems like Trenton Clifford knows we're here," Tickle said.

McCoy showed no reaction. Higgins's face went black with fury. "How you come to know that?"

"I know," Tickle said, "because he sent someone to tell me."

"I take it," McCoy said, "this Clifford's the bad news. So what's the good?"

"Man he sent seems all right," Tickle said. "And could be he's got an interesting business proposition."

George Higgins shook his head. "Ain't no way I'm going to do business with—"

"Not with him." Tickle cut him off before he could speak Clifford's name. "The man I talked to." He leaned in close and lowered his voice. "He wants to make steel and—"

"Evening, boys." Zarina it was, she who had been born without legs. She propelled herself on a board on wheels, so her arms were the size of tree trunks and it was said she could crush bricks with her knuckles. She rolled up to their table and said, "I've been waiting for you."

"Why's that?"

"Had a revelation as concerns you."

"I don't believe in your revelations." Tickle hopped off his stool and headed for the bar. Zarina and her predictions were no match for Maude Pattycake.

Maude swore that was her true name. Not made up the way some who frequented Mama Jack's changed their names because they couldn't change whatever it was they wished was different about themselves. But whatever the name she'd been born with, Maude Pattycake was unique.

She was Mama Jack's one and only child for one thing, her adopted daughter. Mama had taken Maude with her when Mama decided to stop being the fat lady in Barnum's traveling freak show. Once she made up her mind to that hard thing—getting by on her own—taking Maude along wasn't difficult. Mama Jack weighed more than five hundred pounds and Maude, a perfectly proportioned, blue-eyed blonde who stood just two and a half feet tall, would almost fit in her pocket. And Maude could dance like nobody's business.

She wore silver slippers with pearl buckles and pieces of iron on the heels and the toes, so every click and clack would be heard when she tapped out the music's rhythms. She now raised her skirts to her knees so everyone could see her gorgeous shoes, but she didn't move.

"Dance!" the assembly shouted. "Dance, Maude, dance! Tell her, Mama Jack."

Tonio flexed his fingers and smacked his lips and raised his trumpet to his mouth, but he didn't blow a note.

Mama Jack sat on a specially reinforced chair on a cast-iron dais raised above the crowd. She lifted her enormous arm, the rolls of flesh hanging from it shaking and jiggling like a jelly mold, and everything went quiet. Then, laughing so her great belly shook, she called out, "Got to have music before Maude Pattycake can dance. Make us some music, Tonio."

The eight-foot-tall trumpeter started as he always did, with Maude's very own music, an old Irish ditty called "Tom Tiddler's Song." Maude clicked once or twice. Then she clacked a few more steps. And by the time Tonio's trumpet was wailing the second chorus, the tiny dancer was clicking and clacking her way up and down the bar.

Next Tonio went on to the stokers' songs he'd learned back when he shoveled coal into the engines of the trains that ran from Buffalo to New York on Mr. Vanderbilt's New York Central Railroad. The people in Mama Jack's cave knew every note and every word. "I been workin' on the railroad," they sang, and banged their tankards in unison while

Maude danced. And, "Dinah won't you blow, Dinah won't you blow, Dinah won't you blow your horn . . ."

This went on until neither the giant Tonio nor the tiny and perfect Maude Pattycake could find any more breath, and the songs and the dancing ended and Maude finished as she'd meant to do right along. She leapt off the bar into Ebenezer Tickle's strong and waiting arms.

"In here." Josh turned the key in the rusty padlock and ushered Tickle through tall doors into a large brick building behind the oldest of the Devrey docks, themselves an extended strip of waterfront at the place where Wall Street met the East River.

The few windows were narrow and high overhead, and spilled only murky light into what was essentially a shed without interior walls, depending instead on thick brick pillars to hold up a tin roof some twenty feet above their heads. Josh pointed to two stubs of what must have once been massive rafters protruding from the wall at their right, the remains of a long-gone second floor. "Until a century ago this was part of the old slave market. I expect the building was originally two floors."

"Three, more likely," Tickle said, craning his neck to survey the evidence of the original construction. "Cram in more nigras that way. Who owns the place now?"

"The land and the building belong to my family, to Devrey Shipping. It was let to Finnegan's Ironworks for a time."

The dwarf strode off on his short legs, inspecting the hulking metal equipment that loomed in the shadows, touching and tapping and grunting with sounds that conveyed sometimes approval and sometimes the opposite. Knowledgeable sorts of sounds. For his part, Josh could attach only the most general names to what he saw—furnaces and overhead trolleys from which were suspended enormous things that looked to him like huge scoops, everything coated in rust.

Tickle paused beside one of the scooplike things and scraped at the rust with a fingernail. "How long you say it's been since any of this been used?"

"Three years. My brother took the equipment in payment of back rent when the ironworks failed."

"Finnegan's," Tickle said. "Before my time here in New York. Never heard of 'em."

"I'm told it was a small operation, though God knows this place looks vast enough to me."

"Globe and Morgan," Tickle said, citing two of the city's largest foundries, "are at least ten times as big. And Novelty's bigger still."

Novelty Iron Works, Josh knew, was the city's largest foundry. The plant where Tickle had been a foreman covered over five acres of Manhattan Island. "I'm told Finnegan's is successful now they're in Brooklyn. According to my brother, Finnegan was happy to leave this stuff behind. Set up with more modern gear in his new place."

Do what you like with it, Josh. I've never had an offer for any of what that crafty old Irishman left behind. A hurried conversation soon after the wedding ceremony, while Zac was changing out of the morning coat he'd worn as Joshua's best man, and rushing to take ship for Liverpool. He'd pulled the key to the old ironworks off his ring and handed it over along with the one to his house.

Tickle moved off to inspect the furnaces. Josh wandered deeper into the gloom and came across a large, fenced-off square. Mostly empty, except for a small pile of gray and porous-looking nuggets of coal. He picked one up and walked to where Tickle stood. The dwarf was using a piece of string to measure the opening of a massive furnace.

Josh held out the lump of coal. "Seems Finnegan's was burning coked coal in those things. I presume we must do the same." Coked coal burned cleaner and gave more heat, but it cost considerably more than the ordinary untreated sort.

"We must, Mr. Turner. And a deal of it. Only thing burns hotter than a foundry furnace is hell. Can't use regular coal. Don't burn bright enough for one thing. And the smoke would drive off Satan himself."

Josh looked around again, feeling a bit overwhelmed by the ghost-like air of the old ironworks. "Can this place be salvaged, Mr. Tickle?"

"Some of it. Enough to suit your purpose. Big job, though. Take a lot of doing."

"How long before it's ready to go?"

Tickle hesitated. "Tell me again how much steel you need," he said finally.

Joshua had brought the blueprints with him. He moved to a spot under one of the high, slitted windows and unfurled the drawings over the top of an up-ended barrel. "Here's what I'm going to build, Mr. Tickle. And according to Mr. McKim, this is what I need to build it using steel rafters." Josh slipped a second, smaller sheet out from under the first and handed it to the dwarf.

"I take it this Mr. McKim is your architect?"

"That's right. At least in as far as I have one. We're not attempting anything fancy, as you can see."

McKim was a fellow his own age, met through a chance encounter riding in Central Park; a thing possible because Josh had a saddle fitted with a special stirrup, one with a hole that accommodated the peg. He wouldn't call Charles McKim a close friend, but they got on well enough, and the other man was happy to earn a modest fee moonlighting, as they called it these days. McKim had quickly produced the blueprints for the rather simple structure Josh described.

"No doubt about it," he'd said. "You could achieve what you're after if you framed each of eight stories entirely with steel. Though I'm hard put to know who'd want to live there, Josh. Not considering the rent you'd have to charge if you put your building up anywhere a gentleman might be willing to call home. And not considering that you're proposing he live under the same roof with three dozen others."

Tickle seemed as doubtful as McKim had been. He didn't look at the second sheet, the one that listed the steel required for the job. Instead he spent many minutes studying the drawings, tracing out the lines with a hovering finger. Finally, "These here ain't big enough units to be like them French flats over on Eighteenth Street. Not enough rooms. You're building one of them there rookeries, ain't you? One of them places as they cram the immigrants into. Just taller 'n' most."

"Nothing of the sort," Josh said. "It is like the French flats, only a little less grand."

"A rookery," Tickle repeated stubbornly. "For foreign birds. All of 'em chirping different languages and stinking of whatever strange food they been eating wherever they comes from. Be the ruin of the country, all these immigrants will."

Josh leaned against another of the barrels, securing his balance with his elbows, taking the weight off his good leg. "I would think, Mr. Tickle, that you'd know a bit about being the object of derision simply because you're different from the folks around you."

"Here now, ain't no cause to think that. I'm a dwarf, but I'm an American, same as you. My great-granddaddy fought in the Revolution."

In the land of the blind, Josh thought, the one-eyed man is king. No point in trying to change Tickle's politics. They weren't based on reason. "Look," he said, "a rookery of the sort they've got down in Five Points or way uptown is a virtual barracks. Huge sheds, nothing more. The tenements are only a bit better, solid brick rectangles built to cover every inch of ground the landlord owns. Windows front and back, and the only other ventilation a foot-square air shaft up the middle. And, as you say, in both cases people jumbled together like rats in a nest." He pointed to his blueprints. "This is nothing like either of those. These are separate units, each meant for a single family, and each with proper ventilation so there's sunlight and air. And while we'll build on three lots, we can get four flats across the frontage because of your steel beams and girders. It's what we talked about that first day. If I use steel, I don't need to build the bearing walls from brick. That's what you said, Mr. Tickle, and Mr. McKim agrees." The inventory of construction materials he'd handed Tickle remained in the dwarf's hand, the edges curled over his fist. Tickle still made no attempt to unroll and examine it, just kept looking at the blueprints. "I suppose," he muttered after a time.

"Have a look at the list, Mr. Tickle. It will bear me out."

Tickle still didn't examine the paper. After a few moments Josh recognized the problem. The other man couldn't read. "Here," he said quickly, flipping over one of the drawings and taking a pencil from his coat pocket. "It's easier to understand if we do it this way." He began creating a graphic of what was required, indicating beams of different lengths with simple lines, and showing the numbers of each by a system of cross-hatching in groups of five. It took some doing, and once or twice he had to take out his pocket knife and renew the point of the soft lead.

Tickle stood quietly beside him all the while; watching, nodding occasionally as the scope of the project took shape. "Don't need all what's here to make as much steel as you're wanting," he said at last. "We'd only have to restore a few of the ladles," nodding toward what Josh had thought of as giant scoops, "and maybe only two of the furnaces."

"What about the pig iron?" Josh asked.

"We won't try and make that here. Don't make sense when we can buy it."

"Cost?" Josh inquired, this time poising his pencil over a piece of paper meant for his own notes.

"I'll get you the pig iron at a good price right enough. Say half of what it costs regular."

Some sort of private arrangement, Josh realized. Arrived at through Tickle's foundry connections. Everyone but the foundry owners a bit richer than they were before, and so little going out the door each time it wouldn't be missed. "It has to be the best," he said. "I know nothing about making steel, Mr. Tickle, or pig iron for that matter. But I know you can't make first-quality products with inferior raw materials. I don't intend this to be the last building I put up. It has to be safe and sturdy."

"No cause to worry," Tickle said. "Same pig iron as Globe or Novelty uses to make their cast iron."

"Very well. What about the workers? How many and where will you get them?"

"Seven," Tickle said, "including me. Each of the others known to me personally. Experienced. Trustworthy as well."

Josh was prepared to accept this. Being a foreman at Novelty meant knowing what sort of men he needed and where to find them. "And," pencil poised, "I shall pay these seven foundry men how much per hour?"

"Fifty cents."

"That's ten cents over the going rate, Mr. Tickle."

"It is. And they works an eight-hour day."

"Impossible. I need this job done quickly."

"No difficulty with that," Tickle said. "We'll work as many hours as it takes. Round the clock in shifts if necessary. Cost you time and a half for the overtime." The dwarf looked again at the graphic detailing the numbers and sizes of the required steel beams and girders. "Once we get set up, take about three months, I figure. Maybe two if you're a lucky sort of man and we're lucky with you. But I can't get men to leave the jobs they has now and come to work for you if I can't promise a year's steady work."

It was a reasonable assertion, but there was no way Josh could prudently commit himself to employing Tickle plus seven others for a year. His scheme involved too many variables. At best he gave himself a sixty percent chance of succeeding. "Six months," he said. "That's the best I can do. But I'll promise an increase of three cents an hour on the base wage if after six months I see my way clear to extend the contract."

Tickle nodded. "Sounds fair to me. I expect the others will agree."

Josh still hesitated to offer his hand on the arrangement. "One other thing," he said. "And I know I've asked before."

"Mr. Clifford," Tickle said, anticipating the question.

"Yes. Trenton Clifford. Why won't you tell me how you know him, how he happened to send me to see you?"

"'Cause it ain't got nothing to do with this business between us. Like I said when you asked before, I ain't never heard tell of you until the day you first came to my door."

"Will you swear you're not reporting to him, that he's not some sort of silent partner in our arrangement?"

"A partner with me? Trenton Clifford? As God is my judge, that's never how it will be."

The dwarf spoke the words with a look so fierce it was plain Ebenezer Tickle had some dark history of his own with Trenton Clifford, a possibility Josh did not find hard to credit. So fair enough, no cooperation, nothing to do Josh damage. All the same, the dwarf probably wasn't entirely free of Trenton Clifford. Any more than he was.

God knows he'd asked himself often enough why he met Clifford that first time in the bar at the Grand Union, why he kept the card the bastard gave him, why, ultimately, he went to see Ebenezer Tickle, the man Clifford recommended. It was because, Josh had eventually admitted to himself, whatever else he was, Trenton Clifford was a survivor, someone who knew how things worked. And he, Joshua Turner, had it in mind to be not just a survivor but a winner. Meaning he'd take any opportunity that came his way, regardless of the source. As for the dwarf and the onetime commandant of Belle Isle prison camp . . . No way he could know for sure what was between them since Tickle refused to tell him. Josh would just have to wait and watch, and be ready to move if at any time whatever it was seemed to threaten his affairs.

His leg was aching; he'd been standing on it too long. Time to set aside the speculation and move on. "Very well, we're agreed then, Mr. Tickle. You shall make me first-quality steel beams to the exact quantity, dimensions, and shapes Mr. McKim has designated in these drawings. And I shall pay your workers fifty outrageous cents per hour for six months. Fifty-three cents if I've enough business to keep them on longer."

"Up to eight hours in a single day, six days a week, for the base pay," Tickle amended. "Time and a half apart from that."

Josh considered for a moment, scratched a few figures on the notes he'd been making for his own use, then said, "Agreed. And what do I pay you, Mr. Tickle? I presume you expect a greater wage than you've negotiated for those who'll work under you."

Tickle was looking again at the blueprints. "This ain't no rookery? You willing to swear to that?"

Josh put his hand over his heart, impressed that Tickle was apparently so determined to stand by a principle, even if it was a misguided distrust of foreigners. "It is not," he said solemnly. "You and I, Mr. Tickle, are going to build something entirely new, flats for what are called middle-class gentlemen and their families."

"You mean accountants and bank clerks and those sorts of people."

"Exactly."

"Then," the dwarf said after a moment's more consideration, "you pays me nothing."

"Nothing?"

"That's right. Not in cash money as is doled out every week like the rest gets."

"What then, Mr. Tickle?" Josh wouldn't have been surprised if the dwarf asked for Trent Clifford's head on a platter.

"One of them there flats as you calls 'em, Mr. Turner." The dwarf pointed to the blueprint. "I get to choose one for myself. And no rent paid."

"Well, you don't lack cheek, Mr. Tickle. I'll say that for you. Except these flats aren't bigger versions of a rooming house. They're truly private homes. Alternatives to owning a brownstone of one's own."

"Even better," Tickle said.

"You will work for me for a year and—"

"Nope. First six months only. After that, if we're to go on, we negotiates a wage."

"Fair enough. But even so . . . I can't yet be precise, but you can take it as a given that these flats are going to be let for upwards of three hundred dollars a quarter, and a lease of five years required."

"I'd need ten," Tickle said at once. "And I pays nothing."

"Ten years rent free," Josh said. "Does that not strike you as an outlandish wage for six months work?"

A few seconds went by. The dwarf turned and looked at the deserted foundry and its rusted equipment. Finally, he turned back to the man who was proposing to employ him. "Tell me one thing, Mr. Turner," pointing to the blueprint, "can you build these flats without me?"

They both knew the answer.

"Consider something else," Josh said. "Even with your steel beams, it may not all come together. It's a big undertaking, Mr. Tickle. I cannot guarantee this building will ever rise from these sheets of paper to become reality. You might wind up having worked for nothing at all."

"I understand that," the dwarf said. "But I'll take my chances along with yours, Mr. Turner. I'm betting this here building's going to be built. And betting on something else as well. I think, like you said, you're going to put up other buildings, more of these flats maybe. So you're going to need more steel, and I expect you and I can agree a proper wage for me on the next job. And the one after that."

Another few seconds. Then, "Done, Mr. Tickle. My hand on it."

"Done," Tickle said, grasping Josh's hand in his own.

Two days later when Josh returned to the old slave quarters, five men were working inside. Three, including Tickle, were dwarves. Two were black men. Each was stripped to the waist in the stifling heat, though as yet no furnace had been fired. The suffocating temperature was all down to the blazing sun of the August afternoon. The men were pouring sweat, but they weren't slacking. They were using wire brushes and great quantities of sand to scrub the rust from as much of the equipment as they needed.

As Tickle said they needed, Josh thought, realizing yet again how utterly dependent he was on the other man's specialized knowledge to literally get his project off the ground.

The dwarf approached him, wiping his face with a red bandanna.

"I see you've chosen your crew, Mr. Tickle."

"I have. Known 'em all since Eddyville. You've ordered the coke?"

Josh nodded, still watching the others. The dwarves in particular. "It'll be delivered tomorrow morning."

"Good. At least three of us will sleep here from tomorrow night then. Ain't been nothing worth stealing before."

"Three of these men? Do I take it then they are the actual steel-makers, not merely a cleaning crew?"

"Every one's an iron man, Mr. Turner. They'll be here start to finish."

"Fair enough. I'll need time sheets for them, Mr. Tickle. So they can be paid."

"All arranged, Mr. Turner." Tickle turned away and put two fingers to his lips and emitted a shrill whistle. The other men all looked up. Tickle pointed to one of the dwarves and beckoned him over. "This here's George Higgins, been a foundry monkey practically since he came off the teat. Mr. Turner's the man we're working for, George."

Josh put out his hand. George wiped his on his trousers before taking it. "Pleased to meet you, Mr. Turner."

"And I you, Mr. Higgins." The other man was around Tickle's height, with an equally astonishing build. And his grip had much in common with the iron he'd spent his life making.

"George keeps the time sheets, Mr. Turner. Get the ledger, George."

The dwarf moved off into the gloom. Tickle used the pause to introduce the others. The third dwarf was Israel McCoy, and the pair of black men—brothers apparently—were Washington and Sampson Smith. Josh wondered if the Negroes knew the history of the building they were working in, but decided against asking. By the time the introductions were complete George Higgins was back, carrying a board with a sheaf of papers attached by a nail. The top sheet contained the name of each of the workers, along with seven columns headed with days of the week. The hours of labor were indicated by large crosses in particular boxes. The thing was a picture of who had worked what hours, printed in pencil in carefully drawn block letters. The document gave the impression of having been written with much attention and effort, by someone licking the lead pencil every few strokes to be sure of dark and clear results.

"Got a summary sheet next page," George said. "Shows how many hours is regular time, how many overtime. Mr. Tickle here, he makes his mark each day to say I got it right." Pointing to a large letter *T* written at the end of each day's column.

"My responsibility to say everything's as it should be," Tickle said.

Josh hesitated, not knowing how to question Tickle's ability to check George's work, given that the foreman couldn't read. Tickle picked up on the question without it being spoken. "I know how each man's name looks," he said. "It's an honest accounting, Mr. Turner."

"I'm sure." Josh was still looking at the time sheets. "However, there are seven names here. I don't recall meeting anyone named Obadiah or Henry. But they're shown as working. Today and yesterday I note."

"Obadiah Tickle and Henry Tickle. My cousins," Ebenezer said.

Josh peered into the gloom of the foundry's distant corners. "And where might they be, Mr. Tickle?"

"They've gone to Kentucky. To Eddyville. On your business."

"Eddyville, Kentucky. Where you worked for the Kelly brothers?"

"Correct, Mr. Turner."

"And I am apparently paying them fifty cents an hour to make the journey."

"Plus overtime. And feed for them and the pair of horses. The wagon belongs to Obadiah. He said there weren't no need to charge you for its use. Since you're our employer."

"So, a trip to western Kentucky with a wagon pulled by two horses. Sounds as if you're planning to bring something back, Mr. Tickle. Something heavy."

Tickle nodded. "That's right. It'll be here soon enough. That's another reason some of us'll be sleeping on the premises from tomorrow night. It's a thing of value, Mr. Turner."

"How so, Mr. Tickle?"

"Because we can't make steel without it."

"But these furnaces, all this equipment you're so busy cleaning . . ."

"This is my part of the job, Mr. Turner. My part of getting the building off the paper and standing on the ground. You don't think I know what I'm doing, you best get yourself another foreman."

It was all the explanation Josh was going to get and he took it.

The dining-room table was littered with papers of various shapes and sizes. Josh was sitting in his shirtsleeves, making quick notations on first one, then the other. Every once in a while he shuffled them into different piles.

Mollie watched the process for a time, apparently keeping her attention on her embroidery. After a bit she got up and lowered the window. "No breeze whatever today. We may as well keep out the noise."

Josh made a sound that passed for agreement.

She went to stand behind him. "Joshua, can I—"

He interrupted her words by reaching for her hand and bringing it to his lips. He did not, however, lift his head and look at her. "Sorry to be so preoccupied, Mollie. I'm not a very attentive new husband, I'm afraid. Once I've got these flats built we shall have a honeymoon. I promise. Maybe even go to Europe."

"I don't crave a honeymoon, Josh. Truly I don't." She did not say that she expected to be blossoming with his first son or daughter by the time he finished building his flats. Since they had been married only three weeks she could not yet guarantee that to be the case. Though considering the numbers of times they performed the requisite first step, it seemed to her likely. "I was thinking of something else."

"What?" he asked, still looking not at her but at his papers.

Before they were married, Mollie knew, his office and his living quarters had been in the nicest of his rooming houses, the one in Bowling Green. It was in fact two brownstones he'd knocked together into a spacious establishment that maintained the look and feel of the once-fashionable residential neighborhood. Now that he and Mollie were established in Zac's house on Grand Street, Josh had rented both the Bowling Green rooms once kept for his own use.

She was, however, aware of those facts only because he'd told her. She'd offered to keep his books, pointing out she'd been doing so for her aunt since the age of eleven, but Josh refused. *You keep my house, my love. Business is my affair.* "I was going to suggest," Mollie said, "that I arrange a proper office for you. So you need not gather up everything and put it away each time we sit down to a meal."

"A proper office where? One of the bedrooms upstairs, I suppose."

She knew from his tone the idea did not appeal. "No, that's not what I had in mind." All manner of people called on him for reasons of business. Dwarves even. The idea of strangers traipsing about upstairs where she and Josh slept, where someday soon she hoped their children would sleep, was not pleasant. "It does not seem to me we have any need of a drawing room, Josh. And there's room downstairs next to the kitchen to store the parlor furniture. I can see about a proper desk for you. And a cabinet for your papers and some chairs. It wouldn't cost a great deal."

He put down his pencil and raised his head and looked at her. "You are honestly proposing to turn your drawing room over to my affairs? You wouldn't mind?"

Mollie shook her head. "Not in any serious way. Oh, it's nice having a place to receive visitors, of course. But just now no one's coming to have tea and gossip. It's all business. And while the children are small—" She saw his expression and broke off, feeling the heat of a fiery blush. "The children I hope we have, I mean."

"Ah— Then you're not telling me you're . . ."

"I'm not. At least not yet. I mean I may be. I don't know as it's only three weeks." Her cheeks were hotter than before, though that did not seem possible.

Josh stood up and put his arms around her. "I love that you can still blush like a girl, though I can personally attest to the fact that such you are no longer."

"I wasn't a girl when I married you, Joshua Turner. I was a spinster and you took me off the shelf."

"My spinster," he said, kissing her between the words. "And I chose you off a Macy's shelf, where everything is known to be of excellent quality." Then, drawing back his head to look directly at her, "It's probably sensible to wait a bit before adding more expense and commotion to our lives, but I suppose I must prepare myself for the consequences of the exercise of my marital rights. Very well, so be it." He was, meanwhile, fumbling with the buttons that marched up her back. "I have no intention of forgoing them."

"Josh, what are you doing?"

"I'm undressing you. Prior to ravishing you."

"It's barely four in the afternoon."

"Ten past in fact," he murmured, bending his head to nuzzle her neck. "I don't care. I want you right now."

"Josh!"

"That cook you hired starts tomorrow, right?"

"Mrs. Hannity. Yes, but—"

"And the maid is nowhere about that I can see."

"Jane. It's not one of her days. She comes three times a week."

"Excellent. So we're entirely alone, are we not?" He was still struggling to loose the bodice of her dress. And kissing whatever part of her he could reach.

"We are alone, Josh. All the same, I—" Mollie broke off. Auntie Eileen's voice was as loud in her head as if she stood beside them. *If the wives of the gentlemen who come here provided what we provide, mark my words, we'd soon have no clients.*

Mollie reached down and lifted her skirt and the two petticoats that were all she wore because of the late summer heat. "Stop fussing with my buttons," she said. Kissing him back between the words; quick, impatient little kisses as heated as his own. "Pull down my pantaloons," she commanded. "Hurry."

And when he had, she stepped out of them and forced him back in his chair so the peg would present no problems of balance, then herself unbuttoned the front of his trousers before straddling his lap.

Josh's first indication of the return of the Tickle cousins was the presence of a large and sturdy wagon outside the ironworks on Thursday afternoon of the second week of Tickle's occupation of the premises. There was a considerable quantity of straw still evident in the back of the wagon, and a trail of bits and pieces of it leading to the foundry door; indicating that the material had been used to cushion the transport of whatever it was Obadiah and Henry Tickle had brought back from Kentucky, and that the mysterious object was now inside the foundry.

Josh pulled open the door and stepped into the dim interior. Thanks to the thick brick walls it was a few degrees cooler than outside, but reeking of the musk of men's sweat and echoing with the clang of metal on metal as the workers went about hammering the old equipment into working order. Josh had grown accustomed to the appearance and smell and sound of the ironworks. Not, however, to what he was looking at. "Jesus, God Almighty. What is that thing?"

"A Kelly converter," a voice said at his elbow. "Only one of its sort still in existence. You must be Mr. Turner."

"I am. And you are—"

"Henry Tickle, Mr. Turner. Ebenezer's cousin."

He knew there was no reason the dwarf's cousins must be dwarves as well, but he'd gotten it in his head they were. Not so. Henry Tickle was taller than Josh himself, while the man he took to be Obadiah—standing beside Ebenezer, the pair of them working on the half-assembled structure called a converter—was only a bit shorter than Henry. Despite that, the three cousins looked alike; dark hair and square jaws and prominent noses. As for the thing brought back from Kentucky, it was a broad-bellied ovoid some eight feet tall that immediately reminded Josh of the drawing the dwarf had shown him that first day on Dey Street. Just then it was sitting on the ground, though Josh figured the two iron stands not far away were meant to eventually lift it clear of the floor, and would add another four or five feet to the height.

The role of two other pieces of equipment he'd not seen before was less obvious. "Those are trunnions, aren't they?" he asked.

"That they are, Mr. Turner."

He'd recognized them from his army days. Trunnions were the things the artillery used to pivot their big guns. "I take it then that thing you're calling a converter, once it's mounted on those stands, swings in some way."

"It does, Mr. Turner. All topsy-turvy, you might say. Straight over. So's we can pour the steel out from the hole at the top."

"And this converter is somehow superior to the furnaces already here?"

"They's a different thing entire, Mr. Turner. These here furnaces burn coke and melt pig iron. It's that liquid iron what gets ladled into the converter. Then the charge comes. Twenty minutes later we're pouring steel out the top. Converted. From pig iron."

It was an explanation of sorts. "It's enormous," Josh said. "How'd you get it in the wagon?"

"It was all in pieces. Put aside like. And it ain't so big as all that. This was the Kelly brothers' first converter. Only takes five tons of melted pig iron."

"And presto change-o," Josh said, "turns it into steel. In twenty minutes you said."

"That's right."

"This charge you mentioned, what is it?"

"Air, Mr. Turner." The answer came from Ebenezer Tickle, who had left his work to join them. "Ordinary air. As I told you on the first day." Then, turning to his cousin, "Go help Obadiah finish up, Henry. I'll be explaining all he needs to know to Mr. Turner."

Josh was still trying to fathom the process. "If you somehow apply air to that thing when it's full of molten iron, Mr. Tickle, does it not cool and become hard, and therefore impossible to pour out the top? Presuming you manage to use those trunnions to tip over something so heavy."

"Trunnions'll work. You can take that for gospel. Seen 'em do it with my own eyes. Plenty of times. As for the air, I thought the same as you once. Cool everything down and what good's that? But it don't happen like that. Pump air into the bottom of the converter and it sets liquid pig iron boiling fiercer and faster than any kettle on a hot stove. Shoots flames right out the top and burns off the carbon. Thing is to know when you've burned off enough but not too much, then pour it out. Matter of judgment," Tickle said. "Matter of experience."

"Which you have."

"I do, Mr. Turner."

And later, after George had presented him with the reckoning of the cost of Henry and Obadiah Tickle's journey, "Do you realize, Mr. Tickle, that I have paid seven hundred and thirty dollars to bring this Kelly converter all the way to New York by horse and wagon? And neither the wagon nor the men served any purpose of mine on the journey to Eddyville. It would have cost considerably less if we'd arranged a local hauler to get it to a port in, say Raleigh, or even Norfolk. Could have come the rest of the way by sea. Perhaps on a Devrey ship at a favorable rate."

"No, it could not, Mr. Turner."

"Why not?"

"Converter was all in pieces. Stored at different places. Weren't no one in Eddyville knew how to collect 'em all, much less be sure nothing was missing and pack everything for safe shipping. Had to send Henry and Obadiah for that."

New information. Josh considered it, then looked around. He and Tickle were standing on the foundry floor, somewhat apart from the others, but not totally out of earshot. He motioned his foreman to follow him, then walked out the door, waiting until Tickle had closed it behind them to say, "You're telling me the thing was hidden, aren't you? Scattered about down there in Kentucky. And no one knew the whereabouts of each piece except you."

"Not exactly." Tickle had produced his pipe and a portion of tobacco and was preparing a smoke while they talked. "Henry and Obadiah knew as well. That's why they could go and get it. Not nobody else. You'll earn back your seven hundred, Mr. Turner. My word on it."

That nagging something, the one thing he wasn't entirely sure about in the matter of Ebenezer Tickle, started buzzing in Josh's head. "Trenton Clifford's involved somehow," Josh said. "I know he is. How?"

The dwarf had taken some safety matches from one of his many pockets and was busy striking one against the sandpaper strip on the side of the box. Josh waited until the pipe was lit. "You're not denying Clifford's involved, are you?"

"Converter don't belong to him, if that's what you're thinking. Belongs to me. Mr. Kelly gave it to me in return for back wages."

Josh turned his head, as if he could see through the closed door to the thing that lay behind it. "A thing of value, you said. Kelly must have owed you a considerable sum of money."

"Six months' pay," Tickle said, with the stem of the pipe still between his teeth. "But he said the converter weren't worth all that much. Not seeing as how he'd sold the patent to Bessemer."

"Where's Kelly now?" Josh asked after a number of silent seconds, aware that the other man was avoiding a direct gaze.

"Last I heard, Louisville. Makes axes and such like."

"Not steel?"

"Not far as I know. And not unless he's built himself a new converter. Smashed up all the bigger ones after he went bankrupt and sold out. Only this one left."

"And Trenton Clifford's not involved?"

"Not with the converter, no." Punctuated by a puff of smoke that curled above the dwarf's head and hung motionless in the hot, still air.

Josh turned and looked again at the foundry door, then out across the docks to the river. "Jesus," he said.

"That'll do fine, Mr. Turner. You pray. Me and the others, we'll make your steel beams and girders."

Josh spent most of September tramping around the city looking for a building site. Until summer was over and there was an autumn nip in the air, and he still had not located anything suitable that fit his plans or his budget. "Cart got put ahead of the horse," he told Mollie. "Not how I intended it. I got involved in making steel before I'd had a chance to think it through."

"Because the opportunity presented itself," Mollie said.

"Something like that."

"Josh, what about Auntie Eileen's promise? Won't that extra hundred thousand help with the purchase of a site?"

"It might do, but the truth is I've calculated your aunt's loan in ten different ways for ten different parts of the project. And I can't go to my brother yet again. Devrey's is having the devil of a time just staying afloat. Literally and figuratively. What's that expression about borrowing from Peter?"

"To pay Paul," Mollie said. "I understand."

He'd poured himself a small glass of sherry wine and one for her as well, and he brought them to the dining room table where they did most of their living and talking now that the parlor had been made into an office. "Besides," he added, "a hundred thousand's small change what with the cost of land these days. There's a piece not too far from Gramercy Park, Twenty-Seventh Street between Second and Third Avenues, where there are two vacant lots side by side and a third next to them with a ramshackle old two-story building I could take down.

Three years ago I might have bought the lots for four thousand each and the building for fifteen. Now the building's forty-seven thousand and the owner of the lots is asking twenty thousand each."

Mollie nibbled on her lip.

"What are you thinking?" Josh asked. "You're always thinking something when you do that."

Mollie didn't know what he meant for a second, then she realized and stopped chewing. Thinking, meanwhile, that it was quite marvelous that her husband, a busy man of affairs, had noticed such a small thing about her. But she knew this moment was not about romance. "It occurs to me," Mollie said, "that the answer may be boldness. More even than you've already displayed."

"What I've displayed," he said, "might equally be called foolhardiness. C'mon out with it. What's your idea?"

"Your father's lots in the East Sixties," Mollie said. Then, before he could make the customary objection about that land being too far from the heart of the town, "That's what I meant about being bold. You must convince possible tenants that the city is moving north faster than they realized. You can do it, Josh. I know you can. And I'm sure you could work out favorable terms with Dr. Turner."

7

CAROLINA INSISTED THE meeting take place in her bedroom. She was propped against a number of pillows, wrapped in a crocheted shawl, with her silver hair in a braid that hung over her shoulder. Looking, Mollie thought, pale and ill, except that her eyes twinkled rather like her son's, and she was obviously still as clever about business as ever.

"The biggest problem with Papa's lots, Josh," Carolina said, "is that they are miles from anywhere. How will these middling business types you plan to let to get from Sixty-Third Street to where they earn their living?"

"I'm expecting," Josh said, "Mr. Tweed to follow through on his New York Railway Company."

Nicholas Turner sat beside his wife, holding her hand. "Seems like a fair assumption," Nick said. "Apparently nothing whatever can stop Mr. Tweed from stringing an elevated railway right round all of Manhattan. He's got everyone who matters on his board, and the city's pledged five million toward construction."

"The city," Simon Turner said, "had best do something."

At twenty-one Simon was the youngest of Mollie's new family and the only one of Josh's siblings she saw regularly—Zac was still in Liverpool and Goldie had gone to visit him. Nonetheless, she found Simon the hardest to fathom. He had a coolness about him. At least where she was concerned. She didn't think he'd spoken two complete sentences to her since they'd met. Like his father, Simon was a doctor. He'd been graduated from Columbia Medical College a few months before, but had gone on living at home. Mollie thought that was probably because of Carolina's illness; Josh said he simply enjoyed having everything done for him. Whatever the reason, these days Simon traveled daily from Sunshine Hill to New York Hospital on Sixteenth Street and Fifth Avenue. "The horsecar I was on this afternoon," he said now, "had better than sixty people crammed into the space meant for twenty-two. Fully half of them were hanging off the outside at peril to life and limb."

"All the same," his father said, "a railroad that runs over our heads, spilling smoke and cinders while we walk below . . . It seems a rather unsightly choice."

"It's that or we must travel under the ground like moles," Simon said. "There are folks suggesting that, you know. Though I would imagine the upheaval caused by all those tunnels would be as unsightly as Boss Tweed's elevated railway."

"When," Carolina said, "has New York City considered the sightliness of anything? At least when weighed against the possibility of profit. However, given that I've nothing to do but lie abed and read the papers, I can tell you I sense trouble brewing for Mr. Tweed. His enemies are gathering and I think they smell blood."

"May I ask a question?" The others turned to Mollie. All at the same time, rather like a music hall performance. She was still an exotic, a rare bird that had flown into their contented nest up here on distant Seventy-First Street. "When you moved your family to Sunshine Hill, Dr. Turner, did you not require to travel to the city?"

"At least three or four days a week," he agreed. "And my wife as well. She was responsible for all of Devrey Shipping in those days." Patting Carolina's hand in a way that made it obvious he wasn't shamed by her legendary activities in the world of men.

"Then how," Mollie asked, "did you and Mrs. Turner manage to get back and forth?"

"By carriage," Nick said, looking as if he thought the question a bit odd. "There wasn't any other possibility. There still isn't really. Carriage or horseback. Simon rides every day as far as Forty-Fifth Street. Then leaves his mount at a livery stable and takes the horsecar."

"Exactly," Mollie said. "That's what I've been thinking. At least since you raised the point, Mrs. Turner. Josh"—he'd returned to sit next to her—"what about stables? The flats are to occupy three adjacent lots. Dr. Turner owns six. Could you not build a stable beside them?"

He shook his head. "No good would come of it. The sort of people we're hoping will rent our flats are unlikely to afford private carriages or even a horse. The units won't be grand enough to attract those who—"

"You're missing Mollie's point, Josh," his mother interrupted. "At least if I understand her. You mean a commercial stable, do you not, my dear?"

"Exactly, Mrs. Turner. I'm sure Joshua can prevail on one of the omnibus companies to do two or three runs a day from Sixty-Third Street, if they can stable their horses and lodge their cars at a favorable rate."

Josh smelled the smoke of Trenton Clifford's cigar before he heard his voice. "What's this then? Looks like a Yankee barracks. How are you keeping, Joshua?"

"Well enough." He'd wakened with a fierce ache in his left thigh, and a sharp pain in the right leg he did not have. Not uncommon, his father had assured him years before, to feel pain in the missing limb. Science could not explain it, but the phenomenon had been reported countless times. And occasional cramp in the leg that bore the brunt of his weight was to be expected. Worse always when the weather turned cold and damp as it had now that it was almost November. "You're a good way from your usual precincts, are you not, Clifford? What are you doing here?"

"I came to see if the rumors were true."

"What rumors are those?" Though he already knew the answer.

"That you're setting about building your human storage units up here on Sixty-Third Street amid the city's garbage heaps. I declare, son, I'm disappointed in you."

Joshua had pretty much the same thoughts each time he covered the distance between Grand Street and his construction site. Usually he did it on horseback, straight up the Bowery, which became Fourth Avenue, except for the stretch from Seventeenth Street to Grand Central which was called Park Avenue. The name change occurred because for those few blocks grass and shrubbery had been planted to conceal the grates above the tunnel that carried the trains beneath fashionable Murray Hill. Whatever he told Clifford and everyone else, after dark he'd not do the run without a rifle. "The city is moving north at a tremendous clip," he said. "It'll catch up."

"Possibly," Clifford allowed. He was craning his neck to examine the yet unfinished roof above their heads. "So this is what you and Ebenezer Tickle devised between you." Two steel girders stretched the thirty-foot back-to-front length of the brick-framed structure. "Seems a bit of a waste."

"This isn't the flats." He'd had the stable built first because it was much the easier project, and used the steel girders because, given that he was already producing them, there was little expense in doing so.

"I realize that. A livery stable. You've done a deal with old man Hopkins. I heard that as well."

"I expect that's common knowledge by now." The sign was to be delivered and hung outside this week, even though the interior of the stable remained to be finished. HOPKINS AND SONS OMNIBUS COMPANY—DAILY JOURNEYS TO NEW YORK. *You want that in place as soon as ever it can be, Josh. So people will have confidence in the prom-ise.* It's what Mollie had said and he agreed with her.

"Also," Clifford flicked a thick nubbin of ash from the end of his cigar, "that you're counting on Tweed's scheme for an elevated railroad along Third Avenue."

"Eventually there's to be one along Second as well."

"So they say. But there's others as say different, son. You might con-sider throwing your lot in with theirs."

Josh felt himself beginning to totter; the good left leg had taken as much punishment as it could tolerate. His stick, meanwhile, lay atop a half-built stable wall some fifteen feet away. "I'm not, thank God, your son. Is that all our business, Captain Clifford? If so, perhaps you'll excuse me." Josh turned and started for the wall and knew when he took the first step he was more unsteady than he'd realized and might stumble and go down. He did sometimes. Not so bad if he was alone. He could always crawl to something sturdy enough to allow him to haul himself up. But now . . . Dear God, don't let him fall with that bastard looking on.

Clifford guessed what he was after and easily outstrode him and claimed the prize. "Nice walking stick," he said, holding it by the busi-ness end and offering it with the ornate horse's head first. "Looks like an antique."

"Stick's new, but the head's been in my family a time. Thank you." Josh took the stick and planted it firmly on the dirt floor and leaned on it. Most of his weight shifted to his arm. A fair amount of relief, and thank God he was still upright. Though he knew he'd been grimacing, and that his face was damp with sweat despite the autumn chill.

"My carriage is outside," Clifford said. "Why don't we go sit down and talk more comfortably?"

"I thought we were done talking."

"As stubborn as ever. No, Joshua, we are not done. I've come to make a proposition."

"There are no shares of the project for sale. So I'm not interested in any backing you—"

"Not why I'm here." Another glance at the steel girders. "I didn't steer you wrong the last time, did I? About the dwarf, I mean."

"You did not." There was little point in denying it with the evidence stretched above their heads.

"Then at least hear me out this time."

"I'm listening."

"The overhead railway's going to fail. The noise and the stink of it will prove little better than what we've got now with that god-awful clatter running past our front doors." A nod toward Fourth Avenue and Vanderbilt's infernal trains smoking and steaming their way north and south.

"You seem to forget," Josh said, "the Greenwich Street el's been extended up Ninth Avenue as far as Thirtieth Street."

"I'm not forgetting anything, son. But we are standing a considerable distance north of Thirtieth Street. And I declare to you, Joshua Turner, that the way men and indeed women and children are destined to get up and down this thirteen-mile island is in tunnels laid underground. My solemn word on it."

He could be right, Josh knew that. In which case his arrangement with Hopkins—he'd granted the man a twenty-year lease on very favorable terms—would prove to be folly. But Josh didn't think so. There was something a bit too far-fetched about the notion of underground tunnels, too exotic for gritty, workaday New York City. "Blown back and forth by pneumatic tubes," he said, not trying to keep the scorn from his voice. There was a thing of the sort opened the year before in a three-hundred-foot tunnel dug surreptitiously under Broadway. It was a demonstration effort consisting of a single car fitted with velvet cushions and candles, and a grand piano in the station under a building on Murray Street. So decent folk would feel comfortable descending below the earth.

Clifford shook his head. "Nothing like that. No pneumatic tubes, they're a diversion, a novelty show. I'm speaking of proper trains driven by steam and running underground where we neither smell nor see nor hear them. They're already doing exactly that in London.

Here, on Manhattan, it will be a revelation, Joshua. A wonderment for the ages. Something that properly compliments your revolutionary ideas for housing the middling classes."

"And who is to build these tunnels, Captain? They require, I warrant, an amount of capital well in excess of that needed to erect an apartment building." Even with the stick, he really could not go on standing much longer. Josh felt the blood draining from his face.

"Indeed. A considerable amount of capital. Here, you're looking a bit pale. Let me help you. We can—"

Clifford reached out to take his arm. Josh shook his hand away.

Clifford sighed. "Very well, Joshua. We shall do things in the direct and somewhat uncivilized way you Yankees prefer. I'm here to tell you to get a message to your brother. He's in England. He can have a look at what they're doing in London. Once he's convinced himself the enterprise is viable, as indeed it is, I want his backing. The Devrey name attached to it would make an enormous difference."

"I doubt Zac will be interested. He's a much more conventional business sort than I. Underground tunnels will seem entirely too futuristic."

Clifford shrugged. "All I want you to do is convey a proposal. You owe me that much," with another glance up to the steel girder. "Besides, if you've your brother's welfare at heart, you won't refuse."

"How so?"

"Use the brains God gave you, Turner. Devrey's is failing. The entire American merchant marine, if it comes to it. That's what their war of aggression cost the North, the destruction of their commercial shipping. The very lifeblood of their economic power. The English pretty much have the market cornered now. But there's still considerable worth in the Devrey fleet. I'm suggesting the ships be sold, and your brother's company become a major part of a consortium to build underground transportation for New York."

"Wipe out Devrey's and invest the return in some wild scheme of yours? Zac will tell you to go to hell."

"Maybe. Maybe not. He's in Liverpool, I'm told. Scurrying about looking for profitable alliances, and as I hear it, having little good fortune. I'd suggest you write him and convey my offer."

"Boss Tweed's behind the elevated. You won't get his backing for your tunnels."

"We shan't need it," Clifford promised. "Everything's different now, I promise you." He started for the door, then paused and turned around. "One last thing. Please extend my compliments to Mr. Tickle. Tell him I was asking for him."

All during the Macy's years Mollie had gone to her aunt's every Tuesday evening to do the books. After her marriage the visit had been transferred to Tuesday afternoons. She had not, however, visited Eileen for the past three weeks, not since early October. She could not bear the question her aunt never asked—was she with child?— but which was telegraphed by her quick glance at Mollie's slim-as-ever waist. She'd no intention of going on this particular Tuesday either. There wasn't much bookkeeping to be done now that her aunt lived privately. And Mollie had started her monthly flow the day before, so she couldn't even pretend to be hopeful about the immediate future. Then, about three in the afternoon, the doorbell of the Grand Street house rang insistently, as if someone were tugging frantically at the chain. She opened the door herself because neither Jane the maid nor Mrs. Hannity the cook got there fast enough to quiet the summons, and found a small boy repeatedly yanking at the bell.

"Stop that racket this minute. What is it?"

"I've a message, ma'am."

Mollie immediately recognized Eileen's elegant Tiffany's stationery. "Come at once," her aunt had written. "A matter of urgency for your husband."

"Mr. Tweed's been arrested on charges of fraudulent activity," Eileen said when Mollie was hardly in the door.

"I know. I heard the newsboys." *Boss tweed arrested! Bail set at one million dollars!* "I didn't stop to buy a paper because I was sure you'd have one."

"I have, but I've better sources of information than that. Come upstairs where we can talk."

Even with no whores entertaining in the downstairs parlor, Eileen continued to think of her private sitting room as the appropriate venue for confidences. Mollie left her coat in the entry hall and followed her aunt up the stairs.

"Mr. Tweed's already posted bail and been released," Eileen said as soon as they were sitting by the fire. "I imagine he'd have done the same if they'd made the bail five million."

"I don't think anyone," Mollie said, "believes Mr. Tweed to be shy of resources."

"That's not going to matter this time," Eileen said. "The so-called reformers mean to get him and they will."

"Shall they bring down Tammany?" Mollie asked.

"I doubt it."

"Rather a shame. It won't be the same without Mr. Tweed, but if they're still functioning I suppose you must continue to pay seven hundred dollars a month."

"Three fifty since the start of last month," Eileen said. "As you'd know if you'd come to bring the ledgers up to date. I've less need of him these days, as Mr. Tweed agreed."

"Well and good, Auntie Eileen, but surely that's not what you meant when you said urgent. Josh's affairs are not directly involved."

"I know that." Eileen waved away the suggestion that her nephew-in-law's business depended on Tammany good will. "But what happens on Fourth Avenue does matter to him."

Mollie sat up straighter. "It does."

"There's to be a tunnel," Eileen said. "From somewhere just above Fiftieth Street to ninety-something. Ninety-Sixth Street seems to be favored."

"For the trains?"

"Of course for the trains. Whatever else?"

"But Mr. Vanderbilt has flatly refused to—"

Eileen waved that notion aside. "Mr. Vanderbilt has always known he wouldn't be allowed to run his disruptive and noisy trains along the Manhattan streets indefinitely. He is a clever negotiator. That's all his stubbornness was about. Now, with Mr. Tweed about to be brought down and the forces of 'good government' ready to take over, Mr. Vanderbilt's decided it's the right moment to make an arrangement. The proposed tunnel is projected to cost six million dollars. The city is putting up half and Vanderbilt the other half. Construction will begin in the spring."

"Auntie Eileen, are you sure? How do you know all this?"

"I am entirely sure. As I've told you before, Mollie, over the years I've had opportunities to make useful friends."

That was true. Mollie knew Auntie Eileen's influential acquaintances to have guided the investments that allowed her to continue living so well. Whatever information her aunt had, whoever it came from, it was likely to be accurate. "I must tell Josh."

Mollie half rose, but Eileen put out a hand to stop her. "You must, and time is indeed important. I am among the first to know, but I do not deceive myself that I'm the very first. Nonetheless, Mollie—"

"Yes?"

"Your husband is a ticklish sort, my dear. He needs to prove things. Josh copes remarkably well, but surely you realize his ambition is goaded by his loss."

Mollie folded her hands in her lap, looking at them rather than her aunt. "I think so, yes. And I try to be aware of his needs. Mostly without his knowing, though sometimes he discusses business with me quite openly."

Eileen did not seem satisfied with the depth of her niece's understanding. "Times of his choosing," she said.

"Yes, that's correct. Though I don't know—"

"For heaven's sake, child. He's a man. They simply don't believe

women can be trusted in matters of business. And frankly, they seldom grow up, Mollie. Most of them secretly measure themselves by
their physical prowess, however successful they may be in other areas.
That's why all the reckless coaching and racing and, to be honest,
whoring occupies so much of their time."

"Josh isn't like that! He wouldn't—" All the while thinking of
how he'd looked that first day when he took her coaching, and jock-
eyed the modest little phaeton ahead of so many grander carriages.
Beaming like a classical hero, she'd thought, his head circled with
laurel.

"Of course he's not," Eileen said. "But whatever else, my dear, you
and any offspring you produce"—Mollie started to say something, but
Eileen ignored her and went on—"whatever offspring whenever they
arrive, must be financially secure. It's a man's job to provide, Mollie,
but a woman's to manage what's provided. In this case you must take
the reins, but never let Joshua know you're holding them."

Mollie had once asked Josh why he sometimes flourished a whip
when he rode, but never really used it. Whether he sat astride or drove
a carriage, she'd never seen his whip actually land on a horse. "Not
what it's meant to do," he'd told her. "It's the crack of the whip in the
air, feeling the wind and hearing the whistle, that lets the horse know
you're in control."

"What are you suggesting I do?" she asked. There was no doubt but
that Eileen Brannigan knew as much about the proper management of
men as Joshua Turner did of horses.

"First," Eileen said, "bear in mind that your cleverness can sometimes be intimidating. So you must take this information to him immediately, but leave it to him to decide how to best use it."

Mollie shook her head. "A dunce would know how to use it. He
must buy more lots. The thing is, until the flats are built and sold, Josh
has no spare capital to invest."

"I am aware of that," Eileen said. "And there isn't time for me to dip
for what you need. Successful dipping requires thought and planning.

And I would need time to practice, be sure my hand was as steady and as quick as it used to be."

"No, Auntie Eileen, you mustn't! Not ever. I cannot bear the thought of you in that wretched place—"

"I have no intention of returning to the Tombs. And I wouldn't have gone there that one time if it hadn't been exactly what Josh called it, a put-up job with that wretched Teddy Paisley behind it. But dipping isn't what's wanted on this occasion. It's not fast enough, as I said." Eileen was pulling the rings off her fingers while she spoke. "Neither can I liquidate some other investment quickly enough to achieve our end. So, you are to tell Joshua that I do not have as much ready cash as once I did, but I am nonetheless interested in participating in this profit opportunity. He is to use these diamonds to raise capital—pawn them, don't sell them, I want them back. My contribution is an interest-free loan, as with the hundred thousand, but I will have a twenty percent share in whatever lots he purchases with the funds."

"Auntie Eileen, that's—I have no words to thank you."

"I will see a profit out of it, I have no doubt." Eileen spoke brusquely and being who she was did not shed a sentimental tear, but nonetheless produced a handkerchief and patted her cheeks as if she had.

"I . . ." Mollie stopped. "I've just thought of something, but I think you would tell me not to do it."

"Do what?"

"Take these rings straight to a pawnbroker. I'd have cash ready for Josh by the time he comes home this evening."

"The time gained would be valuable, but the price you'd pay is too high. A woman should never be that forward or that obvious. You must let Joshua determine to buy the lots and tell you to go to the pawnbroker, not go on your own." While she spoke Eileen took from her pocket a roll of blue velvet tied with satin ribbon. "I'm giving you as well a diamond bracelet, one of sapphires, and my peacock brooch. Taken all together . . . You'll get a fair amount."

"But unless I go right away it may be too late. You said yourself that other people are bound to know about the tunnel being agreed."

"No doubt of it. By tomorrow morning Josh won't be able to touch anything on Fourth Avenue, however much you get for these stones. But Fourth Avenue's not where he should be looking. I suspect it will soon be entirely too grand for what he intends. The East Sixties, Mollie. Over near Third and possibly Second. Where the elevated railroad is to be. Those are the lots Josh must buy."

Until a few years earlier the streets around Tompkins Square had been a bastion of middle class respectability. These days the area east of Greenwich Village wasn't considered nice enough even for rooming houses. The old single family homes had been torn down and replaced with four- and five-story brick-fronted tenements, each filled with as many of the laboring poor as could be crammed between the walls. The few remaining brownstones had illegal wooden backhouses tacked on behind, the whole jammed with a mix of German and Irish immigrants. It was in precisely such an area that the sort of financial business Mollie intended was regularly transacted.

On the morning after her aunt had summoned her, Mollie stood on East Seventh Street considering her options. "I'll leave to you the matter of which pawnbroker," Josh had said. "I'll be at City Hall meanwhile. Filling out their endless papers. Pretty much everything on East Sixty-Third's owned by the town. They've been known to give huge bits of the undeveloped East Side away to worthy institutions, but not to a private citizen. Not even up there. The standard price is a thousand per lot, though I've no doubt they'll raise it once the tunnel's built."

"How shall you know how many lots to buy, since we can't know how much the pawnbroker will give me?"

Josh had spread Eileen's jewels on the dining-room table and he leaned over and studied them. "Is that peacock's eye an emerald?"

"It is. And those are pearls and rubies in his tail."

"All genuine?"

"Of course."

"Then it looks like a spectacular haul to me, but I don't claim to know much about precious stones. What do you reckon your aunt to have paid for this lot? All together, I mean."

Mollie considered for a moment, recalling the various sums she had entered in Eileen's ledgers over the years. "Something close to seventeen thousand dollars."

"And we know pawnbrokers offer on average a third of retail value . . . I'm going to try for five lots, Mollie. I can always back off one or two if I must. We'll do well out of four thousand dollars, or even three, but we're in clover with five."

Up to her now.

There were two storefronts displaying the traditional three golden balls on the block of East Seventh Street that fronted on Tompkins Square. Mollie's decision about which to enter was based on the dismembered body of what she thought might be a cat. It lay on the pavement a few feet ahead of where she stood. If she chose the second shop she had to walk over it, or skirt it by stepping into the road across a gutter filled with garbage. She chose the closest pawnbroker. WALLACE AND SONS, the sign said, and beneath that, in gold letters on the window, "Always fair and patient."

Patience turned out to be an attribute required by the customers. The shop was narrow and dim, with a counter stretched along one side, and behind it a floor to ceiling array of boxes, each identified with a letter and a number. There was a dumbwaiter in the middle that Mollie surmised to be for carrying larger goods to the storage rooms above, and at the far end three stalls that allowed a measure of privacy for each transaction. It was not yet nine o'clock, but the line Mollie joined stretched halfway down the length of the counter. The customers were all females and each carried something. She saw any number of suits of men's clothes—pawn it on Monday the story went, claim it back on Friday, wear it on Sunday, then start again—and a few tool bags of different sizes. One woman had brought a large chair upholstered in worn brown leather. She shoved it along beside her as the queue moved slowly forward.

"That one's a regular furniture dealer." A woman had joined the queue behind Mollie and she spoke the comment into Mollie's ear. "I saw her bring in a bed and a chest of drawers just last week. She's got five little ones. Must all be sleeping on the floor by now. New here, ain't you, love?"

Mollie turned. Her confidante was dressed in a variety of colors and draped in a series of shawls. She wore as well a large brimmed hat trimmed with full-blown pink and yellow roses. It had no doubt been fashionable some springtime in the past, but combined with the rest of her costume and the fact that it was almost winter, it was ludicrous. The woman didn't seem to care. With one hand she hugged to her breast an ornate marble clock topped with a gold figure carrying a spear. She held out the other and smiled. "I'm Mary Teresa Santucci as was Mary Teresa Maguire, and for a time before that, Mary Teresa MacLachlan. Most folks just call me Tess o' the Roses," lifting her chin to indicate her improbable chapeau. "What's your name, love?"

"Mollie Turner. And you're right, I've never been here before." She'd worn the oldest and simplest dress she owned for this excursion, but even so she felt terribly out of place. Not just her clothes—the fact that she was empty-handed made her stand out.

"Tillie Wallace'll see you right," Tess said. "Not such a thief as some of the others."

"Tillie?" she asked. "You mean the proprietor's a woman?"

"Course she is. Matilda Wallace and her boys, Tommy and Timmy." Tess nodded toward the three booths at the end of the shop. "If I was you I'd go to Tommy. His is the first booth. Wait for him if you have to. Never misses a pretty face does Thomas Wallace. He might give you a bit more for . . . What've you got to hock, love?"

"I . . ." Mollie took a tighter grip on her drawstring bag. "It's nothing very much," she said. She had stripped off her kid gloves and tucked them in the bag as soon as she entered the shop and saw how much better dressed she was than the other clients. So her marriage ring showed. "Here," Tess said, "you're trying to send that wedding band up the spout, ain't you, love?" And when Mollie looked blank, "That's what you're wanting to pawn, ain't it? Your ring. Up the spout," she added impatiently, bobbing the rose-strewn hat toward the dumbwaiter. "My word, you're a right innocent you are. And needing to pawn a wedding ring. Right shame that is. He walk off and leave you, love? For some flashy piece of rubbish, no doubt. And here's you an obvious lady of quality. Right shame," she repeated.

The roses swayed with each word. Mollie kept expecting the hat to fall off, but it did not. "Something like that," she said. It was as non-committal as she could manage without outright rudeness.

The woman pursed her lips, then leaned in closer. "Ain't none of my business, love. But this ain't the right place for that sort of thing. You need old man Ganz. Now I know some as say the Jews only give a fair price to their own kind, but that's mostly talk. And the way I see it, after marrying a Scot and an Irishman and an Italian—all dead now, bless their souls—there's no sort has a corner on badness or goodness. Have to take folks as you find 'em, never mind what people say. Solomon Ganz, Mollie Turner. On Fifth Street and Avenue A. Tell him Tess o' the Roses sent you."

Sol Ganz took the jeweler's loupe out of his eye and set it on the table beside the six rings, two bracelets, and the brooch Mollie had laid out for his appraisal. "Very nice," he said. "Excellent stones." He pushed four of the diamond rings and the peacock brooch to one side. "These pieces in particular . . . All from Tiffany's, I believe."

"That's correct," Mollie said.

"But now you have come to me. Why is that?"

He had a moon face and, Mollie thought, exceptionally white skin, the sort some women spent considerable money and time trying to achieve. Also heavy black brows that beetled across the bridge of a prominent nose, but only a little hair on his head. He stroked the few strands left to him into position across a mostly bald pate and repeated the question she hadn't answered. "Why come to me? Mr. Tiffany is known to buy back his own pieces on occasion."

The truth was the best reply. "Because I don't wish to sell any of these things. Only to offer them as collateral on a loan." He had taken her into a windowless back room as soon as he saw the nature of what she had brought to pawn. It was separated from the actual shop by a heavy velvet curtain. Nonetheless, she nodded in the direction of the three gold balls hanging outside the door. "That is your business, is it not?"

Mr. Ganz put his head first to one side and then to the other, as if he were studying her from different angles. "You do not," he said after some seconds, "look like a thief."

"A thief! Why would you think—"

"What else would I think?" He reached for her hand—she had put her gloves back on—and held it too tightly for her to pull away, and began slipping the rings on her fingers. "Even over your gloves, madam, not one of them fits you. These rings were bought for a considerably larger lady than yourself. And this brooch . . . Mr. Tiffany would not advise such a flamboyant bird for a young bosom."

"I am not a thief." She could think of nothing to do except restate the assertion.

Ganz shrugged. "So you say. And I am not a fence, madam." Then, seeing her blank look, "Do you even know what that is?"

Mollie shook her head.

The pawnbroker sighed. "Someone who purchases stolen goods and sells them on and splits the profits with the *gonoven*—the thieves—who brought him whatever it was in the first place. That's a fence, Mrs. Whoever. And Sol Ganz is not one of them." Then again cocking his head as if to see her better. "It is Mrs., isn't it? I can feel your ring." He had kept hold of her hand and he squeezed his fingers over her wedding band.

"Mrs. Joshua Turner," Mollie said.

Ganz released her hand. "Why do you look familiar to me?"

"I've no idea."

"Yes, you do. Otherwise why would you be blushing? And I have an excellent memory for both faces and names. But right now . . . it is your face I recognize. Not your name." Then after a few seconds when neither he nor Mollie spoke, "Aha! Mr. Leslie's *Illustrated Newspaper*. Some months ago . . . Last spring, I think . . ." Finally, with another exclamation of triumph. "I remember! You are a pickpocket."

It was time to take control. As Josh would do. But using her cleverness, not a whip. "You are remembering only part of the story, Mr. Ganz. I am not a pickpocket. If I were I would no doubt have regular methods to deal with what I acquired. But Mr. Leslie did put my picture in his paper in connection with a story about picking pockets. I was married in August. Before that I was Mollie Brannigan."

Ganz said nothing, merely kept looking at her and nodding his head, apparently mentally running over the story of which Mollie had reminded him. "Yes," he said finally. "You are correct. And these jewels . . . I think it likely they belong to the true villainess of the story. The infamous Mrs. Brannigan."

"My Auntie Eileen," Mollie said with no trace of shame in her voice, "whom I love and cherish. And every item there," she nodded to the array of jewelry, "was bought by her from Mr. Tiffany. None of it was picked from anyone's pocket, Mr. Ganz. You can be entirely sure of that."

"I think," he said finally, "you are again correct. If Eileen Brannigan wanted to fence stolen jewelry, she would know whom to approach. It seems highly unlikely she would send a wide-eyed innocent like her niece to Sol Ganz. So, Mrs. Mollie, what exactly do you want me to do?"

"Take these jewels as security against a loan," Mollie said, "of ten thousand dollars." It took every bit of her will to keep looking directly at him. *I can do with three, but get me five and we're off to the races, Mollie love.* Josh's final words when they parted that morning.

"Hah! Now you are the *gonov*, Mrs. Mollie. Ten is out of the question. Three maybe. And that is very generous."

"It is highway robbery, Mr. Ganz. And you would be earning interest on considerably less than that to which you are legitimately entitled." Legitimate was arguable. According to the sign posted on the wall behind him, Solomon Ganz charged seven percent per month. It was an extortionate sum.

Ganz put his loupe back in his eye and bent over the stones a second time. "How long," he asked finally, "do you expect to leave the jewelry with me?"

"We will reclaim it no later than a year from today. But three thousand is not acceptable, Mr. Ganz. I must have ten."

"Six thousand dollars," he said finally. "And I am to be repaid one year from today. Not a day sooner or a day later."

"That's a hard bargain, Mr. Ganz. It commits us to twelve months of interest whether or not we require it."

Ganz shrugged.

At seven percent for six thousand, they would owe him at the end of twelve months nearly twice what Mr. Ganz was prepared to lend them, eleven thousand and forty dollars. Usury, plain and simple. But once the railroad tunnel was built . . . All Mollie's instincts told her the lots Josh was trying to buy would be worth at least ten times their current value. If necessary he could sell one and pay off virtually the entire debt. "I agree to six thousand for a year," she said, "but at six percent interest, not seven."

There was a pencil on the desk and a small notebook. The jeweler spent a few moments making jottings. "Very well," he said finally. "Six percent interest. One year from today you pay me ten thousand four hundred and twenty dollars. If you do not, the jewels are mine to sell."

"I believe there's an error in your calculation, Mr. Ganz. The amount owed will be ten thousand three hundred and twenty dollars."

He looked at her again, then spent another few moments jotting figures in his notebook. "You are right again, Mrs. Mollie," he said when he put the pencil down. He was smiling. "My wife, may her memory be for a blessing, she could do that too. Any numbers. In her head without even a pencil. Mr. Joshua Turner is a fortunate man."

8

"SOMEONE TO SEE you," Hatty Ellis said. "A gentleman. I put him in the parlor."

"Send him away." Eileen didn't look up from her embroidery hoop. "Tell him we're not in business any longer."

"Tell him yourself. Though I'll wager he's not come looking for whores. Too old."

Eileen knew she'd lost the argument; she frequently did with Hatty, though for the sake of form she continued to protest. "They are never too old. You have surely learned that after all this time." She'd had one regular client, white-haired and bent, who showed up twice a month for years. He simply wanted to sleep beside the young woman he'd selected. Always one of the same two, both endowed with remarkable bosoms. The client slept with his head nestled between his chosen whore's breasts and her hand in the vicinity of his crotch. Paid top rates. But then, they all had. "Send him away," she repeated. "Whatever do I pay you for, Hatty, if not to save me a bit of trouble?"

"To cook, as you know well. Besides, you don't want to send this old gent away without seeing him. Take it from me, what you want is to march yourself downstairs and talk to him."

"And why is that?" Eileen looked up at last. When Hatty adopted that tone attention must be paid.

"Gave me his card," Hatty said.

Hatty didn't read. Which only made the statement more intriguing. "For heaven's sake, why didn't you mention a card? Give it to me."

As soon as the thing was in her hand Eileen understood. What Hatty had recognized were the three gold balls. They were embossed above the name Solomon Ganz, and below that were the words PROMPT PAYMENT AND GOOD TERMS. Eileen had not discussed giving Mollie her jewels to pawn, much less the reason for it. Which, as Eileen had learned over the past quarter century, didn't mean Hatty Ellis was ignorant of the arrangement. Her cook always knew everything that went on under Eileen Brannigan's roof. Pretty much without exception.

"He wrote something on t' other side as well," Hatty said.

Eileen flipped the card over. On the back were the handwritten initials, T. P. "Bring him up here." The words flat and without emotion, belying her beating heart.

"Better if you go down," Hatty insisted.

"Why is that, Hatty?" In that same toneless voice.

"Looks like he's a Jew," the cook said. "You don't want one of them up here in your private sitting room."

"Of course he's a Jew. His name is Solomon Ganz. Bring him up, Hatty. And bring us tea and some of your corn bread and strawberry preserves."

Sol Ganz ate three pieces of corn bread, each piled high with Hatty's superb preserves. "Mrs. Ganz," he murmured, "made wonderful strawberry preserves. You will understand, Mrs. Brannigan, if I say these are almost as good." Ganz carefully wiped his mouth with the small linen napkin she'd provided and set it on the tray. "You've seen what I wrote on the back of my card, Mrs. Brannigan?"

"The initials T. P. Yes, I saw."

"They are familiar to you?"

"I don't think you'd still be sitting there, however good my cook's strawberry preserves, if you did not know the answer to that, Mr. Ganz. What has Teddy Paisley to do with you?"

"I think the question is what he has to do with you."

"Nothing now. Once, many years ago back in the Old Country, in Ireland, we knew each other. Over here . . ." Eileen shook her head. "He's nothing to do with me."

"I don't believe Theodore Paisley agrees with that. Otherwise why would he have gone to such elaborate lengths to do you harm?"

Eileen raised her glance and looked directly at the pawnbroker. "I'm not sure I know what you mean."

"Please, Mrs. Brannigan. Let us save each other the time wasted in playing cat and mouse. For one thing I know the reputation for absolute discretion which made your house the success it was. For another, since saving magazines and newspapers is my hobby, I know that on only two occasions has your name been mentioned in print. In both instances the stories were originated by Mr. Paisley and connected you with a scandal, and each was clearly designed to damage your business. On the second occasion the goal was achieved. Your house is no longer a source of income. Though it does not appear that's the reason you sent your niece to me with a considerable hoard of jewelry. I take it you know the terms we negotiated?"

"I do, Mr. Ganz. For a pawnbroker you were fair. And," glancing at his card which lay on the table next to the tea tray, "prompt. But none of that was my doing. My niece chose you on her own. And it has nothing to do with Teddy Paisley, nor does it explain your reason for taking the trouble to do such careful investigating of the rumors unfortunately attached to my name."

"Rumors . . ." Ganz shrugged. "Forgive me, I don't think that is a fair characterization. You are indeed an O'Halloran from Armagh in Ireland. Your family truly are legendary pickpockets. All exactly as the story said. And you did spend the night in the Tombs for picking the pocket of a gentleman in Tiffany's. Though apparently you never came to trial."

"I never did," Eileen said, "because the authorities were convinced the incident was staged to do me harm. As you have apparently surmised. But what, Mr. Ganz, leads you to associate that incident with Teddy Paisley? That part is a mystery to me, and I confess I want very much to know the solution."

"My business," Ganz said, "is made up of people who share information. It is in our best interests to do so. And while I myself do not deal in goods I am not quite sure belong to the person who is pawning them, that's not the case throughout my profession."

"I know you're not a fence, Mr. Ganz. I made it my business to find that out as soon as my niece told me of her arrangement with you."

Ganz broke into another small smile. "How is Mrs. Mollie? Well, I hope."

"Very well, thank you."

"I am glad to hear it. Your niece is charming. And I hear her husband is building French flats. Way up on Sixty-Third Street. Do you think anyone will want to live so far from the city, Mrs. Brannigan?"

"I think my nephew-in-law believes they can be persuaded to want exactly that, Mr. Ganz. And he's a clever young man."

"Good. I'm delighted. I shall then be getting my money back in November of next year, as we agreed. And you will have your jewels restored to you."

"Teddy Paisley, Mr. Ganz. Why did you write his initials on the back of your card?"

"Ah yes. Your old enemy." Eileen didn't say anything and after a few seconds Ganz continued. "Who unfortunately seems to have brought his grudge with him from Ireland to America. I do not think he is satisfied with what he has achieved, Mrs. Brannigan. Perhaps because you do not seem to be suffering enough from having lost your business. You are obviously living here in comfort. Even without your working ladies."

Ganz paused and patted the few strands of hair that lay across his skull. Eileen still did not respond. "I think you should know," he said, "this Mr. Paisley has it in mind to do more damage."

She had come to the conclusion he'd brought just such news; nothing else made sense. Still, hearing him say the words made her shiver. Someone walking over your grave her mam would have said. Not if she could help it. "Can I ask how you know that? And exactly what you know?"

"I would like to tell you. That's why I bothered to come here rather than simply decide it to be none of my business. I have the jewelry after all, and I acquired it on what are frankly advantageous terms. So if I never see the interest . . . ," he shrugged again.

It took her only a few seconds to see where his line of reasoning led. "Given that it's my niece and her husband who are to pay you the interest, you appear to be telling me that whatever you know concerns them." She spoke calmly, but bright red dots had developed on both her cheeks, and she knew if she reached for anything her hand would tremble. Mollie was only her niece by marriage. She did not share the O'Halloran blood that carried the Paisley curse. But given all that Teddy Paisley knew, it was safe to presume he knew Mollie Brannigan Turner to be the most precious thing in Eileen's life. "Mr. Ganz. Tell me your price."

"Not money," he shook his head. "I have grandchildren, Mrs. Brannigan. And like you, I am a person who thinks of the future. Already I know your nephew-in-law's scheme is clever and likely to succeed. I believe his flats are going to be profitable." He paused. They looked at each other. "What I want is to make an investment. I will pay with something that will make it impossible for Mr. Paisley to threaten you or yours ever again."

"What?" Eileen demanded.

"Not yet," Ganz said quietly. "I'm sure we both agree that good business is based on trust."

Eileen knew that to be so, but that didn't mean she was prepared to go further than she had with a man she'd met in the last hour. Which did not preclude her allowing him to believe she might. "I should like to know what your price will be, Mr. Ganz. For this valuable service I am to take it on trust you will perform."

"Invaluable, I assure you. As for my price, I wish an interest in the buildings Mr. Turner is to erect."

"You speak of buildings. Only one is to be constructed."

"At first," Ganz said. "But you pawned your jewels so Joshua Turner could purchase other lots in, you'll forgive me, the *farshtunkene* East Sixties. He did that because he is planning more buildings. All to be let to a class of people whose housing needs are presently not served in this city. There is nowhere else for them to live, Mrs. Brannigan, so they will rent your nephew-in-law's French flats. However many he builds. I wish to share in the profit that plan will generate. And before you answer, allow me to assure you that without my intervention it is unlikely Mr. Turner's plans will come to fruition."

"Why did you come to me rather than going directly to Joshua?"

"Because you and I are both old and wise. Mr. Turner is young and passionate and in the grip of a dream he will not wish to share."

Eileen nodded. "Very well. I have a twenty percent interest in whatever he builds. I will give you twenty percent of my interest."

"Half of your interest," Ganz said.

She did not hesitate. "Agreed."

"No. Not agreed."

"But you just said . . . Mr. Ganz, I have been dealing with you on the assumption you are a reasonable man of business. If you are a fool or a mad man you are wasting my time. Which is it?"

"Neither. Mrs. Brannigan, I have it on good authority that Mr. Paisley intends to write an article saying that the young man who is building the new flats up on East Sixty-Third Street is not the one-legged war hero he seems to be. He is instead someone who connived with the enemy before the war was ended."

"That's not true." Eileen knew that Joshua's wound had not been gained in battle. Mollie had told her so to avoid her ever asking him about the loss of his leg. But that wasn't particularly damaging information, even if somehow Teddy Paisley was in possession of it. Being some sort of turncoat was an entirely different matter. "Joshua would never have colluded with the enemy. Surely you know his parents were abolitionists and fervent patriots."

"I know," Ganz said, "that Joshua Turner's half sister was Ceci Lee. That she was married to Royal Lee, one of the conspirators who tried to burn down New York before the war ended and was hanged in City Hall Park."

"Those are not secrets, Mr. Ganz. Anyone who cares to take the trouble can ascertain those facts."

"And Mr. Paisley has taken the trouble. But according to my sources— You understand what I told you about talk in my line of business?" Then, after Eileen nodded agreement, "I am given to understand that while the war was still going on, while he was supposed to be a soldier in the army of the North, Joshua Turner spent some months living with his sister on her plantation, and that Mr. Paisley knows this to be a fact and plans to reveal it an article in a newspaper. Her husband was a slaveholder, Mrs. Brannigan, a spy who was to die after trying to burn our city to the ground. What do you think will be made of the information that Joshua Turner lived in the home of such a man, that he had ample opportunity to tell him things about New York City that might aid that man in his attempt to destroy it? Do you imagine that after such revelations anyone will wish to rent a flat in Joshua Turner's new buildings?"

Eileen took a few moments, waiting for her heart to stop its fierce pounding before she said, "One half of my holdings. I agree, Mr. Ganz. As long as you can assure me you can prevent the publication of this story."

"Oh yes, I can prevent it, Mrs. Brannigan. I assure you of that. I need, however, one more question answered before I can be comfortable with an arrangement between us. Why does Teddy Paisley hate you so much?"

Eileen stood up and walked to the window. University Place looked the same as always, but in her mind's eye she saw not the familiar street but the green hills of Armagh. She saw a yard where a boy's body lay broken and bleeding beside a horse trough, and a woman's body was stretched on the ground nearby, her arms reaching toward the child but unable to reach him because she was dead.

"The Paisleys," she said, "were also a dipping family. Like us they made their living by being what the New York police would call a 'ring of pickpockets,' but which, in Ireland when I was young, was considered rather a clever way to earn a living. Particularly if you did most of your work over in England. That said, the Paisleys were not like the O'Hallorans. They weren't as celebrated for one thing. For another we're Catholics and they are Protestants. Have you any idea what that means, Mr. Ganz? Particularly in Ireland."

"I'm a Jew, Mrs. Brannigan. You don't have to tell me what religious hatred can do."

"Years ago, when Teddy Paisley and I were both children, our families were engaged in a feud that had already gone on for generations. One night there was a fight. The O'Hallorans came out the victors. Teddy Paisley's mother was killed and his brother was left crippled for life."

"And were you and Teddy Paisley involved in this fight?"

"Not directly. We were far too young. But I was in the back of the wagon that carried the O'Hallorans to the Paisley's place that night, tucked down in the straw. I was supposed to stay there, but I remember getting to my knees and peeking over the side." She paused, hearing again the shouts of the battle and seeing the blood. Then, long practiced in the art, Eileen pushed the memory aside. "After his mother died," she said, "Teddy's sister brought him to New York. He came when he was twelve, many years before I arrived. I doubt he knew I was here. I was Eileen Brannigan after all. I never used the O'Halloran name in New York. But this place . . . Eventually," her voice grew softer at the memory, "they all came to Mrs. Brannigan's. Teddy Paisley along with the rest. He walked in one evening, saw me, and walked out."

She'd been speaking with her back to him, now she turned. "Will it surprise you, Mr. Ganz, if I tell you that Teddy Paisley and I have never spoken a single word to each other in our entire lives. Not the night he came here and not before."

"But after all these years, he still recognized you?"

"Of course. And I recognized him."

"How is that possible?"

"Because," she said, "some things are not forgotten. There was a meeting back in the Old Country when Teddy and I were children. A formal occasion which required the presence of the entire O'Halloran clan along with that of all the Paisleys. It was to arrange a division of territory, so we could end the dipping war. All we O'Hallorans were lined up on one side and the Paisleys on the other. My da and my grandda spoke with Teddy's da and his grandda. We young ones, we just looked at each other. When the meeting ended everything was said to be settled and an agreement signed. In real blood, mind you. Every single member of the family contributed a drop of it. A week later there was the fight I told you about. The O'Hallorans attacked the Paisleys, but if you believe my da's story, the Paisleys broke the blood promise first." She shrugged. "The dead were dead and the maimed maimed, whoever's fault it may have been."

After a few seconds of silence Ganz said, "So this whole thing, this burning desire to see you ruined and your niece and her husband ruined, this is from a feud in the Old Country?"

"The Irish, Mr. Ganz, are good at a number of things, but they are better at nothing than at hating."

Ganz nodded. "Apparently so, Mrs. Brannigan. Now, here is what you are to do." He leaned forward and spoke quietly for a number of minutes.

"Sign here," the lawyer said. "You on the left side, Mrs. Brannigan. Mr. Turner on the right. All three copies, please."

Josh waited for Eileen to sign and pass him the documents, one after the other. Each time he added his signature and passed the document back to Jeremy Duggan in turn.

For Josh that was the least understandable thing in this whole business. He remembered the day he'd first met Eileen Brannigan. With Mollie in the Tombs. That's when he'd first heard Duggan's name. He was the lawyer who somehow had not shown up to bail out his client, even though her arrest was front-page news. Josh asked about that the night of the urgent meeting Eileen requested, the one he was not to mention to Mollie. "Of course if this is what you want, I'll do it. You've earned the right to a formal agreement, Aunt Eileen."

After four months of marriage Josh was accustomed to calling her that, but not to how agitated she seemed on that occasion. Or to his sense that something had impaired her usually excellent judgment. "I'll do whatever you like, as I said, but why use Duggan to draw up the papers? I seem to recall both you and Mollie thinking he was somehow in the pocket of whoever set you up for that phony arrest in the first place. I can recommend an attorney who—"

"I need this done quickly, Josh. And it's a simple matter. I'm told such agreements are created every day."

He'd had no argument to counter that then, and no reason now to think Duggan hadn't done this exactly the way Eileen wanted it and Josh had agreed it should be. He'd read every word of each copy of the document. Eileen Brannigan nee O'Halloran had a twenty percent interest in the St. Nicholas Corporation, which corporation was established according to the laws of the state of New York for the business of building and managing real estate. It took less than half a page. Pretty sweeping he knew. He could have demanded it be hedged around with whereofs and theretofores and excluding and not excluding. All the lawyer talk that some would argue—Zac for a certainty, his mother probably as well—would protect his interests in the future. Josh was not so inclined. Eileen Brannigan had handed him large amounts of money on nothing but his word. If for some reason she needed that formalized now, then so be it.

Duggan was a small man with a considerable paunch, to which he unwisely drew attention by draping a heavy gold watch chain across the expanse. He had as well an unfortunate, ferretlike face, with too-close-together brown eyes and a thin and pointed nose. A weasel if he'd ever seen one, Josh decided. But he seemed competent enough. The lawyer witnessed one signature. His clerk, a wraithlike figure who seemed to materialize whenever he was needed and disappear thereafter, witnessed the other. "Done," Duggan said. "Is there anything else, Mrs. Brannigan?"

"Nothing, Mr. Duggan. You will keep one copy here, I presume? In my file?"

"Exactly so, Mrs. Brannigan."

"Excellent. And I have my copy and my nephew has his. Good day to you, gentlemen."

She nodded to Duggan and his clerk and stood up. Josh did as well, and offered her his arm. Eileen took it and they walked out of the office on William Street and into the late autumn sunshine. "I've got the phaeton, Aunt Eileen. I'll take you home."

"Thank you, Joshua. I'd prefer a hansom if you don't mind."

Holding him, he thought, at arm's length. Much as she had seemed to do since this business began. "As you wish, Aunt Eileen."

Then, after he'd handed her up into the cab, a moment before it pulled away, she leaned out the window and lay her hand aside his cheek. "All for the best, Josh. I promise."

She was gone too quickly for him to reply.

❧

Eileen waited a few minutes while the hansom struggled through the crush of downtown traffic, then leaned out and looked back to be sure she could no longer see her new nephew. Convinced there was no sign of him she pulled her head back into the cab and lowered the window separating her from the driver. He bent his head toward her. "Not University Place," she said. "I've changed my mind. Fifth Street, please. And Avenue A."

"So," Ganz said, gazing at the document Eileen had laid on the table where her niece had spread out Eileen's bracelets and rings and peacock brooch. "You have been quick, Mrs. Brannigan. I am pleased that you recognize the urgency of the situation."

He reached for the paper, but she kept her gloved hand on it. "This is not yours, Mr. Ganz. It is mine."

"I have no doubt, Mrs. Brannigan. I was simply trying to get a better look at the signature of the witness." He leaned down. "It is that of Mr. Jeremy Duggan, I can see."

"It is. I had him draw up these papers, exactly as you instructed."

"Excellent, madam. You are a woman with whom it is a pleasure to do business. Everything as promised. I too have had the appropriate document drawn." Ganz reached into a drawer and produced yet another piece of paper. "This one states that you make over to me fifty percent of your interest in the St. Nicholas Real Estate Corporation. We must both sign it. I have two witnesses available, my maid and my cook. Upstairs." He started to rise. "Neither of them can read, but they make their mark and that's—"

"Not so fast, Mr. Ganz. I am not ready to sign anything just yet. I have kept my part of our bargain. It is time for you to keep yours."

"I promised," Ganz said, "to give you information that would nullify the threat Mr. Theodore Paisley represents to you and yours."

"So you did. That's what I'm waiting for." Eileen folded the document signed by herself and Joshua and placed it in the black faille pocket clipped to the waist of her elegant suit of gray Donegal tweed.

"I have it right here." Ganz withdrew something else from the drawer, an envelope this time. It wasn't sealed.

Eileen took it. "I presume I'm to open this?"

"Indeed," with another nod of his head. "Please, Mrs. Brannigan. Go right ahead."

There was a single small bit of paper inside. Eileen withdrew it, putting the envelope on the table before she unfolded what it had contained. She read what it said, glanced up at the pawnbroker, then back at the paper that she might read the words a second time. READ THE TIMES ON WEDNESDAY. Written in block capitals. Today was Monday.

"So," Ganz said quietly.

"So . . . That's all you can say? I presume that is when Mr. Paisley intends to publish his despicable—"

Ganz shook his head and held up his hand. "No, no, Mrs. Brannigan. Forgive me for interrupting, but your presumption is not correct."

"I see. What then is the correct interpretation of this . . ." Eileen put the scrap of paper on the desk, as if it were somehow contaminated. "This unpleasant missive."

"It is exactly the information I promised, Mrs. Brannigan. You need only follow the instructions and you will see that you have no further cause for alarm."

"This is unacceptable, Mr. Ganz. Totally unacceptable. We had an agreement."

"Indeed we had, Mrs. Brannigan. You have kept your part of the bargain, as you said. I can assure you I have kept mine. Why would I not? After you and I sign that paper," nodding to the statement that Eileen Brannigan made over to Solomon Ganz one half of her holdings in Josh's company, "it will be as much in my interest as yours to protect your nephew's business."

That was true. But what he was offering as payment for his participation was virtually nothing. Teddy Paisley had shown himself able to do her great harm. Sol Ganz had somehow found out about that and come to her with a story that revealed he knew not just that Teddy was her

mortal enemy, but things about her nephew-in-law that, though perfectly innocent, could be interpreted as damning. Never more so than
in Teddy's hands. Now the pawnbroker insisted this cryptic and unin-
formative note somehow protected Josh and thus Mollie.

"Unacceptable." This time she mouthed the word softly to herself,
knowing even as she did so that she had little choice but to accept
whatever Solomon Ganz was offering because however slim a hope it
might be, it was the only one available.

Eileen had tried every way she knew, used every ounce of influence she possessed, to neutralize Teddy. She'd been doing so for years,
never with more determination than during the last few days. Nothing
she could do had been effective. Teddy was a businessman with small
interests in a great many different activities. No one of them was sufficiently important to him to make crippling it of sufficient importance
to control his behavior. Shut off one source of his income and he had
a dozen others. No one she knew, no one she could imagine, had such
a reach as to systematically interdict Teddy's activities one after the
other until every one of them was destroyed. At least not on the say-so
of Eileen Brannigan.

READ *THE TIMES* ON WEDNESDAY.

Five words. In block letters written in black ink. On a sheet of tis-
sue-thin paper without any identification. It was nothing. But it was
all she had. She felt the unmistakable sensation of someone walking
over her grave. And possibly—God help her—Mollie's.

A quill pen sat in a brightly polished silver holder on Sol Ganz's
table. Eileen reached for it. "Summon your witnesses, Mr. Ganz."

It was at last Wednesday. *The Times* lay folded on the table in front of
her. Eileen had been staring at it for nearly half an hour. She was unable to open it.

What if there was nothing? What would she do then? Go running
back to Ganz yelling "You tricked me"? What good would that do?

What if he had not tricked her, simply failed in whatever he'd attempted. Some sort of preemptive scandal probably. Something that would so blacken Teddy Paisley's name as to nullify his accusations concerning Josh.

What could do that?

A dozen things. New Yorkers sought out scandal almost as avariciously as they chased profit. Whatever it was, they would pounce on it. Devour it. Shun the object of the scandal. Make him or her an outcast.

Until when?

Until they forgot. New Yorkers inevitably forgot. They moved on to the next exciting thing.

But Ganz had been so positive. So sure. And, as he pointed out, it was in his best interest now. As well as hers.

Perhaps Teddy Paisley was to be implicated not in a scandal but a crime. Sol Ganz was a member of a profession that had close ties to the underworld, to the worst gangsters and thieves. He might not be a fence, but he doubtless knew plenty of them.

A crime could send Teddy to jail. Perhaps for years. Maybe for life. That had been a fantasy of Eileen's back when he first announced her background to the city and nearly brought her down. Certainly she'd thought of it again when he sent her to the Tombs on a trumped-up pickpocket charge. She'd had no idea how to arrange that then and she didn't know now. Possibly Sol Ganz did.

Eileen took the paper in hand and unfolded it. She was in her sitting room, beside a lively fire, listening to a cold rain beat against her windows. She lay the paper on her lap and scanned the first page. Shipping news mostly. A story about a diplomatic mission to Spain. And inside, on the next page, a discussion of the proposed Amnesty Act, restoring the civil rights of rebellious Southerners now that the war had been over for nearly six years.

The Gray Lady everyone called *The Times*. It was a name the paper was said to regard with pride. They did not announce shocking or scandalous stories with the black headlines of the tabloids, much less the hawking cries of newsboys. In the pages of the Gray Lady such news was to be found inside, quietly designated by a small and frequently understated headline. Eileen found what she was looking for at the bottom of page four:

BUSINESSMAN FOUND DEAD

Mr. Theodore Paisley, a naturalized American citizen immigrated from Ireland many years ago, was found dead in his home late yesterday afternoon. His housekeeper discovered him slumped at his desk and a glass of whiskey half drunk beside him. The police are testing the drink for poison. Foul play is suspected, but there are as yet no suspects nor any obvious motive.

Dear God in heaven. She had conspired in murder.

. . . give that child suck or I'll tell everyone in the city you tried and failed and your day is past. Not a drop left and here's the starving babe to prove it . . .

She'd have done anything to protect Mollie. Then as now. No difference.

Eileen stood up and tossed the paper on the fire and watched it burn.

Josh was getting a late start that morning. Damned rain always made his leg ache. It had been harder than usual to drag himself out of his warm bed. He'd turned to his wife instead. Now Mollie was sitting across from him at breakfast looking flushed and happy, meeting his gaze occasionally with a small smile in response to his huge and, he imagined, lascivious grin. He'd wanted her to be exactly that sort of woman. One who wasn't afraid to acknowledge her own physical side or his.

"More coffee, Josh?"

"Thank you, yes." He passed his cup over, and when she reached for it took the opportunity to raise her hand to his lips, smiling at her once more in that way that said more than words, and chuckling when she colored a deeper pink. After which he told himself it was time to stop flirting. Eat his breakfast and read his paper and get a move on. He'd visit the foundry first today, then he'd go and—Jesus God Almighty. *Mr. Theodore Paisley, a naturalized American citizen immigrated from Ireland many years ago, was found dead . . .*

Eileen popped into his head immediately. Along with her sudden, unexplained rush to put in writing what had previously been acceptable as a verbal agreement taken on trust. Josh pondered for a moment. There was no connection he could see, but that did not mean one might not exist.

Let it lie. He felt the conviction start in his gut and rise to his brain and knew instantly it was settled. For him at any rate. He had not told Mollie about the visit to Eileen's attorney or the document he'd signed. Perhaps Eileen had. Perhaps Mollie would make some sort of connection. "Take a look at this," he said, passing her the paper. "Bottom of page four. Isn't Paisley the man you and your aunt blamed for sending her to the Tombs?"

"So he is," she said, reading the paper at the same time. She looked up a moment later. "Good riddance," she said. "I know it's not nice to feel so, but I do, Josh. He was incredibly mean to Auntie Eileen and I'm not sorry he's dead."

He read no guile in her open and frank gaze, had no sense of her knowing more than she admitted about his affairs or, for that matter, Eileen's. "Fair enough," he said, getting up and dropping a quick kiss on the top of her head. "Paisley's gone. No need for you or your aunt to trouble yourselves about him ever again."

Not him either. Josh was convinced of that. Teddy Paisley's death could not in any way be connected to him or his affairs.

9

ALL PRAYERS ARE answered. Sometimes, however, the answer is no.

Mollie had read that in a magazine some years past. In this case the answer was yes, though she had to wait for it a bit longer than expected.

That Christmas of 1871, the first after their marriage, Josh and Mollie celebrated at Sunshine Hill so Carolina could participate. The occasion was made more festive because the Turners invited Auntie Eileen to join them, and Zac was back from England. Best of all for Mollie, it was a special holiday because she believed she was at last pregnant.

This was a secret she yet hugged to herself. She wanted to be absolutely sure for one thing. For another Josh seemed to have more on his mind than usual. He'd decided to keep the foundry working, and while the six additional lots he'd bought after they pawned Eileen's jewels were a justification, making more steel than he could immediately use meant tying up still more of his limited capital. "If I have to I can sell a couple of lots. They should triple in value once the railroad people get their shovels in the ground. But that's not going to happen until the cold breaks."

Josh didn't say that to Mollie. She heard him make the comment to Zac soon after the new year, when the brothers were discussing business in the Grand Street drawing room that had become an office. She'd not been invited to their meeting, but she'd gone in to bring them hot cider laced with rum and to borrow the copy of the *Christian Union* sitting on Josh's desk. It wasn't a weekly Josh usually read, but he'd placed the notice of flats to let on Sixty-Third Street in the *Union* as well as half a dozen other journals and newspapers. "May I, Josh? Only until I've read Mrs. Beecher's column."

"Yes, of course. And thanks for this," gripping the pewter tankard. "Very welcome."

"It is indeed," Zac agreed. "This has to be the bitterest January ever."

"And the driest," Mollie agreed. "I don't remember another winter without a single snowflake so late in the season."

Both men agreed. Then, only to keep the conversation going, Mollie was sure, Zac asked her about Mrs. Beecher's column. Advice to housewives, she explained, and he listened politely, though she was sure he'd not a penny's worth of interest. After that there was no more small talk and it was clear her husband and her brother-in-law were waiting for her to go so they could resume their discussion. Mollie took the paper and left.

She settled herself at the dining room table and read the popular column.

> *These days, when there is so much work to be done in a properly furnished home, and when so many can have but one servant to do it, efficiency is the housewife's primary skill. She must learn to manage her household like a business and prepare herself for it as a man prepares for his life's work. It is imperative to keep careful records of everything to be*

done each week: which silvers or brasses require to be polished, which carpets to be beaten, the proper arrangement and spotless cleanliness of the antimacassars and doilies and table coverings, etcetera. Further, you must be certain the domestic you employ understands the order in which these tasks are to be accomplished.

Mollie sighed. She did not find household chores quite so diverse or demanding. She had Mrs. Hannity all the time—the cook slept in a room in the attic—as well as Jane who came on Mondays, Wednesdays, and Fridays. So perhaps Mrs. Beecher wasn't speaking to her.

She put down the paper. Half a minute later she picked it up again and thumbed through the pages until she found Joshua's advertisement. "French Flats to be let on Sixty-Third Street at the tasteful St. Nicholas," it read. "Ready for occupancy in three to four months." It was Carolina, eyes twinkling, who had suggested the building's name, since, as she pointed out, Nick's foresightful purchase had provided the land. "Favorable rates for those signing a lease in advance of completion," Mollie read. And that interested parties were to inquire either at the property or at the Grand Street house.

The same notice had been running every day for two weeks. In at least half a dozen papers and periodicals. All had produced absolutely no result. Not a single person had come to Grand Street to ask about the flats, nor arrived at the building site to see the progress being made.

Mollie read the text a second time. Perhaps if Josh used slightly different wording . . . Her glance went to the announcements above and below. They spoke of ship arrivals. And postal rates. And various dockings and departures of assorted means of haulage. In the column on the left hand side of the page there was a long article about the reliability of paper money.

It could not be more clear. Mollie jumped to her feet.

Since Josh and Zac were discussing men's affairs, she would normally have knocked to signal her arrival. In this instance, in the grip of her flash of understanding, Mollie simply pushed open one half of the connecting doors. "Josh, I've figured it out! I know why no one has come to ask about the flats or gone uptown to see them." Then, to her brother-in-law, "Please excuse me, Zac. I apologize for interrupting. But I know Josh has been worried. And I know what's wrong."

"And what is that, Mollie?" Josh didn't sound angry. In fact he'd not raised his voice to her once in the nearly six months they'd been married. But he'd never sounded quite so distant either.

"It's the position of the notice, Josh. Look, in the *Union* it's here on the page with the shipping news and a discussion of whether silver currency should be eliminated. It's the same with the other papers as well. I know it is."

Josh continued to look at her, but he didn't say anything. Zac seemed entirely occupied with some papers on the desk. He was, Mollie realized, embarrassed for his brother. She should have waited until she and Josh were alone. But it was such an obvious truth, Josh had to see it as well. "You're speaking to the wrong people, Josh. Only men read these pages. You need to have the notice inserted on the pages that women read. Next to Mrs. Beecher's column in the *Christian Union*, for example. Advice to housewives."

"Mollie," still that same quiet and distant voice, "the lease of a flat of this sort, indeed the choice of where to house his family, is a man's affair. It is not the responsibility of a housewife."

"But if she wants the flat, Josh, and if she has reason to believe they can afford it, she'll encourage her husband to at least inquire about . . ." Both Josh and Zac were looking at her now. Rather, she thought, as if she were a small child who had presumed to comment on things far beyond her understanding. Mollie stopped speaking.

"Thank you, Mollie. Now, if you don't mind, Zac and I are busy."

Her husband had dismissed her as effectively as if he'd waved her out of the room as he would a servant.

❧

Mollie waited a few minutes. When he did not come out to apologize she went upstairs.

It occurred to her that he might spend the night in one of the other bedrooms, but after an hour of tossing and turning she heard the door open.

Neither of them said anything and Josh undressed without putting on a light. She wasn't sure if he thought she was asleep, but when he got into bed beside her he said, "Don't ever do that again."

"I didn't mean—"

"I'm sure you didn't. But if you believe me to be inadequate and my business decisions questionable, I would thank you to wait until we're alone to say so."

"How can you say that, Josh? Of course I don't believe you're inadequate. It was simply that I got this idea and—"

"I don't wish to discuss it further, Mollie."

She thought he would turn away but he turned to her instead. Mollie welcomed him, feeling a little surge of triumph because his need of her and the pleasure he obviously took in their coupling reminded her of her aunt's advice.

Except that Auntie Eileen was wrong. You could not fix everything in the bedroom. Her husband seemed to enjoy her as much as ever, but when he was finished he turned over and went to sleep. He did not even murmur good night.

Least said, soonest mended. Nothing would get Josh back to being his customary kind and loving self more quickly than being relieved of the worry that no one would lease his flats. Mollie was, however, quite convinced no one would, if he continued to market them with advertisements only men would see. Very well, she would do what needed doing. When her scheme worked she'd have proved her point, and Josh would be too pleased to be angry with her.

❦

Thursday, Mollie decided, was the best choice. Jane didn't come on Thursdays, and it was Mrs. Hannity's afternoon off.

"I shan't need dinner today, Mrs. Hannity. And the leftover ham pie will do for tonight's supper. You may leave now, if you wish."

The cook went to visit her sister in Harlem Village on Thursdays. In the normal way of things Mrs. Hannity was out the door by one-thirty. It was barely eleven now. So even though Agnes Hannity had been recommended by Auntie Eileen's Hatty Ellis, and Mollie expected the pair of them spent time discussing what went on in Mollie's newly established household, on this occasion Mrs. Hannity was unlikely to ask too many questions, much less refuse an extra two and a half hours of freedom.

"Well, if you're sure, missus."

"Very sure, Mrs. Hannity. Go on. Off with you. It's a long journey to Harlem, I know.

"It is that, missus. The horsecar and then the train, and then another horsecar to Bessie's, 'cause her little cottage is right the way over on 125th Street and First Avenue. I keep saying she should move closer to town, but Bessie loves her garden. And of course you can't grow cabbages in New York City. Still, like I always tell her, it's a wonder she gets anything to grow with them winds blowing off the river and making—"

Moments later Mollie had closed the door behind Mrs. Hannity and climbed the stairs to her room. She chose a traveling suit made of dark red wool, with a snugly fitted jacket trimmed in black silk braid. Never mind that she had to hold her breath to button it over her thickening waist. And even though there wasn't a speck of snow on the ground, she took care to bustle the skirt tightly so no fabric would trail behind her. That, after all, was the point of a fashion meant for going out on the streets, and the reason the jacket flared from the waist and had a fan of deep pleats in the back that expanded sufficiently to cover a substantial bustle. And, since it was so cold, she added a long black coat buttoned from neck to hem and trimmed with black beaver fur.

As a last touch, a gray felt bonnet with a shallow brim edged in black velvet and simply trimmed with black velvet ribbon and a few feathers, pinned in place with two pearl-tipped pins. Then she selected a small black beaver muff, and tucked some money and a comb and handkerchief into the muff's inside pocket and left the house. Forty-five minutes later she was knocking on the door of Joshua's double-fronted house on Bowling Green.

"So you see," Mollie said, "the flats at the St. Nicholas are really entirely different from any rooming house. And they are not restricted to people who can afford grand Fifth Avenue mansions. They are meant for respectable 'white collar' families exactly like yours. The backbone of our city," she added, in a tone of voice meant to convey the pride she took in the accomplishments of her listeners. This despite the fact that there were only women and children seated at the dining room table.

Mollie had quite deliberately timed her arrival to coincide with the midday meal. It was when the people she wished to see would be gathered together, a captive audience, as it were. According to Josh, at rooming houses catering to families the men seldom came home for lunch. Board was nonetheless part of the weekly rent and the men's wives and offspring were fed at a preset time. By long-standing custom they dined together at a common table, and certainly no menu was presented as had become usual in the à la carte restaurants lately grown so popular in New York. The ladies and their children were expected to eat what was set in front of them, though judging from what had been left on a number of the plates, not everyone had found today's offering to their liking. Mutton stew, Mollie thought, sniffing the air. And boiled cabbage.

"On Sixty-Third Street," she said, "each flat has its own kitchen. You can feed your little ones when and what you judge best."

One small girl was nodding off over her half-eaten meal, threatening to land her face in the cold and greasy remains. Her mother, who'd been introduced as Mrs. Jackson, pulled the child into her lap. "All on one floor you said. No upstairs and no down?"

Having decided on her plan, Mollie had spent a considerable amount of time in Josh's office, telling herself she was snooping in an excellent cause. His records were carefully kept, and made her think his idea was in some measure the same as hers. The most likely renters of his flats were families who boarded in so-called family residences; a term preferred to rooming houses, though there was really little difference.

Josh's house on Bowling Green was a family residence, and he maintained a separate ledger dedicated to its occupants, and reserved a half page to each family. The husband's name came first—he was the legal tenant and the one responsible for the debt—and beside it the man's occupation. In some instances Josh had underlined that information in pencil, though the rest of the entries were in ink. Mollie believed the pencil marks indicated someone Josh thought able to afford to rent a flat. Her guess was he'd probably already broached the subject. A quiet word between gentlemen. Bit of a tip really, considering the building wasn't yet finished. Spoken in his most earnest manner. Genuinely so, since Josh believed his flats to be a truly wonderful innovation.

Fortunately, whatever he thought about a woman's right to be heard in the matter, he had nonetheless recorded beside each man's name that of his wife, and the numbers of their children—divided, she had noted, by gender. (Causing her to spare a thought for whether when she told Josh she was expecting—she'd missed her monthlies in January and in February and planned to break her news as soon as the first flat was rented—he would express a preference for a girl or a boy.) The wives were critical. That's what she'd tried to tell him the other evening. It was her justification for disobeying him and poking her nose where he clearly did not want it. And just now, sitting in the dining room of her husband's Bowling Green family residence, it seemed worth the gamble. The women were paying rapt attention.

The one who'd asked about the single-floor arrangement of the flats was Margaret Jackson. She was married to Elva Jackson and they had two girls and a boy. If the records were in her keeping, Mollie thought, she would have noted as well the ages of the children. Josh hadn't done so, but his books did say that Mr. Jackson was the senior accounting clerk at a clothing manufactory; and his name was underlined, so Josh must think him a prospect. There could be no doubt of the value of getting Margaret Jackson's assistance in the matter of her husband moving his family to Josh's new building. She could push, so to speak, while Josh pulled. "That's correct, Mrs. Jackson," Mollie said. "Each flat in the St. Nicholas is conveniently located on one level."

"Och, that means you're away to your bed with all the cooking smells trailing after you." Margaret Jackson's words betrayed a Scots burr, and her voice seemed to rise and fall with the rhythm of her swaying body as she cradled her child's dark head close to her bosom, and rocked back and forth to keep the little girl asleep.

How fiercely would such a woman argue for the opportunity to put her children to bed in a home of her own? Like a tigress protecting her cubs, Mollie decided. "Not a bit of it," she said. "Tasteful and practical, remember. There are windows providing cross ventilation in every flat. You can air the rooms quite thoroughly after meals. And," she added, "there's space for a rocking chair in any one of them."

"But there's something I don't understand . . ." Ethyl Potter this time. Josh's books said her husband was a newly minted attorney. "Since you're under the same roof with a great many others, how is it a private residence?"

"French flats, that's what they're called, aren't they, Mrs. Turner?" The speaker was Mrs. Francie Wildwood, the resident landlady. Josh paid her to run the house, collect the rents, and do the cooking. Auntie Eileen would describe her as *une femme d'un certain âge*, but she still boasted a voluptuous figure, and golden hair Mollie immediately recognized as being helped with a touch of peroxide. Auntie Eileen would never allow such vulgar artifice in her house. *A lady is always a perfect match. As above, so below.* Just now Mollie cared little whether or not Mrs. Wildwood was a lady. She had let Mollie in and shown her into the dining room with something approaching enthusiasm. Now she was being helpful in the matter of the questions. Mollie was prepared to take her allies where she found them.

"Yes, Mrs. Wildwood, thank you. You're correct. French flats. And each is entirely separate from the other. One has total independence in such a home." Mollie let that sink in while her gaze swept the table. "You will have a key to your own front door." It was well known that having to be let in by the landlady after any sort of outing was among the most loathed feature of family residences. "And when you close that door it is locked from the inside. The only rules are those your husband makes for you."

Another blonde, this one natural as well as very young—no more than sixteen Mollie guessed—and obviously *enceinte,* sighed loudly. "The angel of the hearth," she said. Then, seeing the other women turn to look at her, "That's what a wife and mother's supposed to be. The angel of the hearth."

Amanda Jones, Mollie decided. Married to DuVal Jones. There had been a question mark beside his name in the column that listed the tenants' occupations. And nothing in the one indicating children. So Mrs. Jones must be expecting her first. Mollie glanced at the other woman's swollen belly and felt a great urge to pat her own. Barely three months was too soon for quickening, but she had been communing with the infant inside her since those first few weeks in December when her flow did not begin and she became more and more certain she was carrying. She wanted to hug Amanda Jones. Me too, she wanted to say. Me too.

"The angel of the hearth," the young woman repeated in a soft but insistent voice, with her eyes rolling upward like a stage heroine in a matinee performance.

Well, maybe not hug her.

"There are no hearths, I warrant. Not in French flats." Mrs. Buchwald was a no-nonsense sort with graying hair pulled into a strict bun. She had already dismissed her four children, sending them up to the single room which Josh's records indicated was let to the family of Frank Buchwald, post office clerk. "Steam heating, isn't it?"

"Yes," Mollie said. "A furnace in the cellar and radiators in every room. So there's no mess from any sort of fireplace."

"You're sure they're not tenements?" Margaret Jackson again.

"Absolutely not. The plumbing is the most modern available, and there's a bath and a water closet in each flat." Tenements were notorious for providing no bathtubs, and one hall toilet to serve a floor that might house thirty or forty people, all of them crammed in like rats in a nest. "And,"—Mollie was convinced she had saved the best argument for last—"there is an elevator."

Mrs. Jackson shook her head. "Och, I don't trust elevators. Don't see how you can be sure they won't fall."

"My husband has explained it to me," Mollie said. Actually, she'd seen a demonstration three years before arranged for the workers at Macy's. "The cables are protected by a series of knots. If one should break—an almost unheard of occasion, mind—the knots lock everything into place and the cab cannot fall. That's why it's called the safety elevator."

"Almost unheard of," Margaret Jackson said, "is not the same as never."

There was nothing to be gained by this discussion Mollie realized. "As I was saying, the upper floors are as desirable as those below. Nonetheless, they are the most economical." Josh was unwilling to go counter to the convention which priced the ground floor highest.

Mrs. Buchwald had produced a pencil and a slip of paper. "Number forty-two East Sixty-Third Street, is it?" And when Mollie nodded, "Are you going to tell us the price of one of these flats?"

The hard part. She had prepared herself for this, mentally rehearsing her speech about finances all during the long streetcar ride from Grand Street to Bowling Green. "Compared to what even the cheapest brownstone would cost," she said firmly and with a bright smile, "a great bargain. Just imagine, ladies, you get six hundred and fifty square feet divided into two bedrooms and a parlor cum dining room. As well as a kitchen already fitted with a stove and an icebox. And of course the bath and water closet, as I said."

"How much?" Mrs. Buchwald asked again.

"The rent depends on which floor, of course, but it can be as little as two hundred and twenty-five dollars a quarter."

Mrs. Buchwald did not write down the sum. "That's nine hundred dollars a year. It's a great deal of money, Mrs. Turner. And I take it you have to promise to stay the entire year."

Mollie swallowed hard and put a bright smile on her face. "In fact, Mr. Turner is committing himself to maintain that affordable rent for five years."

Mrs. Buchwald put down her pencil. "You're saying it's necessary to sign a five-year lease?"

"That's correct. But only the first quarter need be paid in advance."

"Well, I wouldn't say, Mrs. Turner, that it's all that affordable."

For a post office employee, probably not. Josh had not underlined Frank Buchwald's name. But the new lawyer, and the accountant, and probably the manager of the shop that sold Steinway pianos—his wife hadn't spoken a single word, but she had not once taken her eyes from Mollie's face—all had firmly penciled lines drawn below their names.

"I think it is," Mollie said, "when you consider what you gain. Moving to the St. Nicholas means it's possible for an ordinary family to be in a private home for a modest amount of money compared to the thousands required to purchase. That's every family's dream, isn't it? A home of your own where you serve the meals you choose, and have a Christmas tree decorated to your own taste, and you and your husband can leave a puzzle half done and know when you come back to it next evening no one will have spoiled all your work, or worse, picked it apart. And in summer you can fill a picnic basket with supper and carry it over to the Central Park, and the whole family can have a jolly outing for no extra expense at all. With one of these flats, ladies, you can achieve that goal now, not years in the future when maybe—with no guarantee, mind—you might be able to purchase a whole house."

"Because," Mrs. Buchwald said, rising to leave the dining room, "these places you're talking about are not really in New York City. They're way up in the East Sixties where no civilized people live."

"Och, but you're forgetting about the stable and the horsecars. They make the flats entirely convenient for gentlemen needing to come downtown to work."

It wasn't Mollie who made that argument, it was Margaret Jackson.

By the time Mollie left twenty minutes later, she was entirely satisfied with what she'd accomplished. Of course Mrs. Wildwood would tell Josh his wife had called, but that wouldn't happen for a week or more. Josh was too busy building his flats to visit his rooming houses with any frequency. And by next week or the week after, Mollie was certain, the seeds she'd planted this afternoon would be bearing fruit and it wouldn't matter.

"Sorry, folks, not a hope. This is as far as we go."

The conductor pushed his way through the crowded streetcar with determination. Some of the many standing in the aisles were actually pushed into the laps of the seated passengers. "Everybody out," the conductor shouted. "End of the line for today." The outside straphangers meanwhile, those who anchored themselves to the exterior of the car with the leather harnesses provided for the purpose, had long since jumped free. Because lashings of snow had turned them into moving snowmen in what had become, in a virtual instant, a howling blizzard.

Having boarded at the beginning of the run when she left the Bowling Green residence, Mollie was seated at the back and was among the last passengers to descend from the stalled car. She stepped onto the street and into a blinding white maelstrom. "Please, can someone tell me where we are?" She aimed the question in the direction of the other passengers, mostly men, disappearing into the odd combination of whiteness and encroaching late afternoon dark.

"Fulton Street," someone called. "You'd best find some shelter, miss, else . . ." The warning was lost as the man moved off and his voice trailed away.

Mollie took a few steps forward, clutching her hat with one hand and trying to both lift her skirts and hang on to her muff with the other. She heard the muffled sound of shovels ahead—for the last ten blocks teams of workers had preceded the streetcar trying to clear the tracks—and the snorting of the horses, so she presumed she was heading uptown, but it was impossible to be sure. "Please," directing the question into the white void, "can anyone tell me if there's somewhere nearby I can find a cab?"

The only reply was the whinny of a horse, then the sound of a man gentling him, and the team of four being unhitched, followed by the soft clopping sound their hooves made on the snowy street as they were led away. Mollie started trudging up the road, hoping to encounter a cab, or perhaps someone who could advise where one might be found. Because of the storm, however, the shops and offices that lined this section of Broadway were already shut up tight and this far downtown, there were no private homes on the cross streets. Besides, the regularity of the grid didn't exist down here. If she turned away from the tracks she could get entirely lost. Even heading straight up Broadway she was unsure of exactly where she was. But if memory served, Park Row came after Fulton, and Park Row fronted on City Hall. Which indeed might be open and offering refuge to— How silly! She'd forgotten how close she was to St. Paul's Chapel. There could be no better place to seek shelter.

The path through the graveyard to the church doors hadn't been shoveled, but it did seem to be trodden. The wind shifted and she was half doubled over as she struggled toward the entrance. A gust tore at her hat and it came off but didn't blow away, hanging on instead by one pearl-tipped pin. Mollie made a number of futile efforts to secure it, then gave in and yanked the hat off and let the wind take it. "Hello!" she shouted into the whiteness and the silence. "Hello! Is the rector or someone about? I need—"

A hand grabbed her from behind and an arm circled her throat. "Ain't nobody at their prayers just now, love. So you be quiet and everything'll be fine. I'll take that muff."

Mollie opened her mouth to scream but the arm around her throat reduced the sound to strangled grunts of terror. She tried to kick behind her, but her bustle had come loose and the meant-to-be-graceful trailing skirt of the red traveling suit trapped her foot. "Get those gloves off, love. Let's see what kind o' rings you—" There was a loud thwacking sound and the man's words ended in a squeal of pain.

"Get off with you! Go on! Go rob some other poor soul as is stranded in a storm. You're not even a proper thief, just a coward picking on a slip of a woman all alone in the snow."

The words—spoken in a woman's voice—were accompanied with more thwacking sounds and out of the corner of her eye Mollie saw the rise and descent of a rolled umbrella. Seconds later the assailant had let her go and run off. Mollie fought for breath while mumbling her thanks.

"Weren't nothing, miss. His kind is cockroaches and deserve what they gets." The wielder of the umbrella materialized as a shadowy silhouette in the driving snow, a bulky figure wrapped in numerous scarves and assorted wraps who stooped down and came up holding Mollie's beaver muff. "Here you go."

"Thank you." Mollie had to shout to be heard above the howling wind, "I don't have much money with me, but—"

"Don't mind if . . . Hang on. I know you. Tillie Wallace's pawn shop it was. I'm Tess o' the Roses."

The broad-brimmed hat was thickly encrusted in white snow, but having been reminded, Mollie recognized the unlikely assortment of pink-and-yellow silk roses she'd first seen at the pawn shop on East Seventh Street. "Why, so you are."

Tess reached forward and took Mollie's arm. "C'mon. You can't be wandering around alone in the likes of this. There's more villains about for sure. Candle to a moth you are, love." She was tugging Mollie back toward Broadway meanwhile, both women half-bent against the blowing snow. "It's Mollie as I recall. Now, where's home? Nearby I hope."

"Not very near," Mollie said. "Grand Street. But if we could find a cab, I'd—"

Tess snorted in derision. "Not a chance. C'mon," taking a tighter grip on Mollie's arm, "shank's mare it is. We'll go on together."

On Sixty-Third Street the sky had turned to gunmetal gray soon after the workmen took their dinner break, a meal they brought with them in tin boxes and ate sitting on the ground, leaning their backs against the upright steel beams that formed the skeleton of the apartment house to be. They washed the food down with ale from the keg Josh purchased from a nearby brewery, and provided as a bonus for working this far from the town. It was strong stuff—stand up without a glass, the men said—and the pungent reek of malted hops had become for Josh the smell of his unlikely project as it rose an incredible eight stories into the sky. Not today, however. The ale was overpowered by the metallic smell of the storm, followed by powerful gusts of wind that carried droplets of ice that stung the cheeks and bit into exposed hands. "Ain't but a taste o' what's comin'," someone said and there were murmurs of agreement.

It was not yet three when Henry Tickle nodded at the construction materials scattered everywhere and told Josh, "We'd best get things locked down. Feels like it's going to be a bad one."

Josh was content to let Henry see to what needed doing. The man had proved himself as capable a foreman of construction as Ebenezer was of steelmaking downtown in the foundry. It was the dwarf who'd suggested his cousin take over uptown. Said Henry would be invaluable in getting the steel skeleton in place. Later, when the specialist trades took over—the bricklayers and stone masons and plumbers and steam fitters and carpenters—someone would be needed to co-ordinate their efforts. His cousin, Ebenezer Tickle promised, would do a good job with that as well. *Look out for your interests Henry will, Mr. Turner. Knows as what's best for you is best for him. Won't be noth-ing you paid for walking out the door without you earning a penny for the use of it.*

As usual, it had been good advice worth taking. Particularly since Josh allowed the men who wished to do so to sleep on the building site, just as they did at the foundry. Most of the dozen workers took up the offer, making use of the empty but relatively snug stable, building a charcoal fire in a brazier for warmth, and saving themselves the long trek back into the city at least some nights during the week. Given the weather, they'd probably all stay tonight. If it weren't for Mollie home alone on Grand Street, Josh might have considered doing the same. Or he'd have gone eight blocks further uptown to Sunshine Hill. Either would be preferable to the long ride back to town in a storm. As it was, neither was possible. It was Thursday. Mollie wouldn't have even Mrs. Hannity for company. She'd be entirely alone in a blizzard. Unthinkable.

"Best start back, if you're going, sir." Henry again. "I think we're going to get what Mother Nature's been storing up for the last few months."

"I think so too, Henry. Thing is, Mr. McKim was supposed to meet me here this afternoon."

Henry sucked on his finger and held it up to the wind. "Nor'easter," he said. "Coming over the river and traveling fast. I don't figure any-one's likely to head up to Sixty-Third Street this afternoon."

Down at the foundry Ebenezer Tickle stepped outside just as the bells of Trinity Church tolled three o'clock. Took his pipe with him. He wasn't slacking. They were making less steel these days so there was less to do all around, both work and the supervising of it. Besides, he was thinking on a problem that was, in some ways, more his employer's lookout than his own.

Hard to figure what Trenton Clifford wanted from Joshua Turner. Far as he could see, there wasn't—

Think of the devil and you'll see the tip of his tail. That's what his daddy used to say. Clifford was standing right there. Looking straight at him. "Good afternoon, Ebenezer."

"What are you doing here?"

"Having a look. You cannot object to that, can you, my little friend?"

"A look at what? And I ain't your friend."

"In which case," Clifford said, "I've no need to answer your question." Clifford chuckled when he said it, then turned his back on Tickle and walked a few yards further along the wharf and stood looking at the Devrey Shipping building. No, Tickle decided. He was looking at the Devrey ships.

Three of 'em was tied up at the pier, with four more riding at anchor just beyond. Backed by the great tower of that damned bridge they was said to be building. It loomed on the horizon over on the Brooklyn side. Supposed to be another just like it over here in New York. Going to suspend a structure across. Folks building it said it would be tall enough so any mast could fit underneath. Tickle couldn't see how that was going to prove out. Didn't seem logical to him. Just like it wasn't logical that Trenton Clifford was down here looking at boats as had nothing to do with him. It was the foundry he was interested in. The dwarf had no doubt about it.

Tickle stayed where he was. After three or four minutes Clifford moved off in the direction of Wall Street. Tickle watched him go, then went inside and summoned George Higgins. "You got to go find Mr. Turner. Tell him Trenton Clifford's gunning for him."

"Gunning for him how?"

"Like he was hunting possum. Waiting till he gets things lined up as suits him before he takes a shot. I seen Clifford just now. Outside looking at this place. He made like he was looking at Devrey's ships, or that tower over in Brooklyn. But I think that was playacting."

"That's what you want me to tell Turner? Clifford was down here looking?"

"Ain't the first time. You know that."

Higgins didn't say anything, just nodded.

"Go now," Tickle said. "Go by the house first. If he ain't there, go on up to Sixty-Third Street. Tell Mr. Turner he needs to look out for his interests. Maybe get some folks down here as can keep an eye on things."

"Thought we was doing that," Higgins said. "Sleeping here and all."

"We're no match for a bunch of thugs if Clifford decides to hire 'em. What Mr. Turner needs to do is hire some thugs of his own. Do it fast. Leastwise that's what I think. Go find him and tell him."

10

GEORGE HIGGINS WAS hurrying up Gold Street when the snow began. He increased his pace. Stupid of Ebenezer to have sent him on this errand. Obadiah would have done a better job. Longer legs were sometimes a big advantage. On the other hand, Obadiah didn't know about Clifford. At least not the way he and Ebenezer did.

Most storms started slow and built themselves up. This one was a roaring monster in minutes. Seemed like the wind was forcing him back a step for each two he took forward. George hesitated, considering his situation, then decided he'd come too far to turn back. At this point the house on Grand Street was closer than the foundry. If Turner wasn't home his wife would be. He could ask to wait out the snow. She'd never been particularly friendly, looked at him funny every time he showed up at the house with the accounts or such like. Still, unlikely she'd refuse him shelter in a storm. He turned up the collar of his thick woolen jacket and battled on.

Took him better than half an hour to get as far as Canal Street. By then some of the drifts were taller than he was. Never seen so much snow come down so fast. Leastwise there was no traffic. Just lots of stalled and empty horsecars and streetcars and carriages. Higgins started across the road, head bent against the winds driving straight at him. He felt a hand on his shoulder.

"Hello, George. I've been looking for you."

He looked up at Trenton Clifford's walrus mustache. The twirled ends were frosted with snow. "What for?"

"I just wanted to say hello, George." Clifford tightened his grip. "After all, we're old friends, aren't we?"

"I wouldn't say exactly that. I got to go, Captain Clifford. We don't have no business together anymore."

"Quite so, George. Besides, snow like this could bury a midget altogether. He might not be found for weeks."

Higgins pulled away and Clifford let him go, standing and watching him trudge doggedly on through the increasing fury of the sudden storm. Thought he'd best get out of the weather himself because, Christ Almighty, the north was a cursed place. Seemed like giant hands in the sky were emptying barrels of snow on the world below. Nonetheless, Trenton Clifford did not immediately move on. Not until he made out the man who stepped out of a nearby doorway, tipped his hat in Clifford's direction, and followed the dwarf.

By the time Josh had ridden ten blocks he was fighting a howling blizzard. In other circumstances the occasional hints of life behind doors closed against the fierce storm might have tempted him to give it up and seek shelter in a hotel or even a private home. But however enticing the wink of gaslights and once even a few notes of music, he didn't consider stopping. Mollie was sensible and unlikely to panic, but she was bound to be worried. About him if nothing else. And conditions like this encouraged the worst of the city's villains to go on the prowl. He struggled on, encouraging Midnight with murmurs and whispers, his upper body bent nearly straight over the horse's mane. The going was excruciatingly slow, the pair of them utterly alone in a white world deserted by civilization.

Occasionally he made out the carcass of an abandoned streetcar or carriage, their empty traces outlined by drifting snow. One bit of encouragement were the church bells that tolled along his route. He recognized their distinctive tones: Dutch Reformed at Twenty-First Street, sonorous and steady as they rang in six o'clock; Episcopal Church of the Ascension at Twelfth, chiming six-thirty in prettier, higher-pitched sounds with more flourishes. Soon after that Josh realized the going was getting easier as he traveled further downtown. The more densely packed city provided windbreaks and snowbreaks, and in a few cases the gusts had actually whipped a path along a narrow street, even to the extent of here and there exposing a few cobbles. His progress along Grand Street after he made the turn from the Bowery was achieved at a nearly normal pace, helped on by Midnight's recognition that they were almost home.

The steps leading to the front door of the house were buried in snow, and Josh was glad to see Mollie hadn't been foolish enough to try and shovel them clear. The only light appeared to come from the drawing room that was now his office, a dull glow behind drawn curtains, but just then he had no time to wonder why no light showed elsewhere. The mare was both fractious and determined. She required no urging to use her powerful forelegs to break through the drift in front of the alley that led to the small stable behind the house.

Josh dismounted quickly, grateful for the tight quarters that made it possible for him to bang on the back entrance to the house at the same time he began the job of getting the door to the stable open, cursing meanwhile the fact that he did not employ a live-in stable boy, only a part-time lad who came around to feed whichever horse he wasn't using and muck out once a week. "Mollie! I'm here. Be right in. Soon as I see to Midnight. Got to get her cooled down before I can feed her. Take a good few minutes."

The house was remarkably quiet, and black as pitch, the only light showing as a crack beneath the door of the office. Josh moved along the hall calling Mollie's name and not permitting himself to speculate on the silence that greeted his arrival, or the fact that the dining room where he'd have expected to find her was both dark and empty. "Mollie, where are you love? It's been the devil's own journey, and I'd be grateful for—" He pushed open the office door.

At first the gaslight, even at half power as it was, made him blink. He had to look twice to be sure he was seeing what he thought he saw. George Higgins, the dwarf who kept the foundry books, lay on his belly on the floor beside the desk, his face half-turned as if he'd lain down to go to sleep, so the glow of the wall sconce illuminated him and allowed Josh to know at once exactly who he was. Had been, to be more precise. There was a dagger buried up to the hilt in George's back and he was unquestionably dead.

What struck him first was not the unlikeliness of this victim in this particular place, but the stark evidence that something very terrible had happened under his roof.

Josh ran back to the hall, no longer shouting Mollie's name, but searching for her frantically, expecting the worst wherever he looked. He pelted downstairs to the kitchen first. No one was there but he was able to light a taper from the damped coals of the kitchen stove and thereafter he lit the lamps wherever he passed. At the end the house was ablaze in light and Josh knew he and the dead dwarf were the only people in it.

He went again down to the kitchen and found a large white sheet in the linen cupboard next to the stove and carried it back to the office. This time he lowered himself beside Higgins's body—not an easy task for a one-legged man—and felt for a pulse. The result was what he expected, but he learned as well that the dwarf had been dead for some hours. George's body was cold and stiff. His jacket, soaked through like his trousers—indicating he had struggled through the snow to get here—was thick dark wool and it had absorbed nearly all the blood. There was only a small pool of it beside him on the carpet, and it was already congealed. Josh considered turning the corpse over but decided against it. The police always wanted to do such things for themselves, and sooner or later they must certainly be informed. Given the weather they would understand that he could not summon them as soon as he discovered the body, but they were bound to be less forgiving if he'd trampled all over what they would see as evidence.

Josh spread the sheet over the small corpse, pulled himself up by using the corner of the desk for purchase, and for the first time took a look at the office itself. It was a wreck. The drawers of his filing cabinet had been turned out, the contents left strewn on the floor, and the top of his desk swept clean of ledgers and inkpots and notebooks. As if someone had pushed the entire detritus of his record keeping off the desk and onto the floor in what seemed a fit of pique at not finding what he wanted. Josh had, however, not a clue as to what that might be. Nor what had brought George Higgins up from the foundry in such weather as this, much less who had put a knife in his back or why.

All that registered in the back of his mind, as it were. The front was fighting a terrible and growing fear. He kept trying to convince himself Mollie might have gone to her aunt's, left before the storm, and been prevented from returning because of its onslaught. But she hadn't said anything about such plans, and wouldn't she have left a note or—

His thoughts were interrupted by a series of loud thumps coming from the hall. Someone was banging on the door. Repeatedly and with considerable force.

Josh looked at the outline of the undersized body beneath the sheet and wished he had a pistol, or even a rifle of some sort, but there were no firearms in the house. It had never occurred to him he might require them. Anyway, it was likely all that business about criminals always returning to the scene of the crime was invented by the hacks who wrote the stories for the newspapers and magazines that promulgated the theory. He satisfied his wish to be prudent by picking up a heavy lead blotter and went to investigate.

The snow was blowing straight toward him when he opened the door. At first he couldn't make out anything other than the sheets of white which he'd faced for so much of this day. Then he realized two women stood in front of him, and that one was his wife. Mollie was entirely covered in snow, even her eyelashes were crusted with it, and since she wore no hat it was as if, since he saw her that morning, her hair had turned white.

"Josh, this is Tess o' . . ." She managed only the first words of the introduction, then began to crumple.

That collapse broke his astonished paralysis and he reached for her, catching her before she fell and pulled her toward him, inviting the woman with her into the house only with the command that she close the door behind them. She did that, then strode in front of him, saying, "Here, sir. Let me get that," as she dashed for the door to the office he'd pulled shut when he came out into the hall.

"No! Not in there. The next door." Half carrying and half dragging Mollie, meanwhile. Cursing the fact that he could not pick her up properly because his balance was too impaired by the extent of his own fatigue.

The creature—she was as snow-covered as his wife, but wearing a broad-brimmed hat of some sort that carried half a foot of white frosting—yanked open the door to the dining room and let him go past her with Mollie, then entered behind them. After which she made at once for the tantalus on the sideboard. "Just what's wanted. This ain't locked, is it, sir?" Answering her own question by lifting the wooden lid and grabbing the decanter of brandy. "Where might the glasses . . . Ah, here we are." She helped herself to those as well and poured three generous tots, managing to carry all three to where Josh had put Mollie in a chair and was using the nearest bit of cloth he could find, a lace doily, to both dry her face and rub some life back into it.

"She's a game one," Tess said, putting the brandy down and taking the seat opposite them. "Walked here from Fulton Street we did. I figure it took us best part of three hours. And her in that condition, as she told me on the way. Won't probably do her or the baby no harm, but let her have a sip of that brandy, sir. Bound to bring her round." With that she tossed back the drink she'd poured for herself and stood up to get another.

Mollie grew feverish during the night, sleeping only in fits and starts and frequently calling his name, but apparently not much comforted by anything he said, only by his arms around her. For his part Josh slept hardly at all. He listened for every sound. There were few, the heavy snow muting even the usual creaking of the house, but he was unable to forget that the corpse of a murdered man lay on the floor below. He hadn't undressed, conscious of the fact that as soon as the storm abated and there was some daylight he must go and find, first, the police and, second, a doctor for Mollie. Or perhaps the order should be reversed. Nothing would, after all, bring George Higgins back to life.

"In her condition . . ." the woman had said. Tess somebody. He wasn't sure he'd heard a last name. Presumably that meant Mollie had claimed she was expecting a child. Odd that she'd confided in a stranger when she hadn't told him. Or perhaps not, given the circumstances in which she'd found herself. Struggling through the snow on foot that way . . . it must have felt at times like the last journey she was to take on earth.

She muttered his name again and he stroked her forehead and spoke quiet and he hoped soothing words into her ear. And when she called out, "Tess, don't go!," assured her that the woman who'd brought her home was sleeping upstairs in the room across from Mrs. Hannity's.

He'd gone back earlier and checked on the sorry business in the office where, of course, nothing had changed. Then he'd locked both the hall door and those from the dining room, and tried to shut out of his mind the fact that a man who worked for him, who was in some sense his responsibility, had been murdered under his roof. And for a reason that was, as far as Josh was concerned, totally unfathomable.

Then, around two a.m. according to the tolling clock on the nearby Presbyterian church, the question he'd thus far forgotten to consider surfaced in his mind. What in holy hell had Mollie been doing down on Fulton Street?

Josh woke after a few hours of exhausted sleep to the aroma of frying eggs and bacon and brewing coffee. Mollie was asleep, though her face was still flushed with fever. He got out of the bed and, after a splash of cold water in lieu of a proper wash and shave, went downstairs to see if somehow Mrs. Hannity had managed to get home and resume her duties.

It was, however, Tess who was setting out food in the dining room. "Thought you could use some breakfast, sir. And since there weren't no one else to cook it, I made free. Hope you don't mind."

"No, not at all, Miss . . . Or is it Mrs.? And I'm sorry, I don't remember the name."

"Mrs. Mary Teresa Santucci," she said. "Widow. But everyone calls me Tess. Or Tess o' the Roses if we're being formal. And I'm sure you know why," she added with a bob of her head.

The hat was free of snow and the pink-and-yellow silk roses were dry, and it was apparent she did not intend to take the thing off indoors or out. "I suspect I can guess, Tess of the Roses. And I realize I have not thanked you properly for bringing my wife home. I am quite sure she would not have found her way without you. I'm very grateful."

"You're entirely welcome. And I'm grateful as well. For the warm dry bed," she added, seeing his look of puzzlement. "Now, sir, you sit down and eat some breakfast, and I'll go up and sit with Mrs. Turner until you're done."

"Can you stay for a time after that, Tess? I must go and find a doctor for her, and . . . deal with some other urgent business. You'll be properly compensated, of course."

"Glad to," Tess said gaily. "I'll be here long as you need me."

Josh was torn between rushing to the front door to see if there had been any effort to clear the street—City Hall was notoriously slow to dispatch shovel men to residential streets like this one—and doing something about his empty belly. The judgment was quickly made. He hadn't eaten since a hasty lunch of some bread and cheese the day before and he was, he realized, ravenous. He sat down and practically fell on the food, and only after he'd dispatched four eggs and three rashers of bacon, along with a healthy helping of hashed potatoes and three pieces of toast and two cups of coffee, did he go and open the front door.

The path made by Mollie and Tess when they climbed the front steps was still mostly visible, so the snow must have stopped falling soon after they came home. Now there was bright sun, intensified when it bounced off a gleaming white world. Josh heard the sound of voices, and when he looked to his right he could see gangs of young boys with shovels over their shoulders going from house to house offering to clear a path for the homeowner. "Over here!" he called and three lads made their way to him, wading through waist-high drifts.

"How's Broadway look?" Josh asked.

"Shoveled clear as far as Twentieth Street," one of the boys answered.

"And Fifth Avenue?"

"Only up as far as the hospital on Sixteenth."

"That will do very well," Josh said. "Get started shoveling my front steps and the alley back to the stable. Meanwhile I'm going to write a couple of notes and one of you can deliver them."

When he came back five minutes later the boys had the front stoop clear and were starting on the passage. The biggest of them spotted Josh and pushed the smallest—a towhead wielding a shovel that was taller than he was—into his path. "I take it you're to be the errand boy," Josh said.

"Yes, sir. Where am I to go, sir?"

"First to New York Hospital. Sixteenth and Fifth. Ask for Dr. Simon

Turner and don't put this note into the hands of anyone else." Josh was quite certain his brother would have remained at his post once the storm began, so no question but Simon would be at the hospital now. "After that take this second note to the police office on Broadway. Give it to the first copper you see."

Four hours later the police were carrying George Higgins's body out the front door that according to them had been forced open sometime the previous day—it had never occurred to Josh to look—and Simon was seated in the dining room waiting for him to come and eat a midday meal prepared by Tess o' the Roses. "Course no one's been to the markets yesterday nor today, but I found a bit of leftover ham pie still smells likely and some beans I set to soak, and there's a cabbage and plenty of potatoes, so I can make do if you want."

Josh said indeed he did want, and having seen off the last of the coppers he went gratefully to the table, glad not only for the hot and appetizing food but for the fact that his brother was there to share it with him. Simon had already told him Mollie's fever had broken, and that with proper rest the prognosis was excellent.

"What an unbelievable, miserable business," Josh said as he sat down. "I wouldn't believe it if I read it in a book by some overwrought lady novelist. The mad woman in the attic and the dwarf dead in the drawing room as was."

"You're missing the governess, however. There's always a governess. Seriously, Josh, the dwarf worked for you?"

"Yes. Down in the foundry."

"Making steel for your tower of shelves in which to stack people. Like bags of flour."

Josh blinked. That had been Trenton Clifford's analogy. "I keep telling you," he said, helping himself, meanwhile, to generous portions of the food Tess had spread on the table, "those flats are going to be commodious and affordable for ordinary folk, and a damn sight better than living in one of the family residences that right now is pretty much their only choice."

"Have any been leased?"

"Not yet. And this rotten weather is not going to help."

"It will pass. Listen, about the dwarf . . . You said you hadn't sent for him."

"I did not. I was uptown at Sixty-Third Street almost since first light, and when I came home, I . . . Look here, Simon, I've been explaining this to the coppers for the past few hours. Do you mind if I don't go over it all again? I don't know why he was here, or how he got in, or what reason he may have had for turning over my office the way he apparently did. Though I suppose it could have been whoever killed him. Any further reports on Mollie?"

"She's sleeping now. I've given her a sedative and I expect she'll stay asleep all day, but she's doing remarkably well. She's quite a strong woman, your wife, for all her looking like a reed. Though apparently she won't for much longer."

"Ah. I gather then she told you she was expecting." Simon and Tess and God knows who else; only he, apparently, was not in Mollie's confidence.

"She did," Simon said. "She estimates going on for three months and I concur. She wants a doctor, by the way. Not a midwife as will lock her up for months on end in this 'confinement' nonsense that's their stock-in-trade, and I think she's entirely correct. You should allow it, Josh. A doctor will cost a bit more, but it's much the wiser course than one of these nattering women who have no proper medical training."

"Yes, of course. But . . . Not you, Simon." He blurted out the words, then realized they might sound offensive. "I mean, I'm sure you're a fine doctor. It's just—"

The younger man guffawed loudly. "Of course not me! Don't be stupid. Doctors aren't encouraged to treat their relations. Besides, we don't all do everything these days as it was in Papa's time. Mollie must have a proper obstetrician. I'll ask around if you like. And if you don't mind his knowing, I'll talk to Papa. He's still very much esteemed in the profession. Any number of doctors come to talk to him about what-all. He'll have some ideas on who would be best."

"Yes. Thank you. Do ask him. That would be excellent."

"Good. Settled then. Now, tell me about the murder weapon."

"What about it?"

"Was it a knife from downstairs? From your own kitchen?"

Josh remembered his initial reaction the moment he first laid eyes on poor George's body. His thought had been that the dwarf had been stabbed with a dagger. That's what he'd put in the note summoning the police. *A man in my employ . . . came home at the height of the storm to find him dead in my study, with a dagger between his shoulder blades.* "No. I'd never seen the thing before and it was nothing I'd expect to find in this house. Sort of an oversized bowie knife."

"I see. Plunged up to the hilt, was it?"

"Simon, I know doctors deal with all manner of gruesome details and you read all those scary stories as a boy, but this isn't an exciting adventure as far as I'm concerned. The man worked for me. I'm responsible in a sort of way. And as soon as the roads are passable I have to go downtown and tell the men at the foundry what's happened."

"Mollie shouldn't be alone," Simon said at once. "Can the woman with the hat remain with her? At least until your household's back to normal."

"I'll ask her," Josh said. "But in any case I shall send for Mollie's Aunt Eileen this afternoon. I'm sure she'll come the moment she can get through."

"We was thinking," Ebenezer Tickle said, "that George got hung up somewhere 'cause of the storm. That we'd see him back once the streets was cleared."

"I'm truly sorry, Mr. Tickle," Josh said. "And I came to tell you as soon as I could." It was Tuesday, five full days since the storm. The horsecars were operating on some of their runs, though the streetcars—dependent as they were on following tracks laid on the ground—were still idle. The elevated railroad, meanwhile, had proved itself the easiest means of transportation to restore to normalcy. The sun had a better chance to melt the snow on the tracks suspended above the city over Greenwich Street and Ninth Avenue. Getting around wasn't easy, but it was at least possible. "I take it the police haven't sent anyone to speak with you yet?"

"No coppers, no. Ain't likely they'll trouble themselves too much," Tickle added. "Not about one of us."

Josh didn't argue with that. *These sorts of people, sir, they get up to all kinds o' things a gentleman like yourself wouldn't even imagine.* That from a police sergeant clearly more interested in getting home to his dinner than solving the mystery of what had happened in Joshua Turner's front room. "Mr. Tickle, have you any idea what George was doing at my house? I certainly didn't send for him. I wasn't even home."

Ebenezer didn't answer immediately. Josh looked over to where Tickle's cousin Obadiah stood with Israel McCoy, the third of the original three dwarves who came to work at the foundry. Neither man made any pretense about how avidly they were listening to the conversation.

The foreman waved them off. "Here, you two, show some respect for the dead. Go back there and get George's things together."

Ebenezer waited until they'd moved off, then turned back to Josh. "I sent him," he said quietly. "Didn't have any idea the storm was coming."

"No way you could have known. But what did you send him for? And why at midday when I wasn't likely to be at home?"

The dwarf shook his head. "Poor George. I never thought . . . I'd not have sent him if I'd any idea . . ."

"I know that, Mr. Tickle. I'm not blaming you for anything, I assure you. But why did you send him?"

"To find you. Said he should check your house first, then go on up to the building site if you weren't there."

"From Wall Street all the way up to Sixty-Third," Josh said quietly.

"I think you'd better tell me the reason for that, Mr. Tickle. Given that it was Thursday and except for the storm, which as you say none of us knew was coming, you would have expected me on Saturday with the pay packets, it seems a rather extraordinary errand."

"You might say."

"I do, Mr. Tickle."

The dwarf glanced over his shoulder. The other two men were still occupied at the far end of the foundry. "Trenton Clifford," he said. "He'd been hanging about down here. I seen him twice. Last time was that same day. Before the storm started. He was down here looking around. Before that George had told me he seen Clifford as well. Three times he said."

"And that alarmed you," Joshua said.

"It did."

"I think, Mr. Tickle, it's time you told me the nature of the connection between you and Captain Clifford."

Ebenezer peered into the shadows, though Josh had no idea what exactly he was looking for. "Not here," the dwarf said. "I'll take you to a place."

11

"IT'S A STORY as takes some time for the telling," Ebenezer said. "And this is a good place to tell it."

They were in Mama Jack's Cave. Come not by the entrance through the hidden tunnel at the end of Washington Square Mews, but through a saloon on Eighth Street. Tickle had led Josh along a long, narrow taproom, paying no attention to the many pairs of eyes that followed them. More of the same when they walked through the storeroom at the back where they kept the kegs of beer and ale until they were wheeled to the front to be tapped. Tickle ignored the lot and led Josh down the stairs to a deep cellar lit by pitch torches that cast flickering shadows. And finally, into this remarkable drinking establishment where everyone Josh saw was queerly made one way or another, and a truly enormous woman, her bulging and sagging flesh draped in satins and jewels, sat on a throne raised above their heads, watching over everything that happened.

"Mama Jack," Ebenezer said, nodding his head toward the raised dais. "Used to be with Barnum. Fat lady in his freak show. Got fed up and started this place."

"Were you with Barnum?" Josh blurted the words and was sorry as soon as he said them, but Tickle seemed not to take offense.

"Never. Got me a skill as can be done if you're tall or small. My daddy seen to it I'm an iron man like he was. Don't need to put myself on display to eat. Some here ain't the same."

They were walking through the throng as they spoke and a path, Josh noted, was being made for them. The talk meanwhile was all around them in waves. It abated as they came close, then rose again behind them, so Josh couldn't catch hold of what was being said. Only an occasional word. Murder, he heard. Higgins.

They came to a corner with a low table and stools that were dwarf-sized, and Tickle dragged over another, full-sized, for Josh. When they'd settled themselves a woman appeared and deposited two mugs of ale on the table. She was exceptionally tiny, Josh noted, half Tickle's size, and with no hint of his disproportion. Her hair was long and yellow-blond, like a doll his sister Goldie had when she and Josh were children. The same big blue eyes as well, but not painted on a head made of china. Those real blue eyes looked at him intently. Taking his measure, Josh thought.

"This here," Tickle said, "is Maude Pattycake. She's going to marry me."

"Keep your tongue in your mouth, Ebenezer. I ain't said yes yet."

"You will," he said, no hint of doubt in his voice. Then, "Keep us filled up. I got business to talk with Mr. Turner."

Maude said she'd do that and moved away. Ebenezer took a long swallow of ale, then said, "You been wanting to know about Trenton Clifford. Guess it's time I told you."

Josh was conscious of the attention of everyone in the room. "Why here?" he said. "You were afraid of being overheard at the foundry when it was only Obadiah and Israel, but here there's—"

"Ain't no one here going to take Clifford's part in anything."

"But— Which one?" he demanded as a possible explanation came to mind. "Who don't you trust? Your cousin or McCoy?"

"Going to tell you a story about steel before we get to Clifford," Tickle said, waving the question aside. "You remember who Bessemer is?"

"Fellow who owns the patent on the steelmaking process. I remember very well."

"Like I told you, he claimed he made steel back in England same time as Kelly was making it in Eddyville. Did it the same way as well. Had the identical process down pat according to him, and already had a patent over there. So he didn't have to pay but a pittance to get Kelly's patent. Wasn't worth all that much to him, Bessemer said. Just might be a small nuisance if he didn't have it. Bought it for next to nothing. Didn't even bother to ship Kelly's converters over to London. Said he had the same already. Made locally over there, so why pay for shipping."

"Why did Kelly sell to him if he was offered such a dismally bad deal?"

"'Cause he was broke. Like I told you, Mr. Kelly was a scientific type, not a businessman. Been to school to study what's called metallurgy. Spent years experimenting until he got to understand about taking out some of the carbon—not too much and not too little—and how cooling down the molten pig iron would make it hot. Everything like you seen us do to make steel."

Josh nodded and took a drink of ale. It was good brew, just bitter enough to be refreshing.

"Mr. Bessemer," the dwarf said, "he didn't go to school to study metallurgy. Didn't know nothing scientific about iron and steel. Course he knew steel was much stronger than iron, and how everyone wanted an easy way to make it. Something better 'n the old open-hearth way as takes days and days. But you could stop ten strangers on a street and find six or seven as knew that. How to do it? That's a different matter. So I'm asking you, Mr. Turner, how did Bessemer figure it out? The way he told it, he just came up with the process. Overnight like it were. Figured it out and built himself one converter and it turned out to be exactly the right one, did the job perfect first time. Presto change-o like they say in Barnum's show."

Tickle leaned in. Josh lifted his ale to his lips and the dwarf waited until the other man took his swallow and set the tankard on the table between them. "Best guess how it happened," Tickle said, "is somebody told Bessemer how to do it. Somebody as worked for Kelly and seen how it was done told the tale. That's how Bessemer knew what to do and how to do it."

"Did Clifford work for Kelly?" Josh asked.

Tickle had his pipe going and he sucked on the stem while he shook his head. "Nope. Never. Trenton Clifford, he's a real proper Southern gentleman. Ain't never going to be soaked in his own sweat in a foundry. But Captain Clifford did some business with Mr. Kelly. Had him make a steel door as would take two tons of dynamite to blast apart. Big wheel on the outside and you had to know which way to turn it and how many times in each direction in order to get it to open. Last big thing them Kelly brothers made, that special door. Captain Clifford, he watched the making of it. By then the Kellys was broke and Bessemer was in Eddyville nosing around, getting ready to make his offer for the patent. Seemed like that was two lucky-for-some things happening together and there was questions. Clifford said he didn't know Bessemer. Said he never met him."

The dwarf paused long enough to tap the ash out of his pipe and set about refilling it. "Thing is," he said, "Captain Clifford on his own, he didn't know enough about how steel is made to explain it to some Englishman. All the same, Clifford was in London a year and a half before Bessemer showed up in Eddyville."

"How do you know that?"

"I heard him say so."

"Where? When?"

"Getting there." Tickle refused to be hurried. "First, you got to understand what sort of a man Trent Clifford is."

"Trust me," Josh said. "I already do. He was in charge of the rebel prison on Belle Isle. I was one of the prisoners."

The dwarf considered that for a moment, then nodded. "So it

seems like you got a good idea about the kind of bad he is. It's not the usual sort, Mr. Turner. There ain't no passion in Clifford's evil. It's just the way he sees the world. Like it's set up for his convenience. Nobody else's. The other part of him is that he finds things out. Knows how to get people telling him things he finds a use for."

"I know that as well. How else did I find you? Though I've yet to see the advantage to Clifford in the arrangement."

"That," Tickle said, leaning forward, "is what's been on my mind right along. I almost didn't agree to work for you because of it. Talked to George and Israel about it right here. We decided to take a chance. Guess you did the same."

"I'm not sure I follow," Josh said.

"You were willing to take a chance on me, even though it was Clifford as put us together."

Josh nodded. "I was. I judged you were worth the risk, Mr. Tickle. Frankly, I'm glad I did. But it appears George has been considerably less fortunate in the arrangement than either you or I."

Tickle lifted his hand and signaled to Maude Pattycake and she brought them two more tankards of ale. "That's what I'm trying to tell you about. George's bad luck. How it might o' happened. Like I said, no doubt in my mind it was Clifford gave the information about making steel to Bessemer. Told him what Mr. Kelly figured out after years of studying and experimenting. But somebody had to have told him first. Clifford wouldn't get enough information just by watching. Not unless somebody explained about the temperatures and such, and how to build a converter."

"And you think those details might have come from either Obadiah or Israel." There seemed no other explanation for the dwarf's reluctance to tell the story at the foundry.

"I don't," Tickle said. "For one thing, Obadiah and me, we got the same grandma and grandpa. Same blood. And Israel . . . It's just not his way. I guess I just feel more comfortable talking about all this here. With my sorts of people."

Josh knew the other part of the story was coming. The thing that had made the dwarf's face go dark with rage the day they first visited the foundry together, when Josh demanded to know if Tickle and Clifford were somehow partners. What was extraordinary was that the people around him seemed to know as well. Their talk first quieted, then died away. Until finally Ebenezer Tickle's voice was the only sound in the place.

"That door Clifford had Mr. Kelly make for him back in Eddyville, it fit a cave in the woods near the lake. Not outside where it could be seen, door was halfways in. So's you only knew it was there if you already knew about the cave and you was inside. Even then, you couldn't open it unless you knew how the turns of the wheel went."

"Which you did."

"Yes. I helped make the door. So I knew." After that the other man sat silent, puffing on his pipe.

Josh waited, but Tickle seemed to have run out of words, seemed to be sinking into his thoughts. Maude Pattycake had moved closer to their table and Tickle reached over and took her hand, then raised his head. "There was a wide open space behind that door," he said. "All stone, hollowed out kind of. Big waterfall at the far end. A sort of flat place in the middle. And sloping walls all around. Lots of rocks and such jutting out here and there. Sort of like benches. Folks sat on them rocks so they could watch what went on down below."

"A natural amphitheater," Josh said. "That's what you're describing, isn't it?"

Tickle nodded. "I think that's the word, yes."

"In classical times," Josh said, "among the ancient Greeks and Romans, an amphitheater was meant for shows. Performances. Like the Colosseum in Rome."

"Place they fed the Christians to the lions," Tickle said.

Mama Jack's was warmed by a few charcoal braziers and the body heat of all the drinkers, but Josh felt cold. Back on Belle Isle, watching Clifford and the guards using prisoners for target practice, he'd felt cold as well. "What did Clifford do in the Eddyville woods, Mr. Tickle?"

"He had chariot races. There was a track marked out on the flat place, a big stretched-out circle."

"An oval," Josh supplied.

"That's right. Clifford and his friends, they ran the chariots right round that oval in sets of two. Went hell for leather. Never mind who got tipped up, or run over by the metal wheels. Cracked them long whips at the team pulling their chariot and the other team as well. In the end the winner would be whoever beat all the other drivers, one by one."

Josh heard the whispers all around him.

Long whips.

Metal wheels.

Hell for leather fast.

The entire room was listening and repeating the story, telling it as a sort of dirge. It was something most had heard before, but which had not lost its power to both terrorize and inflame.

"Did Clifford keep the horses in his cave?" Josh asked.

Tickle shook his head and the smoke of his pipe made wreaths in the air. "Weren't no horses. Not enough room for 'em," he said. "You'd have to take horses out into the woods and run 'em around the lake to keep 'em healthy. Someone would see. Them chariots was pulled by little people."

Then, as if he wasn't sure Josh understood, "By dwarves. They was paid seven dollars a night. A little man with no skill, maybe no daddy to put him in the way of earning a living in the big people's world, that's what he has to do to eat, Mr. Turner. One way or another, put himself on display."

"Mr. Barnum's freak show," Josh said. Barnum sometimes took his spectacle on the road. Not just in America, all over the world. Crowds paid good money to come and look.

"Barnum's museum and his traveling freak show, that's bad," Tickle agreed. "But nobody dies. Least not regularly."

"I take it," Josh said, "some of the dwarves pulling Clifford's chariots did die."

"Yes. At least one was killed most nights they was racing. Sometimes three or four. It was a thing you could bet on. Not just which team would win, how many would be dead when it was over. Clifford and the others, they whipped the dwarves something fierce. Made it so they had to veer over and drive the other chariot up against the wall, upend it maybe if it was going too fast. The edges of the wheels were kept sharp as knives. Drivers used their whips to make the team of little people pulling one chariot drag them sharp wheels over the team pulling the other. Best thing of all as they saw it was their team running those sharp wheels right over the neck of a dwarf on the other team. Cut his head off. When it was what they called a clean cut the driver, sometimes he'd reach down and lift up the cut-off head. Clifford, he always did that. He'd hold that dwarf's head up by the hair and yell and shout while his team pulled his chariot right round again. Blood everywhere. Plenty of it running all down Clifford's arm. He seemed to like that."

"And the other dwarves?" Josh asked, his voice flat, the smell in his nose that of the riverbank in the fetid heat of Belle Isle. "What did they think of committing murder for the sake of spectacle?"

Tickle sucked on his pipe before he answered. When he did the smoke came out with his words. Circled them. Like underlining and exclamation points in a newspaper. "Can't say what they thought, but I know what they felt, Mr. Turner. When there was a kill the little people on the team as made it got a dollar-a-man bonus. Two if it was a clean cut. Them dwarves, they felt richer."

There was silence in Mama Jack's when Tickle stopped speaking. It lasted a good while.

Finally, Josh said, "I take it you never pulled a chariot."

"Never. Not Israel nor George neither. But me and George, we got in sometimes. We knew about what went on and we knew how to open the door. So we went to see. Did it twice. Shamed by it, I am. But that's what happened. Thought maybe we could tell others what it was like. Get 'em to stop coming. But that was foolishness. Maybe just an excuse. They already knew. Seven dollars a night. Sometimes eight or nine. No dwarf thinks he'll get that for nothing."

Another silence, but this one didn't last as long. After a few seconds Tickle said, "That's where I heard Mr. Clifford talking about having been in England. At the chariot races. Heard him say he'd met a man as wanted to make steel and didn't know how. Me and George, we both heard."

"And you think Clifford somehow got the information? He found out exactly how the Kelly brothers made steel, and sold the knowledge to Bessemer?"

Tickle shook his head. "It's not what I think, Mr. Turner. It's what I know. Just like I know how it was about a year and half after me and George heard Clifford talking about an Englishman who wanted to make steel but couldn't that Bessemer showed up. Right there in Eddyville, buying Kelly's patent for a few dollars because he was already making steel over in London. Finishing touch that was. Put the Kelly brothers right out of business."

The talk around them started up again. Faster and louder than before. As if having heard the tale anew was a catharsis for the misbegotten sorts drinking at Mama Jack's. Maude Pattycake whispered something to Tickle, then left. The two men were alone and no longer the focus of attention. Josh leaned down so he was looking into Ebenezer Tickle's eyes. "That's what you think Clifford is planning to do to me, isn't it? Put me out of business in some way."

"That's what I think, Mr. Turner. And that won't be to my advantage neither. That's why when we discovered Clifford hanging about down by the foundry, George and me, we thought it was important to tell you."

❧

Josh took a much abbreviated version of the story to the police office on Broadway. "I can't say what motive Captain Clifford may presently have for murdering George Higgins, but I do know there was bad blood between them that went back to Kentucky some years past. And Clifford's an evil bastard. I can attest to that."

The copper listening to the tale—a Captain Willis in a belted, knee length frock coat with his star-shaped copper badge pinned to his chest and a top hat sitting near to hand—nodded. "Captain Clifford's a reb. I know that." He leaned forward over his desk. "Seems like you'd have no cause to like him, would you, sir?" No way to see the peg, given that both men were seated and facing each other. Still Josh had no doubt about the copper's meaning.

"I bear Trenton Clifford no grudge, Captain. Certainly nothing that would induce me to falsely accuse him of murder. I merely suggest that I know he was in the vicinity when George Higgins was killed."

"Begging your pardon, sir, you know he was down near Mr. Devrey's Wall Street docks earlier that day."

"My brother's docks and my foundry," Josh said. "Where Higgins worked."

"Making steel for you."

"That's right."

"But the midget was killed later. In your house."

Josh could see no point in continuing the discussion. He stood up. "Look into it, Captain Willis. I'm sure I can trust your diligence in the matter."

He didn't need to mention Zac's prominence directly. That was already well established.

A couple of days later another policeman, a Sergeant Hoyle, came to see him up on the building site. "We wanted you to know we done what you asked, Mr. Turner. Checked on Captain Clifford's whereabouts the day of the murder."

"What did you discover?"

Hoyle was craning his neck, taking in the remarkable skeleton of the future St. Nicholas flats, and he seemed more interested in the building than in a discussion of the murder. "This building, sir, it's—"

"What about Clifford?" Josh interrupted.

"Trenton Clifford was at Kate Meacham's establishment from close to four, soon as the snow started that would be, until the next morning."

"Rather a long time to stay at a place like Kate's, wasn't it?" Everyone called Mrs. Meacham's whorehouse by her first name. It was well-known for catering to any sort of notion, however bizarre. Sex with animals, with children, involving whips or chains or whatever. Anything at all. For a price you could do it at Kate's. Or just watch it being done, if that's what you fancied. Not the sort of homey place you might spend an afternoon and a night and eat breakfast the next morning.

"In the regular way, sir, yes, it would be. Figures to be only so long you can spend doing things with donkeys and freaks and such. But that's just it, Mr. Turner. Captain Clifford was stranded 'cause o' the storm. Everyone at Kate's was. Has to be a dozen different people as saw him there from when I said, before four, until after breakfast the next day. So don't seem like any way he could get away and stab the midget up at your house, then get back to Kate's without no one knowing he was gone. Not on a day and a night like that one."

Josh had heard the stories about police corruption. Tammany was said to have infiltrated the force and all but taken it over. But if that was operating here, he had no means to counter it. Clifford's alibi seemed unassailable.

It was Mollie who prepared the pay packets Josh distributed on the third Saturday after the storm. She'd taken over that portion of George Higgins's duties since his murder because Josh had no one else to do the work. "Only until I can find someone else," he'd promised.

"I don't mind doing it, Josh. I'm delighted to be of some use to you. And just now it can't hurt to pay one less wage each week."

"That's certainly true, but . . ." He'd spoken the words with a nod in the general direction of her midsection, thickened enough now so he couldn't pretend not to notice, though given her delicate health after the storm, and his preoccupation with getting his building crews working again, the subject had not yet been discussed, simply assumed between them.

Mollie knew she was cornered. "I am quite well, Josh. Truly. The physician Simon recommended, Dr. Thomas, says I am none the worse for . . . for the storm," she'd finished. And waited to be asked why she'd been caught in the snow in the first instance, and what had she been doing on Fulton Street. Josh asked nothing of the sort.

"May I ask when you are expecting the child?" He didn't look at her, only continued tying his cravat while gazing into the old mirror above the dresser.

"Towards the end of the summer, Dr. Thomas thinks," she said. "Late August, or perhaps early September."

"Time enough then."

"For what, Josh?" With a look at once startled and perplexed.

"To be in our own home. I would hope, Mollie, to have our first son . . . if indeed it's to be a boy," he'd added hastily, "to be born under my roof, not Zac's."

"Are you proposing we move to one of the St. Nicholas flats?"

"Nothing of the sort." Josh sounded astounded at the notion. "I shall do a bit better than that for us. I promise, you shan't live as if you've married an office clerk. But," he added as she stepped closer to remove a speck of lint from one broad shoulder, "the flats must be built and sold before I can make other arrangements. So, about the books . . . ," with a hand to her cheek, "I know it's beyond wifely duties, but if you truly don't mind . . ."

"Of course I do not. It makes no difficulty, Josh. I'm happy to take it on."

"That's my girl." And he'd dropped a quick kiss on her forehead and headed down the stairs and into the front hall where his freshly brushed hat and the old cloak that was better for winter riding than his fashionable overcoat, and his gloves and his cane all waited by the door. Mollie held the hat while he flung on the cloak, then took charge

of his gloves and cane while he adjusted the topper. Finally, ready to
meet the world, Josh reached for the door, but paused before opening
it. "The bookkeeping's only temporary, Mollie. But since you'll doubtless need extra help what with it and your . . . the circumstances . . . Do
you find Tess agreeable?"

"I do, Josh. Very. She's always cheerful, and she does whatever I
ask."

"Why not keep her on then? Tell her I'll pay a wage of forty-six dollars a month. Plus room and board. My only condition is that she stop
wearing that ridiculous bonnet indoors. Let me know if she agrees."

"I will do that, Josh. I'm sure she'll agree, it's quite generous. And
thank you." Then, after a moment's hesitation. "Josh, there's something
I should tell you."

"Is it urgent? I'm already delayed."

"No, of course not." A great whoosh of relief flooded up from her
toes at the let-off.

"Fine, then we'll leave whatever it is for later. Not tonight, though.
I'll be late home. I'm planning to go down to Bowling Green after I've
seen everything's as it should be on the site. I haven't been since before
the storm. That's much too long."

Bowling Green, Mollie thought looking at the door he'd closed behind him, where Francie Wildwood would tell the story Mollie had
not had the courage to confess.

She spent what seemed a very long day rehearsing in her mind what
she'd say when Josh finally returned. How she'd explain herself and
what he would doubtless deem her interference in his affairs. With
such nearly disastrous consequences. Six o'clock came, then seven
with no sign of him. Tess—empowered by her new, more regular place
in the household—persuaded Mollie to eat something, but she only
picked at the food. Finally, close to ten, Mollie went upstairs and undressed and climbed, quite miserable, into bed.

The hall clock had just chimed half-ten when she heard the front door open, and a few minutes later the uneven rhythm of her husband ascending the stairs.

At first she pretended to be asleep. Until, when he had finished undressing and was sitting on the side of the bed releasing his peg, she whispered, "I'm awake, Josh."

"Sorry to be so late. And for waking you."

"You didn't. I've been lying here waiting for you."

"Have you then? Well, that bodes well, I must say. You are a loose woman, Mrs. Turner. And I delight in it."

He was chuckling. And turning to her. And kissing her cheeks and her neck and soon pushing up her nightdress so he could suckle her breasts. He smelled of brandy and cigar smoke and it seemed he'd passed a congenial evening, but one that left him hungry for still more pleasure. He took her swiftly, with surpassing vigor and at the end a gleeful shout that made her cheeks redden, for she was sure Tess and Mrs. Hannity, sleeping above their heads, must have heard. After which he fell immediately asleep.

Leaving Mollie to lie awake wondering what Francie Wildwood was playing at if, as appeared to be the case, she had said nothing to Joshua about his wife's visit on the day of the storm.

12

THE CLANGING BELL announced the approach of a horsecar, the very first run to be made by Hopkins and Sons Omnibus Company between New York and the St. Nicholas flats.

Josh was standing by the door of the building, holding his pocket watch. "Ten past two, Washington. Excellent, don't you think?"

"If you say so, Mr. Turner."

Josh grinned at the other man. "Indeed I do, Washington. Providing the car left Forty-Second Street at half past one as Hopkins promised, we'll have proved the claim that the journey can be done in less than an hour and— My word, what's this?"

Three men and one woman descended to the pavement and stood with their heads thrown back, staring at the tall building—its steel frame now fully wrapped in slabs of pale gray granite—rising improbably on Sixty-Third Street. Meanwhile the driver, aware that his skills were on display, deftly pivoted the team of four, turning them with a few tugs on the reins and some low-spoken commands, and omnibus and horses disappeared into the stable. "Crikey," Josh heard someone say. "It's a stunner."

"It will be." Josh hurried through the wide-open double doors onto the sidewalk.

"It will be a fine building, and the first in New York City designed for genteel folk exactly like yourselves. May I ask how you knew about the car's coming today? It was meant to be a trial run. I didn't think it had been announced."

"Wasn't." Josh recognized the speaker as Mr. Jackson from his Bowling Green residence. And he was fairly certain the woman with him was his wife. "We went to inquire about coming here and were told there was a car leaving imminently, so we took it."

The same explanation was offered by Mr. DuVal Jones, also from Bowling Green, and by a third man, a Mr. Anthony Wolfe. Josh had mentioned the flats to Jones and Jackson. But Wolfe was a stranger. Tall, well dressed, and good-looking despite a black eyepatch.

"Good luck for all of us, then," Josh said. "Me certainly. I assume, Mr. Wolfe, you've seen my notices and you're here to inquire about the leasing of flats? All of you? You're all interested in living here?"

There were murmurs of assent.

"Excellent," Josh said. "Let me show you around together, then I can speak with each of you privately and answer individual questions."

The underboarding on all eight floors was in position—though none were yet overlaid with the oak floorboards McKim specified—and the plasterers and the gas fitters were working in tandem on the interior walls. They were finished as far as the fourth floor, but Josh led his potential buyers up the stairs only to the second. "We needn't go higher since every floor's the same, and as you can see, the elevator's not yet installed." The last with a nod to the yawning chasm where the elevator was to go.

"I've never lived where I had to ride in an elevator to get to my bed," Margaret Jackson said. "I canna' say I fancy it."

"Then you've no need to do so," Josh said. "You can choose a flat on the second or third floor. Or even the first."

"First three floors are dearer, are they not?" Her Scot's burr sounded offended by each syllable.

"Yes, Mrs. Jackson, they are. So perhaps you'd prefer using the elevator after all. I'm sure you've had the experience at Macy's or Stewart's or one of the other stores."

"Not to get to my bed," she said stubbornly.

"No," Josh agreed. "Of course not. But—"

"Bit out of the way, isn't it? And I hear you've not yet rented any of these places." This from Wolfe. He'd wandered off on his own to look at the arrangement of the rooms, then rejoined the group.

"Not yet," Josh admitted cheerfully. "But as you can see, we've only just begun the interior construction. The framework is made entirely of steel—first of its kind in the city, I believe—and that had to be erected before we could do anything else. Then there was the storm. Naturally, we were held up a bit by that. As for being out of the way, since you came here by horsecar you can see what an easy and speedy journey it is. Particularly once you're past Forty-Eighth Street. And at the end you're here at home away from the congestion of the city."

"First time we heard about these wee flats," Mrs. Jackson said, "was the day of that fearful blizzard. I've been thinking it was a bad omen."

"Not a bit of it," Josh said. "We were back at work within three days. And no serious damage done. Now, let me show you how each flat is to be laid out. I think you'll find they're not so wee as all that. Over here is your own front door, and to the right, the parlor."

He took his time about it. He'd come up without his cane and his good leg was aching badly by the time he finished, but he was too elated to care. He had, he was quite certain, all but definitely rented three units.

"According to Wolfe, he's living with his wife's family on Fourteenth Street and Seventh Avenue. Seems they have two children and expect a third. No wonder they think it's time to move to a place of their own."

Mollie wrote down all the information, repeatedly dipping her pen and careful to blot away any excess ink. She was quite sure this was a ledger that would someday be a family heirloom. The first flats Joshua ever built and rented. When he was the king of Manhattan property she knew he would be, they would show it to their child. Their children, she amended to herself, keeping her free hand in her lap all the while, pressed tight against her belly. According to Tess and Mrs. Hannity she should be feeling a kick any day now and she was terrified she might miss it. "Which flat are the Wolfes to have?"

"Six A," Josh said. "Corner flat closest to Fourth Avenue. At least that's what he said he'd have if he decided to go ahead. Mind you, he's not yet put down a deposit. None of them did, unfortunately."

"It can't be expected, Josh. Not on the first visit. I'll make a column that indicates how many times you see a potential tenant before the lease is signed. That way you'll be able to establish guidelines. You can know what to expect for the future."

"Do that, Mollie. That's quite clever."

She smiled, but went on with the business at hand. "Mr. Elva Jackson, isn't it? And his wife's name is Margaret. They've three children as well, I believe."

Another glance at his notes. "The names are right, but I don't know how many little Jacksons there are. They may have said, but I didn't write it down."

He was looking at her quizzically. It was, Mollie knew, her moment. She could tell him the whole story right now when he was so happy about the enormous breakthrough that meant so much to the future of his business. He'd be sure to forgive her. Even if it turned out Francie Wildwood had spilled Mollie's beans and Josh had for whatever reason kept silent about it, she'd get credit for doing so herself. She could do it. She would. Except . . . "The ledgers for the house on Bowling Green," she said, her courage deserting her. "You've noted the numbers of children in each family in those records."

"That's right, so I have. Well remembered, Mollie. And after only a week." Despite his earlier reluctance, Josh had slipped into having her keep the books for the rooming houses as well as the flats. Hard not to when she did it with as much ease as skill. "You're a wonder, my girl."

And a coward, Mollie thought.

On the Tuesday evening following his first visit to Sixty-Third Street, Elva Jackson arrived at the house on Grand Street and placed a check for two hundred and fifty-five dollars in Joshua's hands.

The two men conducted their business in the drawing room turned office. Josh had been reluctant to use the room for some time after the murder, but nearly six weeks had passed since he'd found George Higgins's body. Meanwhile the police had let the matter drop, and Jane had managed to scrub the carpet clean of bloodstains. After that the room had been thoroughly aired and put back together by Mollie, who refused to be either sentimental about a man she barely knew, or fearful about bad omens. Auntie Eileen's upbringing had given her a bit more spine than that. Besides, no one could arrange Josh's disturbed papers better than she.

Josh found it easier than he expected to slip into his old ways of doing things. He was waiting in his office when, as expected, the bell rang promptly at seven and Mollie showed Mr. Jackson into the front room.

After which she promptly ran around to the dining room where she could press her ear against the double doors and hear every word the men exchanged.

"Flat Four B," Joshua said. "To be leased to at a sum of eighty-five dollars a month payable in advance in quarterly installments of two hundred and fifty-five dollars each. This first payment to serve as a deposit against damages. The first quarter's rent due the day you move in."

Four B. A canny choice, Mollie thought. Cheaper because it wasn't a corner flat, and less expensive than the flats on the floors below. But three flights were manageable if one didn't wish to use the elevator. She heard nothing for a moment or two. Presumably both Josh and

Mr. Jackson were looking over the lease. Then Josh asked, "Are we agreed, Mr. Jackson?"

"We are, Mr. Turner."

Mollie couldn't see the handshake, but she knew it had happened, and that both men had signed, and she twirled around the dining room in a single and silent waltz of triumph.

By week's end DuVal Jones had agreed to lease the ground-floor flat closest to Fourth Avenue. It was now well known that Vanderbilt would start sinking a tunnel for his trains come spring, and Josh had assigned One D the highest rent of any of the units, one hundred and ten dollars a month. Mollie had paled when he mentioned the sum. "It's not as exorbitant as it sounds," Josh insisted. "For one thing it looks west to Madison and Fifth. They'll be grand avenues one day, even as far uptown as Sixty-Third Street."

"Still, Josh, it's so much more than they're paying at Bowling Green."

"Jones didn't quibble over the price and he's chosen to pay me a year in advance. Plus the security deposit. That's sixteen hundred and fifty dollars cash money."

"If he can afford so much, Josh, why doesn't he buy a house?"

Josh shrugged. "Can't rightly say, but the price of real estate is on the rise everywhere in the town. Mr. Drexel of Philadelphia has just bought a building on Wall Street for three hundred forty-eight dollars a square foot."

"Good Lord."

"Exactly. Meanwhile, Mr. Jones is leasing six hundred and fifty square feet for what—?" Looking to Mollie to supply the sum.

"Two dollars a square foot per annum," she said instantly. "Plus a fraction." She picked up her pen to enter DuVal Jones's name in the ledger that listed the St. Nicholas tenants. "I shall mark it down as a bargain." Then, as her pen moved across the columns, "Do we know what Mr. Jones does for a living, Josh?"

"No idea. But he's never been late with the rent in the years he's lived at Bowling Green."

"And you gain a tidy bit in interest by having a year's rent in advance." She wanted to cut out her tongue as soon as she spoke the words. *Never forget, Mollie, Joshua has more to prove than most men. You must not put yourself forward in the matter of business.*

He didn't bristle, just said with the exuberance that marked him since things began going so well, "The devil with the interest. It's folding money, my love. Working capital. That's a lot more important to me right now. But," with a quick kiss planted on her forehead, "nothing for you to be concerned with in any case."

"So," she said, "the only one of the prospects we haven't heard from is the one-eyed Mr. Wolfe."

"Not another word from him," Josh said. "But two out of three's a fine result. I am certainly not grousing. And I'm told another prospect came by yesterday when I wasn't at the site. Mr. Stanley Potter who, according to Samuel, says he'll return next week."

"Stanley Potter, recently admitted to the bar? Who also lives at Bowling Green?"

"That's the one. And why are you smiling like a cat with a bowl of cream?"

"I'm thrilled for you, Josh. For all three of us," she added with a shy smile.

"All three of us," he agreed, reaching out to pat her swelling belly.

She had to find a way to visit other family residences. There were dozens in the city. Of course they weren't owned by her husband so she wouldn't have such easy access. Perhaps she should see if Francie Wildwood might introduce her. It might even be an opportunity to discover what it was Mrs. Wildwood wanted, and how come she had apparently kept Mollie's secret.

"I trust you don't object to bringing the papers here," DuVal Jones said.

He and Josh were in an oyster bar on South Street, typical of many
on the waterfront. The sign outside said Hanrihan's and inside a long
counter with stools accommodated men wanting a quick half dozen
and a glass of beer. It was lunchtime and there were many more customers than stools. Josh and DuVal Jones, however, were seated at
a small table beside a window. Jones sat with his back to the room.
Josh where he could see everything. His topper, he noted, was pretty
much the only one in the place. Some of the patrons were laborers
in the nearby fish market, or men who worked on the ferry pier a
few steps away. They wore caps. Like many of the others—men who
managed the ferry traffic and the market stalls—Jones wore a hard
round bowler, the sort of hat sometimes called a derby, and a black
overcoat with a velvet collar. Proof against the cold March winds. "I'm
not likely," Josh said, "to object to meeting a man any place he chooses
when he's prepared to pay me a large sum of money."

Jones responded with a tight-lipped smile. It occurred to Josh that
he'd known the man since he moved his blonde and dimpled young
bride into the Bowling Green rooming house, but he'd never actually
heard DuVal Jones laugh.

The clang of the bow slamming the dock announced the arrival of
the Brooklyn ferry. A few of the men went out to meet it. The window
was foggy with warm breath and Josh used the side of his hand to
rub a clear space. The glass was crusted with salt spray, but he could
make out the crew securing the mooring lines, and beyond them, on
the opposite shore, the rising tower of the audacious bridge some said
would make the ferry obsolete. "Do I take it we meet here because
you're on your way across the river, Mr. Jones?" Francie Wildwood
had reported Amanda Jones saying her husband worked in Brooklyn.
She never mentioned at what.

"No, Mr. Turner. On this occasion it happens I've just returned. It
is a journey I make frequently." Jones took an envelope from his inside
pocket.

"Am I to assume, Mr. Jones, your business is based across the
river?"

Jones didn't answer, merely laid the envelope on the table between them and covered it with his hand.

"It might be thought," Josh said, "that a flat way uptown on Sixty-Third Street is particularly inconvenient for a gentleman who makes regular ferry trips to Brooklyn." He did not reach for the money.

"I do not expect to find it so, Mr. Turner." The envelope edged closer to Josh, but Jones kept his hand over it. "In any case, it is a trade I am willing to make."

Josh lay his hand over that of Jones. "In return for what? If you don't mind my asking."

"Not at all." Jones slid his hand out from under Josh's. "I believe Mrs. Jones will be most comfortable further uptown. If you care to count that, Mr. Turner, it is quite safe to do so here. And I will certainly understand your caution. I can assure you, however, that it is all there."

"I've no doubt of it," Josh said. He slipped the envelope into his pocket and produced the lease. Both men signed it and pocketed a copy of the document. Jones rose to go. "It's always a pleasure to do business with you, Mr. Turner."

Josh insisted the pleasure was his.

Stanley Potter, Esquire, was short and thin. Looked, Josh always thought, like a paper cutout of a man. As if you could fold him up and put him in your pocket. He had, however, a surprisingly deep voice. Twice the size of the rest of him.

"I have decided to lease one of your flats, Mr. Turner. I will have Four B. I am, as you know, an attorney, and I've prepared an agreement for the transaction." His comments were made on the site, in the hearing of every laborer within twenty yards.

Josh was delighted. Couldn't hurt for the men to know the flats were being spoken for. "That affords me great pleasure, Mr. Potter. You're precisely the sort of man to anchor a new direction for the city. With residents such as yourself, the East Sixties have a great future. I cannot, however, rent you Four B because it's already spoken for. Four A is available. Also Four C and D."

"Mrs. Potter will be disappointed. She told me Four B was the one she'd set her heart on."

"Four C is the same price, Mr. Potter." How the devil could his wife know which flat she wanted when she'd never been to the site? "And have you considered the advantages of Four A or D? They're corner flats. That means more light and air."

"More noise as well," Potter said firmly. "Mrs. Potter discussed the question with your wife. They agreed the middle flats would be quieter."

"My wife?"

"So I'm told, Mr. Turner. When you sent her to visit the ladies of your Bowling Green residence." The attorney had wandered over to the elevator shaft while he spoke, and was peering up at the newly installed cables and pulleys. The cab wasn't yet in place and the tall empty space acted as an echo chamber for his booming voice. "I take it Mrs. Turner got home safely despite the storm. Took a bit of a risk, didn't you, sending a woman on that sort of errand? Though of course you couldn't have predicted the weather."

"Stanley Potter has given me a deposit on Flat Four C," Josh said. "He wanted Four B, but I had to tell him that's gone to the Jacksons."

"Another one rented! Josh, that's wonderful."

"Yes, it is rather." There was a bowl of apples on the dining room table and he reached out and took one. "These look like Roxbury Russets. From Sunshine Hill."

"They are. Your mother sent them, along with a note that they're the last of what's been stored from the summer's crop. We're to savor every bite since we'll have no fresh apples again until August next year."

"Right." Josh agreed. "Mollie, does it seem remarkable to you that

I've so far rented three flats, and each has gone to someone who presently lives in my Bowling Green residence?"

There was something in his voice, a quietness that was somehow more sober than his usual tone. She was embroidering tiny daisies around the hem of a white lawn, infant-size nightgown with a beautifully smocked top, and she went on stitching while she spoke. "Not really, Josh. After all, they're exactly the sorts of people you intended the flats for, aren't they?"

"Exactly the sort." He took a large bite of apple. "Thing is, not every prospective tenant for a flat at the St. Nicholas is presently a resident in my place on Bowling Green. So it's a bit of a coincidence, isn't it? Three out of three, as it were."

Mollie kept sewing. "But one will probably have told the others. Besides, you spoke to those men, didn't you? The ones you thought likely prospects."

"Yes. Exactly." He'd finished the apple and he tossed the core into the large brass bowl Mollie used to collect the bits of thread she discarded.

"It was an excellent idea."

"I thought so. Thing is, how did you know?"

She didn't look up. "Know what?"

"That I'd spoken with the men who live at Bowling Green."

"I guessed. Because you'd underlined their names in the ledger."

"Right. And you've been keeping the books for more than a month now. So it's no surprise you looked back at my earlier entries."

"Yes. That's what I did."

"No," he said quietly. "It's not. Because back in January, the day of the big storm, you weren't responsible for the ledgers and at that time you'd had no call to look at them. But that's the day you went downtown and talked with the wives of my tenants. That's how come you got caught in the blizzard." And when she didn't say anything, only stopped sewing, "I know, Mollie, because Potter told me. Said you called at the house and spoke to all the women. Even discussed finances, how much the flats would rent for and the terms of the offering. He didn't say as much, but it's obvious he thinks I must be a bit of a cad to have sent my wife on such an errand. Not the sort of thing a gentleman does. At least not in the opinion of Stanley Potter, Esquire."

There was a long silence after that. Mollie secured her needle in the exquisitely soft fabric of her unborn baby's nightdress, then folded it neatly and put it in the basket along with the rest of the layette she was so carefully preparing; the bonnets and booties she'd already made, and the knit bunting Auntie Eileen had finished and delivered a few days before. When she at last looked up her eyes were shiny with tears, and her husband was staring at her. He looked, however, perplexed rather than angry. "And you, Josh?" she asked. "What's your opinion?"

"I don't know. I've been thinking about it all the way home. And it's a good thing Midnight knows the way, because I was so preoccupied with the question I didn't notice a single thing between Sixty-Third Street and here. But the puzzling did me no good. I'm no closer to understanding than I was when I started."

"I wanted to help, Josh. I knew you were worried about the flats not renting, and I was sure getting the wives involved, getting them to tell their husbands they'd love to live at the St. Nicholas and it wasn't financially out of reach . . . That would be sure to promote business."

"According to the evidence," he admitted, "it did."

"Yes." Two big tears were rolling down her cheeks. Mollie wiped them away. "But now you hate me."

"No, I don't. Far from it. I'm simply very disappointed. I can't believe you'd lie to me in such a fashion."

"I never lied to you. Not once."

"You kept the truth from me, and that's the same thing. It undermines my—"

There was a quick knock on the dining room door. It opened and Tess appeared. "Mrs. Hannity sent me up to lay the table for your supper."

They didn't say much during the meal. Tess was in and out serving it for one thing, and Mrs. Hannity herself brought up the custard pie she'd made for dessert. That way Josh could shower her with praise for making him all the things he liked best. A woman of any age, Mollie had long since noted, basked when Joshua smiled at her, missing leg notwithstanding.

Eileen Brannigan insisted that a clever woman could fix anything in the bedroom. Mollie didn't get the chance to try. That night Joshua slept down the hall.

It had gotten to the point where the workmen at the St. Nicholas were tripping over each other as the different trades applied their diverse arts to the finishing of the building. Interesting as well, Josh thought, how various immigrant groups gravitated toward one or another skill. Just now the site was crawling with half a dozen Italians laying the tile floors of the lobby and corridors. Last week it had been all Irish carpenters, except for the two days when not one of them showed up. First because it was St. Patrick's Day; second, because it was the day after St. Patrick's Day.

"What do you think, Washington?" The black man was pulling a wagon piled high with stacks of tiles, heading for the elevator when Josh stopped him. "Are there any Italian holidays coming up?"

"Can't say, Mr. Turner. Don't know much about Italians. Never met none before."

"Nor I," Josh said. "But they do remarkable work if this is an example." It was Charles McKim who had recommended the Italians to do the flooring, and their precision at executing the architect's design was splendid. The center of the lobby had a sunburst pattern that required expert cutting and fitting of the tiles. Two older men had done all the work, leaving the four others to get on with the simpler checkerboard effect of the border and the solid sections between. Now that the sunburst was finished the pair of superior artisans were occupied with the precise trimming of the edges. "Those two," Josh said nodding toward them, "don't speak a word of English, but I expect they won't want for work here in New York."

Washington braked the wagon with his foot and looked at his employer. "Got something going for them 'sides how good they does their jobs," he said.

Josh was intrigued.

Washington didn't turn his head, but his dark eyes darted in every direction. No one seemed to be paying them any attention, but there were workmen everywhere.

Josh nodded toward the wagon. "Leave that," he said. "Come outside with me. I want you to carry something over from the stables."

And once they were on the street, standing between the St. Nicholas and the Hopkins horsecar barn, "All right, no one can hear us out here. What are you saying?"

"Nothing. I ain't saying nothing 'cause I don't know nothing."

"Yes, you are, and yes, you do." And when the other man made no reply, "I've treated you fairly, haven't I? You and Sampson. No different from the others. Seems to me it's in your interest as well as mine to see nothing gets in the way of our getting this building done on time and as it's supposed to be."

"Don't know any reason why it won't."

Josh was unwilling to credit that denial. "Tell me," he urged. "Whatever it is, whatever I do about it, I won't involve you. You've my word on that."

Washington turned and looked back at the entrance to the St. Nicholas. One of the Italians came out carrying a bucket of something—grout it looked like—and dumped it on the road. "Them fancy flats as is going up downtown on Broadway," Washington said, pitching his voice a bit louder than it needed to be and looking at the tile mason.

"Mr. Hunt's flats," Josh said. "What about them?"

"Got a canopy over the front door. So as folks is protected from rain and snow and like that. When they come and go."

"That's a good idea," Josh said, "but Hunt's building is much grander than ours. Still, I'll consider it."

The tiler had gone back inside and they were again alone. Josh waited.

"The Italians," Washington had gone back to speaking in a tone barely above a whisper, "they got protection."

"From whom? And from what?"

"Ain't nobody going to ride 'em about not speaking English or nothing like that. Got other Italians what looks out for 'em. For a fee o' course. Way I hear it, they pay twenty, maybe thirty percent of everything they earn to an Italian gang. Protection."

Josh nodded. "Could be true," he said. "There are enough other gangs in this city. Why not one made up of Italians? But that's got nothing to do with you or me, has it?"

Silence.

"Maybe not directly," Washington said finally, and then, after a few more seconds of hesitation, "Back in Eddyville, when Sampson and me first knowed Tickle and Higgins and the rest, when we were all working for Mr. Kelly . . . You know about how Mr. Kelly sold his patent for almost no money?"

"Yes. Ebenezer Tickle told me about that."

"He tell you there weren't no way that made sense? How that Englishman what bought the patent, he didn't go to school to learn about steel like Mr. Kelly did?"

Josh nodded.

"Man named Trent Clifford," Washington said. "You know about him as well?"

"I do. What's more, I think you know that I do. You know a lot about what goes on, don't you, Washington?"

"Keep my eyes and ears open," the other man said. "Don't mean my mouth got to be open too."

Joshua again nodded agreement. It seemed to be enough to keep Washington talking.

"Captain Clifford," the black man said, "he spent a lot of time hanging around the Kelly brothers' foundry in Eddyville. He was there a lot the year before the Englishman showed up and said he'd take the Kelly patent, since Mr. Kelly, he was broke. Didn't pay a lot for it, mind. Didn't have to since he said he already knowed how to make steel in a converter."

So far he was confirming Tickle's entire story. "That's what I heard," Josh said. "You think Captain Clifford told the man from England how to make a converter? That he figured out the process just from hanging around the Kelly brothers' foundry?"

Washington shook his head. "That ain't sensible. I think . . ." One more glance up and down the street, and when he saw that they were entirely alone, "I think George Higgins told him."

"For money?" Josh said.

"Course for money. Ain't no other reason any dwarf had for getting mixed up with Captain Trent Clifford."

"What about Tickle? Couldn't he have been the one to tell Clifford how the converter worked?"

"Could have been, but he wasn't. Known him a lot of years and that ain't Tickle's way. Never takes a crooked path when there's a straight one available. George Higgins, he was a different sort. Not bad long as things was going how he wanted them to, but not one to pass an opportunity by neither. Long as it didn't mean he had to get whipped and maybe killed."

"You know about the races then, the dwarfs being used to—"

"I know. Ain't nobody was in Eddyville back then don't know."

"Fair enough," Josh said, "and say you're correct about it likely being George Higgins and not Ebenezer Tickle who sold out the Kellys, what's any of it to do with me or the St. Nicholas?"

"Captain Clifford started coming to the old ironworks down on Wall Street, hanging around. Couple of times I seen him talking to Higgins. Outside when they didn't think there was anyone around."

"But you were around," Josh said quietly. "Watching and listening."

"Tell you something about being a black man in a white man's world, Mr. Turner. Far as white folks are concerned, if you're a Negro, you be pretty much invisible."

Josh had no difficult believing that and he let it pass. "Are you saying you think Clifford was paying Higgins to spy on my business, and that somehow caused Clifford to murder him?"

Washington shrugged. "Maybe not exactly like that." He turned and looked back at the St. Nicholas. "And I'm not saying nothing 'bout these tilers. They ain't been here but a few days and a week from now they'll be gone. But the way I hear it, there be some kind of connection 'tween Captain Clifford and the Italians."

13

THE ROOM WAS thick with cigar smoke and the rich aroma of malted whiskey. An elaborate Chinese screen decorated one corner; a mahogany bar occupied another. Wine-red velvet curtains were drawn across the far wall, shielding the constant tumult of the intersection where Fifth Avenue crossed Broadway to form Madison Square, keeping the focus on the power gathered within. A dozen men, all wearing evening dress since it was after six, took each other's measure. A tall black man stood behind the bar. He wore black trousers and a waist-length white jacket, and poured drinks according to the murmured instructions of another black man—older, white-haired, his face lined with years—who carried them round the room on a silver tray. *Your Kentucky bourbon, sir. Your Tennessee sour mash. Your scotch, sir. Yes sir, a single malt. Immediately, sir.* The tray, like each of the heavy lead crystal glasses and each gold button on the uniforms of the servers, was etched with the initials "FAH," Fifth Avenue Hotel.

The guests clustered in small groups of two or three. Trenton Clifford stood alone. He had a cigar between his teeth and a drink in his hand, and he listened with no specific interest to the fragments of conversation floating in the air around him.

"A good thing Congress nullified the Indian treaties and made the savages wards of the nation."

"Wards, hell. Criminals more like."

"Damned Apaches are slaughtering whites in the Arizona and New Mexico Territories, and what is wrong with our Army that there are still live Indians to be dealt with?"

"Tweed is bound to be convicted."

"The man was reelected after being indicted, he'll never come to trial."

"Thirty million according to The Times. *No great city can ignore such theft."*

"Then how is it Gould's still a free man?"

"Grant is bound to be reelected, the public doesn't care about the scandals of his administration."

"Wrong, Grant is vulnerable. His policies are bringing the damned nigras north in numbers. The Democrats stand a chance if they nominate someone other than a rabble-rouser like Greeley."

"Word is the various elevated lines are to put their shares together in a holding company. Give them the necessary clout to get it done."

"Fools if they do. Gould will swallow their company whole."

Clifford heard that last comment and smiled. It was, as Barnum would say, time for the show. He took a few steps closer to the curtained wall. "Gentlemen." And once more, a bit louder, "Gentlemen, if you please."

The room quieted, the only sound the tinkle of ice in glasses as sips of smooth whiskey soothed throats made dry in anticipation. Eleven pairs of eyes, all dark with avarice, looked toward the tall and broad Southerner with the walrus moustache and the fair hair that curled just above his collar.

"Thank you for coming gentlemen. I shall get straight to the point." Clifford turned and pulled a cord. The red velvet curtains rippled into motion and parted. "Take a look at that."

The men surged toward the windows. They framed a dizzying turmoil of streetcars and horsecars and private carriages and wagons and
people on foot and on horseback, a scene so clogged it seemed as if
everything and everyone was squirming in place. All struggling frantically to get ahead, but going nowhere. "What is it?" An elderly fellow
in the rear was convinced he was missing something. "I don't see anything unusual. Is it an accident? Are there bodies? What's happened?"

"Nothing has happened, sir." Clifford's voice carried over the rising murmur. "Nothing can happen. That is exactly the point. What
you see out this window, that stagnating intractable tangle of traffic,
is not simply typical. In the matter of moving from place to place in
this town, it is by no means the worst. Right now it takes upwards of
an hour and a half to get from Twenty-Third to Wall Street. If a man
wishes to traverse Fourteenth Street east to west he must take three
different horsecars and pay four separate fares. Five if he goes west to
east. Should he choose to hire a hansom his journey will be dearer and
take longer, since a private cab does not have even the small advantage
of the horsecar tracks. Your city, gentlemen, this great New York, is
rotting in situ. Pretty soon your laborers will be unable to get to your
factories, and your clerks won't arrive at your workrooms and offices.
Your businesses will become as putrid as the metropolis around them.
They will stink of manure and crumble into decay."

"What's this about, Clifford?" A single voice speaking the question
on every mind.

"It's about saving yourselves from total ruin. It's about transportation at a speed swifter than that of the tortoise. It's about the thing
New York desperately needs, and as you can readily see simply by
looking out this window, does not have."

"Whole business is settled." The old man again, the one who'd
thought he might be missing some bloody mayhem beyond the glass.
"Tweed got his law through. Going to be trains forty feet in the air.
Banging on above our heads."

"I'll get to Boss Tweed and his Viaduct Railway shortly, sir," Clifford assured him. "But first . . . ," a pause while he looked at each man in turn, "I've asked you here this evening because I think you are men with the foresight to recognize the only way to genuinely solve this problem. If we're to secure swift transit for this enormous city, we must carry passengers on trains through tunnels."

"Underground?" someone asked.

"*Where the hell else would you build a tunnel?*"

"*Pneumatic tubes. Asinine. As likely as flying pigs.*"

"*The idea works. Beach proved it with that demonstration on Broadway.*"

"*Cost him thousands an inch.*"

"Gentlemen," Clifford again, "if I may. Please forget pneumatic tubes, or belowground horsecars, or all the other nonsense. We must run proper trains powered by steam through our tunnels. Exactly as they've been doing in London for the past seven years, in a system they are busy expanding even as we remain paralyzed."

A man standing beside the bar made the point that London was not an island but a sprawling mainland metropolis. "Over here we'd have to dig below the most heavily used thoroughfares in America, right up against its tallest buildings."

The fellow couldn't have said it better if Clifford had written him a script. The Southerner smiled and with only a slight flourish—mustn't appear too cocky, that would only put them off—produced an easel from behind a portion of the velvet curtains and exhibited a series of colored plates. Different views of the same thing: London's Euston Road with its many tall buildings and busy shops, all untroubled by the railroad running twenty feet below the street. Someone asked about ventilation and Clifford found yet another drawing, this one diagramming the thirty-foot grids that occurred in the pavement every three-quarters of a mile. "Steam rises and almost instantly dissipates, and fresh air descends. Problem solved."

The talk continued for maybe fifteen minutes, until one man—younger than most, dressed in impeccably tailored swallowtails, wear-

ing a black eyepatch over his left eye—brought the discussion back
to Tweed and his elevated railway. "Forgive me, sir. I mean no disrespect when I ask, what's the point of this discussion? As has been
mentioned, Albany already passed the Viaduct bill. We're to have Boss
Tweed's elevated railways whether or not the scoundrel himself goes
to trial. Indeed, it's my understanding the city is soon to pay his consortium five million to start the building of them."

Quiet after that. With everyone looking to Clifford for a rebut-
tal. "Exactly," he said. "That five million is what will get the Viaduct
law repealed. It is greed beyond common sense, gentlemen. A classic
overreach."

"How so, Captain Clifford?" The young man again, rolling a cigar
by his ear meanwhile, listening for the crackle of freshness. Then, obviously having heard the question murmured by a number of the others, he switched his single-eyed gaze from the man beside the easel to
the assembly. "My name's Tony Wolfe for any as don't know me. And
like yourselves I'm a businessman. I came because I was invited by
Captain Clifford, and like you I know he's got a nose for profit, but,"
turning his attention once more to Clifford, "this time I fail to see how
it's going to work. Once the city's paid over five million it will be com-
mitted. Nothing you say will change the mind of anyone who matters."

"The Gray Lady, Mr. Wolfe," Clifford said. "*The Times.* And Greeley's *Tribune.* The moment that check is drawn, both papers will be for
once on the same side of an issue. They'll send up such a thunderous
cry as to drown out the hounds of hell."

"Too late then," someone said. "Tammany will do their dirty business in the dead of night and before anyone knows about it. The check
will be cashed and the money unrecoverable. Same as always."

Clifford closed the cover of the book of drawings. "Not," he said,
"if someone is to let the papers know before the money's paid over. A
few days before, perhaps a week. Allow enough time for the reaction
to build."

"Are you telling us, Captain Clifford," Wolfe paused with a match halfway to the tip of his cigar, "that you will know when the payment is to be made? Before it's to be made?"

"I am," Clifford said.

He let them chew on that for a while, gave them their heads, and let the talk go its own way. Then, "Let me tell you the one thing worse than having Tweed and his crowd get their five million before they lay an inch of track." Not raising his voice, just letting his breathy Southern vowels nip at the awkward angles of the strident Northern voices all around him. Waiting for his words to do their job and call the combined attention back to where he stood. Finally, when every eye was on him, "The thing, gentlemen, that would be worse, that would be a catastrophic mistake of the sort Lee, to my everlasting regret, made at Gettysburg, would be to drum up a huge opposition to the Viaduct plan. It could be a terrible blunder to encourage a great wave of public disgust at the thought of those noisy and dirty elevated trains running above the heads of every man, woman, and child on Manhattan Island."

"But you just said—"

"What's the point of having the papers get a stink going, if—"

Clifford raised his hand. The objections died away. He had an almost irresistible urge to call out *Heel!* No doubt he'd see every damn one of them pull up short and open his salivating mouth, ready for whatever tidbit he chose to throw. "A blunder," he said, the silence so total he need not raise his voice, "if we alert the public to the stench of the Viaduct law, and then have nothing to put in its place. If the papers and the public are to demand the bill be repealed, we must give them something—someone—who has both the wherewithal and the reputation to stand behind a different method of transport. We cannot achieve our aims simply by destroying the overhead railroad. We must offer a superior alternative."

He could see them all sizing each other up after that. Thing is, none of them quite fit the bill and they knew it. Rich, yes. Influential even. Everyone in the room knew everyone else, knew exactly where they all

fit in the pecking order. Except, of course, for Wolfe, the fellow in the
eyepatch. He was a stranger to all of them. So by definition they did
not credit him with the stature to pull it off, even if unbeknownst to
them he had the power. As for any of the rest having both the money
and the distinction to take on Tammany? Not a one of them. Trenton
Clifford least of all.

"I think we've gone about as far as we can this evening, gentlemen.
I'd like to believe you're all going to be thinking on this. Mulling it over
in your minds. Bringing your individual intelligences to bear upon
the problem, so we may eventually apply our collective wisdom to the
solution. I shall be in touch and we will meet again soon. Meanwhile,
I am sure you all recognize what a serious disadvantage it would be to
have the wrong people made privy to our ideas before we've brought
them to fruition. Such an error, gentlemen, could cost every man here
an enormous profit. I'm sure I can rely on your discretion."

A general exodus after that, each man shaking Clifford's hand as
he left, murmuring something about an interesting evening, and how
he hoped to hear more if the plan looked to be going forward. Clifford
waited until the sound of the last pair of polished patent-leather evening pumps had clattered down the marble staircase before turning
back to the room.

The waiters were gathering up the bottles of whiskey on their way
out. "Leave the Kentucky sour mash, boys," he told them, nodding to
a half-full bottle of Old Fitzgerald's. Then, after they'd gone, he poured
two glasses and turned to the opposite corner. "We're entirely alone,
sir. May I invite you to a drink."

Zac Devrey emerged from behind the Chinese screen.

In some circumstances, Josh learned, success was like the pox. It
spread by contagion. By the middle of April he'd leased thirty-seven
of the St. Nicholas's forty-eight flats and he had a clutch of inquiries
for the remaining units, some of them quite promising. He'd put a

series of notices in the papers and requested they be run on the pages women were likely to read. Unquestionably, it did the trick.

Churlish of him not to actually thank Mollie for the idea, but he couldn't bring himself to do it. Not after she'd lied to him about her visit to Bowling Green. It still rankled whenever he thought about it. If she'd simply confessed once she got over the immediate effects of her adventure, he'd have forgiven her for not consulting him beforehand. (Though he could not honestly say he'd have given his permission for her to talk to the women, and it had turned out a useful exercise in terms of the flats.) But he could not understand that after she went to Bowling Green, after the potentially dire consequences for her and their unborn child, she did not own up to what she'd done. It was that which planted seeds of doubt Josh ignored with difficulty, even allowing for her condition, which Simon had warned him could lead to all sorts of female irrationality.

Fortunately he had little time to dwell on the matter. The flats were looking to be finished by the middle of April. McKim had done some drawings for him of a similar project to go up on Sixty-Eighth Street, on three of the six lots he'd bought with the money raised by pawning Eileen Brannigan's jewels. The new building would be closer to Third Avenue. And while it would be served by the same horsecars, residents would have five further blocks to walk once they were dropped off at the end of the line. Those things made Josh think he must rent the second lot of flats for slightly lower sums. "You can save a bit on finishes," McKim advised.

"Better still," Josh said, "we can go up a story. I can afford that this time, and additional flats will protect my margin."

"Nine floors," the architect said.

Josh detected some hesitation. "Can we go up that high with no safety issues?"

"Keep the steel coming and you can go up twice that high. The only difficulty would be finding men who wish to install their families among the clouds."

"People told me no one would want to live above and below each other. The St. Nicholas is two-thirds leased."

McKim smiled. "You're right and I was wrong. May I, nonetheless, offer a suggestion? One that might even qualify as an apology of sorts. For doubting you originally."

"No apology required. I'm interested in your suggestion because I trust your skills and admire your talent."

"Thank you. In that case . ." McKim's pencil flew over the paper in swift and certain strokes. "Square the new building off. Build it over the three lots on Sixty-Seventh as well as those that front on Sixty-Eighth and have back-to-back flats."

"It'd be like a tenement." Josh could not hide his astonishment. "No cross ventilation."

"Nothing like a tenement," the other man insisted. "Those abominations run an air shaft up the center that's so narrow you can reach across it. You," more pencil strokes, "will have this." He turned the sketch so Josh could see it more clearly. It was drawn as a bird's-eye view and he was in effect looking down at a clearly defined space with trees and benches and what he took to be grass. "A central courtyard," McKim said. "It will provide an amenity for the residents, as well as proper ventilation in each unit. At the same time you will not simply double the number of flats by doubling the building space. You will triple them. And you can make each nine hundred square feet rather than six fifty. So you can rent them for the same amount or perhaps more, despite their being further from the stable."

He went on to explain the structural realities, the gains made by creating additional bearing walls, and differing configurations of plumbing and heating requirements. Joshua listened intently for twenty minutes. "Do it," he said finally. "It's brilliant."

"I shall design and draw it," McKim said. "Doing it, my friend, is up to you."

❧

Josh doubled the work at the foundry and Tickle hired two new men. He did so under the terms of the contract the two had negotiated that first day in the old slave quarters turned foundry. Base wage increased to fifty-three cents an hour for a forty-hour week. Time and a half for overtime. "I must pay you a wage now as well, Mr. Tickle. That was our agreement."

"It was, Mr. Turner. But I don't want an hourly wage. I'm a manager here, not just a supervisor."

"That you are," Josh agreed.

"Should have a salary, then." And when Josh made no objection, "I'll settle for thirty-five dollars a week. To start," he added.

"A year at thirty-five a week," Josh said. "No overtime, mind you. Not if it's a salary. And no increase for twelve months. Though I've a mind to pay a bonus if the steel for the second building is ahead of schedule."

Tickle nodded. "That's fair. Now, what about the other part of our arrangement? I'm to have a flat in return for these past six months with no pay."

"So you are, Mr. Tickle." It was the first time the little man had mentioned it, but Josh never thought Tickle had forgotten their unusual agreement. Any more than he had. He'd just been glad not to be asked to make good while the project was in the early struggling stages. It had always worried him that Tickle might demand his right and want to move in immediately in the bargain. Could have given the project a bad name if the initial resident was someone who looked to have come straight from Barnum's freak show. "Tell you what," he said, "why not choose your flat in the new building? We can call it the Eddyville Arms."

"Our agreement was a flat in the first building," Tickle said. "The one as is already built. I'm not bothered by the name."

"I've only six flats left in the St. Nicholas."

"Don't need but one," Tickle said. "I'll come pick it out this Sunday. Noontime. I'll be bringing Maude Pattycake with me. We're betrothed."

Josh accepted the inevitable, since going back on his promise was out of the question. "Congratulations, Mr. Tickle. Sunday noon it is then."

Tickle and his bride-to-be were at the flats before Josh arrived, waiting outside the building, craning their necks as most people did when confronted with the structure. It must, Josh thought, look taller to them than to most. "You can take much of the credit for the fact that it's been built, Mr. Tickle," he said by way of greeting. And, tipping his hat to the tiny creature holding Ebenezer Tickle's arm, "My best wishes to you, Miss Pattycake. Mr. Tickle is a most remarkable maker of steel. I am, as I said, the beneficiary of his excellent work."

"Wedding's in three weeks," Maude said. "At Mama Jack's. We'd be most pleased if you'd come, Mr. Turner. And Mrs. Turner, of course."

"I'm honored, Miss Pattycake. Thank you."

"Come along." Tickle was pulling impatiently at Maude's hand. "Let's go pick our new home. Tell us which ones are still available, Mr. Turner."

"I'll show you," Josh said, leading them into the lobby where he had a schematic plan of the flats tacked to the wall. "Those with red crosses through them are rented," he explained.

"We get our pick of what's left," Tickle said. "Whichever one we want." He aimed the words at his fiancée, but he was looking at Josh.

He'd waited purposely, Josh realized, gambling that the last flats to go would be the dearest. And in some measure he'd been right. Two A and D and Three A were still available. They were all priced at over a hundred a month. "So you do, Mr. Tickle. That's what I promised."

The dwarf nodded, then turned to the drawing. "These two here," pointing to the second floor of the plan and the two corner flats. "They're not taken, are they?"

"They're not, Mr. Tickle."

"What about them top two floors," Maude Pattycake said. "Looks like some of them are still available as well."

"They are," Josh agreed.

"Those are cheaper units." Tickle looked grim.

"That's correct," Josh admitted. "Sixty-five dollars a month on the corners and forty-six each for the middle two. Plenty of light and air on the upper stories," he added, but went no further. It wasn't just Tickle's obvious displeasure that stopped him. He didn't like the feeling of encouraging the man with whom he'd made a good-faith arrangement, who'd come through for him in every particular, to make a choice that others found undesirable.

Maude Pattycake meanwhile had stopped studying the drawing. She was looking around at her surroundings. "The corridors on the upper floors are black and white tile as well," Josh said. "And there will be mirrors and gas lighting, just as here in the lobby."

Maude nodded. "That's an elevator over there, isn't it?"

"It is," Josh said.

"Can you run it?"

"Yes, I can."

She turned back to the plan. "I want to see that one up there." She pointed to the uncrossed corner flat on the top floor, Eight D.

"But the ones lower down are the best ones," Tickle insisted. "That's why they're the most expensive."

"That one," Maude said pointing again to the eighth floor.

Twenty minutes later Josh ceremonially drew a red X through the unit on the top corner overlooking Fourth Avenue. "I'll have the papers ready for you by week's end," he promised. Then, unable to contain his curiosity, "Can you tell me why you chose that flat, Miss Pattycake?"

"All my life, Mr. Turner, I've been looking up to folks. Now I have a chance to look down."

These days Mollie mostly slept alone and Josh in another bedroom down the hall. He came to her occasionally, did what he wanted—it was in her mind to say he used her, though she hated the thought—

then left. At first their separate sleeping arrangements were dismissed with a murmured word about her needing her rest after the ordeal of the storm. Eventually it was clear that Josh suffered more from the memory of that adventure. Though they did not discuss it after he reported what he'd been told by Stanley Potter. *It's obvious he thinks me a cad to have sent my wife on such an errand. Not the sort of thing a gentleman does.*

It was in Mollie's mind to ask Auntie Eileen what advice she might offer, but she kept putting off the discussion. It wasn't so much their nighttime habits that made her cringe with embarrassment. It was her disregard of all her aunt's good counsel concerning the business of not putting herself too far forward.

She had not yet found the courage to broach the topic, and had yet to profit from whatever good advice her aunt might offer. So she was alone on that Monday morning well before dawn when she was jolted from sleep by someone ringing the bell and banging on the front door.

Mollie pulled on a robe and hurried into the hall. Her husband was there before her. She sensed his presence in the dark. "Who is it?" she asked.

"No idea, but sounds like he's in a hell of a hurry to talk to me. Go back to bed. I'll deal with it."

She heard the approach of either Tess or Mrs. Hannity starting down from the attic, heard Josh dismiss whoever it was.

He hadn't strapped on his peg. The soft shuffle of whoever it had been returning to her room did not muffle the heavy, asymmetric sound of Josh descending the stairs with only his cane for balance. Mollie held her breath, listening for the thud that would indicate a fall. There was none.

She stepped into the hall, leaning over the banister so she could see. Josh had reached the front door. He tucked the cane under his arm, standing on one leg while he used both hands to deal with the bolt and the chain he'd had installed right after poor George Higgins was murdered. "Hang on," he said. Then, "Good God, Mr. Tickle.

Come in. What's happened?" And turning to the stairs, as if he knew Mollie would be in the hall despite his instructions that she return to bed, "Come down, please. Bring some bandages and carbolic."

"There was five of 'em," Tickle said. His face was cut and bruised and one eye was swollen shut. "Stompers, with them black kerchiefs tied around their faces. Me and Obadiah and Israel, we weren't no match for 'em."

Stompers were one of the Five Points gangs. They were known for having steel blades fixed to the heels of their boots, and masking their faces when they went on a job. "I should think not," Josh said. Then, to his wife, "I believe Mr. Tickle's arm is broken. He'll need a doctor to set it. Will you write a note to Simon, please. Perhaps Tess will take it to the hospital. If Simon's not there she can leave it for when he arrives."

He waited until Mollie had gone into the office, then turned back to the dwarf. "How are the others?"

"Obadiah got a mean crack on the head with one of the billies them thugs had. Put him straight out. That's why I was the one as come to tell you. Otherwise I'd have sent him. Longer legs can be useful sometimes."

"Is he still unconscious?"

"He was coming around when I left. Israel will look after him. I suppose I could've asked the new men to sleep at the foundry as well. Didn't 'cause they both got families and—"

"You and your men are paid to make steel, not do guard duty," Josh said grimly. "It's my job to protect my business, and you can be sure that after this I shall."

"That'll be a good thing, Mr. Turner, but what I didn't tell you . . ."

"Go on." He steeled himself for what he knew was going to be worse news. "Tell me now."

"It's the Kelly converter, Mr. Turner. That's what them thugs was aiming at. Smashed it up right proper and weren't nothing we could do to stop 'em."

"What's the plan then, Josh?" Zac had a way of sitting back in his chair and folding his hands, rather like Solomon waiting to pass judgment Josh always thought. "Tell me what you need. If I can help I will."

"Not money," Josh said quickly. The Devrey Building was as impressive as ever, a white marble temple of commerce built in 1835 when the city's oldest shipping company was at the height of its power, but these days there were half as many clerks in the various offices, no new vessels under construction, and at any given time fully a third of the fleet riding empty and at anchor. Josh reckoned his boarding-houses and building projects were probably showing a greater profit for the year than his brother's fabled company; certainly he had more liquidity. "I'm not in a bad position as far as cash goes. I've taken deposits on all but six of the flats at the St. Nicholas, and ten percent of those at the new building are spoken for."

"I thought you hadn't broken ground for that one yet."

"We're supposed to get started in a couple of weeks. I think we can maintain that schedule. There's a supply of steel at the foundry. Enough to begin building at any rate."

"I take it then the inventory wasn't damaged?"

"Pretty damned hard thing to do, damage steel beams with billies and sledgehammers. Time-consuming as well, since you'd have to go after them one at a time. According to Tickle, the Stompers went straight for the converter. Attack the means of production, a good strategy the generals tell us."

"Tickle's the dwarf, isn't he? Your foreman."

"That's right. He and the others, there's not much they don't know about a steel converter. They can fix this one, but it will take time." Josh got up and refilled his glass from the decanter of sherry on the table beside Zac's office window. "And before you ask," he turned back to face his brother, "I'm pretty sure I know whose idea it was, but I've no proof."

"This isn't a court of law. Who?"

"Man by the name of Trenton Clifford. Captain in the rebel army. He was commander of the prison on Belle Isle when I was there. I think he murdered George Higgins as well. As a way to get at me. Can't prove that either."

"I see. Josh, about Clifford, I . . ."

"Yes." Josh waited.

After a few seconds Zac shook his head. "Nothing. Except I'm wondering what you might have done to cause Captain Clifford to hold such a potent grudge all these many years."

"I concentrated on staying alive, nothing more. It can't be about Belle Isle or anything that happened during the war because as far as Clifford and I are concerned, nothing did."

"What then?" Zac rose and came to join him by the window.

"I'm not sure," Josh said. "But I don't think Clifford wants to beat his chest and sound the rebel yell. He's done with all that. What he wants is to make a fortune, like everyone else in this town."

"By somehow taking over your business? Constructing flats?"

Josh ignored the slightly disparaging tone and shook his head. "No, though mark my words, there's a fortune to be made in real estate if one has sufficient capital. Clifford's got a different idea, however." He gestured with his drink to the hubbub below the window where the junction of Broadway and Canal Street was seething with traffic. "He came to me a few months ago with a scheme for building an underground railway. You were still in England at the time. He wanted me to write and suggest you sell all the Devrey ships and bankroll his plan. Lend it the Devrey prestige."

"Did he now? And what did you tell him?"

"To go to hell." Then, when his brother didn't say anything, "Zac, he's not just an ordinary bastard. Clifford's wicked to the core. I've seen him do things that would chill your blood. I knew you wouldn't have anything—"

His words were cut off by the chiming of the Carolina clock. Zac had installed it before the war. The clock did more than toll the hours; it set up a moving display running along the top of the five-story building, models of the fabulous clipper ships Carolina Devrey Turner had commissioned in the 1840s. Reproduced on a scale of one to one hundred with meticulous accuracy, the clippers crossed a churning ocean under the full cloud of sail that had once transfixed onlookers standing on the New York docks. These days people made the journey to the Devrey building just to see the simulation.

"Five o'clock," Zac said when the noise faded. "I've plans for later, Josh. Let's get this sorted, shall we?" He moved back to his desk. "Tell me exactly what I can do."

"I need to put guards at the foundry. Hoods as tough as any to be found in the city. A match for whomever Clifford sends."

"Presuming you're right and he's the one sending them."

"Presuming exactly that. Though it doesn't really matter. I've no doubt that once we start producing again, we'll get a second visit, whoever's behind it. They made their intentions clear."

"Have you thought of going to the police?"

Josh recalled his interviews with Captain Willis and Sergeant Hoyle, and their willingness to accept an alibi provided by the most notorious whoremistress in the city. "You're joking, aren't you?"

Zac nodded. "Point taken."

"After all these years running the New York waterfront," Josh said. "If you don't know which toughs are the right ones for the job, no one does."

"Happens I do." Zac made a note on the pad on his desk. "I'll send someone to see you at the house tomorrow evening. Name's Frankie Miller. You'll never meet him in church, but as long as you pay him what you've agreed, you can trust him absolutely. Anything else?"

"Yes. I want to move the inventory. I'm having a shed constructed on one of Mother's lots. I'll arrange to have that guarded as well, of course, but the easiest way to get the steel there is by boat. I need to transport it from Wall Street uptown to Ninety-First Street."

"Done," Zac said, making another note. "Is that it?"

"It is. I'll be on my way and leave you to your evening's plans." Josh picked up his topper and his cane and started for the door, pausing before he opened it. "Zac . . ."

"Yes?"

"Clifford's every bit as bad as I said. Worse maybe."

"I've no doubt," his brother said quietly. "None at all."

"Not Stompers," Frankie Miller said. "Word is it was one of the Italian gangs been taking over around Mulberry and Bayard and Hester. Mulberry Bend they call it, not that a gentleman like yourself would know much about the Bend or the Eye-ties. Anyways, they tied on them black kerchiefs to make it seem like they was Stompers, but according to my sources, they wasn't."

Josh was astounded. He'd never seen Frankie Miller until ten minutes earlier when the man showed up at his front door. Now they were sitting in his office on Grand Street and Miller was making it clear he'd already taken it on himself to investigate the source of Josh's woes. "I presume my brother told you what happened."

Miller nodded. He looked like a bank clerk, or perhaps an accountant. Certainly not a criminal. Medium height, thin, not particularly muscular, with pale skin and black hair parted on one side and carefully combed and oiled. He wore a tweed jacket and matching trousers, and the hat clutched in his hand was a bowler.

The hat sparked a train of thought. "Mr. Miller, if the men who attacked my foundry weren't Stompers . . . Is it possible some gang from Brooklyn could be involved?" There wasn't much logic to it, only his memory of having met DuVal Jones in an oyster bar near the Brooklyn ferry landing the day he leased a flat in the St. Nicholas. And his conviction at the time that Jones was some kind of thug. Though it made no particular sense that he should want to delay construction on another of Josh's buildings.

Miller put paid to that idea. "No reason whatever to think so," he said.

"Then who were they? And why pretend to be a gang they were not? According to the newspapers the whole point of the distinctive clothing is to brag about their violence."

"That's the Irish gangs." Miller spoke softly, each word receiving equal emphasis. Rather like a judge pronouncing sentence, Josh thought. "They're what you might call playing at being baddies. Oh, I know they kill folks and whatnot, but it's not the same. With the Irish, mostly it's because they love to fight. Bigger the dust-up, more it suits 'em. The Eye-ties, they're professional criminals. Seems most of 'em are from some island. Sicily, I think it's called. They do business in a regular way. Got a price list. Two dollars to punch somebody, four if both eyes is blacked. Twenty-five for a stabbing. Unless it's to be fatal. Then they call it doing the big job and it costs a hundred."

Josh glanced at the place on the rug where he'd found George Higgins's body. If Miller noticed he didn't say. "I take it you want guards down at the Wall Street docks, Mr. Turner. Near Mr. Devrey's pier."

"The old iron foundry next to it, yes."

Miller nodded. "That's what Mr. Devrey said. I'll put four men on it. One inside, three out. You won't see the three. Nobody will unless they're needed."

"Is that enough? According to my foreman they were attacked by five of these Stompers, or Sicilians, or whoever they were."

"Four of my men's enough," Miller said quietly. "You can trust me."

Exactly what Zac had assured him to be the case. "I need guards as well on Ninety-First Street. I'm going to store the finished steel in a shed up there. It's closer to where we'll be using it and perhaps it won't be so obvious a target. My brother told you that's the object of all this thuggery, interrupting the production of steel?"

"Nope, just said I was to guard your interests. Said they were the same as his. I'll look over the uptown location, put as many on it as is called for. But it's a far ways to go. I'll have to charge you extra for that."

Miller paused while he calculated his costs and profit. "A hundred and a half a week," he said finally. "Four weeks in advance to start."

Josh was prepared. He counted six hundred-dollar bills from a roll in his pocket and passed them over. "When will you start?"

Miller smiled. "We already started. I got my men in place down at the foundry right now. Mr. Devrey told me what was needed and that I was to do for you exactly like I would for him. When can I see the Ninety-First Street location?"

"Whenever you like," Josh said. "We're to move some steel up there a couple of nights from now."

They spent another few minutes discussing how to find the shed Josh had built on his mother's lot, and Miller's suggestion that he also provide two guards on the boat that would carry the beams and girders upriver. "The numbers you're talking about," Josh said, "two to guard the shipment, four at the foundry. Two on the boat. It doesn't sound like enough."

"My men carry pistols, Mr. Turner. Latest-model Colts. Some of 'em got rifles. And they're all sharpshooters. We're a match for anything that's out there. Fists or knives or billies or broken bottles, even sharpened teeth . . . none of it can compete with bullets."

Jesus God Almighty. A corrupt police force against hoodlums with firearms and some new form of organized Sicilian criminals who published a price list. The town would soon be under permanent martial law. Not his lookout. If they posted Seventh Regiment pickets on every damned corner, people still needed somewhere to live. Unless, of course, he'd actually added the bad apple to his own bushel. "Does the name DuVal Jones mean anything to you?"

The answer was immediate. "Sure it does. Jones works for the Brooklyn mayor."

"What?"

"Not the real mayor. That's what they call the man runs the Brooklyn lottery offices. Jones organizes his collections. Oversees the boyos who go to each office and collect the money coming to the mayor."

Only quasi criminal in that case. The lotteries were legal and hugely popular, particularly with those who could least afford to gamble. But dealing in that much cash—reportedly the business generated millions each year—invited every kind of leech to suck his share of blood. "I take it the man you call the mayor is being paid protection money?"

Miller nodded.

"And have you any idea, Mr. Miller, why a man working for this so-called mayor would want to live on Sixty-Third Street. Uptown Manhattan is a good ways from Brooklyn."

The other man's face lit up. "I get it. Jones is taking one of your flats, right?" And without waiting for a reply, "It makes perfect sense. Word is, Jones got married a while back. Pretty little young thing from some place out of town. That's what he's after, Mr. Turner. A place to stash his wife. Keep her tucked away, so to speak."

Confirming pretty much what Jones himself said. "Mr. Miller, you are a genius." Josh got up to show his visitor out, then, just before he closed the door, "My brother told me you're the best there is at this sort of thing. It seems he was right."

Frankie Miller smiled. "Appreciate the compliment, Mr. Turner. Happens your brother gave me my start when I was just a lad. Made me what I am today, Mr. Devrey did."

14

EVEN SIX MONTHS with child and her belly sailing ahead of her like an inflated balloon—or so it seemed to her—Mollie could still wear most of her regular clothes. Her bosom was fuller and her middle thickened, but there was so much fabric in the skirts of her fashionable suits that once she let out their waists and moved the buttons of the short fitted jackets that had always flattered her, the sort *Harper's Bazaar* referred to as a cuirass basque, she was still presentable. This despite the fact that Dr. Thomas had made a point about not lacing her corsets too tightly, even suggested she dispense with the garment entirely until after the child was delivered.

He discussed such things through a woman called Miss Palmer, a nurse who was always present when Mollie went to his office. *Miss Palmer, please tell Mrs. Turner about not wearing restrictive clothing whilst expecting.* Looking at the nurse all the while, though Mollie was right there in the room with the two of them. Miss Palmer duly repeated the instructions after the doctor left the room. As if, Mollie thought, she herself had been stricken with temporary deafness while he was present.

Mollie was quite willing to forgo her corset, but she had not expected to be getting herself up in party finery when that final three
months was just beginning. Josh, however, had invited her to accompany him to a special event. "Ebenezer Tickle is marrying an extraordinary little woman named Maude Pattycake. She's half his size if you
can believe it. Maude herself invited me, and she specially asked that
you come as well."

"But it's not, you say, a wedding in a church?"

"No. It's being held in what's known as Mama Jack's Cave. Frankly,
it's a tavern of sorts. With a clientele who are . . . I guess distinctive's
the word. All happy in each other's company and making merry as
if they were any regular assortment of New Yorkers. Not a place I'd
consider taking you in the ordinary way of things, but this isn't ordinary. I'll understand if you think it impossible in your condition. But
if you're feeling well enough, I'd like to show Ebenezer the respect he
deserves. Nothing would make that more apparent than the pair of us
attending his wedding."

She knew he was right on both counts. The dwarf was responsible for much of the success that was lately coming their way, and the
presence of his employer and his employer's wife would do Mr. Tickle
honor. Besides, she was curious. A wedding of dwarves in a disrepu-
table cave that sounded like a bawdy house was the sort of occasion
she'd expect to read about in Mr. Leslie's *Illustrated Newspaper*, not
see for herself. She was also gratified. It had been a great many weeks
since Josh actually expressed any desire to be in her company. "I'll
be delighted to accompany you, Josh. Dr. Thomas says women can
do many of the things they're accustomed to doing until a few weeks
before the child arrives."

Including some things she'd not had the nerve to tell him were
permitted. Like all the rest, that instruction came from the doctor
through his nurse. He'd kept his eyes on Miss Palmer while he poked
and probed at Mollie's nether regions with the unspeakable instru-
ments she glimpsed on entering the examining room. And it was dur-

ing those sessions that he issued his peculiar third-party advisories and admonitions.

"According to Dr. Thomas," she told Auntie Eileen, "women need not be locked away for months on end. And their husbands need not be banished to a separate bedroom."

Eileen snorted in derision. "Well, that won't please many women. Is that truly what he says?"

"It is." Mollie imitated the doctor's sonorous tones, "Miss Palmer, please tell Mrs. Turner she may perform all the duties of her marriage until one month prior to the delivery. It is a privilege I extend to all my patients."

"Ha! A privilege given to the men who are paying the bills more like. Mind you, the women are the real fools. I've taught you better than that, surely. You haven't sent Josh to sleep down the hall, have you?"

"Of course not." It was true after a fashion. Josh had changed bedrooms of his own accord.

This business of the dwarves' wedding, coinciding as it did with the start of her being unable to wear a corset, was an opportunity Mollie recognized entirely on her own. Helped along by a sketch she happened on when looking at one of Auntie Eileen's books of fashion. The whole thing came together in her mind as a chance to see if she could remind Joshua Turner how it used to be between them. She had wounded his pride. Very well, she would give it back to him.

"Prepare yourself for a series of surprises," Josh said when they approached Eighth Street. "And don't be alarmed, I promise you're entirely safe."

She smiled up at him. "I'm with my handsome husband. I know I'm safe."

Auntie Eileen would be proud of her. But it did take some doing to keep the smile in place when Josh ushered her through not just a taproom, but the storage space behind it, then down a stone passage into what had to be a low-lying cellar of some sort. Mama Jack's Cave, Mollie reminded herself. Where would it be but belowground?

Her eyes adjusted to the long dark passage, and by the time they entered Mama Jack's she was able to see quite well. Her glance fastened first on a woman whose arms stopped at her elbows. Then she spotted a black giant with a brass trumpet who stood so tall he had to stoop, and at least a dozen dwarves. Another creature, a woman judging from her dress and her voluptuous bosom and handspan waist, had a full beard. She was speaking with a man whose face was . . . mixed up was the only way Mollie knew to think of it. His nose was off to one side, his mouth to the other, and he had only one eye that seemed to be placed close to the middle of his forehead. "Oh dear."

She barely breathed the words, but Josh tightened his grip on her arm. "Steady."

"I'm fine," she managed, meanwhile opening the purple lace fan that hung from her wrist and waving it vigorously.

"It's warm in here," he said. "Shall you take off your coat?"

Now or never. She could say she preferred to keep it on. Josh wouldn't find that particularly odd. No, she wouldn't back down. "I shall," she said, lifting the hem of the long garment known as a polonaise and beginning to unbutton it. Josh waited patiently behind her. Until the job was done and he slipped the coat from her shoulders and she was revealed.

Perhaps, she told herself, she was imagining the murmur of surprise.

Mollie had made the frock herself, copying a fashion that had not been stylish for sixty years. During the War of 1812, when a British blockade made it difficult to bring in the woven silks and satins and taffetas that in those days were mostly imported from Europe, American dressmakers had copied a provocative look popular at the time in Paris. *La mode Directoire* it was called, and the great advantage of dresses so fashioned was that they required a third as much fabric as other styles. For a brief time the *Directoire* look totally captivated the women of New York City, though it was far too daring for the rest of the nation. Even New York ladies dropped it as soon as the war ended and they could get sufficient quantities of cloth to again make elaborately bustled suits and dresses. The thing that so attracted Mollie when she first saw the plate in Auntie Eileen's book was the freedom. Only after that did she think of how the style would suit her purpose. A woman wearing a *Directoire* gown was celebrating her natural shape.

The dress Mollie wore to the wedding of Ebenezer Tickle and Maude Pattycake was a rich and shimmering purple that seemed to change hue when she moved. The neck was scooped low front and back, and the sleeves were short and puffed. There was a strip of olive green silk just below Mollie's breasts—so much fuller now that she was expecting—and it was embroidered with silver leaves and purple flowers. Below that a scant few yards of chiffon simply fell loose, emphasizing every aspect of her form. The gown ended in a series of ruffles, but before any eye could be drawn to that flourish it had to stop at her rounded and very obvious belly.

The legless woman Josh saw the first time he visited Mama Jack's rolled up to them on her board and looked Mollie up and down. "Hello, dearie. Looks like you've a bun in the oven." She laughed raucously and turned toward Josh. "So you're to have a prince or a princess for them beehives you're building uptown, are you? And this looks to be your queen bee. Well, what's it to be, bride or groom?"

Josh was still trying to accept that his wife was standing there in what looked to be a sort of nightdress, and a very daring one at that. "Groom," he mumbled.

"Follow me."

The woman swiveled her contraption around and wheeled herself off to the right side of the room. Mollie followed her, chin high. Josh went behind them, carrying Mollie's coat. And somewhere to the side of him someone said, quite loud enough for everyone to hear, "Well, he may have only one leg, but looks like he can get it over."

Mollie glanced back at him. Josh hesitated. He should challenge the fellow, defend his wife's honor. But . . .

For the briefest possible moment of time, no more than a heartbeat, he would have sworn Mollie had winked at him.

Jesus God Almighty. She didn't mind. She was cool as you please. She could have kept the damned coat on, he realized. Hell, she could have worn something more concealing to begin with. But . . . she wanted everyone to know. She might never speak the word, certainly not to him, but he'd made her pregnant and she wasn't hiding it the way women were taught to do. She was proud of it. Proud of him. *Only one leg, but he could get it over . . .*

Holy damn but you're a wonder, Mollie Popandropolos Brannigan Turner.

They were seated close to a bar that ran the length of the room, though no drinkers stood at it just then. "Look," Josh whispered, raising his chin toward the ceiling.

Mollie glanced up and saw the dark silhouette of what appeared to be a larger than life statue. No, it was a live woman and she was sitting on a sort of throne suspended in midair. Mollie didn't get a chance to ask who she was because a trumpet fanfare called the room to silence and what light there was dimmed further. "Ladies and gentleman, your attention please." It was the black giant, and he was speaking from just to Mollie's right. "Welcome to the wedding of Mama Jack's adopted daughter, Maude Pattycake, and her groom, our own Ebenezer Tickle."

At precisely that moment a series of rope pulleys were activated and four lanterns rose behind the oaken bar, illuminating its full length. "Trained by Barnum many of them," Josh whispered in his wife's ear. "They're showmen to the core." The point was underlined by the appearance of a dwarf atop the bar at the far end, fiddling madly as he danced toward them down the narrow strip of wood.

"Groom's next," the giant announced. "With his best man." He sounded another fanfare and Ebenezer appeared, walking the length of the bar with his cousin Henry beside him. But the dwarf walked on the bar and his over-six-foot cousin beside it. The effect was to make Ebenezer the taller.

The giant blew a few notes on his trumpet. A voice somewhere in the rear sang "Swing Low Sweet Chariot . . ." Just the opening words, then the singer fell silent and so did the trumpet. "Ceremony," the giant said into the hush, "will be done by the preacher, Willie Sykes." A hunchbacked man dressed entirely in black and carrying a prayer book rose from the back of the audience and walked forward to take his place beside the Tickle cousins.

"And the maid of honor is none other than Mama Jack herself." Another lantern rose to the ceiling and swung across the room to illuminate the woman seated on the dais above the heads of Mollie and Josh. She was draped in baby blue lace. Yards of it—acres of it, Mollie thought—fell over and around and below her. A crown of tiny pink rosebuds topped her huge head, and she held a matching posy, dwarfed by her enormous hands.

The trumpeter raised his horn yet again and blew the notes familiar to most everyone in the room, "Tom Tiddler's Song," the announcement that Maude Pattycake was going to dance, but she didn't immediately appear. Instead the fiddler took over and Mollie heard what people now called "Here Comes the Bride," the same music she'd chosen for her own appearance at the head of the aisle of majestic Grace Church. It was from a German opera by the composer Richard Wagner. "Faithfully guided, draw now near," the aria began, and brides everywhere had begun using that melody to accompany their walk toward the most fateful moment of their lives.

A lantern moved slowly to the far end of the bar and created a pool of light. Maude stepped into it. She wore white silk, tight-waisted and drawn back into a bustle from which flowed a white lace train. Her veil fell from a circlet of white roses, these full blown, and she carried a spray of them in her tiny hands. The beam of light from the lantern followed her slow and deliberate walk along the top of the bar, and when she drew level with the Turners Mollie saw the tips of silver slippers peeking from below the hem of her gown.

"Dearly beloved," the preacher began.

A man's head appeared between Mollie and Josh. He was behind them, leaning over so he could whisper something in Josh's ear. She heard Josh say "now" in an incredulous tone, and the man say "Yes, right now."

"But the ceremony's just starting," Josh protested.

"Right now," the man repeated. "Or they're going to shut you down and confiscate the lot."

". . . holy estate," the preacher was saying, "not to be entered into . . ."

Josh got to his feet, pulling Mollie up beside him. "My wife will need an escort home."

"Thought of that," the man said. "Follow me."

Mollie heard the preacher ask Maude Pattycake if she would take Ebenezer Tickle to be her husband, but nothing more. Josh was pulling her along beside him and in seconds they had left the cave, not, however, by the way they'd come in. Their exit was through a different and steeper tunnel. It avoided the taproom on Eighth Street, Mollie realized. "Josh, what is it, what's happened?"

"I'm not quite sure. Something to do with the police."

"But who is this man? How do you—"

"Name's Frankie Miller, Mrs. Turner. I work for your husband. Watch yourself, ma'am. Pretty narrow going here."

She had to turn sideways to fit through an opening in what looked like a solid rock wall, then Josh guided her up a set of stone stairs and into a narrow alley. She had no idea where they were, and for a moment it seemed Josh was equally puzzled. He looked around, getting his bearings, then said, "Washington Square Mews?"

Miller nodded. "Secret way in and out of Mama Jack's. Saves a bit of trouble." He was hurrying them to a small rig, a buggy, drawn by a single horse and driven by a slim, freckle-faced boy who looked no more than twelve. "This here's Eddie the Babyface, Mrs. Turner. He'll see you safe home. I guarantee it."

Mollie spied two horses a bit further down the alley. Each was saddled and ready to ride. "Josh, I—"

"Please, Mollie. I'm told this is an emergency and I accept that it is." He wrapped her coat around her as he spoke, and lifted her into the rig. It had only a single bench, so she had to sit beside the driver. Close up, she thought he might be older than she'd first thought, a speculation that faded in importance when she saw a rifle lying lengthwise at her feet. "Josh . . ."

"Later. I'll explain. I promise."

Eddie the Babyface jerked the reins and they moved off down the alley. Mollie turned and looked between the metal struts that held a gaily fringed leather canopy above their heads. Josh was already astride one of the horses. Frankie Miller was mounting the other. The buggy made a sharp turn to the left and she lost sight of both.

They were on lower Fifth Avenue, the road lined either side with substantial brownstones, many of them sold when ultra fashionable New York moved north. Miraculously there was not a great deal of traffic and they flew past the Hotel Brevoort and Miss Lucy Green's, the school Mollie had once attended. Eddie kept turning his head and craning his neck to look back the way they came, urging the horse to go faster all the while. "Mr. Babyface, why are we in such a great rush?"

"My job's to get you home safe," he said as they entered Washington Square Park. "It's what I mean to do."

The buggy was lurching from side to side meanwhile, and Mollie started to protest that there was greater safety with less speed when she saw the pistol in his hand. "Dear God! What—"

"Here, take the reins. And scrunch down as low as you can."

"I've never—"

"Take the reins."

She had to, otherwise he'd have dropped them and the horse would be without any control at all. Mollie had never driven any kind of vehicle. Josh had promised to one day teach her to guide the phaeton, but so far he'd not done so. She had no idea what she was supposed to be doing and she simply held on as tight as she could, astonished at the weight and power she felt pulling against her. The horse seemed to realize it had virtually been given its head and surged forward.

She heard the crack of a shot and saw Eddie hanging over the side of the buggy, clinging on with one hand while he aimed with another. "Mr. Babyface, you are surely going to—"

"Get down. As low as you can. Like I told you."

There were two more shots in quick succession. One seemed to whistle past her cheek. A bit of the canopy's fringe landed in her lap and the peacock feathers of her coiffure floated by and drifted away. Impossible unless . . . Eddie the Babyface, Mollie realized, was not the only one shooting. "Who is following us? Why?"

He was fully back in the buggy for the moment, bending down to get the rifle. "It's the Eye-ties. Tony Lupo himself. It's you they're after, not me." He reached over while he spoke and gave the reins a sharp jerk, almost but not quite pulling them out of her hand. The horse neighed loudly, rose for a moment on its hind legs, then dropped back and swerved. The buggy went up on its left wheel. She'd never put the polonaise on properly and it slipped off her shoulders and fell into the street. "Hang on," Eddie shouted. "Don't let us tip over." He was on one knee now, facing backwards and aiming the rifle out the struts.

Mollie gripped the reins, bracing both feet against the front lip of the rig, wishing to heaven she had on proper boots, not patent-leather slippers with silk rosettes. The buggy righted itself with a thud that bounced her six inches off her seat and back down again.

"Down," Eddie shouted. "Scrunch down."

She tried to do what he said and control the buggy at the same time. It was nearly impossible, and the horse was definitely stronger than she. "Mr. Babyface, I can't—"

He reached over and took the reins from her hands. "It's all right now. Too much traffic down here. He's backed off."

The horse slowed some in response to the return of a firm hand. Mollie sat up straighter. She reached up and touched her coiffure, a silver band decorated with iridescent bird feathers that had been the outfit's crowning glory. The feathers were gone. Shot off her head by someone of whom she'd never heard, much less met. "Who is Tony Lupo?" she demanded.

"Head of the Sicilian gang. You must be important, missus, for him to come himself."

Mollie turned her head. She was just in time to see a rig not unlike the one she was in slow and start the turn into Spring Street. The man driving it, she saw, was well dressed and had an eyepatch. Nothing else to identify him and on any given day she passed a dozen men who looked exactly the same.

Moments later they were on Grand Street and Tess came to the door in response to Eddie's knock. "Mrs. Turner . . . What's happened? Well, I never . . ."

Mollie walked through the open door and headed for the stairs, looking neither right nor left and not pausing to say hello to Tess or goodbye to Eddie. Tess stared after her for a long few seconds, then realized the man was gone and closed the door. "Are you all right, love? What's happened? I don't—"

Tess stopped speaking. There was a trail of something behind her mistress. At first it seemed to be bits of purple chiffon dropping from the extraordinary gown the girl was wearing. Then Tess realized she was looking at splatterings of blood. They grew larger and closer together as they progressed. By the time Mollie reached the top of the stairs, blood was puddling in her wake.

There was a police cordon stretched across the entrance to the foundry, seven coppers standing elbow-to-elbow, all holding their billies at the ready. Josh pulled the horse up in front of them. "Just what are you doing here? I'm a businessman and these are my premises. I've broken no law."

A man in civilian clothes appeared at Josh's side, standing and looking up at him through spectacles that caught the midday sun. "I'm afraid that's not true, sir."

"And who are you to be calling me a liar?"

"I'm an attorney, sir. Acting for Mr. Henry Bessemer of London, England."

"And just what is Mr. Bessemer's complaint?"

"I believe men in your employ have been making steel inside this building." The lawyer nodded toward the foundry.

"That's correct." Out of the corner of his eye Josh could see Frankie Miller still sitting his horse, but hanging back, remaining out of the direct view of the coppers. He couldn't see anyone else, but he knew Miller's men were nearby. Not much good to him in this situation. An armed battle with the police would eventually land all the survivors in jail. Himself included if a bullet didn't finish him first.

"And is your steel," the lawyer asked, "made in what's known as a converter?"

"It is made," Josh said, "in a Kelly converter." He was conscious of someone walking up behind him, but he did not turn around to see who it was.

"Mr. Bessemer," the lawyer said, "bought Mr. Kelly's patent some years past. Making steel in that way is now known as the Bessemer process. It is protected by patents Bessemer owns. Here in the United States as well as abroad."

"No doubt about that," a voice said. "Afternoon, Josh."

"I'd ask what you're doing here, Clifford," Josh still didn't turn around, "but I'm quite sure I know."

"I'm a fair-minded citizen, Josh. Only that. Helping the police to enforce international law."

Clifford moved into his line of sight. "Fair-minded," Josh said.

"That's right. Sorry to interrupt the festivities. I'm sure you'll be missed. Your wife as well."

For the first time Josh felt a frisson of fear. "Leave my wife out of this. You're not fit to mention her name."

Clifford chuckled. "High dudgeon suits you, Josh. Goes with your red hair. But it's not much use just now. You have been making steel in violation of Henry Bessemer's patent and Mr. Clark here," Clifford nodded to the attorney, "has a court order to close this foundry. He'll also be confiscating the building on Sixty-Third Street known as the St. Nicholas flats. Given that it was built illicitly with his steel, Mr. Bessemer has a substantial legal interest in that building. No one is to be permitted to move in until the courts have decided the issue of how much of the property Mr. Bessemer can claim. Is that not correct, Mr. Clark?"

"It is." The lawyer took a folded document from his pocket. "I have an order from the judge to do exactly that. Close down the building as well as the foundry."

"What do you reckon, Mr. Clark?" Clifford asked the question without looking at the attorney, keeping his gaze fixed on Joshua all the while. "Given how backlogged the courts are, how long do you think it'll be before this case gets heard? Just an estimate, mind you. Based on your long legal experience."

"Could be months and months, Captain Clifford. Maybe even years."

Clifford sighed. "I'm genuinely sorry to hear that, sir. This gentleman has leased all but a few of the flats in that building. And being a young and ambitious man of business, he has of course used that money to get started on still another building. Which, incidentally, also uses the illegal steel. So Mr. Bessemer will have a claim on it as well." Clifford shook his head. "It's a right mess, Mr. Clark, a possum stew as we might say down home. Mr. Turner here, he's going to have a hard time untangling himself from all that twisted-up legal business. Not to mention dealing with those rightly indignant folks who rented his flats. A right mess. Wouldn't you agree, Josh?"

"I might, Captain Clifford." Josh took out his pocket watch and glanced at it. A few minutes past one. He turned his head and looked at Frankie Miller, who nodded. The police cordon, meanwhile, hadn't moved, just stood their ground and stared straight ahead. Josh turned back to Clifford. "I might agree, except that nothing is actually the way you described it."

"How so?" Clifford gave no hint of being less sure of his ground.

"Well, for one thing, Mr. Clark here isn't acting for Mr. Bessemer in London. He's acting for Trenton Clifford, late an officer in the rebel army, now in New York. Isn't that so, Mr. Clark?"

"A formality," Clifford said before the lawyer could answer. "I am an associate of Mr. Bessemer's and I have engaged counsel on his behalf."

"For another thing—" Josh heard the sound of a horse galloping toward them. Frankie Miller had told him to expect delivery sometime around one. Damned close to spot-on. "For another thing," Josh began again, "contrary to your assertions, this is a properly licensed facility. I have paid Mr. Bessemer for the right to make steel using what is, I entirely agree, his patented process. Did it before we produced a single ounce of the stuff."

Clifford tipped his head back and studied Josh's face. Then he took off his hat and wiped his forehead. "Son of a bitch," he said very softly. "Son of a high-tailed bitch."

"Something like that," Josh said. He turned his head just as Zac reined in beside him. "Excellent time to arrive," Josh said. "Thanks."

"Don't mention it. Haven't ridden like that in years. Exhilarating. Up to Sunshine Hill and back in less than two hours. Mind you, the traffic's impossible south of Forty-Second Street or I could have done it faster. Afternoon, Captain Clifford." Then, to the lawyer, "I believe this lot of coppers are here at your behest, sir. However, I own this property and I'll thank you to have them clear off."

"I have a court order, Mr. Devrey. Signed by a judge—"

"Who's no doubt in Clifford's pocket, just as you are. But you've all acted on misinformation and wrong assumptions. I have the license from Bessemer right here." Zac slid from the saddle and took an envelope from his inside pocket and held it out to Clark. "You can see for yourself, sir."

"Here," Clifford grabbed for the document. "Let me see that."

"Happy to oblige," Zac said. "But take care, please. This is valuable," jerking his head toward the police cordon, "as is proved by all this carry-on. Mind you," he added. "We have other copies. In case something should happen to this one."

"What you're holding, Clifford," Josh wasn't waiting for him to read the document, "is permission to make steel using the Bessemer process. A license granted for three years from August of 1871. My brother was in England when we set up down here. At my request he saw Bessemer in London and arranged the legalities on my behalf."

As long as there was any chance of a fight, Josh had stayed on his horse. Same as always, he was the equal of any man as long as he had four legs under him. No chance now of a dustup, but he remained in the saddle. It was enormously satisfying to look down at the commandant of the Belle Isle prison camp. "That's what was behind the ransacking of my office, wasn't it, Clifford? You were in my house looking for something exactly like this when poor George Higgins somehow got in your way. So you murdered him. And when you found no evidence of a license on Grand Street, you decided to go ahead with your little drama." Josh jerked his head toward the police cordon. "Ebenezer's wedding must have seemed a perfect opportunity since the foundry would be empty."

"I had nothing to do with the murder of the dwarf or the break-in. I was at Kate Meacham's whorehouse from the start of the storm until the next morning. At least a dozen witnesses will swear to it." Clifford handed the letter back to Zac and turned and left.

"Bit early for brandy," Zac said. "Sherry do you?"

"It will not. Brandy. Damn the hour."

"You're quite right. I'll join you." Zac poured two generous snifters and carried them to where his brother sat. They were in Zac's office on Canal Street, finally rid of the police and the oily little lawyer and Frankie Miller and his men. On their own. "Thank you," Josh said.

"Don't mention it." Zac raised his glass in a toast. "Shall we drink to Ebenezer Tickle and his bride."

"Good idea. Well married by now, no doubt. And the groom no idea how close he came to being both jobless and homeless on his wedding day."

"Clifford never had a chance of pulling it off," Zac said. "You headed him off at the pass. Last year when you had me get hold of Bessemer in London."

Josh shrugged. "A man would be daft to risk an entire enterprise in order to save a few thousand for a license. The thing I still don't understand—" The chiming of the Carolina clock cut off his words. Two o'clock. He should be getting home to Mollie. She must be beside herself with curiosity about the whole remarkable incident. But there were parts of it he found every bit as mysterious as she probably did. "Thing I don't know," he repeated when the echo of the clock faded, "is what Clifford stood to get out of it all. He ruins me, fair enough. But from his point of view, to what end?"

"You're still sure you did nothing to earn his enmity? Back in that rebel hellhole prison camp?"

"Absolutely nothing."

"Has to be me then," Zac said.

"You? What's Clifford to do with you?"

"His underground trains." Zac swallowed the last of his brandy and headed back for a refill. "I haven't given him an answer yet. I assume he's looking for a way to force my hand."

"Given him . . . Jesus God Almighty, Zac, are you actually considering doing business with Trenton Clifford?"

Zac returned carrying the decanter. "Top up?"

Josh held out his glass, saying nothing, waiting for an explanation.

"It's a possible way out," Zac said.

"Of what?"

"Financial ruin."

"Surely things are not that bad. I know Devrey Shipping's been on its heels for a while, but you're still in control of a huge amount of quite remarkable assets. The property here in the city is worth a fortune, not to mention the fleet and all the goodwill you've— Zac, you haven't hocked it all in some way, have you? Mortgaged everything to the Wall Street money men or something of the sort?"

Zac shook his head. "Not yet. That's precisely what I'm trying to avoid. But there's no future in shipping, little brother. Not American shipping at any rate. The New York docks are being 'organized,' or so they call it. Labor unions are taking over. We're going to have to pay more to employ our stevedores and land-based personnel than any European nation. Next it'll be the crews. And I can't say they don't have a case as far as their treatment is concerned. Mind you, it doesn't matter a great deal. The war pretty much finished American merchant shipping. The unions are administering what might be called the *coup de grace*."

"But Clifford's—"

Zac held up his hand. "He's got essentially what I think to be an excellent idea. An underground steam railroad. It's the perfect answer to our intractable traffic, though I can't say I like his manner of doing business. However, whether I throw in my lot with him or do something else, I need to transform Devrey Shipping into a different endeavor. I've considered passengers rather than freight, luxury steamships carrying people across the ocean, but Sam Cunard and Bill Inman pretty much have that tied up. I'd be late to the party, and it'd take years to recoup the cost of refitting the fleet. Alternative is, sell it all. Both Cunard and Inman would bid for our New York docks, that's for sure. I'd squeeze a fair sum out of their rivalry. Then I could sail the fleet across to Asia and sell it piecemeal to a cartload of thieves and pirates in countries you've never heard of. Put the capital into rolling stock, underground trains. It just might be a solution."

Josh couldn't get his mind around the notion of Devrey Shipping simply disappearing, whether or not Zac called it a transformation. "Tammany's opposed to an underground railway. Tweed and the others are backing the elevated. Besting them's not easy."

"I know. And you're entirely correct about Clifford. I know that as well and I'm looking for alternatives. I just wanted to see if—"

There was an urgent knock on the door. Zac looked up, but it opened before he could ask who it was.

"Mr. Turner. Thank God. They told me I'd find you here. Been looking everywhere."

A clerk loomed behind Tess, half hidden by her bulk and her roses, speaking over her shoulder. "I tried to stop her, Mr. Devrey. Said I'd announce her and see if—"

Tess shook off the man's restraining arm. "You've got to come home, Mr. Turner. Right away. It's Mol—Mrs. Turner. She's right poorly. Doctor Thomas is with her now, but frankly it's—" Tess's voice choked with sobs. "Blood everywhere, Mr. Turner. She's hanging on by a thread."

It had been a week, and Mollie was not after all going to die, though it had been a close-run thing. She would not, however, see him or speak to him. "You can of course insist," Eileen Brannigan said, "but frankly, I don't think it would be wise. She is . . . I believe the best word is fragile, Josh. And still quite ill."

He did not fancy himself the sort of man who would push his way into his wife's sickroom. He did, however, seek medical explanations from Simon.

"The straight of it," Simon said, "is she went into premature labor. It seems to have been brought on by something that happened. I take it you've no idea what?"

Josh shook his head. "None. I wasn't with her. The business at the foundry, with the Bessemer patent—"

"Yes, of course. Zac told me. You had your hands full. I understand. Look, she's going to get well, Josh. We can be fairly certain of that now. But—" Simon broke off and looked away.

"What?" Josh demanded. "Come on, flat out."

"The labor went on for so many hours and she was losing so much blood . . . Thomas had to withdraw the infant with forceps to put an end to it. No choice unless she was going to be allowed to die. It was a boy, but far too premature to survive." He did not mention the crushed head, though Thomas had been quite graphic. "Thing is, Mollie's uterus was damaged. There will be no other children, Josh. I'm sorry. Truly."

"Thomas went through a lot of rigamarole I knew was meant to tell me something. I understood about six months being too soon and no chance the baby could live. But, Mollie . . . Frankly, I couldn't fathom all his polite roundabout. I needed it spelled out. That's why I asked you to involve yourself. Thank you, by the way. I'm grateful."

"Not at all. Sorry I couldn't bring better news."

A tragedy caused by something that had happened, which ruined the chance of Mollie giving him a son now or in the future. The "something" was, however, an event about which he knew nothing at all. Not good enough.

Frankie Miller operated out of Roach's Tavern on the bottom end of the Bowery. Used to be where hogs and cattle raised on farms in Queens or Brooklyn came across to be slaughtered and sold in New York City markets. Place had been the Bull's Head Tavern in those days, but that trade was dead. First the Erie Canal, then the expansion of the railroads, made it easy to bring in beef and pork from bigger and better spreads in the West. Butchers were still a vital part of a city, but these days the purveyors and slaughterers congregated on the other side of town.

The portion of the Bowery to which Josh came in search of Frankie Miller was now a no-man's land, hovering in the shadow of the colossus rising a short distance away. The half-built Manhattan tower of what everyone called the Brooklyn Bridge already cast a perpetual pall over Roach's Tavern.

Mr. Roach, however, seemed to be living in the past. A taxidermist's steer stood at the entrance to the taproom, the beast's hide mangy and moth-eaten, and both glass eyes lost over time. "Blind as well as deballed," Miller said. "But you can't expect old Roach to stuff one of his namesakes and put it by the door. What can I do for you, Mr. Turner? Everything all right at the foundry and the warehouse?"

"Everything is fine at both locations, Mr. Miller. Your men do an excellent job as far as that goes."

Miller's eyes narrowed. "What I hear you saying, Mr. Turner, is that maybe it doesn't go far enough. What's on your mind?"

Josh looked around. A pair of drinkers stood out of earshot at the far end of a long and heavily scarred wooden bar. There was no one else. "I want to know what happened when your man drove my wife home from Mama Jack's place. Eddie somebody."

"Eddie the Babyface."

"Yes, he's the one."

"There was a small fuss of some sort," Miller said. "But Eddie saw the troublemaker off. Nothing came of it."

"Something indeed came of it. My wife nearly died. She's still quite ill."

"I'm sorry to hear that, Mr. Turner."

Josh had the impression Miller knew all about Mollie's illness. There didn't seem to be much he did not know. "This fuss you mentioned," Josh asked, "what was it exactly?"

"Somebody followed Babyface and your wife. Took a few shots."

"At Babyface?"

Miller shook his head. "The way I hear it, Eddie's sure Lupo was after Mrs. Turner."

"Good God, why should anyone want to shoot my wife?"

"I got no idea why, Mr. Turner. That's your business. I figured if you wanted to talk to me about it you'd bring it up. Only thing I know is Tony Lupo was after her."

The only conceivable explanation was that somehow Clifford was behind it. It happened, after all, at precisely the same time the bastard was making his move on the foundry. Could be part of a larger scheme for taking over Josh's business—leave him a grieving widower as well as tie him up in endless litigation. Or perhaps Zac was right, Clifford's real aim was to exert further pressure on Zac and the assets he controlled. "This Lupo, I take it he's a gunman for hire. Rather like your men."

"Not exactly. Tony Lupo's head of the biggest of the Sicilian gangs. The Eye-ties I told you about. From Mulberry Bend."

"And it was he himself, you're quite sure?"

"Eddie the Babyface wouldn't make a mistake about that, Mr. Turner. He knows Tony Lupo. We all do. Kind of fellow, once you see him you don't forget. Always dressed in the best. Tall. Good-looking. Wears an eyepatch, but a lady's man despite that."

Before her second son took himself off to war, Josh's mother entertained the notion he might study at Princeton in New Jersey, as Zac had done. It was Nick who suggested Carolina's expectations were unrealistic. "He's barely surviving at the Trinity School. Frankly, if it were not for Zac having excelled in his day, and Simon looking to do quite well, I think I'd long since have been invited to educate Josh elsewhere."

His lack of fitness for university had made Josh's romantic notion of signing up with the cavalry less outrageous than it might have been. But however poor a student he'd been, Trinity had managed to cram a certain amount of Latin into his head. *Lupus*, he knew, was the Latin word for wolf. Italian being the modern language closest to Latin, it didn't take a lot of imagination to get from lupus to *lupo*. So Tony Lupo and Anthony Wolf, or Wolfe as he'd insisted it be spelled, might well be the same person with an Italian name translated into English. Add to that the presence of an eyepatch and it seemed certain.

Josh couldn't remember any more about the man who'd come to look at the flats in the St. Nicholas, but never actually took one. Fortunately Mollie kept very complete records.

"ST. NICHOLAS FLATS—PROSPECTIVE TENANTS," she'd written on the cover of the ledger. Every inside page was filled now he'd rented all but three of the units, but Josh had no need to thumb through them to find what he wanted. Wolfe had been with the initial group of potential lessees who arrived at the building that Saturday after the storm. His name was on the first page. Two children and a third on the way, Josh read. Living with his in-laws on Fourteenth Street and Seventh Avenue.

Nonetheless, over an hour combing both sides of that block produced no sort of connection. "The gentleman I'm looking for lives with his wife's family," Josh explained repeatedly. "They have two children and possibly a third. A newborn. Or will have soon. And he wears an eyepatch. I simply want to ask him some questions."

No one knew anyone in the neighborhood who met the description, whether the name was Lupo or Wolfe.

"Tony Lupo," Josh said. "Head of some sort of gang from Mulberry Bend."

"And he shot at Mollie?" Zac looked incredulous.

"So I'm told by Frankie Miller."

"In God's name, why?"

Josh paused, choosing his words with some care, "I suspect he might have been put up to it by Trenton Clifford."

"Going after you, in other words, to get at me."

"Possibly. Don't look like that. It's not your fault."

"It is rather. I shouldn't have given Clifford any reason to think I might go along with—"

Josh dismissed the words with a gesture. "No point in dwelling on that. Anyway, I know you don't credit my business with much, but I promise you it's going to be worth a fair bit someday soon. I believe Clifford's of the same opinion. He might have been seeking simply more leverage over me."

"Look, I didn't mean to disparage—"

"I know. That's not why I'm here. I was thinking you might ask around. Perhaps some of your waterfront people might know something."

Zac nodded. "They might. And if they do," he said quietly, "what will it gain you?"

Josh stood up, pacing the office without the aid of his cane, coming down hard on the peg every other step, so each time he moved off the colorful Turkey rug there was the staccato beat of wood on wood. "I want to know," he said. "I realize it won't change anything as far as Mollie and I . . . our future . . ." He saw Zac's sympathetic nod and knew Simon must have told him that Josh and Mollie would now be forever childless, "but I want it nonetheless."

"I'll make some inquiries. Give me a day or two."

"Excellent. Thank you." Josh lifted his topper and his cane from his brother's desk and started for the door, pausing just after he opened it. "One other thing, probably not relevant. A while back a man came to see the flats at the St. Nicholas. Happens he also wore an eyepatch, and he gave his name as Anthony Wolfe. Lupo's Italian for wolf, so I thought maybe—"

"Good God." Zac stood up and leaned forward supporting his weight on his knuckles. "Anthony Wolfe, you say? With an eyepatch?"

Josh closed the door. "You know him don't you?"

"Not exactly. I saw him. Once. At a meeting Clifford convened to get backers for his scheme."

"Did you speak with him?"

"No, nothing like that. I didn't want anyone to know I was there. Told Clifford it would start talk about the stability of Devrey Shipping.

Actually, I didn't want it to look as if I was ready to participate in his scheme. So . . ." Zac sounded a bit sheepish. "I hid behind a screen."

"Pity," Josh said. "You might know more if you spoke to him. As it is . . . Well, what did you think of him? Could it be the same man as came to look at the flats in the St. Nicholas?"

Zac shook his head. "It's hard to credit it. He was slick, very well dressed. Well spoken. Not the sort to live in a place like your— Sorry, but you know what I mean."

"I do."

"And he certainly didn't strike me as an immigrant criminal."

"I don't think," Josh said, "the two words necessarily go together."

"No, of course not. But . . . The fellow at the meeting, I presumed he had money. Everyone appeared to have been invited for the purpose of forming a consortium. But thinking about it now, whenever Wolfe opened his mouth it turned out to help Clifford make one or another point."

"So acting for Clifford somehow," Josh said, his face darkening with anger. "On both occasions."

The next day the brothers went back to Fourteenth Street near Seventh Avenue, but though they prowled around for half an hour, there was no sign of Anthony Wolfe. Dead end. At least for the moment.

Josh might have spent longer on the problem had Eileen Brannigan not changed her advice and shifted his focus.

Eileen gave him lunch on University Place. It was, Josh noted, four weeks to the day since Mollie had lost the child. "I take it," she said, "your wife remains unwell."

She visited her niece three or four times a week; she was fully aware of the state of Mollie's health. Nonetheless, Josh decided to allow her to guide the conversation. "Dr. Thomas says she is healing well, but that her spirits remain low."

"And she still refuses to see you?"

Another thing he was sure she knew. "She does not wish me to visit her sickroom, no."

"That must be difficult for you."

"It is." He was about to say something about his affection for Mollie when Francie Wildwood popped into his head. He shook off the vision and blamed it on some vestigial aura emanating from the walls of this onetime brothel. He'd been married for less than a year and been entirely faithful. He fully intended to remain so. Besides, that's not what he'd meant. "I would like to share her sorrow," he said. "It's mine as well, Aunt Eileen."

She said nothing, only lay her hand over his. Joshua had the extraordinary feeling he might weep. He couldn't remember doing so since he was perhaps six. Not even when the farmer's wife was hacking at his leg with the cleaver she used on the carcasses of her stuck pigs.

"More rhubarb pie, Joshua?"

"No, thank you, Aunt Eileen."

She got up and carried the pie dish and the silver server to another table. By the time she returned to sit across from him, Joshua was composed. "It's time," Eileen said, "you did something to bring Mollie out of herself."

"You're the one who told me not to force the issue."

"I did, Josh. Now I'm suggesting an alternative approach. She must do something other than sit in a chair in her room and brood. I was hoping you might think of some activity that requires her involvement."

He would not demand her bed, but it struck Josh with sudden and remarkable force that he had not actually seen his wife, physically looked at her, since they came out of Mama Jack's in those tense and hurried moments after Miller came to get him. Nearly a month. That, coupled with Eileen's advice, brought him to the door of the bedroom they had once shared.

He knocked once, then went in. And knew at once that this was a new and somehow lesser Mollie. She had become someone different from the woman who got herself up in a remarkably revealing gown and flaunted her blooming figure before a crowd of people she'd never met. *Only one leg, but he can get it over.*

Mollie sat beside the window of her bedroom, hands folded in her lap, gazing out into Grand Street and, he'd warrant, seeing nothing of it.

"Leave us please, Tess. I'd like to speak with my wife."

Tess gathered up her darning and disappeared into the hall, closing the door behind her. Mollie did not turn her head.

"It's a fine spring day," Josh said. "Would you perhaps like to go for a walk? Or a drive?"

"No, thank you." Still not facing him. "I prefer to stay where I am."

He took the seat Tess had vacated. Mollie's profile had sharpened, a factor of how drawn she was. "Dr. Thomas says you should be eating a bit more. And getting some fresh air."

"I'm eating quite as much as I need, thank you."

"No, you're not, you . . . Mollie, look at me."

She turned her head obediently. Her eyes were opaque.

"Look," he said, "I want to tell you—" He could not imagine how to finish the sentence.

"Yes?" Her tone was polite, as noncommittal as a stranger's. "I'm listening. What is it you'd like to tell me?"

"Mollie . . ." Josh leaned forward, taking both her hands in his. "I'm so sorry, my love. So very sorry. It was abominably bad luck, but we'll make a li—"

She made no move to pull away from him. "I do not believe 'it,' as you call it, was a matter of luck. A man shot at me. Someone I'd never met and to whom I'd done no harm whatever. I presume it was all to do with your business."

"Perhaps. I'm not sure. It may have been about making Zac do something. Or . . . Look, do you recall the fellow who came to see the flats that first day after the storm? Anthony—"

"I'm afraid I have not been concentrating on the flats of late. Is there anything else you wish to discuss?"

He let go of her hands. "Your Aunt Eileen says you must have an interest, not just stay in this room grieving all the time."

"I'm sure Auntie Eileen has good intentions. She does not, however, understand."

"And neither, you think, do I. That's it, isn't it, Mollie? You blame me for what's happened, and you imagine I do not share your sorrow over our loss."

"Blame changes nothing. I am trying not to consider it. As for the loss . . . You can still father a child, Joshua. If you wish to divorce me and take a wife who can give you children, I will fully understand."

"Divorce! In God's name how can you think I'd even consider such a thing?"

She turned away from him to look out the window once more. "As you wish."

"No." He stood up. "Nothing is as I wish at the moment. Please do everything you can to regain your strength. You shall need it. I will have certain requirements of you in the not too distant future."

It would be good for Mollie, no doubt about it. But face it, he wanted it as well. A home of his own, something that said he'd arrived, that the one-legged middle son who'd never been as clever as his two brothers was a man of property. Why the hell not?

His second building was well underway on Sixty-Third, seven stories already in place and going up at a wonderful clip. A third of the flats were spoken for, never mind that he'd erected the sign only a few days before. THE CAROLINA—PRIVATE HOMES A NEW YORK GENTLE-

MAN CAN AFFORD. DESIRABLE LEASES AVAILABLE. Naming the new
building for his mother had seemed both inspired and obvious once
the idea came to him. Particularly after she'd refused to sell him two of
her lots on Eighty-Seventh Street and Fourth Avenue at market rates.
"You must have them, Josh. A dollar a lot, just to make it legal."

"Mama, that's very kind, but are you quite sure? That land's not
worth a great deal now, but someday . . ."

"Someday it will be worth a fortune. I always thought so, Josh.
That's why I bought it. But you have looked after it all these years. And
if you're worried about your brothers and sister, don't be. Papa will
deal with the legacy issues."

He protested that such concerns were well in the future, but Josh
suspected only his father's extraordinary care had kept her with them
this long. Something else he could do nothing about. A home of his
own, however . . . that was entirely possible.

No denying the area remained a trash heap superimposed on a
wilderness, but Vanderbilt was digging his tunnel. Not as deep as
anyone would like and the smoke and fumes and cinders escaping
through the vents remained a problem, but the fortunes of upper
Fourth Avenue were, Josh was convinced, sure to follow those of
the downtown portion. Someday it would be fashionable Park Avenue up here just as it was in Murray Hill. And not all that far
in the future. Particularly if he helped it along by building a fine
house in advance of the crowd. The pattern, after all, was a New
York commonplace. One pioneer broke ground and others arrived
in his wake. He'd put up the basic structure—get McKim to design
something not too grand, but very nice—then insist that Mollie
see to furnishing and equipping it. It might make him seem like a
tyrant to demand her involvement, but he was convinced it was in
her best interests. And he'd hire a clerk, but require she oversee the
bookkeeping. It was getting into a terrible state with him trying to
do everything himself.

A man of property. Yes, indeed.

15

"SUBSTANTIAL," JOSH HAD told McKim that June of 1872 when they met in the bar of the Grand Union Hotel. "But simple. Dignified."

"Elegance, my good man, is always simple." The architect had pulled a notebook from his breast pocket, moved aside his whiskey, and sketched furiously while he spoke. "Something with classical influence, like this? What do you think?"

Josh leaned forward. "A bow front?"

"Yes. Gives you the best light as well as adding some grace to the exterior. And a pediment above it."

"Looks vaguely Greek," Josh said.

"Any objection to that?"

"None at all." Josh smiled. Mollie Popandropolos memorialized.

"The bay to go up two stories, I think." McKim added more pencil strokes. "Better proportions. And that will allow you a balcony outside the third-floor windows."

"You're thinking four stories?" Josh asked the question while catching the eye of a hovering waiter and pointing to their glasses.

"Yes. Or perhaps five. If you're planning for children and—"

The waiter brought the refills, depositing the fresh glasses and removing the old in one smooth gesture. The break was just long enough for Joshua to control both his tongue and his feelings. "Four stories is plenty."

"Fine. You're sure about only building on one lot? We could do something quite splendid if—"

"One lot," Josh said firmly. "My mother was exceedingly generous, but I believe in husbanding my resources."

It was October when he took Mollie uptown to see the finished house. "Quite grand," she said, accompanying him on a tour of the twelve spacious rooms.

"Quite empty," Josh said.

He'd tried repeatedly to get her to come during the summer of construction, but though she'd resumed responsibility for his bookkeeping—overseeing a rotund clerk named Hamish Fraser lately come from Edinburgh—she almost never left the house. Until today when he had absolutely insisted. *I mean for us to move next month, Mollie. You'll have to see the house before furnishing it.*

"Next month?" she asked now, her voice seeming to echo through each bare room, obviously aware of the enormity of the task he'd set her. "You're quite sure?"

"Absolutely certain. I mean to carve my Thanksgiving turkey under my own roof."

"But there's nothing here."

"Nothing," he agreed cheerfully. "Not a bed to sleep in nor a plate to eat off. No tables, no chairs. No desk for my papers—I should like my study to be the large room in the rear of the second floor, by the way—no chests for clothing nor lamps to read by. Not a curtain on any window or a sheet or a coverlet for the nonexistent beds. It all needs choosing and ordering and arranging. Over to you, my girl. Do me proud."

Mollie stared at him as if he had lost his mind.

Josh ignored her stunned silence and opened the front door. The hansom that had brought them uptown was waiting to return them to Grand Street. "I've a brougham on order, by the way. Being up here requires you to travel in more comfort than the phaeton provides and we can't rely on cabs this far uptown. The stable will be finished by week's end." He pointed with his cane to a brick structure at the rear of the second lot. "Mr. McKim is arranging to fence the whole property as soon as the construction is done. And all the building scrap will be cleared away, of course."

Mollie was staring in the direction he indicated, across a weed and rubble strewn expanse. "Lilies," she said.

"I beg your pardon?"

"Lilies would be lovely. White lilies and blue delphiniums. Perhaps some dark purple irises as well. In a border just there. And one or two small trees of the sort that flower in spring."

He had the feeling she was speaking more to herself than to him. But there was a degree of animation in her voice he had not heard since the day they followed Frankie Miller out of Mama Jack's Cave.

"You know quality, Auntie Eileen. Exactly as you've always said. I trust you to make the choices."

"I'm not sure," Eileen said, "that's exactly what Joshua had in mind."

Mollie waved the objection aside. "Josh wants the house to be furnished and livable in the shortest possible time. And if you do it, so it shall be. Why should he object?"

"Because he wants you to be as you were. That's the goal of everything he's done, dear child, surely you know that."

"I do. I should like to be as I was, Auntie Eileen. If there was any way to make it be so, I promise I would take it." *Miss Palmer, please tell Mrs. Turner that certain interior parts were injured during the difficulties. And that regretfully there can now never be children.*

The past could not be changed, but the future might hold some small possibility not of happiness—she no longer expected that—but perhaps . . . relief.

The vision that came to Mollie in those few moments when she looked across the waste space between Josh's grand new house and his stable was born of articles in *Godey's Lady's Book* and *Harper's*, implanted in her mind over many years. The magazines frequently featured sketches of beautiful gardens attached to houses in places where such things were considered the normal surroundings of a fine home. In New York City, where however much a man might spend on pleasure, it would never occur to him to allow a building lot to be without a building, Mollie never actually saw any flowers that were not in a florist's window, or a vase, or an indoor pot on a sunny sill. Perhaps that's why so much of her needlework featured nature. She hadn't sewed a single stitch since that terrible day when she bled away her motherhood, but the possibility of a garden sparked a small but insistent flame of interest.

Eileen recognized the opportunity and took it. She set about furnishing the house in a whirlwind effort that brought her to the Ladies' Mile six days out of seven—"Please send the bill to Mr. Joshua Turner on Grand Street"—all the while keeping an eye on her niece's even more remarkable activity.

Mollie took a cab to Eighty-Seventh Street each morning, stopping along the way to pick up various urchins and idlers willing to spend the day digging at her direction. She chose the most likely looking from among the impoverished gaggle hanging about in front of the uptown rookeries, and paid them in coins at the end of each session, making careful note of those who had done the best job. The following day they were the ones she selected. After two weeks she had assembled a reliable crew who were quickly becoming skilled groundsmen. Meanwhile, she sat with a stack of back copies of the journals that had provided her inspiration and thumbed through them, stopping each time she encountered a notice offering horticultural necessities or plants or seeds. *"Dear sir, I write in response to your announcement in* Godey's *of March 1871. Do you still offer specimens of the white lilium regale? . . . Dear Sir, I am most interested in the dark blue delphinium you offered in* Harper's Bazaar *earlier this year."*

When she discovered a publication called *The Gardeners' Chronicle,* full of advice and extensive instructions for nurturing every type of growing thing, she was ecstatic.

Gradually Mollie's vision matured. Since by happy chance she had conceived her plan in the autumn, the best time for planting many perennials, shrubs, and trees, the garden in her dreams made a faint but swift impression on the lot marked in the city rolls as number 1062 Fourth Avenue. Meanwhile, a steady procession of delivery vans—most of them blazoned R. H. MACY and A. T. STEWART, though there were some from Mr. Constable's establishment and an occasional visit from an anonymous carter dispatched from a small draper's shop with no fleet of its own—arrived next door at number 1060, and off-loaded every conceivable sort of household furnishing and necessity.

At first Mollie was charged by her aunt with accepting the deliveries, but when Eileen found the beds and chests meant for the third and fourth floors all left willy-nilly in the drawing room because no one had troubled to give the haulers more specific instructions, she arranged for Tess to go uptown with Mollie in the mornings and be on hand to receive the merchandise Eileen spent her days acquiring. That suited Mollie, who was then free to devote as many hours as were required to deciding if the blush pink of the climbing Bourbon rose Lady Antoinette would, on maturity, blend well with the creamy blossoms of the Virgin's Bower clematis she planned to grow up the side of the stable. No, she concluded. Too insipid. She would instead plant the deeper-colored Bourbon, Souvenir de la Petite Malmaison.

She sighed with pleasure at the thought of the two blooming together. As for hunting down the preferred rose, the quest made her tingle. Rather like what it felt like after one's hand or foot had "fallen asleep," as was said, and after much shaking and rubbing, sensation returned.

The sign above the door said SOLOMON GANZ, and beneath it hung the traditional three golden balls of the pawnbroker. Joshua had a moment's pause. He could have sent Hamish, except the clerk knew nothing about last year's desperate attempt to raise capital. No reason he should be made privy to the details now. Mollie would have been a logical choice since she was the one who had arranged the original transaction, but the garden she was creating had brought on the first signs of genuine recovery he'd seen since she lost their child. He was reluctant to interrupt that healing for even a few hours.

Josh pushed open the door.

A bell tinkled.

A small, thin man with a mostly bald head appeared from the rear, pushing aside a heavy velvet curtain and smiling at him. "Good afternoon, Mr. Turner. I am Sol Ganz." The man took a few steps forward and extended his hand. "It's a pleasure to see you here."

"The pleasure is mine, Mr. Ganz. Though I didn't expect to be so easily identified."

Ganz's smile got wider. "You are distinctive, Mr. Turner. A large red-headed man with—" The pawnbroker broke off.

Josh's turn to smile. "With a wooden leg. You're quite right, I should expect to be recognized."

"Besides," Ganz said, "I was expecting you today. Or perhaps your wife."

"She's otherwise engaged at the moment, so I—"

"Ah yes, soon you will be moving to your new home. Ladies are always busy at such times."

"You know a great deal about me and my affairs, Mr. Ganz."

"We have," Ganz said, "a moderately large transaction between us.

At least it is so for a small businessman like myself. These days the sum is very modest for you. See, I know that as well."

"Your loan went a long way to making that possible, Mr. Ganz. And as you indicate, it is due today. I've come to pay you and reclaim my property."

Ganz showed him into the room behind the curtain and indicated a chair. "When your wife came to see me she sat right there." He took his own seat and reached into a drawer and produced a roll of soft chamois leather. "And gave me this." Ganz loosed the tie, and allowed the roll to unwind on the table between them. Eileen Brannigan's rings and bracelets and her peacock brooch sparkled in the light of the gas lamp that provided the only illumination in the windowless space.

"And you gave her," Joshua said, "six thousand dollars in paper currency."

Ganz offered a slight shake of his head. "Not exactly. I gave her a banker's draft for that amount. And accompanied her to Mr. Cooke's bank on William Street and saw that it was cashed."

"Yes," Josh agreed. "I recall her explaining that." Her hand had trembled when she handed over the thick roll of bills. *Six thousand, Josh. What shall you buy? Six lots, you magnificent creature. Back to back on Sixty-Eighth and Sixty-Seventh, and our fortune made.* From that flowed McKim's clever and enormously profitable square with a central courtyard. Had he bought fewer lots, the Carolina would not exist. Josh withdrew a piece of paper from the breast pocket of his coat and put it on the table beside the jewels. "I can go with you to Drexel's bank on Broad Street and perform the same service if you wish."

The pawnbroker did not touch the draft, only leaned forward and examined it. "That won't be necessary, Mr. Turner. Ten thousand, three hundred and twenty dollars. That is the correct amount."

Josh put his hand over the roll of chamois leather, which he knew without checking would include everything Mollie had pawned the previous year. Sol Ganz would not still be in business if he indulged in that sort of blatant thievery. Ganz put his hand over the draft, knowing that a man of Joshua Turner's sort would not write it had he not the funds.

The exchange was made.

The pawnbroker accompanied his visitor to the street in front of his door. "It has been a great pleasure doing business with you, Mr. Turner. If I can be of help anytime in the future . . ." He stretched out his hand.

Josh shook the other man's hand, and put on his topper. "Thank you, Mr. Ganz. I do not see any immediate need for a pawnbroker, but one never knows."

"Indeed, Mr. Turner. One never does. So just remember, Sol Ganz is here on Avenue A. Waiting only to be of service."

The newness of everything had a particular smell. Not in the least unpleasant, Josh thought, but quite different from every other house he'd lived in. Sunshine Hill was built by his parents from the ground up, but in his earliest memories it was already full of people and much lived in. Even his rooming houses had been occupied before he acquired them and transformed them to his purpose. Number 1060 Fourth Avenue was pristine.

Thanksgiving fell that year on the twenty-eighth of November. The last of their things—clothing, toiletries, papers, and the like—were brought up from Grand Street two days before. The final transfer of the household goods came in the form of a carter's wagon that arrived bearing Agnes Hannity and what appeared to be the contents of at least six pantries.

"Careful with them there pies," the cook was shouting as Josh rode up on Midnight. He reined in and watched while the haulers carried box after box through the basement level tradesman's entrance to the left of the front door. "Hey! Them's my summer pickles and they won't be improved by your jouncing 'em this way and that."

"I fear she thinks no one has discovered fire this far uptown," a voice said at his elbow, "and we must survive on picnic food from now on."

It was the most normal remark Mollie had made to him since the previous April. Josh slid from the saddle and put an arm around her waist. "I have not been this excited," he admitted, "since I was six years old and it was Christmas Eve, and I was convinced St. Nick was coming down the chimney."

A young boy appeared. "Stable your horse, Mr. Turner?"

"And who are you?"

"This is Oliver Crump," Mollie said. "He's called Ollie and he's been working with me for two months. I thought to keep him on as a combined gardener and stableboy. Subject to your approval I told him."

"Well, he looks suitable enough." He was small but wiry. And no doubt, thought Josh, plucked from one of the god-awful rookeries. "I take it you've convinced Mrs. Turner you can dig, Ollie Crump, but do you know anything about horses?"

"Yes sir, happens I do."

The boy was stroking Midnight's muzzle all the while, and the mare was nuzzling up to him, apparently content with his touch. "How," Josh asked, "has that familiarity come about?"

"My pa was a blacksmith, sir. I worked with him sometimes."

"Was?" Josh said. "And is he not a blacksmith now?"

"No sir. He got the fever and died two years back. Left me and my ma and four sisters what's littler'n me."

Followed by abject poverty, and the fetid, criminal environment of those places where the poorest of the poor were warehoused and left to their evil. The whole sorry story laid out in two sentences.

"There's a room in the stable where Ollie can sleep," Mollie said.

"A month's trial," Josh said releasing the horse to the care of his new stableboy. "See she's properly brushed and cooled down before you feed her, Ollie."

"Yes sir, Mr. Turner. I will."

The boy led the mare away. The carter's wagon was at last empty

and rolling down Fourth Avenue. Agnes Hannity and Tess and whoever else was part of his newly established household had disappeared.
He and Mollie were alone. "Shall we go in?" he asked.

Through his own front door. And just before he crossed the thresh-
old Josh swept his wife into his arms and carried her into the house.
"Not bad for a fellow with a peg," he said as he put her down.

She didn't say anything, but at least she was smiling.

Josh had not been inside the house for two weeks. It was a quite
deliberate act of restraint. He'd wanted to be as surprised as he was
right now, seeing the warm yellow gaslight bathing polished wood
and softly draped damask, and occasionally reflecting a sharper gleam
as it encountered marble and the hard sheen of satin. And everywhere
that wondrous smell of newness and beginning.

They ate a cold supper of mutton pie off trays on their laps in a
comfortable family sitting room on the second floor, where the more
formal fabrics of the downstairs drawing and dining rooms gave way
to flowered chintz and checked gingham. "Your study is through
there," Mollie said, indicating a door behind them. "Just as you said
you wanted."

"Excellent. Incidentally, I've set up an office for Hamish down at
the foundry, but he'll come and work with you here two days a week."

She nodded agreement. Then, the trays cleared and the room quite
empty of anyone but themselves, "Will you show me the bedrooms,
Mollie."

He followed her up to the third floor. "Two here and two on the
floor above," she said. "Proper bedrooms up there. Not servants' quarters. Agnes and Tess have rooms downstairs near the kitchen. Jane as
well. She's agreed to live in now that we need a full-time maid."

"Downstairs," Josh repeated. "They don't mind that rather than the
upper floor?"

"They haven't said if they do. And Mr. McKim says that's how it's
being done in all the better New York houses these days."

"Makes sense," Josh said. Looking meanwhile at the bed big enough for two in the room in which they stood. It had four tall posts but no canopy or curtains.

"I'm told," Mollie said, "that with modern heating there is no need to enclose the beds in drapery. But if you prefer—"

"No. This is fine. It's a handsome room."

"The one next door is exactly like it," she said, speaking quietly and turning her back to him as she did so, while making a show of adjusting something on a dresser top.

He was, he realized, dismissed.

He could not, however, fall asleep in the room next door to his wife's. There was a chiming clock in the entry hall and he heard it strike ten and then eleven. After that he got up and prowled about the place, not bothering to strap his peg back on, managing with only his cane and feeling more excited with each hopping step. By God, it was a place to do a man proud. Never mind that Mollie had wriggled out from under the task he set her and gotten her aunt to do the selecting and buying and arranging. He loved the way the house looked, and tonight, eating supper with him, showing him around, Mollie had been closer to her old self than anytime in the past six months.

More than ample time for what Simon called her female parts to have healed.

He did not knock but let himself into her bedroom as quietly as he could, grateful for the thick rug that quieted the tapping of his cane. He could hear her breathing. Soft and steady and not startled. Either she was asleep, or awake and expecting him.

Josh made his way to the side of the bed and slipped out of his robe and his nightshirt and lifted the quilt and crawled in beside her and whispered, "Mollie, are you awake?"

"I am."

"I thought . . . It's a new beginning, love. I want us to be as we were." She did not answer.

He reached out and stroked her cheek, leaning forward after a moment to kiss first her forehead and then her lips. "I thought I'd taught you to kiss me back," he said, a hint of teasing in his voice. "Have you forgotten so soon?"

She shivered. Not with that welcoming tremble of the virgin girl who despite her inexperience had delighted him by daring to come naked to her bridal bed. She was crying. He could taste the salt of her tears on her cheeks. "Mollie, please . . ." Then, because he knew he could not live with himself if he did not make the offer, "I'll go if you wish."

"You're my husband, Josh. It's what you wish that matters."

Damn her. She wouldn't even meet him halfway. He'd been celibate for months and he was not a monk; she should not expect him to act as such. "Look, I don't want—"

"Yes, you do. And you can. So you may as well go ahead."

He rolled on top of her without another word.

He felt rotten about it the next day and perhaps if things had worked out differently Josh might have tried again to effect a rapprochement with Mollie. As it was, events intervened.

A note was delivered the following morning. It was from Zac. Josh was at once summoned to Sunshine Hill.

He knew something was desperately wrong as soon as he approached the house; the gates at the foot of the long steep driveway were flung open. Zac met him at the door, his stricken face conveying the news before his words. "She didn't wake after the night. It was very peaceful. We can be thankful for that."

They buried Carolina from Trinity Church and interred her in the churchyard. Joshua was astounded at the numbers who showed up for the funeral. All the New York waterfront it seemed, everyone from an aged Greek named Socrates Paxos—the last survivor of the trio who had captained her clippers—to any number of gray-bearded stevedores who remembered her with affection. A goodly number of black people as well. Confirming the truth she had never been willing to discuss, how active she'd been in the dangerous work of the underground railroad in the days preceding the war. Old friends as well, Papa's old business partner, Dr. Klein and his family, and much to Josh's astonishment, a contingent of Catholic nuns, as well as a Chinese woman. His father, he noted, spent a good amount of time talking with one of the nuns, and embraced the Chinese woman with obvious and genuine affection.

"Your mother was a woman of many parts," Mollie murmured.

"Apparently so."

Eventually, the graveside ceremonies were done and a verger in a white cassock and a purple cape began ushering them past the many worn and moss-covered headstones of this oldest part of the burial ground. Most were original and undisturbed, though the church itself had been rebuilt three times since it was erected in 1697.

Josh caught a number of names as he walked by. Sally Turner Van der Vries for one, and Lisbetta Van der Vries Smythe for another. Lisbetta had been known to the town as Red Bess, he remembered, and one way or another deeply embroiled in the feud that originally tore the Devreys and the Turners apart. Death, however, was the great leveler. Not far from Red Bess was the grave of her brother, Willem Devrey. Born Van der Vries, he'd been the one who anglicized the name. And there was Christopher Turner, and beside him Samuel Devrey—not Zac's father, the ancestor he'd been named for—and Sam's brother Raif. And nearby a stone that was aslant and had a corner knocked off. Jennet Turner DaSilva it said, 1715–1783. Someone had left a single rose at its base, dead now but the browned petals not yet blown away. Josh bent over to examine the card beside the flower. *Heroine of the Revolution R.I.P.* He knew Jennet was his many times great-aunt, and according to family legend, in her time the most notorious woman in the city. It pleased him that someone in his own day had remembered the other part of who she'd been.

Everything passes, dearest Joshua. Try and leave behind more good than bad.

He would have sworn it was his mother's voice whispering those words in his ear, and when at last the slow file of mourners went through the churchyard gate to Wall Street he felt as if he'd trodden through his own history and somehow emerged on the other side.

"I intend to carve my Thanksgiving turkey at my own table," he'd said. And so he did.

Mrs. Hannity produced a bird of uncommon wonder, golden brown and succulent, and a series of accompanying dishes—chestnut stuffing and roasted potatoes and onions in cream and buttered squash and cranberry sauce—that showed no hint of having been made in a kitchen she'd not seen until forty-eight hours before. The family gathered and ate with gusto and exclaimed over the glories of the new house.

At the end of the meal both the cook and Tess arrived in the dining room, each bearing a pie in either hand. "Mince and apple and pumpkin, and custard," Mrs. Hannity announced. "Course custard ain't traditional for Thanksgiving, but it's Mr. Turner's favorite." There were three Messrs. Turner at the table, but no one was in doubt that Josh was the Mr. Turner Mrs. Hannity wanted to please.

Master of all he surveyed.

The thought actually crossed Josh's mind. He had the grace to, first, color, then chuckle to himself, though he didn't think anyone but Aunt Eileen noticed. Probably his mother would have as well, and smiled at him in that knowing way she'd had.

They were, of course, all trying not to think of Carolina's absence, nor the fact that Nick looked twenty years older now he had buried his wife.

For her part Mollie sat at the foot of the table and did everything expected of her. But she did not once meet Josh's glance, and she disappeared upstairs the moment the guests left.

On Friday she did not join him for breakfast and he saw her outside, bundled up against the raw November wind, wearing a broad-brimmed hat and a long coat and a scarf that was whipped about by the wind. She was using a sharp stick to mark places in the soil, while the stable boy came behind her with a narrow spade, digging a hole in the places she indicated. She seemed to be issuing a string of instructions and she spoke to Ollie Crump, Josh noted, with more animation than she'd mustered for her husband in six months. Certainly more than she'd exhibited the other night when he shared her bed.

He went outside through the pair of glass doors McKim had added to the breakfast room as an afterthought. *Given that your wife is making such a feature of the plantings, French doors might be pleasant, don't you think?*

Neither the boy nor Mollie acknowledged his arrival. "I thought gardening was a warm-weather activity," Josh said. "What are you doing?"

"Planting tulip bulbs," Mollie said. "They arrived from Holland only a few days ago. They must be planted now if they're to flower in the spring."

"I see. And what's that?" He pointed to a small tree, its leafless branches showing above the burlap wrapping tied over its roots.

"A young Roxbury Russet apple from Sunshine Hill. Your father sent it over. We shall plant it later today. Over there."

She used her pointed stick to indicate a spot some ten feet from where they stood. It looked to Josh not unlike any other place on the lot and he started to ask her why that was the favored position, but she had turned back to Ollie and was saying something about the depth of one of the holes. Joshua had come out without a coat and the wind was freezing. He turned and went back into the house.

That evening he called on Francie Wildwood.

Francie was exultant. She'd bided her time and kept her mouth shut, knowing that to be a wiser course of action than simply telling of Mollie's arrival at the house on Bowling Green. (She'd suspected from the first the visit was made without his permission. Joshua Turner was far too proud to send his wife to drum up custom for his business.)

At the time she had weighed her options carefully. If she told she would have the momentary satisfaction of seeing his face darken with anger and disapproval. But though the chief cause would be the almost-spinster who'd got him to propose marriage, the anger would quickly be directed at her as well. Francie, after all, was in charge of the rooming house, and she had allowed the meeting to take place. So she'd stayed silent. And here he was back in her bed not fifteen months after he married that skinny, drawn-out creature who, as it turned out, hadn't managed to give him a child in all that time, and according to what she heard never would. And thanks in part to Francie helping to rent those first flats and saying nothing of it to him or anyone else, the Joshua Turner who'd returned to her was a lot richer than the one who'd smacked her bottom and given her pearl earrings to mark the last time he took advantage of her charms. "I mean to keep my vows, Francie. But I'd be happy to have you stay on running this house."

"Course I will," she'd said. "And if you change your mind or just get lonely, I'll be here on Bowling Green like always."

And so she was.

16

INSUFFERABLE HEAT ON the August day of 1873 when Eileen Brannigan summoned Joshua to tea at University Place. She let him in herself and ushered him upstairs to her sitting room, and sat him down to one of Hatty Ellis's sumptuous midafternoon repasts. Beaten biscuits on this occasion, and peach preserves with candied ginger. "Please have another, Joshua. You're looking quite peaky. I think you are working too hard." According to Mollie, the pattern of the nine months since they had moved into their new home did not include many meals taken in the opulent dining room Eileen had furnished with such care. Business, her niece said. Restaurants for both lunch and dinner most days. *Joshua prefers it so, Auntie Eileen.*

He nonetheless was falling with abandon on Hatty's home-cooked delights. So as not to draw attention to the fact, Eileen made constant small talk while he ate. "Do you think, Joshua, Mr. Darwin's latest theory is correct? He says human beings have also evolved, not just turtles and lizards and whatever else he reported on a while back."

"Evolved from animals, not simply like them," Josh said, heaping preserves on his fourth biscuit. "We, apparently, were once apes. Darwin is very convincing. Why does that make you smile?"

"I'm thinking that some men have not evolved all that far. Ah, I'm embarrassing you. Never mind, I see you've finished your tea so I must get to the point before you go rushing off."

Josh sat back, content to wait until she spoke her piece. Eileen Brannigan never wasted his time.

"I have a . . ." Eileen hesitated, as if seeking for a word, "a colleague," she said. "He is very clever and has certain connections."

"As have you, yourself," Josh said.

"Indeed. But these days I don't see as much of the important gentlemen who once visited regularly. I have come to rely on this particular colleague for business advice." She had dinner with Sol Ganz once a month. Always at Delmonico's on Chambers Street where he arranged a private room. The food was unfailingly superb, but the talk still more interesting. Mr. Ganz, she had discovered, for all his folksy manner, was a man who knew just about everything about just about everyone. Their discussions always finished with him inquiring after her niece and nephew-in-law. *Mr. Turner's business is still doing well? Very well, Mr. Ganz. Good, good. I am delighted to hear it.*

Eileen was convinced Mr. Ganz already knew everything there was to know about Mollie and Josh, but since his fortunes were now in some measure tied to theirs, she no longer found his interest alarming. She believed instead that he was looking out for them. An opinion confirmed the night before when Mr. Ganz did more than simply ask after their well-being. "I have things to tell you. I can explain only a limited amount, but you must pay close heed to what I say and act on it swiftly." Following that announcement he spoke earnestly for a number of minutes.

As soon as she got home Eileen wrote to ask Joshua to come to tea at his earliest convenience.

So here he was, awash in excellent tea and stuffed full of delicious biscuits and jam. And though there was no one in the house other than the two of them and Hatty Ellis, Eileen got up and closed the door, then returned to sit across from him. "I have something of great urgency to tell you."

"I'm listening, Aunt Eileen."

She nodded, but she did not speak. In another example of that caution Josh found remarkable, Eileen reached for a piece of paper and a pencil, wrote something, and passed it to him.

Josh was looking at two letters. A *J* and a *G*. Both capitalized. "Initials?" Josh asked.

"Precisely."

He thought for a moment. "I'm sorry. I can't think of anyone I know who—"

"Someone you know of," Eileen interrupted. "In the world of business and finance. Very high finance."

"Jay Gould."

She snatched the paper back and began tearing it into tiny pieces. "Yes." Spoken quickly, as if it might be a curse and she didn't want the gods to overhear. "Him."

"Aunt Eileen, Mr. Gou— That particular gentleman operates in circles far above mine. I have no connection whatever to—"

"Please, just listen to me. I believe it is the intention of Mr. J. G. to arrange things so that he can acquire whatever he wants anywhere in the country at the lowest possible price."

"Nothing new in that," Josh said. "He's been doing it for years."

"This is different. More . . . extreme. The market, Josh . . ."

"Yes."

"At the moment it is not reliable."

He thought for a few seconds. "You're talking about a run, aren't you? A panic. Like '57, or even '37." Her silence was confirmation. "Aunt Eileen, I assure you, rest easy. There are new laws in place. The Treasury Department promises such an event can't occur again."

"My friend," she said quietly, "is extremely reliable. I am myself sometimes astonished at the extent of his knowledge. And
his . . . influence." *Mr. Theodore Paisley . . . found dead in his home . . .*
"Please take this information very seriously, Joshua."

So, his choices were Eileen Brannigan and the high-level friends
she had cultivated over better than three decades, or a Washington
politician who might well be gone in the next election. "I shall take it
very seriously indeed, Aunt Eileen. I promise."

September 18th was a Thursday. Still warm for so late in the season.
Sticky as well. It seemed the men on the floor of the New York Stock
Exchange on Wall Street were doing business with something less than
their usual exuberance. The weather, someone said. Another pointed
to a character called Two-finger Tommy—the other eight digits had
been lost at Second Bull Run—a trader known to act for a number
of different principals. When the market was about to leap in one or
the other direction Tommy inevitably got itchy. No explaining it, he
insisted, but it was as if biting insects were crawling up and down his
body. At just after ten that morning Tommy was scratching like mad
and jerking up and down as if possessed by a devil.

There was never any evidence that Two-finger Tommy had advance
knowledge of the meeting a short distance away at the New York office
of Jay Cooke and Company, a Philadelphia investment bank believed
to be among the strongest in the country. It was held in strict secrecy
and only a handful of the most important bankers and brokers in the
city, men who made the market, had been invited. Once assembled
they listened to Cooke's senior people plead for an investment of capital to keep their bank from going under. It did not take long for the
leading lights of finance to make clear their refusal to bail out a firm
that was the victim of its own bad judgment.

Vanderbilt voiced the explanation most everyone believed. Jay
Cooke had overreached. He'd hired fellows—advertisers they called

them these days—to convince people that the stark badlands of the Dakota and Minnesota territories through which his Northern Pacific Railroad ran were ripe and luscious and accessible, a courtesan waiting to be enjoyed. The extravagant tale sold some stock in the short run, but the price collapsed once people saw the actuality. "If people will carry on business in this madcap manner," Vanderbilt insisted, "they must run amuck."

The moneymen left Cooke's office at eleven, convinced they had done the right thing. The bad tidings were telegraphed to Jay Cooke in Philadelphia. He immediately closed his doors and suspended all business at every branch of his bank.

The news was announced on the floor of the Exchange at 11:22, and like a wounded beast the market roared in pain and plunged into frenzy. The vast majority of traders couldn't sell fast enough. Jay Gould made an instant fortune on the decline. Vanderbilt opposed him and bought with abandon, desperate to start the bulls running. He succeeded in hanging on to the New York Central line, but Gould grabbed much of the rest of his rival's holdings. Brokers large and small failed in a matter of hours and a dozen banks collapsed.

Friday, despite a driving rain, seething crowds churned the downtown streets into mud as they dashed from one bank to another trying to withdraw their funds. Lines formed around entire blocks and the police had all they could do to maintain order. The banks, meanwhile, had pretty much run out of cash. Their vaults were stuffed with railroad bonds, each of which was losing value as the seconds ticked by.

On Saturday at eleven a.m., forty-eight hours after the panic began, the governors of the Exchange shut down trading. Someone asked for how long. The answer was a shrug.

Zac found Josh at the foundry. Frankie Miller's men, usually hidden, were in plain view around the perimeter. "You're expecting trouble?" Zac asked. "Here?"

"Not really," Josh said. "I'm just being cautious."

"Well, you've been right so far. Prescient I might call it." Zac's voice betrayed a new respect for his younger brother. "How the hell did you know?"

"I can't tell you a lot. Just that Mollie's Aunt Eileen has some remarkable connections."

"Jesus God Almighty. It certainly seems so."

Zac had not at first credited Josh's warning. Until in mid-August, a few days after their initial conversation, his brother brought four suitcases full of currency to Zac's office in the Devrey Building. "Except for 1060 Fourth, my rooming houses, my flats, and the land each stands on, I'm now entirely in cash. And not a penny of it is in any bank. This is it, Zac. All I possess. In four leather satchels."

Zac stood up, peering into the cases as Josh snapped them open. Each was full to the top with greenbacks.

"United States bills," Josh said. "Every one, so our government assures me, backed by gold."

"The gold," Zac said, "is in Fort Knox. With an army to protect it. What are you proposing to do with all this?"

"I think Mama will look after it for me."

"Now I know you're mad. Surely you don't mean to bury—" Zac had broken off and sank back in his seat, the light of revelation dawning in his eyes. "The Carolina clock," he'd said softly.

"Exactly."

Three hours later, eleven minutes before nine in the evening and the building all but empty, Zac went through the door beside his office and up a short ladder into the rooftop structure that housed the clockworks. Josh rested his left foot on the ladder's second rung and his peg on the floor and hoisted one satchel at a time for Zac to stow away. At two minutes to nine the brothers were on Canal Street, gazing upward, intent on seeing that nothing they had done had interrupted the clock's functioning. The seconds ticked by, with the hands moving in what appeared to be an entirely normal fashion. The hour struck. *Hell Witch* sailed majestically across the sky, followed by *West*

Witch and *East Witch* and the clock chimed nine times. "Mama," Josh said, "approves."

The next day Zac began raising as much cash as he could—less than Josh's stash he was fairly certain—and hid his suitcases next to his brother's.

Now, some four weeks later, the whole incredible drama was playing out exactly as Joshua had predicted. Pandemonium on Wall Street and a run on the banks.

The tension in the foundry that September Saturday morning was real, but more controlled than what was happening on the streets. Zac had arrived on an old swaybacked nag. He'd added seven hundred to his supply of cash when he sold a fine mare a month previous.

There were only four men standing near the Kelly converter—Tickle and the other dwarf, McCoy, and two normal-size men he didn't know—because Josh had cut back on his payroll over the last few weeks. The four continued working, but Zac knew they were eyeing him with apprehension, anxious for any word from the world of finance.

"What's the latest?" Josh asked.

"Well, it took me about an hour to get from Canal Street down here. Crowds everywhere, and I heard thirty-two different stories along the way. Only thing I'm sure of is that Grant and Richardson are in the city. At the Fifth Avenue Hotel, meeting with the governors of the Exchange. Apparently the federal government is being asked to put some forty million in cash into the banks."

Josh turned to his men. "You hear that? The president and the secretary of the treasury have come to New York to help us. We'll be fine." Never mind how rapidly he'd dismissed the promises from Washington when Eileen issued her warning. Nor how right he'd been.

No different this time as it turned out. The administration announced it would not pony up hard cash in the form of deposits—not morally defensible, Richardson said, to reward the profligacy that had created the situation—but Washington would buy government bonds on the open market and that would put some cash in the system.

The Exchange stayed closed for a week. The bears ran rampant nonetheless. Men traded on the street under the trees as they had in Colonial times. And always, it seemed, they were forced to sell for less than they'd bought. Stocks sank to new lows. Brokerage houses disappeared overnight, their clients finding them open for business one day and their premises empty and bolted shut the next. Banks defaulted one after the other—in a few cases the bankers disappeared with what little cash the bank still had. A week later a number of the insurance companies closed their doors. By then the crisis had spread from New York across the nation. Chicago, for one, was entirely without a banking system and the town resorted to barter.

Zac still could not quite believe that his younger brother had predicted the chaos, and managed to somehow protect them from the worst of the carnage. "So," he said over mugs of grossly inferior dark and cloudy brew in a taproom on Fifty-Second Street and Fourth that catered to the workers in the block-square Steinway Piano-forte Manufactory across the road, "what do you have in mind for your next miracle?"

Josh chuckled. "It wasn't me. I told you. Mollie's aunt tipped me wise. If it were not for Eileen Brannigan, I'd be in as much trouble as everyone else. I suppose I told you I didn't at first believe her."

"I'm glad you were persuaded." Zac looked around. One of Frankie Miller's boys was standing by the door. "The beer in this place is god-awful and it's up here in the back of beyond. I wouldn't think they'd need a bouncer."

Josh saw the direction of his brother's glance. "He doesn't work for the taproom. He's with me."

Zac shook his head in wonder. "I spotted Frankie's potential when he was nine, but you've made more use of him than I ever did."

"He credits you with making him what he is today. Worships you. In the matter of underworld connections, I'm destined to be forever in your shadow."

Zac did not rise to the bait. "Tell me why you believe you need a bodyguard."

"First, not just me. I'm arranging for you to have full-time protection as well."

"Josh, I don't need—"

"Yes, you do."

Zac recognized that tone. It was his younger brother when nothing would change his mind. "Why?"

"Because I mean for us both to do very well out of all this misery. Some people are bound to be jealous."

"That seems to indicate a plan. Mind telling me exactly what it is?"

"Not at all," Josh said. "We are going to buy as much of Manhattan as we can get our hands on."

❧

"Even Macy's," Rosie O'Toole said, "is beginning to feel the pinch."

"Bad times for everyone," Eileen agreed.

Rosie looked at her friend with some degree of speculation. It was early November and the nip of oncoming winter was definitely in the air. They were in a tea shop on Broadway and Seventeenth Street. Eileen wore a small fur over her dark purple wool suit; a mink appeared to have draped itself around her neck. The creature's mouth gripped its own tail in the effort to keep Eileen Brannigan from feeling a chill. And when she lifted her cup Rosie saw that the customary array of rings yet sparkled on Eileen's fingers. "Some of us," Rosie said, "more than others."

Eileen set the cup back on its saucer without bothering to take a sip. "Are you having difficulties, Rosie. I could help if—"

The offer stung more than its omission might have done. A little wave of spite rolled in from somewhere, and for once Rosie didn't beat it back for fear of rupturing this generally satisfactory friendship. "Oh no, I am managing very well, thank you, Eileen. I have a skill, don't forget. A talent I can always call on. I still see a few select clients who prefer made-to-measure, you know."

"No, I didn't know." Eileen's antennae were quivering. "What sort of clients might they be? Anyone I know?"

"Well . . . Perhaps some as you should know."

Eileen sat back, aware that Rosie was dying to tell her whatever she'd made up her mind to reveal.

"Down on Bowling Green," Rosie said. "That rooming house your nephew-in-law owns . . ."

"The family residence. Yes, what about it, Rosie?"

"The woman in charge is quite good-looking in her way. A statuesque sort. The blond hair's peroxide, of course, but I must say it suits her. Has me make her a gown now and then. Pale rose satin the last one was, and cut so low I had to put in extra stays to make sure it held up."

"I can attest to your being very good at that, Rosie. You always were. I rather doubt the Good Lord has made a bosom too big for you to keep it from spilling out."

Rosie smiled. "That's true, Eileen. I daresay He has not. But in the case of Mrs. Wildwood as she calls herself—"

"And what do you call her? Is she not Mrs. Wildwood?"

"Who can say? When they make themselves out to be a widow, well, it's anyone's guess, isn't it?"

"I suppose it is."

"Francie Wildwood." Rosie spoke the name, then paused to see if there was a reaction. There was not. "Your nephew-in-law has never mentioned her, I take it?"

"He has not."

"I see. Well, according to Mrs. Wildwood, Mr. Turner is specially nice to her. Much nicer than he need be simply because he's her employer."

"And she," Eileen said quietly, "is nice to him in return?"

The other woman nodded and reached for the teapot, taking on the role of hostess though, in the usual manner of these outings, it would be Eileen who called for the check and paid the bill.

Later, sitting and thinking about the information which she knew was probably true, Eileen decided to do nothing about it. It would not, she decided, make Mollie any more inclined to mend things with her husband. Far from it. As for Josh, Eileen thought it quite good of him to choose such a relatively discreet liaison.

17

MOLLIE HAD SURVIVED playing hostess at a second Thanks-giving dinner, thankful that this year as last, she was not required to make Christmas at 1060. It would, she thought, have been more than she could bear. Josh did have two large fir trees delivered; one for the drawing room and one for the help's enjoyment downstairs in the kitchen precincts. Mollie left the decorating of both to Tess, and avoided looking at either lest the shades that lived in her heart materialize with their nonexistent toys and ghostly joy and torment her further.

She had become adept at turning her mind from that which she did not wish to see. Not just the longing she could never entirely sup-press, the reality as well. The occasional whiff of perfume from her husband's clothing, for example. Or the blue box marked Tiffany that was once delivered to the door—she left it on the table in the foyer and it was gone next morning. An error, Joshua said in passing. He would deal with it. Perhaps he did so on one of the many evenings when he did not arrive home until well after midnight.

Mollie asked no questions. Why bother? She knew the answers, and she did not pretend she could expect it to be otherwise.

The new year brought bitter cold but no snow. It had been a not-quite white Christmas, with only the remains of a couple of early December dustings. In January Mollie walked around the bare and brown garden finding it hard to imagine that anything would be green again.

The Gardeners' Chronicle had taught her that most plants could winter over successfully no matter how extreme the weather, if they were insulated from rapid changes in temperature. *Contrary to intuition, snow is therefore the gardener's friend.* Their first winter at 1060 there had been snow from December right through to the middle of April; this winter of 1874, the garden's second, there was only brown earth. Mollie imagined she could see the bare branches of her trees and shrubs and vines shivering in the icy wind, and the cut-back plants in her perennial border shaking with cold.

"Perhaps hay," she said staring out the window of the breakfast room in mid-January.

Breakfast was the single meal they regularly took together, and while Josh might comment on something he read in the paper, it was rare for Mollie to initiate a conversation. The sound of her voice caused him to look up from *The Times*. "What about hay?"

"Can you spare any from the stable?"

"I suppose so. And there's more to be had in the town if necessary. What do you want it for?"

"Tucking in my garden," Mollie said.

Josh shook his head. "I do not understand what—"

"Plants need insulation from the cold," she began. "It's the thawing and freezing at the roots that causes—"

He had given up trying to muster any enthusiasm for the details of horticulture. The results were quite pretty, but the minutiae failed to interest him. "That fellow Edison," he said, returning to the paper. "Says here he's close to inventing a single wire that can carry four messages." Mollie looked blank. "It will revolutionize communication," he added. His wife went back to spooning up her soft-cooked egg. Josh suppressed a sigh. "Take as much hay from the stable as you like."

"Thank you. I shall tell Ollie."

He turned the page of *The Times* and found an announcement, prominently displayed and impossible to miss. The Bethlehem Iron Works in Pittsburgh wished to inform its many customers and the general public that it was now Bethlehem Steel.

Josh read the words a second time. No mistake. And next to that notice, an article saying the name change made perfect sense since these days steel accounted for the company's major output. Mostly for the railroads according to the reporter, but it was thought likely that once the slump ended—and business cycles inevitably end—there might be call for steel to be used in ". . . constructing newer and taller buildings than are currently common in our city."

Mollie had finished eating. She stood up to go.

"Listen to this," Josh said. She paused and turned to him, but her expression lacked any genuine interest. "Never mind," he said. "Go see to your hay."

In the face of the terrible economy that followed the financial panic of September, the kinds of men for whom the Carolina had been designed were fortunate if they were still working. They were not inclined to take on new burdens of heavy debt. Joshua had seen that coming. He was prepared to wait out the slump in terms of new tenants, but not to cope with mass defaults on the leases already in place. "I cannot," he told Zac, "survive empty flats and buildings allowed to go to ruin."

"What do you propose to do?"

"A few things," Josh said.

He'd begun by sending a notice to the residents of every flat. Henceforth they would be able to pay their rent monthly, even weekly if that made budgeting any easier. "I'm dealing with men who live on their salaries. In hard times it's got to be difficult for them to come up with a large quarterly payment." Additionally, he announced he was taking two dollars off the monthly rent of each flat for the next year. The twenty-four dollars of additional debt would be added to the final payment. A loan of sorts, and interest-free.

Inevitably, word of the new arrangements got around. "How come," Ebenezer Tickle demanded, "I didn't get one of them letters you sent?"

Josh didn't mention the fact that Ebenezer could not read. "Why should you have, Mr. Tickle? According to our arrangement you pay no rent for another three and a half years."

"Me and Mrs. Tickle won't be able to stay here," the dwarf said glumly, "if all the other tenants pack up and go back to boarding. Who's going to run the elevator and clean the halls and the lobby and such? Word is, you're going to cut back on the building staff."

"I shall have to do so, Mr. Tickle. But the point of the letter was to prevent a mass exodus from the building. I believe it will be successful and the flats will remain occupied."

"Even so," Tickle said, "seems to me you won't be doing any more building for a time."

They were conducting this conversation in the foundry, where not a single furnace was operating and the repaired Kelly converter hadn't been used since well before the holidays. "That may be so, Mr. Tickle."

"They tell me nobody's hiring down at Novelty. Not over at Globe neither. Nothing doing at any of the ironworks."

"There are few businesses in the city hiring these days," Josh said. "But that's not your worry, is it, Mr. Tickle? You are still being paid your weekly wage."

The dwarf nodded. "I am."

"Well then?"

"How long?" he asked. "I'm a married man. Got responsibilities. I need to know if you're planning to let me go."

"At the moment, no," Josh said. "I plan to keep my original crew intact as long as I can. With any luck, until things are on the uptick again. This is New York City, Mr. Tickle. There is always an uptick."

"But we won't be making steel, will we?"

"Not for the moment," Josh admitted. He had clipped the article about Bethlehem Steel from the paper. It was in his pocket as they spoke.

"Iron and steel," Tickle said, "they're all we know."

"It's a special skill, Mr. Tickle. But it's not the only thing you know. You, for instance, can run the elevator at the St. Nicholas, can you not?"

"I can. Nothing much to it. Keep the cables running smooth and the weight and counterweight in balance, and you go up and down like you mean to. No stops and starts."

"Exactly. And keeping my buildings clean and in good repair, nothing much to that either. But it has to be done."

"You're proposing we do that?" Tickle nodded to the other men, making a pretense of work by cleaning the idle equipment of the foundry. "Me and my cousins and Isaac and Washington and Sampson?"

"Yes. That's exactly what I'm proposing. You'll be the elevator men and maintenance crew for both buildings until things are better. Then we'll see."

The dwarf nodded. "Could be all right. I think the others will agree."

The streets were full of newly made beggars and tramps and half-naked children become urchins overnight. Work or bread was the cry. The response was a demand for patience, and the customary diatribes about the evils of overmuch charity. "I would think so, Mr. Tickle."

"Same pay as before?"

"That's not reasonable. Fifty-three cents an hour for running two elevators and general upkeep . . . I could hang on to the maintenance men I have for considerably less. But they were hired well after you and your crew, so . . ."

Tickle hesitated.

"I'm thinking thirty-five cents an hour, Mr. Tickle. Each man to work a twenty-hour week. What do you say?"

"For the others or for me as well?"

"You're a salary man, Mr. Tickle. Not a wage earner. Let's say twenty-five dollars a week for running the elevator at the St. Nicholas and overseeing the work of the others."

"It's a big drop in pay, Mr. Turner. And I'll be having to go back and forth 'tween the Nicholas and the Carolina at least once a day."

"It's work, Mr. Tickle. When thousands have none."

After a few moments the dwarf nodded. "I'll put it to them. See what they say."

That conversation took place on a Monday morning. By Tuesday the thirteenth of January, outside events pretty much assured Josh getting his way.

A rally had been called in Tompkins Square to show "solidarity with the suffering poor."

The goal was a labor relief bureau to be established by the city and granted a hundred-thousand-dollar fund to alleviate the misery of those who had no work. The idea had been in circulation throughout the long hard autumn and the already difficult start of winter. According to the press, creating such an entity would be capitulating to the thriftless and improvident who were influenced by European socialism.

It was well below freezing that Tuesday morning, but the crowd wasn't daunted by the weather. Wave after wave of men and women without work arrived, bringing their hungry children, filling the park and spilling into the surrounding streets. One man foolishly unfurled the red flag of the Paris Commune. The coppers needed no further reason to weigh in, billies flailing. Chaos followed and the clubbing went on for hours as mounted police charged the crowds, and those on foot chased those fleeing their hooves. An orgy of brutality according to the organizers. The press, however, hostile to the out-of-work, mostly agreed. From the point of view of the mayor and the leaders of the business community, the best thing that could have happened. There would be no more nonsense about labor bureaus and government handouts in New York City.

Whatever he thought of the violence, Josh knew his interests to have been served, same as every other man of property in the city. Unlike most of them, however, he did not believe in rubbing the noses of his employees in their take-it-or-leave-it choices. He let Tickle come to him, and allowed the dwarf to seem to agree rather than capitulate.

"Me and the rest's in agreement," Tickle told him on Thursday. "Thirty-five cents an hour and twenty hours a week. Until things get better. Your word that you'll go back to the old contract once we're making steel again."

"You have it," Josh said, putting out his hand. "The old contract when we're again making steel."

Tickle eyed him. Rather as if he thought it had been a mite too easy. "Here or any place else," he said, nodding his head to include the old slave market turned foundry.

Josh agreed as how that was correct and they shook hands on the bargain.

Zac was once again impressed with Joshua's business acumen. "So you get to hang on to your skilled crew, with considerably less outlay and temporarily doing a different job."

"Maybe not temporary," Josh said.

Zac was surprised. "You think things won't improve?"

"Nothing of the sort. Of course they'll improve. They always do. But that doesn't mean they'll be exactly as they were before."

"What then? Come, my brother the oracle. What do you think it means?"

"The answer for ninety-nine percent of things is, I've no idea. But for me . . . I doubt I'll be making any more steel."

"Why the hell not? You've got us buying lots all over town, and you keep talking about buildings of ten, twelve, and more stories. How can you do that without steel?"

"I didn't say we wouldn't need it, just that we wouldn't make it." He passed the notice about the steelworks in Pittsburgh across Zac's desk. "Take a look at this."

Zac read it quickly. "You're saying you'll be able to buy it cheaper than make it. You think these Bethlehem people are using the Bessemer process?"

"I'm going to go and talk to them, but yes, that's what I think. And if I'm wrong it doesn't matter. They're obviously doing something that allows them to make steel in quantity at a competitive price."

Zac nodded. "You're probably right. And if you can get it by rail from Pittsburgh to Philadelphia, we can bring it up the coast on Devrey ships."

"Which reminds me," Josh said, "have you spoken with Trent Clifford lately?"

"Why in hell would I do that after what he tried to do to you, not to mention that you think he might have been behind what happened to Mollie? Josh surely you don't think—"

"—that you're in league with Clifford? Of course I don't. I just know what a persistent bastard he is. I wondered if he was still trying to get you to take part in his scheme."

"I haven't spoken to him since he tried to close down your foundry. Mind you, I've no doubt, given how bad things are, that his plans are on hold along with those of everyone else."

"Hmm," Josh said.

"Mind telling me what 'hmm' means?"

"Only that my plans are not on hold. Full steam ahead. Devil take the hindmost."

Zac was quiet for a moment, then, "Sounds impressive, Josh, but you're venturing into unexplored territory. Keep in mind what the old sailing charts used to say. Unknown waters, here there be demons."

"Over there, Ollie." Mollie gestured to the Chinese wisteria she had recently planted to climb the north side of the house. It might not get quite enough sun to flower, but if it did it would be so lovely . . . Worth a try.

The boy wheeled his barrow in the direction she indicated, then deposited a quantity of hay at the foot of the wall. "You want me to put it all in this one place?"

Mollie glanced at the leafless stems of the wisteria. They were some two feet long and she had tied them to a wooden trellis when she put the vine in the ground. They were not in the least impressive at the moment, but the drawing of the pale purple blossoms hanging in graceful eddies—racemes she'd learned was the botanist's word for them—had enchanted her. "I believe the wisteria needs all you have there, Ollie. You must bring more hay for the rest." There were still a few sapling trees and young shrubs standing with their feet naked to the cold; though the crescent-shaped perennial border was covered in the thick straw blanket she and Ollie Crump had spread with pitchforks and determination.

"Ain't no more hay," the boy said. "Not if I'm going to have feed for the horses tonight."

"No more? But Mr. Turner said . . . You must go downtown, Ollie. Order a load of hay to be delivered at once. Tell them we must have it today or—" She stopped speaking and looked up. The sky was dark gray and covered in dense cloud. A few flakes were beginning to drift through the air. A few more appeared and then more, swirling around her until she and Ollie were standing in a shower of snowflakes.

Since that terrifying day three years before, she had shuddered with horror every time it began to snow. This time she wanted to laugh with delight. "Shall it last do you think, Ollie? Are the gods of winter playing with us, or are they serious?"

"Not sure about God, Mrs. Turner. Never heard nothin' about him being different in the winter than in the summer. But this looks to be a fair enough snow."

Mollie opened her mouth and stuck out her tongue and tasted an icy prickle. "Go right now, Ollie," she said, but with less urgency than before. "Get as much hay as we need for a month and ride home with the carter."

"Much as we need for the garden, or just for the horses?"

The needles of a small blue-green fir—Abies balsamea—a narrow but clotted evergreen about as tall as she that would someday have sufficient size and substance to mark the turn of a brick path, were already frosted, and there was a coating of white on the hay spread on the perennial border. "Enough feed for the horses only. I do not believe the plantings will require more."

The boy hurried off on his errand. Mollie stayed where she was, watching the garden fill up with snow. Dreaming different dreams from those that had once filled her mind and soothed her heart. But dreams at least. Something. She stretched out both arms and held them open, as if she were welcoming someone. A child.

No, never.

But her embrace was not quite as empty as it had been before.

Book Two

1880—1883

18

THE TELEPHONE WAS attached to the wall beside Josh's desk, a wooden box about a foot square. When he wanted to use it he lifted the earpiece and turned the crank and somehow, in what seemed miraculous even after a year, a man's voice said, "Exchange."

"Please connect me with Mr. Devrey."

There was a long and mostly silent pause, followed by a loud buzzing. Josh took out his watch and observed the movement of the minute hand. When after sixty seconds nothing had happened he jiggled the metal cradle of the earpiece. On the third try a different voice said, "Exchange."

"I was connected previously. I asked for Mr. Devrey but did not reach him."

"You weren't connected to me, mister." The rudeness of the phone men was already legend. "What's the number?"

"I can't remember the number. But I believe you have the list." There were, he knew, some two hundred fifty subscribers. At sixty dollars a month he suspected there might not be many more. "Mr. Zachary Devrey in the Devrey Building on Canal Street."

The phone man grunted. Another pause. Then Zac shouted hello in his ear.

"It's Josh, Zac. Can you hear me?"

"Loud and clear." With that hint of glee that still accompanied every one of these extraordinary communications.

"Are we set for this afternoon?"

"Can't hear you now. Speak up."

"This afternoon," Josh shouted into the funnel-shaped mouthpiece fixed above the crank. "At Sunshine Hill."

"Yes, what about it?"

"Is the auctioneer coming? Are we still on?"

Zac shouted still louder, as if to emphasize the affirmative. "I'm assured he'll be there at three."

"Good. I'll see you then."

Followed by the satisfying click when the connection was broken.

Thirty-two miles in all directions from City Hall; connected by cables buried underground which somehow carried spoken words, not merely Morse code. A marvelous leap of progress that came after Western Union funded Mr. Edison's improvements to Mr. Bell's invention.

Josh hung up the telephone and turned to the window. His office of the moment was on Seventh Avenue and Fifty-Third Street, on the fourth floor of a building that climbed five additional stories above his head and housed fifty-four flats. He'd occupy this one until he rented it, then he'd move on.

Steel-framed buildings remained his unique achievement. His detractors found their straight-up facades entirely too austere to be worth copying. Western Union's "tallest office building in the world" was ten floors, finished four years earlier downtown on Broadway and Dey Streets, but built entirely of masonry. It rose in tiers like a wedding cake, with similar furbelows and flourishes.

Josh cared nothing for his critics. Let them carp about Spartan exteriors unworthy of a great city. He housed people who without him would not have a private home. And he made a comfortable profit doing it. He no longer, however, made his own steel. The girders came from Pittsburgh by rail and coastal steamer. Caused a lot of dissension within his crew. "We're iron men, not janitors, Mr. Turner," Ebenezer Tickle fumed. "And you gave me your word we'd have our old jobs back at our old pay rate." Josh pointed out that he'd promised they would make his steel if he made it. Not the same thing.

He might not have prevailed had he not been able to put them back to work on construction and raise them a dime an hour. "That's forty-five cents an hour for your men, Mr. Tickle. Time and a half for anything over forty hours as before. And your salary up five dollars a week to thirty. Do we have an agreement?"

"It's six cents an hour less for the others and five dollars a week less for me. Since before the panic."

"It is," Josh admitted. "But economic upheavals of that magnitude have consequences."

The dwarf considered for a moment. "An extra two years rent-free on my lease," he said finally. "And I have to talk to the others 'fore I can say."

"An extra year," Josh said. "Not two. And I'll wait as long as a week for your decision. No longer."

It took three days, then their customary ritual of contract. *Done, Mr. Tickle. Done Mr. Turner.* Accompanied by a handshake.

Now he was considering putting up a new building on Fourth Avenue in the Nineties, something that seemed possible because civilization was marching toward 1060, and had in a few instances even moved beyond it. Why not? He could call the building the Park Avenue Flats. There was no reason not to appropriate the name the street bore in Murray Hill. These days there were plantings down the middle of the avenue uptown as well as down. For the same reason, disguising the venting of an underground train tunnel. Better still, he could call his new project the Park Avenue Apartments, the fashionable word of the moment.

But putting up a building of fifty or more flats in a place where probably no one but he imagined any gentleman would want to live . . . Yes, it was risky, but the thought got his blood going in a way that nothing else did. Particularly on a cold gray day that didn't feel at all like the middle of June. Josh opened the window and leaned out over the street. Below him Seventh Avenue seemed busier, more alive than he remembered it being in some time.

An economic uptick? He thought so, thought he could smell it in the stink of coal dust and hear it in the clattering rumble of the elevated railways.

Boss Tweed had coughed out his lungs and his life in Ludlow Street jail the year before, but his legacy was celebrated in every speck of ash that landed on the heads of pedestrians walking below an el. Building and running what the romantics called trains in the sky—a bit of a stretch for something only forty feet up—not only provided desperate New Yorkers with jobs, the els had at last made it easier for other workers to get to the jobs they already had.

Josh could see the tops of two of the lines from where he stood. The Ninth Avenue went as far as Eighty-First Street, and they were talking about extending it to Harlem in a few years. It was a grubby, workaday conveyance used by laborers employed along the great mercantile corridor that clung to the Hudson River, the mostly Irish dock workers and haulers of freight who manhandled the necessities of life on and off Manhattan Island. If he turned his head to the right, he saw the cheerful green stations and graceful wrought-iron roofs of the Sixth Avenue line. It offered comfortable cars not unlike a Pullman train, and heated, gaslit waiting rooms meant for ladies on their way to the Mile. As well as the very sorts of middling gentlemen who rented his flats.

The el further east on Third Avenue was neither as grimy as the Ninth nor as elegant as the Sixth. It passed through largely residential parts of the city along an avenue lined with four- and five-story tenements, which were barely livable, but a huge improvement on the barracks-like squalor of the rookeries. Josh couldn't see the Third Avenue el from his window, but if he turned to the wall behind him it was carefully drawn on the map for which he'd paid a printing company called Galt & Hoy the outrageous sum of twelve dollars and fifty cents.

Exorbitant, but worth it. Three feet wide by seven feet long, the map showed every street and almost every building in the city. Josh had stuck pins with brightly colored heads in his own property. They formed a satisfying and very private rainbow. Yellow was for the five rooming houses he still owned, green signified his house at 1060 Fourth, and the five red pins indicated his apartment buildings in the East Fifties and Sixties. The one in which he was standing also had a red pin. It was an anomaly both because it was on the West Side—he'd picked up three contiguous lots for a song when the original owner went bankrupt—and because it was not actually pictured on the Galt & Hoy map. He'd built it after their cartographer did his survey. Another curiosity was that both the St. Nicholas and the Carolina were obscured by the draftsman's quixotic notion of showing Lexington Avenue continuing above Forty-Second Street and obliterating them. Josh stuck his red pins in nonetheless. He trusted reality more than the mapmaker's imagination. Hell, the man had chosen to show the Second Avenue el as completed when it had been started only a few months before, and he'd made a major feature of the Brooklyn Bridge. "And God knows if that will ever be finished."

"What's that, sir?" Hamish Fraser sat at a desk on the opposite side of the office, head bent over the accounts, and so quiet Josh had forgotten he was there.

"I was speculating on whether," Josh reached for his topper and cane, "the Brooklyn Bridge will eventually cross the river the way this map has it."

The Scot shook his head. "Och, it dinna' seem likely, Mr. Turner. If a man gets so ill he might die going beneath the thing, what will he suffer from being a hundred and thirty-five feet in the air on top of it? It's some evil sickness coming out of the river. Has to be."

June, Mollie thought, was her garden's moment. At least that's what she thought now when luscious purple and red roses twined among the lacy white blossoms of the clematis, and a drift of late-blooming tulips followed one of the garden's brick paths. The tulips shaded pale peach to deep pink, and shimmered with color despite the unseasonably cool and gray afternoon. Mind you, in a few weeks when the lilies and iris and peonies and hydrangeas of high summer were at their best in the perennial border, she would doubtless think that the perfect time in her private paradise.

Private was a relative term. Most days people of every size and sort stood peering through the bars of the iron fence that surrounded the property. They craned their necks to see around the artfully laid-out corners and curves, and inhaled the scents, and made appreciative sounds of pleasure and amazement at this thing of beauty crafted from an ordinary New York City building lot.

Mollie had little option but to tolerate the gawkers and gazers. Mr. McKim had suggested building a high stone wall, but that would create shadows and shade where she might not want it. Besides, she had long since admitted to herself that she rather enjoyed the attention.

She had become adept at looking toward the fence without seeming to do so, but a covert glance revealed no onlookers today. Instead Mollie saw a shabby van. It had a wooden sign that read DEANGELO BROTHERS hanging on its side and it was heading north on Fourth Avenue, pulled by two horses of the sort usually dismissed as nags.

She went back to her pruning, but when she looked up she saw that the driver had turned his horses onto the vacant ground next to the garden. Presumably he was taking advantage of the opportunity to turn around and head back downtown . . . no, perhaps that was not his intention. He had reined in beside the small gate she'd had cut so Ollie could conveniently carry plant trimmings over to the empty lot for burning. "Delivery," the driver called out. Then he got down on the far side of his rig and busied himself with his horses.

Mollie made her way to the gate. She had no idea who these DeAngelo brothers might be or what they could be delivering, and at closer view the van was not just shabby, it was mud-spattered and dirty and the horses were in need of a good brushing. "Yes, can I help you?"

"You Mrs. Joshua Turner?" The man had moved around to the rear, and he was bending his head over some papers. His trousers, she noted, were torn and patched, he wore no coat, and his shirt was stained with sweat.

"I'm Mrs. Turner, but I'm not expecting a delivery and I've never heard of DeAngelo Brothers. What do you have there?"

He continued to riffle through his papers, as if she were one of a series of customers. "Statue," he said at last, apparently having found the information in his documents.

"What statue?"

"Says here it's Venus."

"Well, if that's what it says, I've no doubt it's true. But I did not order a statue of Venus or any other goddess, and I have no need of one. I'm afraid you'll have to take it back to wherever it came from."

He turned to her. She saw that he wore an eyepatch, and that his face matched the rest of him. He was scruffy and unshaven and as much in need of grooming as his horses.

"According to these papers, Mr. Joshua Turner ordered the statue. Paid two hundred for it as well. So you may as well have it."

"Are you quite sure," Mollie demanded, "your customer is Mr. Joshua Turner of 1060 Fourth Avenue? And that he has requested a statue of Venus to be delivered to our home?"

"That's what it says. Statue of Venus for the flower garden what's on lot number 1062."

"How extraordinary."

"You want to come around back and have a look 'fore I take it off?

It's pretty heavy. Wouldn't want to unload it only to have you tell me to put it back on."

Mollie looked around. Ollie had gone downtown to buy some new tack required for the horses. The other members of the household were women, and they were all inside. "Perhaps I can get you some assistance, but—"

"Sure would like you to take a look yourself first," the man insisted. "See if you want it. I can take it back otherwise."

"Yes, all right. That's sensible." Mollie unlatched the gate and stepped through it. She was now near enough to the man to smell his body odor and a pervasive miasma of alcohol. She tried holding her breath during the few seconds it took him to unlatch the van's rear door. How extraordinary for Joshua to purchase a statue for the garden. Venus of all things. At such a huge cost and without saying a word about it to her. The only explanation she could think of was that her birthday was next month, but she could not remember the last time her husband had bought her a gift to mark the occasion.

"In here," the man said, holding open the door.

The van's interior was in deep shadows, and appeared empty. "I don't see any—"

There was a sense of movement, a whooshing noise that lasted perhaps a second, then darkness as the cosh made contact with her skull and she crumpled.

"Caisson disease," Simon said when Joshua reported Hamish's remark about something evil in the river holding up the building of the Brooklyn Bridge. "There's a doctor named Andy Smith on the project, and that's what he calls it. Comes on after the workers have been some time in caissons below the water."

"Why didn't it show up on the Brooklyn side?"

"They only had to go down forty-some feet to reach bedrock over in Brooklyn. This side of the river they're down nearly seventy and they're still digging through mud. Tell that to your clerk."

"I shall, but I don't think it will convince him. Hamish prefers his evil river spirits."

Simon shrugged. "Even today people don't think of medicine as science." He broke off because a tall and fleshy man with a red nose and a swallowtail coat shiny with age brought his hammer down with a sharp crack on a sort of lectern, on top of a dais erected in the middle of the spacious foyer of the house Nick and Carolina had built in 1845 and named Sunshine Hill.

"Sold for fifty cents," the auctioneer said, and a stranger claimed a box of old and rusty lanterns for which Nick and Carolina's children had no use.

A practical way to dispose of what was left, Josh knew. Necessary. Nonetheless, incredibly painful.

A new Avenue A had been pushed up from Fourteenth Street. The effect was to level the steep driveway and leave the house on a precipice. Both it and the land on which it stood were slated for the wrecking ball. So nothing to do but get rid of the furnishings and personal effects none of them wanted.

"Lot number three," the auctioneer intoned. "Two painted wooden chests. What am I bid, ladies and gentlemen? A dollar to my right. Can I have two? Excellent. Three fifty. Four. Four twenty-five behind you. Nothing more? Sold." The hammer came down and a couple of porters hauled in two iron bedsteads that had been stored in the attic. "Lot number four, ladies and gentlemen."

They had buried Nick in the winter of 1875, on the same day the hand of the huge monument to be called the Statue of Liberty was installed in Madison Square, in a ploy meant to help raise the capital needed to erect the full statue on Bedloe's Island. Josh remembered thinking how much his father would have enjoyed seeing the thing. Not, however, this sad dispersal of the last of his possessions, however old and unloved.

The auctioneer was getting set to bring down the hammer on a carton of children's books. Josh wondered if Simon might be going to bid. He and Rachel had two sons and expected a third child any day. His brother, however, showed no sign of moving. Josh raised his hand.

"Pure drivel," Simon murmured. "I had a look. Not a proper mystery in—"

"Mr. Turner," a boy's voice called from somewhere near the front door. "Mr. Joshua Turner."

"That's me." Someone topped his bid for the books and Josh let them go and pushed through the crowd to where the lad who'd called his name waited. "Yes," quietly, so he wouldn't interrupt the auctioneer's spiel, "I'm Joshua Turner. What do you have for me?"

"This note, sir." The boy held out a small envelope.

There was no name written on the front. Nothing on the back side either. "How am I to know this is meant for—" He broke off because when he raised his head he discovered the messenger had disappeared.

"You cannot," Zac said, "know that Trent Clifford is behind it."

"My gut tells me he is." Josh and both his brothers were in Josh's second-floor study at 1060. The note was the only thing on the desk. WE HAVE YOUR WIFE. YOU WILL BE CONTACTED. "Using a defenseless woman is exactly the sort of thing he would do."

"If it's him," Zac said. "And you've got no proof that it is, what do you think he wants? Look, I can talk to a few people. Find out which of the police is likely to be honest and—"

"No coppers," Josh said firmly, repeating what he'd been saying all along. The unsolved murder of little George Higgins was as fresh in his mind as if it had happened yesterday not six years before. "If you find any that are honest they'll probably be incompetent. And the others are all in Clifford's pocket. I've sent for—"

There was a tap on the door. Frankie Miller opened it, said something to the two men with him, then stepped inside. "Evening, gents. Sorry to hear the bad news, Mr. Turner."

Joshua had sent Ollie Crump to Roach's Tavern with instructions to explain what had happened and bring Miller back to 1060, glad to have something for the lad to do. Since Mollie disappeared Ollie had spent every minute downstairs in the kitchen, cursing himself for not being with his adored mistress when she needed him. Which only sent Tess and Agnes Hannity and Jane into further floods of tears.

"Is that the ransom note?" Miller asked.

Simon handed it over. "The nearest thing," he said. "But there's no demand for ransom."

"Not yet," Miller agreed, reading the terse message. "And nobody saw nothing?"

"No one," Josh said. "My stableboy had gone downtown as he probably told you." Miller nodded. "The rest of the household were all inside. Mrs. Turner was in the garden and no one thought to look for her until well after four when Tess went out to see if she wanted tea. Tess is—"

"Tess o' the Roses," Frankie Miller finished for him. "I remember. From when me and my boys was looking after you, Mr. Turner."

Josh flushed; there was no mistaking the reproach. He had ended the bodyguard arrangements a year before, when the economy became more stable and New York City no longer felt like the Western frontier. He'd kept Miller's men on as security guards in a number of his buildings, but no longer had anyone posted to 1060. Just now, however, he had no time for arguing past decisions. "I'm sure you remember everyone, Mr. Miller. But it's your other contacts that make you valuable just now. We need to find out who's behind this and what he wants."

"My brother thinks Captain Clifford may be involved," Zac said. "There's bad blood between them from way back. I'm sure you remember that as well."

Miller nodded. "Clifford's the one who thought he could shut down the ironworks, I remember."

"There's something else," Simon said. Miller and his brothers looked at him expectantly. "I'm not a detective or anything of the sort, but . . ." He sounded embarrassed.

"But you're the one who has read every mystery story ever written," Josh said. "What are you thinking?"

"The note," Simon said. "It's written in capital letters so presumably we shall gain no knowledge from the handwriting, but it doesn't look to me to be the work of a thug or a lowlife."

He looked apologetically at Miller, but the gunman—who as always looked more like an accountant than what he was—merely nodded. "Why's that, Dr. Turner?"

"The letters are neatly drawn," Simon said. "There are no smudges, no false starts. It looks rather as if an educated person was pretending not to be so."

Miller picked up the note, looked at it again, then replaced it on the desk. "I'll start asking some questions downtown. Let you know as soon as I find out anything."

"That has to be very soon," Joshua said. He was standing and leaning on his cane and his grip on it was white-knuckled. "I cannot imagine," he said softly, "what Mollie must be going through."

She could neither stand nor stretch out, only sit with her back against what felt like a wooden wall, her knees drawn up toward her chest. She was blindfolded and her hands were tied behind her back. Her ankles were also roped together, and her toes were pressed up against the other side of whatever this thing—Mollie thought of it as a cage—actually was.

After a while she realized she could hear street noise. A hubbub of people calling to each other, but in a language she could not identify, and the occasional clop of a horse's hooves and the rumble of wagon wheels over cobbles. Apart from that her only company was her terrible, soul-destroying fear.

She had no real sense of time, only of anguish and cramping pain, but she suspected it was a couple of hours later when the door to her cage was opened a second time. "You need toilet?" the gruff voice asked.

"Yes, oh yes, please." She had been praying she would not soil herself, praying that would not be added to her indignities.

The rope around her ankles was removed and a hand grasped her shoulder and pulled her free. "Stand up."

There was sharp pain as the blood rushed back to her legs, and dizziness from being so quickly yanked to her feet. Mollie fought off both. She had to make the most of any opportunity to improve her situation. To do so she knew she must remain alert.

Her jailer had hold of her arm and was pulling her along. Mollie let him guide her steps, willing herself to get as much information as possible from this time of relative freedom. There was a certain resilience to whatever was underfoot. A carpet perhaps, but her senses rejected that conclusion. She thought herself to be outside. There was a dampness in the air, and the noises of people and traffic did not seem filtered through a window. She was aware of another sound as well. Less familiar. Steady though, a kind of constant drone.

She was distracted by the screech of metal on metal. After a second she recognized it as curtain rings moving across a rod. "Here," the voice said pushing her forward. "There is bucket. Use it."

"My hands," Mollie said, "I can't lift my skirts."

This was greeted with a word she did not understand, though it was clearly a curse. She took that as confirmation of what she'd already supposed, that her jailer was a foreigner. And since the name on the side of the van had been DeAngelo, perhaps she'd been taken by Italians. That's why she couldn't understand what was being said on the street. Everyone was speaking Italian. Most likely she'd been brought downtown to the slum known as Mulberry Bend. Having divined that much despite the conditions of her captivity was a triumph of sorts. It gave her courage. "If you untie my hands," she said quietly, "I swear I won't do anything except what I must to use the bucket."

"If you lie," the voice said, "in your own filth you will sit. As long as it takes."

The words were meant as a warning but they were a promise of an ending; her captors had a purpose other than to make her suffer. That too was information. And given her circumstances the bucket was a luxury beyond price. Even when her hands and feet were once more tied and she was bent in that dreadful position in the cage, Mollie felt something other than despair. It might almost be called hope.

When her jailer came again she was unsure how much time had passed or whether she had slept. Once more she was pulled out of the place they'd left her, and her hands were untied and released from behind her back. "Here. Eat," the gruff voice said. "Hurry."

Coffee and bread. Breakfast, she decided. She was as tightly blindfolded as ever, but she could sense light, and there was a certain early freshness to the air. The street sounds were different as well, busier. So she'd been in this place for what . . . sixteen hours perhaps. She must be careful to keep count. That she decided was critical.

She took as long as she could over the food, but eventually it was gone and her hands were retied. "I come back soon," her jailer said, "take you to the bucket."

The door to the cage was closed after that. The darkness was again complete. Then, very soon, she heard more footsteps. Not those of her jailer. Someone else. They did not come toward her but stopped some distance away.

Should she cry out? If she did, would she gain an ally or merely enrage her captors, perhaps make things worse?

She smelled something. Smoke. Dear God, was someone setting a fire? She would be burned alive. She opened her mouth to scream, but bit back the sound. The constant drone that had been in the background since she was brought here had changed. It was louder, more insistent. A distinct buzz. Bees! Someone kept honeybees nearby. Perhaps she was in a yard behind a house.

She'd read about beekeeping in her gardening books. These days the hives were not made of straw and didn't look like the pictures in the books she'd read as a child. Modern hives were wooden boxes with open slats on the top. When the keeper wanted to check on how much honey had been made he pacified the bees with smoke.

Her theory was instantly confirmed. The droning sound was lower, less angry. She could hear a murmuring voice. The keeper, she decided, was speaking to his creatures, almost crooning to them as if they were pets. So perhaps she could find an ally after all? She opened her mouth again, still unsure, but leaning toward making some kind of sound. Then she heard the footsteps she recognized as those of her jailer and a whispered conversation.

The beekeeper was in league with her captors. Mollie choked back tears of disappointment and, when she realized they were speaking English, strained to hear their words. She could get only fragments. *Not now . . . I told you . . . No matter about the bees . . . What do you think he will do if . . .*

She did not hear anything that told her who "he" was, or what might be the penalty for disobedience, but apparently Mollie Turner was more important than honey.

The next time she was taken to the bucket she identified the faint resilience of the surface she was walking on. It was tar. She was not in a backyard. She was imprisoned on a roof.

Ollie could remember when there'd been eight or ten rookeries and a few shacks in the Sixties and Seventies. Nothing else. Things changed once Mr. Turner put up his tall buildings. Besides, Central Park was finished now, and so was St. Patrick's Cathedral, and the new Seventh Regiment Armory occupied the entire block between Sixty-Sixth and Sixty-Seventh Streets on Fourth Avenue. He'd heard that pretty soon some kind of fancy museum was going to move to Fifth Avenue at Eightieth Street. No place for rookeries in among all that. Most were gone, but three remained in the Seventies.

Ollie knew his way around such places better than Mr. Turner or his brothers, or even Frankie Miller and his gunmen. On Thursday morning, the day after Mrs. Turner was snatched, Ollie began his mission. His intent was to prowl every hall and climb every stair within the dark and cavernous interiors of these worlds that were within the city but entirely outside its laws and customs. "You seen anything? Yesterday afternoon after two and before four? Anything or anyone looked like maybe he didn't belong up here?"

"Don't belong how?"

"I don't know. If I knew I wouldn't be asking you, would I? You want this or not?" Flashing a shiny nickel.

They always told him something. One boyo said he'd seen a big bird flying by with a woman in its beak. Another that a witch on a broomstick had ridden back and forth at ground level, then sailed off into the sky. He knew they were lying just to get some money, but though he reduced the bribe to two cents, Ollie kept on paying. "More where that came from," he kept saying, "but you got to get me something works out to be the truth. How it really was."

Once a couple of boyos tried to rough him up and get money without bothering to lie for it. At fifteen Ollie was still small for his age, but he'd not forgotten the survival skills required in the rookeries. He kicked the largest of his two assailants in the groin. Recently, Mrs. Turner had bought him new work boots. They were made of tough leather with a metal reinforced toe, so the tactic was particularly effective. The boyo he'd kicked howled in pain and doubled over. The other one started coming for him, but backed off when he saw the knife in Ollie's hand. "I don't care two turds about you," Ollie growled, clutching the pruning knife with the lethally curved blade. He'd honed it for an hour before he set off on this venture. "I just want information. Get me something I can use and there's a ten-dollar reward."

He hadn't cleared that with Mr. Turner, hadn't even told him what he planned to do. But if his employer wouldn't pay the reward, Ollie would. It was a week's pay, but it was thanks to Mrs. Turner that his ma and his sisters no longer lived in one of these hellholes. Mrs. Turner sent his ma all the laundry from 1060, and paid her three dollars every week for the washing and ironing. With that and what Ollie gave his ma out of his wage, she and the girls had been able to move to a couple of rooms in a tenement on Third Avenue and Forty-Eighth. There was a bathtub in the kitchen and a stove so they could boil a kettle to get hot water, and they had their own toilet in a tiny little closet beside the front door. The el went right by their fourth-floor windows. His ma didn't like the noise, though his sisters thought it was exciting. Everyone agreed the new place was a palace compared to the rookeries.

He and his family had Mrs. Turner to thank for everything. Ollie wouldn't give up.

"I didn't wish to worry you, Aunt Eileen." Joshua's hand had been forced because it was Thursday afternoon. Every Thursday since they moved uptown Mollie had gone to visit her aunt. He'd been reluctant to leave the command post his study had become, but he could not allow Eileen to get such news from a messenger.

"They can't want anything but money," Josh told Eileen. "Once I pay they will bring her back." He tried to sound confident; Eileen was nonetheless white-faced with shock. He poured a tot of brandy from the ever-full decanter on the table in her sitting room. "Here, drink this. It will help."

She took the glass. "Mollie disappeared yesterday, you say?"

"Yes." The mantel clock showed twenty past two. "As near as we can make it, some twenty-four hours ago exactly."

Eileen tossed back the brandy. When she put the glass down her hand trembled, but her color had improved. "But why . . . Who . . ."

"I don't know, Aunt Eileen. I thought perhaps you might make some inquiries. Among your influential friends."

"Most of them are dead," she said with some bitterness. "Or forgotten they once knew me. Or they're so old they've lost what wits they had." Eileen was fifty-eight. Her hair had turned entirely white but her face was unlined and her mind undiminished. "There is, however, someone who may be useful. I shall speak to him immediately."

"Anyone," Josh said. "Any possible ray of hope. Please, Aunt Eileen."

Eileen was silent for a time. Then, "Go home, Joshua. Whoever has taken Mollie will try to contact you there or at your office. Not here certainly."

"Yes, you're right." He stood up. "You'll do—"

"Whatever I can," she said. "Immediately. You can rely on it."

Half an hour later a hansom cab discharged her at Avenue A and Fifth Street.

The bell above the door tinkled when she opened it, but the pawnshop was empty. "Mr. Ganz," Eileen called. "It's Mrs. Brannigan. I wish to speak with you on a matter of some urgency."

Sol Ganz appeared from the rear. "Ah yes, my dear Mrs. Brannigan. I have been expecting you."

There was no point, Ollie decided, in offering a nickel or a dime to a lady like this. Not even ten dollars. She lived in a splendid new house on Fourth Avenue and Sixty-Ninth Street, and she wore a lace shawl around her shoulders and a dress made of shiny silk, and her white hair was perfectly arranged. But according to the man in the house next door, this old lady sat at the window all the time and watched the street. So she was a good prospect to answer his questions. "Please," Ollie said. "It's real important."

"A lady being taken somewhere against her will. I should think it's important. And you're quite sure she didn't live in one of the rookeries? Those sorts of women might choose to be carried off somewhere by a stranger."

"No ma'am. This lady absolutely didn't choose to go away. She'd never leave her garden. Maybe you seen it. Up on Eighty-Seventh Street."

The woman clapped a hand to her cheek. "Oh, of course. I thought

I'd seen you somewhere before as well. I don't get out much, but my nephew comes sometimes and takes me for a drive. We always go up to see the garden next to 1060 Fourth. I've seen you working there. And your mistress. That lady. My goodness. Who would do such a thing?"

"Nobody knows. Not Mr. Turner—he's her husband—nor nobody. There ain't been no ransom note nor nothing like that. But I thought if somebody seen something, I could maybe tell Mr. Turner and that would help."

The woman pursed her lips and thought for a moment. "I must say . . . This did occur to me as soon as you asked, but I didn't want to get anyone in difficulty without knowing . . . It's such a beautiful garden. Those pink roses that bloom over the fence on the south side—"

"Those are the damask roses," Ollie supplied eagerly, seeing that talk of the garden seemed to produce the effect he was after. "We grow Bourbons and Gallicas as well, but Mrs. Turner had two damasks sent over from England. Tiny little things they was when they came, but now they're doing fine. The damask rose comes from Persia originally. Mrs. Turner told me."

"Persia, my word . . ." The woman had gone back to clutching her shawl with both hands, as if she thought maybe he was going to try and pull it away, and she stared over his shoulder for what seemed a long time. "Yesterday afternoon," she said finally. "It happens there was one delivery van . . . Of course, there are often delivery vans on Fourth Avenue, but this one looked not exactly the sort one sees here. This neighborhood is becoming quite fashionable, you know." And, after Ollie nodded agreement, "At least I'm sure I've never seen this particular van before . . . DeAngelo Brothers. I remember quite clearly. That's what was written on the side."

"Thanks, lady. I'll bring you a bunch of the damask roses soon as ever I can." Ollie turned and began running up the avenue.

❧

There were only three hitching posts outside the St. Nicholas. Josh had balked at more. He said he liked the clean sweep of the pavement, and that anyway Hopkins's stable was right next door and a horse that needed tethering for a short period could be left there. He had, however, no need of the stable when he rode up to the building a few minutes before seven in the evening. All of the hitching posts were available. Josh secured Midnight's reins to the first of them and went into the lobby.

An elderly couple were waiting for the elevator. He joined them, murmuring a greeting and touched the brim of his topper. Moments later the elevator arrived and Ebenezer Tickle opened the doors.

"Good evening, Mr. Tickle."

"Evening, Mr. Turner. We wasn't expecting you."

The couple turned to give him a second look. Josh was always surprised at how well known he had become. It had started a few years back when he built on Seventh Avenue and Pulitzer's *World* published an editorial titled "Housing for the Common Man." The paper mentioned his having lost a leg in the war and made him out to be a hero. He hated it, but there was nothing he could do. "I'd like a word, Mr. Tickle. Perhaps after you take this lady and gentleman to their destination. I'll come along for the ride, if I may."

The dwarf nodded. Somewhat warily Josh thought.

"Fourth floor, please," the man said. The couple went into the elevator. Josh followed. Both men immediately removed their hats. The lady sat down on the red velvet banquette that went around three of the dark mahogany walls of the cabin. The words Otis Safety Elevator were inscribed on a polished brass plaque. They gleamed in the light of four gas sconces. Tickle reached up and grabbed the leather strap that pulled shut the lobby door, then yanked the door across and secured the strap on the opposite side. The inner door, a folding metal grid, slid closed soundlessly on well-greased runners. The dwarf shot a sideways look at Josh and he nodded acknowledgment.

Tickle took hold of the brass handle that operated a large black wheel and spun it a quarter turn. There were a couple of clangs and a hissing sound, then the elevator began slowly to rise. The little man kept his gaze fixed on the indicator high above his head. When it was just past three he eased back on the wheel, bringing it to a full stop when the moving arrow pointed to four. "Here we are," he said, sliding open the metal door and unhooking the leather strap that freed the solid door leading to the hallway. He pulled that open as well and glanced down. The floor of the elevator was precisely level with that of the hallway. He smiled. Sometimes the operator had to play with the crank repeatedly to get that right.

The couple got out. Josh wished them a good evening. Tickle closed both doors. "Visitors," he said. "Their grandson lives in Four A."

"I see. I wasn't expecting you to be running the elevator, Mr. Tickle, but it's just as well. You're the man I came to see."

"Regular man's sick," Tickle said. "I took his shift since it was right here in my own building. Anyways, the elevator stops running at eight. What can I do for you, Mr. Turner?"

"I need a favor, Mr. Tickle."

Josh hadn't seen Mama Jack's Cave since the Tickles' wedding six years before, but nothing had changed. Certainly not Mama Jack, sitting on her throne on a platform suspended above their heads. She acknowledged the arrival of the Tickles and their guest with a nod of her huge head. Tickle nodded back—almost bowed Josh thought—then turned to Josh. "Stay here. Me and Maude, we'll move about, talk to folks. Anybody says they maybe know something, I'll send 'em over to talk to you."

Josh took a seat. The lady with the luxurious beard brought him a tankard of what turned out to be best-quality ale. Five minutes or so went by.

He was conscious of a number of people staring at him openly, particularly after Ebenezer Tickle talked to them. He felt the covert gaze of others against the nape of his neck, but no one approached him with information. Josh had protested the Tickles' plan, said he didn't think he should accompany them to the Cave. "Surely you'd do better on your own. I'm the outsider. Why should they help me?"

"Not such an outsider as all that," Maude had said, nodding at his peg. Her husband added that if he hinted at Trent Clifford being one of the villains, Turner would gain plenty of allies.

Josh could see Ebenezer moving through the room, but Maude seemed to have disappeared. Another dwarf started in Josh's direction, but either he changed his mind or Josh had misread his intent. The dwarf stopped in front of the giant with the trumpet. Big Black Tonio reached down and lifted the man into his arms so they were face-to-face. For a few minutes they spoke earnestly, then Tonio set the dwarf down and he turned and went back the way he'd come.

"Psst. Mr. Turner." Josh looked around.

"Up here, Mr. Turner. Mama Jack's roost."

He glanced up. What the voice had called the roost, Mama Jack's floating platform, had swung into position just above his head. Mama Jack was in the shadows, but he could see Maude standing at the platform's edge and leaning towards him. "Her," she said, pointing somewhere off to Josh's right. "Go with her."

He turned his head and saw the woman whose hands were attached to her elbows. She reached him after a few seconds. "Come with me," she said. "Mama Jack wants to talk with you."

He was bad with heights. Always had been unless he was sitting on a horse. And there didn't seem room on the roost for one more person. Nonetheless, he followed what Barnum had called the "Incredible Armless Lady." *See her use her feet to drink a glass of milk and comb her hair!* She went through a door beside the bar, then up a steep flight of stairs. After which she led him along a narrow stone ledge that circled the tavern some twelve feet in the air. The ledge was no more than two feet wide, and made of dark stone like the walls. Had to be why he'd not noticed it on either of his two previous visits. The Incredible Armless Lady turned back toward him. "You managing? Peg leg and all?"

"I'm managing." He didn't add that he was gritting his teeth and leaning so far into the wall he thought his shoulder might be carving a furrow in the stone.

"Almost there," she said. Then, stepping onto a spot where the ledge was slightly wider, "Come out onto this bit here and wait."

Josh did as she instructed, fighting off nausea, trying to press himself back against the wall. The woman turned, squeezed past as if they were on an ordinary sidewalk, and went back the way they had come After a few seconds he heard a soft grating sound and looked up. A series of cables crisscrossed the ceiling—he could reach up and touch it from where he stood—and Mama Jack's roost was whirring toward him. For a moment he thought he'd be crushed between the woman's great bulk and the stone wall, but the platform halted a few inches from the ledge. "Good evening, Mr. Turner. My sympathies for your ill fortune."

"Good evening, Mama Jack. Thank you for talking to me."

A match flared and she lit a candle in a holder fastened beside her. The flickering light revealed the many chins that obscured her neck, and made her huge head seem to grow out of her shoulders. But in the candle's light her skin was flawless and alabaster pale, and her eyes large and black and long-lashed. She would have been a fine-looking woman without the fearsome burden of her mountains of flesh, and that was somehow the most shocking thing about her. He wondered if she knew she was pretty. "Please," he said, "whatever you know. I'll be extremely grateful. If there's anything—"

"Be on your guard, Mr. Turner. Do not make any rash promises. You have a dwarf couple living in one of your buildings and apparently their fellow residents accept that. I do not think you could rely on that degree of accommodation if you sprinkled a variety of freaks among the other of your flats."

Her quiet voice and her educated speech astonished him more

than her appearance. There was no reason to think only the poor and the ignorant were prey to such misery as hers, but he'd nonetheless made the assumption. "I didn't mean to imply a promise beyond my ability to deliver."

"No, of course you didn't." She waved the apology away with a slight motion of a hand the size of a dinner plate. "Now, I must be direct and return to my post." Mama Jack leaned in, fixing him with her dark stare. "Two of the people involved in this affair are not strangers to you. One is a pawnbroker, a Jew named Solomon Ganz. The other is an attorney. A Mr. Jeremy Duggan. You must be very careful with both, though one profits from your downfall and the other from your ascendance."

"Who told you such things? How can you possibly know—"

Mama Jack tugged on a cable attached to one of the arms of her chair. The platform whirred off across the ceiling. Josh was left standing alone in the semidarkness.

19

THE NOTE HAD been pushed under the front door some time during the evening. Tess saw it first and sat in the front hall with it clasped in her hand until Josh returned from Mama Jack's Cave.

"From them what's got her? It is, ain't it, Mr. Turner?"

"Yes, Tess. It is."

"Is she all right?" Holding an already sodden handkerchief to swollen eyes.

"They say she is. We can only pray they're telling the truth. Get Ollie, Tess. Hurry." Cursing meanwhile the fact that he and Zac had telephones only in their offices.

"Well," Zac said, "at least now we know what the villains are after."

"I've been thinking," Josh said. "I've one suitcase left in the clock-works. It's only half full, but that's a hundred thousand." He'd left it in place all these years. His fund of last resort, insurance of a sort.

"You think they'll take cash rather than the lots?"

Josh was standing beside the window of his study looking north across the garden. It was nearly midnight. A bright sliver of moon illumined a patch of white petals that had drifted to the grass, blossoms of the late flowering Roxbury Russet apple. Something he knew only because Mollie had told him. "I'm hoping so," he said. "I can't think Mollie will care much about surviving if I sign away all this. The garden has become her reason for living."

"All the lots you own west side of Fourth Avenue," Zac said, looking at the note that now lay on Josh's desk. "Eighty-Seventh to Ninety-Fifth."

Josh nodded. He'd bought the remainder of his mother's uptown lots from the estate soon after his father died. Goldie had remained in England all these years—some sort of unconventional liaison, her brothers assumed—and she needed cash. The purchase of the additional Fourth Avenue lots had served her purposes and Josh's, and neither Zac nor Simon had objected.

All for this. He glanced down at the ransom note, then out through the window. He'd been too long on his feet and his right leg felt like it might give way, still he stared out at what Mollie had spent five years creating, the child that comforted her childless sorrow. A cloud covered the moon and the garden seemed to be disappearing before his eyes. "They're specific," he said. "We have to give them that."

Zac was scratching something on a pad. "What's your reckoning? Is forty thousand for each lot fair market value?"

"At the moment it is." Josh's voice was heavy with something close to despair. "They're going up every day. But even at the present rate . . . That's three hundred and twenty thousand, isn't it?"

"Look," Zac said quietly, "I've nothing remaining in the clock-works, but I can raise about a hundred and fifty thousand in cash fairly quickly. A day or two perhaps."

"Cunard," Josh said, knowing the passenger line had for some time been trying to buy a couple of the Devrey piers.

"Probably."

Zac had been struggling to keep the Devrey assets whole for years.

Now, because of Josh, Zac's defenses were about to be breached. And whatever was happening to Mollie, that was his fault as well. "Damn! Damn! Damn!" It was a litany of impotent rage and frustration. "The bastard knew exactly what to ask for and when to do it. In good times I could sell something else to raise the cash. With the market as it is . . . It could take weeks."

"What bastard?" Zac asked. "Clifford?"

"I think so, but . . . I'm not sure, Zac. I can't be." His good leg was about to collapse. Josh hobbled to where he could catch hold of one corner of the desk and swung himself into his chair. "I've told you about Mama Jack's Cave?"

"You've told me."

"I was there earlier and according to the woman who owns the place, Mama Jack, there are two others to be—"

The door burst open. Ollie was red-faced and panting. "Mr. Turner, sorry sir. But I found out something. Important. Maybe. I mean . . ."

"Come in, Ollie. Sit down. I thought you'd gone to bed. Zac, would you mind . . ." Nodding to the pitcher of water on a table across the room.

"Haven't been to bed, sir," Ollie said, gasping out the words between noisy breaths. "I went back to the rookeries. Found a boyo down on Seventy-Eighth said he'd been sick and that's why I didn't see him yesterday." Zac brought Ollie a glass of water and he stopped speaking only long enough to gulp it down. "This boyo, he says he saw the DeAngelo wagon as well. That's what he called it, Mr. Turner. Said it was a beat-up old thing. More like a wagon than a proper van. But it had a sign hanging off the side said DeAngelo and—"

The brothers exchanged looks. "Well done, Ollie," Zac said. "Was that what you wanted to tell us?"

Ollie shook his head. "No, sir. That's not it. It's about the driver. The boyo said the fellow driving the van was wearing an eyepatch." Ollie turned to Josh. "I know lots of men do, but it's something, ain't it? It might help us get her back, mightn't it, Mr. Turner?"

It was the morning of the third full day of her captivity.

The wind had shifted and today she fancied the bees were more active. Buzzing loudly and, she thought, flying closer to her cage. Perhaps they were somehow aware of her sharing the rooftop with them. A bit later, when she was taken for her first visit to the bucket, she felt sunlight warm on her skin and realized that was what had stirred up the bees. It was the first time in a week there had been a break in the clouds. As for her, she might have enjoyed the warmth were she not so distracted by the pain in her feet and legs.

"Hey! You no fall down!" Her jailer grabbed her arm as Mollie stumbled.

"I can't help it. You are keeping me in such a cramped—"

"No talk. You no talk."

She was half-shoved and half-carried the rest of the way, then she heard the sound of the curtain being pushed aside and her hands were untied. "Here. One foot like this. The other here." In what had become an established routine, she was set into position straddling the bucket, then—in a gesture for which she supposed she should be grateful— she heard the sound of the curtain being pulled closed.

Her hands were numb and swollen, but she could still use them to lift her skirts. Her feet were in much worse condition. The boots she'd been wearing in the garden when she was abducted were old and well worn and usually comfortable. Now they were so tight she knew her feet must be swollen as well. Perhaps she should ask to take them off. No, she would be even more helpless if she were barefoot. She leaned forward to lift her skirts and— Oh!

Her blindfold slipped down to the bridge of her nose.

Mollie caught her breath.

She had kept her word not to touch the thing because the thought of being denied the privilege of the bucket was intolerable. But now, without her having done a thing, she had been given the gift of sight.

"You done in there?"

"Not yet."

"Hurry. I got business."

Mollie tipped her head back. She saw a bright blue sky, but it told her nothing she did not already know, that she was being held outside on a rooftop. She looked down. The curtain didn't quite reach the tarred surface. She could see the hem of a black skirt and the scuffed and pointed toes of a woman's boots.

Her guard was not a man but a woman with a gruff voice.

She shivered, but this time with anticipation rather than fear. She was stronger than she'd ever been in her life. Working each day in the garden had made her so. It was conceivable she could overpower another woman.

"You hurry!"

"I am. I'm hurrying." She lifted her skirts with one hand, fumbled the blindfold back into position with the other. It was, she realized, the tension of the knot that had slipped. The guard—the woman as she now knew her to be—had never thought to tighten it. She was unaccustomed to her role, acting on instructions. Another tiny advantage.

She pushed the blindfold back into place, but just the merest bit higher than it had been. She had a sliver of vision beneath one eye. "Almost done," she called, dropping her skirts and yanking the knot tighter so the blindfold would stay as she'd arranged it. "All right. I'm ready."

On the way back to her cage she was able to peek at the bees. They were in two wooden boxes side by side, hived exactly as she'd imagined. Just beyond them, of much greater interest, she spotted a door.

"There ain't no sign nowheres of Trenton Clifford," Frankie Miller said. "My boys have checked every one of his usual hangouts and plenty that ain't usual. He can't be found. You ask me, he ain't in New York. Went back to wherever he's from."

"Back to Virginia. It's possible, Josh." Zac was stretched out in the leather armchair in Josh's study. Like Josh, he looked as if he'd not slept for days. "The Union troops are pulling out and the rebels are ready to pick up the pieces. Plenty of Southerners are going home."

The morning sun was streaming in the windows, already warm enough for Josh to feel a sheen of sweat covering the stubble of beard he'd not yet shaved. He was of no mind to let Clifford off the hook because Rutherford Hayes had declared an end to Reconstruction. "Tony Lupo," he said stubbornly, "works with Clifford. That's his only connection to me and mine. It has to have been Clifford who told him to take Mollie."

"You can't be sure this Lupo is the one who took her," Zac said. It was the third time he'd made the assertion.

"Look," Josh would not be shaken, "we already know Lupo is a chameleon, someone good at playacting. He was a white-collar worker when I first met him, and a wealthy man at that meeting where you saw him being Clifford's foil. Now we find he got himself up to look like the driver of a delivery wagon and—"

"Josh, the only thing we know for certain about those three men is they all wore an eyepatch. There are any number of men in this city who wear an eyepatch. For all I know, hundreds."

"He used the name Anthony Wolfe on two of those occasions," Josh insisted. "That translates to Tony Lupo. And the eyepatch was a common thread. That's unlikely to be a coincidence."

"That's the other thing I got to tell you," Miller said. "I tried to set up a meet with Lupo. Couldn't find him neither. He's gone to ground."

"Does it matter?" Zac was reading the latest ransom note. "You're supposed to hand over the deeds tonight." He glanced at the clock. "In twelve hours. Who you give them to doesn't seem to me the most important element of the transaction. How do you know you're going to get Mollie back safe and sound when you do? That's the question."

"Me and my boys will be there," Miller said. "And I guarantee no one will see us unless we're needed."

Josh grimaced. The instructions called for him to be at Ninety-Fifth and Fourth, the northernmost of the lots he was transferring as Mollie's ransom, at ten p.m. He was to bring the deeds and wait.

"Anything ain't like it should be," Miller said, "we'll jump right in."

And, Josh thought, God alone knew what would happen then.

It was lunchtime, just after noon, when Josh got to the oyster bar near the South Street docks. The place appeared to have changed hands—the sign read CLANCY's, not Hanrihan's as it had previously—but it was pretty much the same inside. Men stood four and five deep at the counter, behind the fortunate front row who occupied the stools. All were slurping oysters and drinking beer, accompanied by loud talk and laughter, and the occasional shout. Josh craned his neck, peering over their heads to the corner where eight years before he'd sat with DuVal Jones. The little table by the window was still there. Jones was not, but despite the crush the two chairs were empty.

He worked his way through the crowd to the bar. "What's your pleasure?" The barman didn't look up, just continued polishing the counter.

Josh ordered a brown ale and half a dozen bluepoints.

"Raw or roasted?"

"Raw." He put down a gold quarter eagle.

The barman raised his head. "Don't cost but a dollar."

"The extra dollar and a half's a bonus. For information. I'm trying to find Mr. DuVal Jones. I was here with him once before and—"

A hand clasped his shoulder and a voice behind him said, "Mr. Jones would like you to join him, sir."

The barman pushed the quarter eagle back in Josh's direction. "You go ahead, sir. I'll bring your food in a minute. Brown ale and half a dozen slick and shinys. On the house, since you're a friend of Mr. Jones."

Josh turned around. DuVal Jones had materialized at the window table and the crush of men had fallen back to open a clear path between them.

The floor was covered in sawdust, nonetheless Josh had to rely on his cane to be sure of not slipping. He was conscious of being watched, but by the time he took his seat the space he'd traversed was once more filled with bodies. "Good afternoon, Mr. Jones. I asked for you at the St. Nicholas and Mrs. Jones said I might find you here."

"Just came over." Jones nodded to the ferry beyond the window. "What can I do for you, Mr. Turner?"

"Does the name Tony Lupo mean anything to you?"

Someone brought a large platter of oysters to the table before he could answer, and crackers and a pot of horseradish, and two old-fashioned pewter tankards of ale. Jones waited until they were again alone before he spoke. "I know the name," he said, "but to my knowledge the gentleman does not have any business on the other side of the river, and I have never made his acquaintance."

"What about Trenton Clifford? Used to be a captain in the rebel army. Has his finger in various schemes here in New York now."

"Trenton Clifford." Jones repeated the name and for a moment Josh thought he was going to say something meaningful. In the end, he simply shook his head. "No, can't say I know anything about him."

Disappointment was a sour taste in his mouth. "Am I to take it," Josh asked, "you are quite sure?"

"Positive." Jones selected a plump bluepoint and tossed it back. "Have some oysters, Mr. Turner. I'll warrant they're the best and freshest in the city."

Josh ate three in quick succession, without accompaniment, tasting their sharp briny edge, and surprised that despite everything he was hungry.

"A man," Jones said softly. "Needs to keep up his strength in times of trouble." He shook his head in a gesture somewhere between sadness and offense. "I disapprove of those who would intrude on the sanctity of marriage, use a man's wife against him . . . If I knew anything at all, Mr. Turner, you could rely on me."

"Apparently," Josh said, "you know a good deal."

"In my business," Jones said, "word gets around."

"That's why I came."

Jones offered another shake of his head. "Nothing to do with Brooklyn, but . . ." He leaned forward, then paused and stood up. "I'll walk you out, Mr. Turner."

Once more a path was opened for them.

Outside, the Manhattan tower of the Brooklyn Bridge loomed above their heads, mirroring the one across the river. Jones led the way deep into its shadow. "A hundred and seventeen feet tall here on land," he said, "and a hundred and thirty-five above the water. So even the tallest mast can pass beneath it." He had his bowler in his hand and he used it to indicate the men working high above the river, on what looked to be a raft of roped-together wooden planks that swayed in the wind. "They tell us," Jones said, "that when it's done it will be stable. And strong enough to drive a carriage over. Hundreds of carriages and even trains. Remarkable, isn't it?"

"It is. But they're using steel cables. A lot stronger than iron." Tamping down his impatience, trying not to concentrate on how fast the hours were ticking away and how little control he seemed to have over everything that was happening. Trying not to concentrate on what Mollie must be feeling. "I don't think we're out here to talk about the Brooklyn Bridge, Mr. Jones. Is there something you want to tell me?"

"I'm making a point, Mr. Turner. About connections, and the fact that sometimes what we think we see," pointing once more to the swaying structure above the river, "is not the reality."

Josh waited. His companion turned to the bustle of the road behind them where workmen were digging into the city's crust, swinging pickaxes in revolving twelve-hour shifts to create an approach ramp as far back as Chatham Street, because that's what was required for this miracle in the sky. Jones put a hand on Josh's arm. "Look just over there." The bowler indicated a horsecar stopped to discharge and board passengers. "Wait till the car has left," Jones said.

Josh waited. When the horsecar moved on he was staring directly at a pawnbroker's shop, identified by the requisite three gold balls.

"Something to think about, Mr. Turner," Jones said.

"Is ready now," the woman said. Mollie heard the scrape of the bucket being moved into position and the swish of the curtain closing. "You hurry. No take too much time." The voice sounded obviously female to her now that she knew the truth. "I got business," the woman said. "No time for waste up here."

Mollie made a wordless sound of acquiescence. Her heart had been pounding in her chest all the while she sweltered in her cage. The change in the weather she'd at first welcomed had many times increased her misery and made her plan seem even more urgent. Now, moments away from actually putting it in practice, she was calm.

"You no take too long," the woman repeated as she tugged the curtain closed. "Hurry."

Mollie lifted her skirts with one hand and yanked the blindfold off with the other. She blinked furiously, willing her eyes to adjust to the return of normal sight. Then, in a voice as normal as she could make it, "I am done."

The woman pulled the curtain open. Mollie had a swift impression of black hair and all-black clothes. She flung herself onto that dark vision, using both hands to shove as hard as she could, widening her own stance to secure her balance. The woman lost her footing and fell to the ground.

Mollie ran across the roof, ignoring the stabbing pain in her legs. She looked back over her shoulder. The creature in black was scrambling to her feet and uttering a string of Italian curses. Mollie expected her jailer to shout for assistance, from the beekeeper perhaps, instead she seemed to deliberately keep her voice low. No time to worry about that now. Speed, Mollie had told herself when she made her plan. Run as fast as you can, however much it hurts. Speed and surprise are your only weapons. She knew that success depended on getting to the door before the woman caught up to her. And that—dear God in heaven let it be so—the door must be unlocked.

"You come back. Bitch! I get you and I kill you!"

In English. As if she thought Mollie would obey if she understood.

"After this you sit all day and all night. No food. No bucket."

She was level with the beehives and the door was maybe a yard away. A hand grabbed her skirt from behind. "I got you, bitch!" An arm around her waist. Incredibly strong. Mollie jammed both elbows back behind her and made contact with soft flesh and hard bone. There was a whooshing sound, like letting the air out of a balloon, then a thud.

Still not a shout, instead a kind of breathless whisper of rage. Mollie lurched forward. A hand clutched at the hem of her skirt. She reached out and pushed the nearest beehive. She was off balance and couldn't get much force into the gesture, but the thing tottered and half fell against the hive beside it. A swarm of angry, buzzing bees rose up and filled the air, forming a cloud around her head. Mollie bent one arm across her face to protect her eyes and pulled forward again. She heard the ripping sound as her dress tore free. She willed herself to disregard the stings and fumbled around the top of the hive. A frame heavy with honey came free in her hand and she held on to it despite the furious attack of the enraged bees. She half turned and saw her jailer getting to her knees and reaching out to grab her again. Mollie brought the frame crashing down over the woman's head. Honey dripped down her hair and her face, and the bees swarmed in her direction. In seconds Mollie could no longer see the other woman's head, only the yellow and black bodies of the bees. She hurled herself forward and grabbed the handle of the door.

It turned. The relief—this had always been the thing she couldn't know—was almost too much. The calm she'd mustered deserted her and heart pounding she raced down the narrow stairs.

The stairwell was dark and the place smelled of things she could not recognize, but which were not unpleasant. Mollie went down one flight and then another. Despite everything she'd heard and read about the crowded condition of the tenements, she neither saw nor heard another human being. The house seemed entirely empty. On the first floor the door at the end of the hall was open and she could see pots boiling on what looked like a modern stove, all polished black iron and gleaming cream-color enamel. *You hurry. I got business.* The woman probably wanted to tend to her cooking. The only other door in the hall was closed, but she heard the soft drone of voices speaking on the other side. English she realized. She didn't care. Nothing mattered except getting away. She had to will herself not to run, only creep to the front door.

There was no stoop. As soon as she pushed open the door she was standing on a street bathed in sunshine and filled with bustling activity. A man was selling tomatoes off the top of a pair of overturned ash cans directly in front of her. The road behind him was lined with pushcarts. The sidewalk was thick with people. Most jostled past her, seeing nothing and caring less. One, a woman carrying a bag made of mattress ticking, stopped to confront her. "*Pane,*" the woman said, pulling a round loaf of bread from her bag and waving it under Mollie's nose. "Bread. Good. *Del giorno. Fresca.* Five cents only." Mollie was hungry, but she had no money. She pushed past the woman, terrified lest someone appear from the house behind her and she be dragged back into captivity. She knew if that happened she would find no allies in this crowd. They would turn away because their survival depended on seeing as little as possible.

There was a break in the crowd and she could see a sign across the road that said BAYARD STREET SALOON. She was where she'd thought herself to be, in Mulberry Bend. She turned left because her instincts told her that was the way north. She'd have run except the throng of people made it impossible.

"Excuse me," she kept murmuring as she struggled through the crowd. "I'm sorry. Excuse me." No one paid any attention. There was a horse just ahead of her and it was harnessed to a hansom cab pulled up to the curb. That seemed miraculous in this neighborhood. Mollie pushed and shoved her way toward it. Finally, near enough to where she thought she could be heard, she called out, "You, cabby. Over here." And when the driver looked in her direction, "Can you take me please?"

She was level with the cab by then and the man peered down from his perch, grinning a mostly toothless grin. "Well now, can't say as I'd refuse if my time was my own, miss. Though looks like you been busy enough for so early in the day. Sorry, sweetness, I'm waitin' for the fellow already hired me."

Mollie put a hand to her head. Her hair was hanging loose. And she knew her dress to be torn and filthy. She made no apology for her appearance. "I am Mrs. Joshua Turner," making her voice calm and her tone as authoritative as if she were speaking from the security of her own home. "I will pay you fifty dollars if you take me to 1060 Fourth Avenue immediately."

The driver stared at her, obviously beginning to doubt his original assumption. "Show me the money," he said finally. "You don't sound like a doxy, but you don't look like you got no fifty dollars neither."

She started to respond, then saw him looking over her head in the direction from which she'd come. She had run out of time. Mollie reached for the door of the cab and hauled herself up and inside.

"Hey! I didn't agree to—"

"A hundred dollars," she said, slamming the cab door closed and shoving down the front window so she could talk to the driver. "But only if you get me out of here right now."

The driver made up his mind and cracked his whip over the horse's rump. They set off at a pace that scattered everything in their path. Mollie ignored flying fruit and vegetables and the clatter of over-turned tin cans and peddlers' carts, and peered out the window as they passed the house from which she'd just escaped. It was red brick, three stories tall and two windows wide, and there was a white granite lintel above each closely curtained window. She saw laundry hanging from the windows of buildings either side, but there was none in the house where she'd been held. And no number on the door. No matter, she knew she'd recognize it again if she saw it. More important, she re-alized with a profound sense of shock that she knew the man standing in the doorway staring after her.

"Mrs. Turner! It's you, ain't it?" Ollie flung open the garden gate and ran toward the hansom. "Mr. Turner! Come quick, it's Mrs. Turner. She's home!"

Two of Frankie Miller's men appeared out of nowhere and flanked the cabby, grabbing him by either arm. "No!" Mollie was almost too tired to speak but knew she must. "He helped me. He wasn't one of them."

Then Josh was there, lifting her out of the cab, refusing the assis-tance of any of the others milling about in the street.

"I promised the driver a hundred dollars," she murmured. "I'm sorry to have been so extravagant. It did seem required."

"He shall have two hundred," Josh said, "if he'll stay until I have time to talk to him." The cabby nodded eagerly. Josh turned to the stable boy. "Ollie, saddle Midnight and go at once to Dr. Turner. Tell him we need him." Then, remembering that Simon was waiting for his child to be born. "If he can't leave, ask him to send another doc-tor as quickly as possible. After that go to the Devrey Building and get word of what's happened to Mr. Devrey." All the while he was is-suing these instructions the implications of the event—that Mollie had somehow escaped from her captors—were becoming clear in his mind. Josh turned to the gunmen, speaking over Mollie's head, lolling now against his chest. "Send someone to Mrs. Brannigan at fifty-three

University Place. Please say her presence is urgently required at 1060, and I'd be grateful if she would return with you at once and be prepared to remain a few days."

Everyone moved in response to his orders and Josh started for the house, still carrying Mollie, his gait jerky and asymmetrical, but the great strength of his upper body and his urgency prevailing even over gravity.

She was so still he thought she might have fainted, except that as they approached the door she moved one hand to his shoulder.

Josh lowered his head and kissed that available hand. Mollie sighed softly.

Ten minutes later she lay on her bed in exactly the same position as he'd set her down, seeming not to have the strength even to move. He sat beside her and ran a gentle finger over the red and angry-looking bumps on her cheeks and forehead. "What did they do to your face?"

"Nothing. Bee stings. How I escaped . . . I tipped over a hive and . . ."

The words stopped, dammed, he realized, by her total exhaustion. "It's all right. You'll tell me about it later. Tess will be up in a minute with hot water and cloths. And Simon will be here soon. You're a heroine, my dearest Mollie. Quite remarkable. And you are going to be fine. I shall not permit anything else."

She smiled but seconds later the expression changed to a wince of pain. "Josh, my shoes. Do you think you might . . ."

He started at once on the laces, but even after he'd entirely freed them from their hooks he couldn't pull the shoes off. He saw her grimace when he tried. "I need to cut them off. Scissors?" She directed him to the bottom drawer of a small chest and he found her old sewing basket sitting on top of a number of tissue-wrapped parcels. It occurred to him that it had been many years since he'd seen her with a needle in her hand, but the basket yielded a choice of scissors and he picked the pair that looked to be the strongest.

He'd freed her right foot, taking off her stocking as well as her shoe, and was finishing the left when Tess arrived with piles of towels, a bar of lavender soap, and a large pitcher of steaming water. "Good Lord Almighty," she murmured looking at Mollie's swollen and purple foot. "However did she walk on that?"

"I'm guessing she ran on it," Josh said. The second boot came off while he spoke and he removed that stocking as well, revealing a left foot as deeply purple and misshapen as the right.

"The bumps on her face and arms are bee stings, Tess." He was working hard to control his rage and the words came out quiet and subdued, but edged with steel. "I'll have Jane bring up some chamomile and the doctor will be here shortly. Meanwhile, please make her as comfortable as you can."

"Josh, wait . . ." Mollie's voice was a faint and exhausted whisper. "Something I must tell you."

He had to bend over to be sure her heard her. "Yes. What is it? I'm listening."

"I saw him," she murmured. "In the doorway, watching me leave." Then she told him the name.

"I've been working out the connections," Josh said, turning the pad on which he'd been making notes so Eileen, sitting across from his desk, could see what he'd written. Her name was on one side of the paper, that of Solomon Ganz on the other. A dark and purposeful line had been drawn between the two.

Eileen leaned forward and peered at what he'd shown her, then sat back. Her face was deeply flushed, a pink contrast to her white hair. "You cannot think I would be behind any kind of harm coming to Mollie. Or to you, for that matter. Surely you realize—"

"I know you would not consciously harm either of us. Far from it. But Mollie saw him. There's no mistake. Solomon Ganz really is the villain of the piece, and from the first his connection to Mollie and to me has been through you. Did you suggest him as the pawnbroker Mollie should approach?"

Eileen shook her head. "Absolutely not. I have no idea how Mollie chose him, but once she pawned the jewels Mr. Ganz figured out they were mine and paid me a visit. I thought at first he was threatening you and Mollie, but I was wrong. He was after profit. For his grandchildren he said. It was a motive I understood. And there was something else." She hesitated. "Mr. Ganz claimed someone was going to print calumnious lies about you. He said he could prevent it."

"What sorts of lies?"

"That you colluded with the enemy during the war. The time you spent with your sister, on her plantation . . ."

Josh nodded. The pieces were beginning to come together. The article from nine years earlier, *The Times* of November 1871, was still in his desk drawer. *Mr. Theodore Paisley, a naturalized American citizen immigrated from Ireland many years ago, was found dead in his home . . .* "I presume the someone of whom you're speaking was Teddy Paisley," he said. "And Paisley appears to have died shortly after Mr. Ganz paid you a visit."

"Josh, I did not—"

"Of course you didn't. Such an idea never occurred to me. But there is a connection, is there not? Between Ganz and Paisley's murder."

"I have always thought so." Eileen was pale now, but her cheeks were stained with two bright red dots. "I had no choice, Josh. I could not allow you and Mollie to suffer at the hands of someone who wanted only to use you to get at me. All her life I have protected Mollie. I hope you understand."

Josh leaned forward and covered Eileen's hand with his own, then withdrew. "You said Ganz was after profit. How was that to be arranged?"

"I sold him half my interest in the St. Nicholas Corporation. I thought that way he would have a reason to want you to succeed. I was right, Josh. Solomon Ganz has earned thousands from your ventures

these past six years." She glanced at the piece of paper that had started
the conversation, the one that showed a connection between her and
Solomon Ganz and was meant to be related to Mollie's disappearance.
"Why do you think he would be involved in such a terrible scheme?"

"First because two different sources told me so." He would not
try to explain about Mama Jack or DuVal Jones. "More important,
Mollie says she saw Ganz standing in the doorway of the house where
they kept her. Right after she ran away. And the cabby who brought
her home was only on Bayard Street because the fare he'd picked up
on Avenue A asked to be brought there, and required that he wait to
bring him home. Mulberry Bend is, after all, an unlikely place to get
a hansom."

She shook her head, still unwilling to grant his interpretation of
events. "Five years ago. The panic. Mr. Ganz was the one who warned
me it was coming and instructed me to warn you."

"Protecting his investment," Josh said. "Until such time as he decided it should be cashed in. Eight city blocks, Aunt Eileen. On what
many believe destined to be one of the finest avenues in all New York.
A king's ransom. In this case, a queen's. Mr. Ganz, as you pointed out,
is in this for profit."

"Joshua, I cannot believe he—" Eileen stopped speaking, drew a
sharp breath, and pressed a hand to her face. A single tear rolled down
her cheek.

*I have never seen my Auntie Eileen actually cry, Josh. She is the
strongest woman I know.* "You've thought of something, Aunt Eileen?"

"As soon as you told me what had happened." She whispered the
words. "The moment you left. I went to Mr. Ganz. I knew him to be a
man of extraordinary resources and I wished to enlist his aid. But . . ."

"What is it?"

"He knew," Eileen said. "About Mollie having been taken. I've been
so distraught, I never made the connection, but . . . I remember now. I
called out to him as soon as I walked into the shop, and he said, 'Come
in, Mrs. Brannigan. I have been expecting you.'"

20

"SHE'S SLEEPING NOW," Simon said. "I gave her something, so it will be a good long while before she wakes. I gave your Tess a sedative as well, incidentally. Couldn't stop her sobbing otherwise."

"What about Mollie's feet?" Joshua asked, unable to shake the memory of those purple stumps so distorted they looked like hooves.

"Three and a half days should not have done any permanent damage. Mollie is strong, not to mention determined. Do you know how she actually got away? She said something about having knocked over a beehive and covering someone in honey."

"That's more than I know. Why would honey be a weapon?"

"The bees, I expect." Simon was meanwhile repacking his black bag with various pincers and wooden sticks, all the gear modern medicine demanded physicians carry with them to a house call. "Think about it. The little stingers are going to descend en masse wherever their stolen honey lands."

"Good God."

"Quite resourceful, I must say. I think perhaps you'd best not make your wife angry." Simon grinned as he tucked away his syringes and needles, then remembered that Josh and Mollie had been angry at each other for a number of years. "In a manner of speaking, of course. I don't mean she would defy your auth—"

Josh waved away the awkward apology. "It's all right. I know what you meant. She was indeed astonishingly resourceful, as well as brave."

His brother nodded. "I was a bit concerned she might be concussed, but there's no indication of that. She's simply suffering from complete exhaustion. As near as I can make out, they kept her in some kind of wooden rooftop structure where she could neither stand nor stretch out. She was bent into an accordion shape and had to remain so."

Joshua clenched his hands into fists, but said nothing.

"You're looking rather beaten and bent yourself," Simon said. "You need to get some rest." He folded his stethoscope away, but hesitated before closing the bag. "Would you like something to help you sleep?"

"I think you are considering drugging this entire household. No, thank you."

"Fine. But I mean it, Josh. You must get some proper sleep."

"I shall," Joshua promised. He walked Simon to the door, pausing just before he opened it. "Thank you for coming so quickly. I know it wasn't an easy time for you to leave."

"Rachel," Simon said smiling, "does this sort of thing rather on her own. With no help from me and as I understand it, not much from Dr. Thomas. But," checking his watch, "I think I may have a third child about now. So I'll go home and become acquainted."

It was after nine when Josh had his last consultation of the day with Frankie Miller and dragged himself up the stairs. There was a soft glow coming from beneath Mollie's door and it was not closed all the way. He pushed it open and stepped inside. An oil lamp was lit but turned low. Eileen was sitting in a chair beside the bed. A book lay open on her lap but she appeared to be dozing. Josh put a hand on her shoulder. "Go to bed, Aunt Eileen. I'm going to stay with Mollie."

She blinked a few times, then looked up at him. "If you're quite sure . . ."

"I am. Go on."

Mollie lay on the bed, rather as he'd last seen her, but the lacy edge of a pale blue nightdress peeped out from beneath the summer quilt, and her hair had been brushed to its customary dark gleam and curled softly around her face. She seemed to him to look as young as when he'd first seen her, when all that silly talk of spinsterhood at twenty-two had her believing he wouldn't want to marry her. But he'd wanted to very much indeed, and looking at her now he could remember the exhilaration of that extraordinary trip to the Tombs to rescue Eileen. Followed by the bargaining over Mollie, which he'd allowed because it tickled him to see her so discomforted by it—and the way he'd dared to pat her bottom because he knew they were going to be betrothed when the little game he was playing with her aunt was done.

She sighed and shifted her position slightly. Josh watched for a moment, then decided she was as deeply asleep as before. He sat in the chair Eileen had occupied and began taking off his clothes. They felt stuck to him after this long and emotion-filled day. His peg as well. He had to yank it off and the stump itched something fierce when it was finally gone. "Massage, don't scratch," his father had told him early on. "You mustn't tear at the scars or they'll fester. It's loss of circulation that causes the itching. Rub the stump hard to get the blood flow back." After they'd been married for a time Mollie cottoned on to the routine and offered to rub it for him. He'd refused at first. Permitting her to touch what was left of his right leg was in a way a more intimate thing than even their sexual congress, but he'd come to allow her the liberty. Even to celebrate it. Almost always such encounters finished with her yielding to him with that breathless eagerness that had marked their early years together.

Dear God, how had they come to where they were now? At least where they'd been until three days ago when she was snatched away. All unbidden, Josh seemed to see a parade of perhaps irrelevant visions of Mollie throughout the years he'd known her. The prim dark dress of her days as a Macy's employee, the saucy hat she wore the first time he took her coaching, the ruffles and bows of her bridal dress as she stood beside him in Grace Church. Then, with a stab of intense feeling, the memory of how she'd come naked to their marriage bed. A tremendous act of trust and giving, exceeded only by the audacity of the purple chiffon frock she'd worn to Ebenezer Tickle's wedding, designed quite obviously to flaunt his male prowess. *Only one leg, but he can get it over . . .*

He knew he bore the blame for the deed that precipitated all that came after. Mollie lost their child and the possibility of any others because someone—Trenton Clifford, he was more than ever sure— wanted to harm Josh and thus hold Zac hostage. Now Clifford was the reason his wife had been abducted, and subjected to such terror and misery.

Josh did not shrink from those truths, but what of the intervening years, the estrangement that had sometimes bordered on overt hostility? Partly his fault as well, but also partly hers. How much? He was honest enough to know he couldn't say. It was impossible for him to compare his absence of fatherhood to her loss of motherhood. He regretted not having an heir, but he didn't fool himself that meant he knew what she felt.

He was undressed save only the bottom half of his undersuit, and he declined to remove that. Instead, as he was, he slipped silently and easily under the covers and into the bed beside her. Mollie sighed and moved a bit, then settled. Josh propped himself on one elbow and looked at her for a few long moments, seeing the way the veins traced faint blue lines in her temples, and how the pink of her cheeks looked normal now, no longer the feverish flush of earlier in the day. He bent over and kissed her forehead. She sighed again. Josh turned and lowered the wick of the oil lamp, watching the flame die and the glow disappear. Then he put his head down beside that of his wife, sharing her pillow and putting one gentle hand against her breast, and allowed himself to sleep.

"Thirty-two Bayard Street," Miller said, handing Josh a carefully drawn sketch. "As much detail as that daguerreotypist would have gotten. With a lot less chance of making trouble."

The photographer had been Josh's idea. Miller had discouraged him. "Don't matter how many other pictures he takes, walking around with that big box and putting that cloth over his head ... it won't work. Not down in Mulberry Bend, Mr. Turner. I know someone who can do as well with a pad and pencil."

That someone had improbably turned out to be Miller's younger brother. "He's a budding artist for sure," Josh said, examining the drawing. "And you don't think anybody spotted him?"

"Never said that." Miller shook his head. "Course they spotted him. But everyone knows Joe's my brother and nobody bothers him. He's always walking around the city drawing things. Illustrations he calls 'em. Sells 'em to Leslie for his journal, sometimes the newspapers. So no one's likely to have taken any special notice."

Josh was not entirely sure that was accurate. Solomon Ganz, he was beginning to believe, had eyes everywhere. Josh, however, was more focused on getting information than he was in concealing his interest. He knew which house was likely the right one because the driver of the hansom that brought Mollie home had been able to describe it. "No number on the door, sir. And all my fare said was, 'Bayard Street just near Mulberry.' But I'm fairly certain the one where that gentleman went in and Mrs. Turner came out was third from the downtown corner. Looking north, I guess you'd say. Oh, and on the west side of the street. I'm certain of that." Then, by way of a second thought, "Could have been the fourth house from the corner. Sorry, sir. I'm just not sure 'bout that part of it. Never seemed important until after everything happened the way it did. And by then we was driving up Bayard Street as fast as Bessie could take us and I didn't think about nothing else."

"So it's number thirty-two," Josh said, bending over the sketch.

"That's what Joe thinks. But he made a sketch of thirty-four as well." Miller passed over another drawing. "According to Joe, thirty-six sells bread on the ground floor, and nobody said nothing about that. So it's not likely, is it?"

"No, it's not." Mollie would surely have mentioned a bakery. "What about the roofs? Did he manage to see those?"

"Absolutely. Joe's clever. Like I said." Miller reached out and turned over both sketches. "Number thirty-five across the road is five stories, so he climbed up to the roof there. That's what he saw across the street. Roofs of thirty-two and thirty-four. Respectively, like they says."

"No beehives," Josh said, examining the reverse sides of the drawings. "He's quite sure?"

Miller shrugged. "Joe ain't sure he knows what a beehive looks like. Me neither, come to that. I mean . . . here in the city . . . But he says he drew exactly what was there, and you can rely on that, Mr. Turner. Joe wouldn't give you nothing wasn't the straight stuff."

"Yes, I'm sure." It was nonetheless a disappointment. The beehives would have been positive identification simply because Frankie Miller was correct—they were not a commonplace in New York. There was, however, one other likely clue. "This boxy sort of structure here," Josh said, pointing to one of the drawings. "What did he think it was?"

"Hard to say. Some kind of storage place maybe. Some four feet long and three feet tall, Joe reckons. That's about the right size, ain't it? For the way Mrs. Turner was kept, I mean."

"Looks likely," Josh said, flipping the picture over and checking on the identification written below the sketch. "And that would make thirty-two the right house."

Miller nodded.

"I'll try for a bit more confirmation," Josh said. "Meanwhile, you push forward on the other fronts."

Merely the way he let himself into her bedroom was, Mollie thought, different from before. There was a certain ease to it that had been lacking for many years. And when he sent Tess away with a kind word for her attentiveness, his manner expressed that same . . . Recovered intimacy? Yes, perhaps. She felt her cheeks flush.

Josh waited until Tess had left and closed the door behind her, then, "How are you feeling? Your color is high. Not feverish I hope."

"Not a bit feverish." His words, however, turned her a deeper pink. They had not been alone since the early morning when she opened her eyes to find him lying in the bed beside her. His hand was on her bosom and somehow during sleep she had laid her head against his bare chest. As if the past years had never happened.

He'd wakened soon after, kissed her forehead, and hobbled off down the hall.

"Glad to hear you're improving," Josh said now, sitting beside her on the bed.

Mollie was propped up on a number of pillows. She moved her bottom half a bit, giving him more room. The flush traveled down to her bosom, somewhat exposed because the warmth of the day had made her leave the top of her nightdress unbuttoned.

"Are you up to looking at something I'm sure won't be pleasant?" he asked. And when she said she was, "Frankie Miller's brother is an artist, however odd that seems. He went to Bayard Street and did these drawings for me. According to him the number of the house where you were kept has to be either thirty-two or thirty-four, because the only other possibility is thirty-six where the ground floor's occupied by a bakery. You didn't say anything about that."

"I didn't see it. The stairs led down to a hall and there was a kitchen behind me and a closed door on the right, as I told you."

"And you heard voices behind the door?"

"Yes. Mr. Ganz and someone else. Maybe more than one other person. I don't know. My only thought was to get away."

"Indeed. Quite right too. But you're sure it was Ganz you heard?"

Mollie shook her head. "No. Actually, I'm not sure at all. I just assumed so because I saw him in the doorway when we drove past."

"Fair enough." He handed her the two drawings, both with the front facades of the buildings facing up. "Can you say whether either of these is the house where they kept you?"

Her reaction was unhesitating. "This one." She handed him back the drawing of number thirty-two.

Josh flipped the paper over. "This is the roof of that building as viewed from across the road. It's entirely possible the structure we see there is where you were held. But there do not appear to be any bee-hives."

"They are portable," Mollie said. "I expect they've been taken away so as not to be evidence."

Josh nodded. "My thought as well. But I didn't know if it was practical, or even possible. Portable, you say? How do you know so much about bees?"

"My gardening journals and books often discuss them."

"Of course. I should have thought of that." He folded the drawings, tucked them into his pocket, then started to rise.

Mollie put a hand on his arm. "Josh, please. There's something no one will tell me. Not Auntie Eileen or Simon or Tess. Why was I abducted? I presume there was some sort of ransom demanded. What was it?"

"The deeds to some lots I own." He had expected to have to tell her, though perhaps not quite so soon. He had forgotten Mollie's sharp intellect, the way she always went straight to the heart of the matter.

"Which lots? You must tell me, Josh. I have a right to know."

"Yes, you do. All the Fourth Avenue lots my mother bought at the end of the war. Eighty-Seventh to Ninety-Fifth."

"All the Fourth Avenue lots," Mollie said quietly, "including our house and my garden?"

"I'm afraid so. Yes."

"It was the thing he most agonized over," Eileen said. "Signing away your garden to get you back. He thought it would destroy you. In the end, he agreed because he'd no other choice."

"Dear God."

Eileen glanced up from her embroidery. "He wasn't doing it lightly. That's exactly my point. You mustn't think he was being hard-hearted because—"

"Auntie Eileen, what do you imagine Joshua has done for female companionship these past eight years?"

The question could hardly have startled her more. Eileen's jaw dropped. Then she bristled. "Mollie, for such a clever girl as you've always been, you can sometimes be the most extraordinary fool. Given everything you've seen, how I brought you up . . . Surely you didn't think that denying your husband your bed would cause him to take a vow of celibacy."

"What did he do?" Mollie insisted, ignoring her aunt's reproach.

"This is not the time to berate Josh for—"

"Did he have a favorite whorehouse? I know you know. It's exactly the sort of thing you and Rosie O'Toole always find out about and discuss for hours."

"I do not gossip about my prominent nephew-in-law," Eileen insisted, then set her lips in a prim line.

"Rubbish. Not with strangers perhaps. But definitely with Rosie. Tell me. One of the Seven Sisters on Twenty-Fifth Street? I wouldn't think all that pretension was Josh's style, but I've sometimes seen him leaving the house in evening dress and—"

"Not a whorehouse at all." Eileen bent her head over her needlework and avoided looking at her niece. "A regular companion. A lady who works for him. Calls herself a widow, but who's to say?"

"Francie Wildwood," Mollie said. "Of course. I should have worked it out years ago."

"Rosie makes her a gown every once in a while. Mrs. Wildwood has a clattering tongue."

"Do you think Josh has switched all his affection to Francie Wildwood?"

This last spoken in a voice so small and frightened it brought Eileen's head up as sharply as a shout. Perhaps this was not, after all, about Mollie having more about which to feel aggrieved. "I can't say, but if I were to venture a guess . . . The man who was so distraught over his wife's abduction . . . Frankly, my dear, I think it is only the baggage between his legs your husband brings to Mrs. Wildwood. But if you are honest with yourself, you must admit to having packed it for her."

"I know," Mollie whispered, turning her head aside so her aunt would not see her tears.

Josh thought of Mama Jack's warning as he looked at the information Hamish Fraser had brought. He said only, "Excellent, Hamish. You've done well. It must have taken a long time to get all this."

"Och, not so long as all that, Mr. Turner. It's nay the first time I've been to the Registry of Deeds on your behalf."

Josh looked up from the array of papers—each one stamped as a fair copy—Fraser had spread across his desk. The Scot was staring straight ahead, not meeting his employer's gaze. "You devil, Hamish," Josh said with a chuckle. "You've got the registry clerk on our payroll, haven't you? C'mon, own up. You may as well, I'm considerably impressed."

"It comes out of petty cash, Mr. Turner. I dinna hide it. Mrs. Turner has approved the transaction every week."

"Has she now? And how much am I paying the registry clerk?"

"A dollar a week, sir. Fifty-two dollars per annum."

"Well, it's hardly a fortune . . ." Then, as the thought occurred, "The registry clerk's not the only one is he?"

"I canna say he is, Mr. Turner. But I am judicious in my choices. Mrs. Turner has—"

"—approved every expenditure. Yes, I've no doubt." Josh was less annoyed than amused to discover that behind his back Hamish Fraser and Mollie had been paying minor bribes in the name of the St. Nicholas Corporation. Apparently for years. But those emotions were a pinprick compared to his disappointment with the information Hamish brought him today. Because however thorough a job the Scot had done, the facts were not what he wished them to be.

He sent Hamish away, promising he could come back and visit Mollie later when she'd had more time to convalesce, and asked Tess to tell Mrs. Brannigan he wished to see her.

Eileen came at once. These last few days had aged her. There were dark circles under her eyes and her bearing was less erect than he was accustomed to seeing. "Please sit down, Aunt Eileen. I wish to show you what my clerk just brought me. This is the deed to the house where Mollie was held captive."

Eileen looked down, then pressed a hand to her cheek. "I cannot believe it."

"I've been thinking the same," Josh admitted. "But there it is. Quite plain, and I have no reason to doubt it is the true and fair copy it attests to being. The owner of number thirty-two Bayard Street is Jeremy Duggan. Your attorney."

"My attorney as was," Eileen said with some feeling. "I hardly ever use him these days. Not since he deserted me in my hour of need in the Tombs. And you must admit, the owner is not Solomon Ganz. That's what you expected, isn't it?"

"It's what I hoped for," Josh admitted. "It would be straightforward. But . . ." He hesitated, remembering how agitated Eileen had been when they spoke of this before. "Aunt Eileen, as you've just said, this man proved himself disloyal years ago. How did it happen that when you and I formalized our arrangements concerning your part ownership of the St. Nicholas Corporation, you chose Duggan to draw up the papers?"

She had been staring at the deed, now she looked up. "Those were Mr. Ganz's instructions," she admitted. "I was to use the services of Mr. Jeremy Duggan and no other."

Jeremy Duggan, Joshua suspected, was not a villain. Rather a man too weak to resist being used by villains.

"It was an ordinary transaction, Mr. Turner. The sort of thing attorneys regularly do for their clients."

"Indeed, Mr. Duggan. I am, as you're aware, accustomed to buying and selling property and I too use a lawyer to attend to the details. But it is my name that finishes up on the deed. In this instance City Hall says you own not just number thirty-two Bayard Street, but a considerable number of other lots and buildings in the same vicinity."

Josh pulled a second piece of paper from his breast pocket. The first—a copy of the deed to the house where Mollie had been held captive—already lay on Duggan's desk. What he produced now was a list of addresses. He handed them to Duggan. "The deeds of each of those properties has your name on it. The majority are in Mulberry Bend, some in what I believe is nowadays called Chinatown, and yet more in the heart of Five Points. Odd sorts of investments for a man of your sort, sir. I should think simply collecting the rents would be problematic. As in you'd be lucky not to be beaten to a pulp when the attempt was made."

Duggan was studying the list of properties as if he'd never seen it before. "So many," he said softly. "I did not realize . . ."

"You've never totted it up, have you?" Josh asked. "Never done a reckoning of all those accommodating misrepresentations of the facts you've entered into on your client's behalf." He reached out and retrieved both documents, folding them carefully and returning them to their secure place in the inside pocket resting against his heart. "Seems to me the newspapers would find this an interesting story. One more example of our city's terrible corruption. Astonishing how today's reporters have no sense of propriety, no restraint. They can hound a man to despair. Don't you agree, Mr. Duggan?"

"What do you want? I don't have much money. As you've implied, I take no profit from any of those buildings."

"I'm not after money, Duggan. I want to know who is behind all this official lying."

The lawyer shrugged. "Don't use that tone with me. You did not get where you are, Mr. Turner, by sweet purity and innocence. Why the hell do you care, anyway?" He stood up. "I think it's time for you to go."

Josh rose as well, but he did not turn to go. He leaned forward, planting both hands on the other man's desk and putting his face close to Duggan's. "I care because my wife was held captive in thirty-two Bayard Street for almost four days. Under the most appalling conditions. Murderous conditions. That's a rather more serious charge than simple corruption. So if you weren't the one who ordered her abduction, I'd suggest you tell me who did."

Duggan drew back. "Jesus God Almighty."

"He is not, I'm quite sure, behind any of this."

"You've a quick wit, Turner. And a good deal of bravado. Especially for a man who must hobble because he cannot run. But I haven't seen your wife since she was a girl. I certainly had no hand in imprisoning her, nor indeed any reason to wish her ill. From what you said, it sounds like you've retrieved her. Count your blessings and forget about it."

Josh reached out and grabbed the other man's shirtfront. The gesture caused a silver ink pot to be swept off the desk. It landed with a crash. The door flew open. "You need anything, Mr. Turner?" The tone was conversational, with no hint of threat, but Frankie Miller's arm was outstretched and he held a pistol, cocked and ready.

Duggan did not struggle out of Josh's grasp. His calmness with a gun pointed at his head indicated less distance than he'd implied from whatever he was involved in. "I guess, Turner, this proves you're no better than I. Back off. Both of you. You've no idea who you're playing around with, or what kind of a hornet's nest you're stirring up."

"Honeybees," Josh said, "not hornets." He let Duggan go, watching for any reaction. There was none. The lawyer shot his cuffs and brushed his lapels, seeming more concerned with his appearance than with Miller's weapon. "I believe you're telling the truth when you say you had nothing to do with my wife's ordeal," Josh said. "Give me a name and I'll go. You'll hear nothing further about any of this. Otherwise I take the story to the press. After that I warrant you'll have seen your last client."

Duggan glanced from Josh to Frankie Miller and back again. "Why not?" he said with a shrug. "Since it seems we've both learned the value of alliances. The name you're after is Tony Lupo. But I don't think that information is going to do you a whole lot of good."

They had been sitting in the back of the carriage for close on to ten minutes, ever since they left Duggan's office. Josh and Frankie Miller. Not saying a word. Miller had started to speak on at least three occasions; each time Josh waved him silent. Ollie sat at the front of the brougham, awaiting Josh's instructions.

Finally, Josh leaned forward and pushed down the window separating him from the driver. "Take us to Avenue A, Ollie. Between Fifth and Sixth."

The carriage moved into the traffic. Josh leaned against the tufted red leather of the interior bench. "Head to head with Ganz," he murmured. "Otherwise we shall go on playing cat and mouse for God knows how long. I've been the mouse long enough, time to be the cat." It was unclear whether he was speaking to himself or to Miller, but his tone did not invite conversation.

Half an hour later they were trotting south along Avenue A, leaving Tompkins Square Park on their left. A block ahead, on the west side of the street, were the three gold balls that identified Sol Ganz's pawnshop. Josh lowered the front window, preparing to suggest Ollie rein in where they were. Miller touched his arm. "Mr. Turner. Look to the right, sir. Just now."

Josh turned his head. An improbable broad-brimmed hat piled high with silk roses was coming toward him.

Tess was busy putting something into the drawstring bag she carried on her arm. She did not look up and it was apparent she had spotted neither the carriage—there were half a dozen black broughams on any New York block at any given time—nor Ollie nor Frankie Miller. Certainly not her employer. Frankie made a move as if to open the door and jump out. "No!" Josh said quickly. "Stay where you are."

The flow of traffic urged them forward. Josh turned his head so as to keep Tess in view as long as possible. She kept on walking north, concentrated on drawing her bag tight closed, and did not look back.

"That was folding money she was tucking away," Miller said. His face was dark with anger. As if he, personally, had been betrayed.

"I know," Josh said calmly. Then, leaning into the brougham's open front window, "We've got what we came for, Ollie. Take us home."

21

"YOU SHOULD HAVE let me grab her," Miller grumbled half under his breath.

"No," Josh said. They were a few yards from 1060 and it was the first word he'd spoken since they reversed direction on Avenue A. He dropped the brougham's window. "Don't stop by the door, Ollie. Drive straight into the stable."

Ollie did as he'd been told, approaching the stable from the vacant lot beside the garden, then jumping down to open the carriage door.

Josh climbed down first, Miller right behind. Ollie made a move toward the horse. "Just a moment," Josh said. "I want to speak to you both. You must keep this entirely quiet. Particularly here at 1060. I believe I've been handed an advantage in this business, but I'll lose it if either of you says anything to Tess or anyone else about seeing her on Avenue A. Is that clear?"

Miller hesitated for the space of perhaps two short breaths, then nodded. "It's one way to play it. I can see that."

"It's the way I choose to play it." Josh turned to Ollie. "You understand, don't you? I want your promise, Ollie. Not a word to anyone."

The boy looked stricken. "Seeing Tess where we did means she had something to do with Mrs. Turner being snatched," he said. "It does, doesn't it, Mr. Turner?"

"It might," he admitted.

"I can't believe it. Not Tess." The boy's voice was choked with tears.

"I think we should be careful about jumping to conclusions." Josh had wrestled with that same incredulity all during the drive home. "But our first priority is protecting Mrs. Turner. You do see that, don't you Ollie?"

"Sure I do. But Tess . . . I can't believe . . ." The boy turned his face to the garden, visible in all its early summer glory beyond the open stable door.

Josh put a hand on his shoulder. "As natural as you can be with Tess, Ollie. Try really hard. Mrs. Turner's continued safety depends on it."

"Tell me again," Mollie said, "what my ransom was to be."

Josh was reclining in a thickly upholstered chair covered in flowered chintz, resting both his peg and his good leg on the large ottoman in front of it. As far as he could recall this was the first time since the day they moved to 1060 that he and Mollie had actually spent time together in what McKim had designated the family living room on the second floor. "Everything I own on upper Fourth Avenue," he said. "If the town's development goes as I expect, that's a queen's ransom. You might even consider it flattering."

Mollie grimaced.

How would she look if he were ever forced to tell her of Tess's involvement? Considerably worse, he reckoned. Simon had advised that she not be allowed to dwell on what happened. Such thoughts, he'd warned, would pull her spirits down.

Now, five days after the event, there didn't appear to be anything wrong with Mollie's spirits. She was sitting across from him on a smaller chair with a straight back and wooden arms. Josh remembered someone referring to it as a lady's sewing chair. "You never sew anymore," he said. "Not since—" He broke off, appalled that he'd brought up such a painful subject. "I'm sorry."

"It's all right. That's part of the difficulty, isn't it? That we pretend it never happened."

"I suppose it is." He remembered trying to talk to her about their loss, but he didn't remind her of that now.

"I was making a layette," she said, her voice low but calm. "For our child. When that ended as it did, I could see no reason to again take up a needle. Then, when we moved here, the garden gave me something else to think about, to . . . I think the word is to nurture."

He nodded. "I understand. I always have. That's why I was trying so hard to get you back without giving him what he asked."

"Him, I take it, is Mr. Ganz."

"I think so. There's every evidence."

"But no proof."

"None," he admitted.

"Josh, does it matter? Now that I'm home and we have Mr. Miller's men guarding us again, can we just forget the whole wretched incident?"

"I wish I thought that wise, Mollie, but I know it's not. Men such as Ganz and his cohorts—there's a gang leader called Tony Lupo involved, and I'm convinced Trenton Clifford's part of it as well—such men are not likely to give up simply because they've been thwarted. And they have shown themselves capable of pretty much anything."

"Yes, I've been thinking the same," she admitted. "When I'm not indulging in wishful fantasies that the whole affair will simply disappear into the past." Then, after a few seconds' pause when the realities of the dilemma hung heavy between them, "Auntie Eileen tells me Rachel has produced a little girl this time."

"Yes. Simon is quite enchanted to add a daughter to his brood, and—Mollie, you mustn't worry about them. I can see what you're thinking, but I've got Miller's men watching the houses of everyone in the family."

"That can't go on indefinitely. I know it cannot, Josh. Don't forget, I have continued all these years to oversee the bookkeeping of the St. Nicholas Corporation." She ticked off the various households on her fingers. "Simon and Rachel, Zac, Auntie Eileen . . . it's a huge drain on your resources. It cannot continue."

"We're working on getting some proof," Josh said. He did not add that Miller kept reporting no progress.

"But you are not," she said, "using your best resource."

"What's that?"

"Me."

"You? I don't understand." Then, as the thought occurred, "Do you mean you as some sort of bait? Like in one of those stories Simon reads? I will never agree to—"

"Not bait, no. I'm afraid I am not that courageous." She got out of her chair and came to kneel beside his, putting her hand on his leg—the good one—in a gesture that seemed without premeditation. "I saw things, Josh. On Bayard Street in those few minutes after I ran out the door and before the cab drove me away. I heard the street sounds as well, for three days and four nights. Take me downtown again. Let me walk around and look and listen. As long as you and Mr. Miller are at my side every instant I will feel perfectly safe. I may see something, Josh. Or perhaps remember something useful."

Her face was turned up to his, glowing with earnestness in the lamplight. He was conscious of her hand resting on his thigh and he reached down and put his own over it. "You are a brave and wonderful woman, but I will never permit you to be in danger again."

"That's just it, isn't it Josh? Exactly as you said earlier. As long as the men who seek your downfall are free no one who cares for you—for whom you care—can possibly be entirely safe. Bodyguards are useful, but one need only read the New York newspapers to know they are not infallible."

She was, he knew, entirely correct.

"You and Mr. Turner," Miller said. "You walk along arm in arm. And don't worry about nothing, Mrs. Turner. I'm right behind you." It was after four and the sun was dropping, but the July day remained oppressively hot and sticky. Miller, nonetheless, had both hands tucked in his pockets. As if, Mollie thought, he were fighting a chill.

Josh craned his head, scanning the roof lines to his right and left, then realized he could be drawing attention to the presence of Miller's men. Besides, he couldn't see anything. That was their great strength, how well hidden they always were. He focused on the block in front of them, Bayard Street between Mott and Mulberry. Number thirty-two was a few doors up on the left. "Here we go," he murmured. "A genteel couple come to see the sights."

Mollie managed a tight little smile. She was the one who had convinced everyone that was the only excuse they needed. "It's common enough," she'd insisted. "All the ladies' magazines speak of it. Educating oneself by going to actually see the slums. It's supposed to make one more aware of one's blessings." Stupid and ill-advised she thought, but no time for that now. Concentrate on putting one foot in front of the other, on adjusting her gate to Josh's. After all, she'd been adept at doing that since the very first time she saw him, when she ushered him through Mr. Macy's display of ladies' crinolines. The memory eased her.

Mollie twisted her head this way and that. Since she was pretending to be a gawker, she might as well gawk. Much was as she'd seen it ten days previously. Now, as then, pushcarts lined both sides of the road, leaving only a narrow lane for horse-drawn traffic. No incongruous hansom cabs today, only wagons pulled by swaybacked nags. Pedestrians— frequently small children—darted in and out among them.

Josh and Mollie, with Frankie Miller close behind, drew level with number thirty-two. Mollie took a long breath, held it, and deliberately turned her face to the house. It was exactly as she remembered. Curtains drawn shut, no laundry hanging from any window. It was a closed place, rejecting the surrounding bustle, hiding secrets she knew to be cruel and ugly. She concentrated on the space between the front door and the street, the spot where she'd seen Solomon Ganz staring after her. There was no sign of him today, but closer to the curb the display of tomatoes on top of two overturned ash cans was as it had been. Presumably the same vendor was standing beside them hawking his wares, but Mollie hadn't paid enough attention to be sure.

Like most of the peddlers the tomato seller wore no jacket, only a shirt with the sleeves rolled above his elbows, and a cap rather than a hat. The shoppers were mostly women in long, full-skirted dresses of brightly printed fabrics, sometimes with a shawl, frequently covered by an apron, never a hat. Mollie was acutely aware of her dove-gray summer suit—tight-waisted, carefully bustled—her white kid gloves, and her small black hat trimmed with gray and white ribbons.

No one, it seemed, paid them any mind.

They continued up the road. She spotted the bakery Mr. Miller's brother had mentioned. And next to it—

A bee was buzzing around Mollie's head.

She looked up. There was nothing to see, certainly no swarm of bees.

"What is it?" Josh drew her arm closer to his side, holding her tighter to him.

"I don't know. I . . . There's a bee."

"Where?"

"It's gone. I wasn't sure if— Oh."

"What? Mollie, tell me."

She nodded to a crush of people around a wagon where a man was hauling small whole fish out of barrels and throwing them into the crowd. As soon as one was caught another man approached to collect payment. The excitement seemed to be as much about catching the slippery and squirming fish as anything else. Josh watched for a few seconds. Mollie was rigid beside him. "What?" he asked again, conscious that Miller had moved in closer.

She pointed to the ground. "That black skirt," she whispered, "and the boots. It's her."

The woman's upper half was hidden by the throng, but Josh could see the swathe of solid black among the vivid colors and patterns of the women's frocks. "The one you called your jailer?" he asked. "You're sure?"

"Yes, I—"

A fish flew through the air and half a dozen hands shot up to catch it. They all missed. The crowd fell back so as not to trample the prospective dinner, then a number of the women went to their knees, squabbling over whose fish it was to be. The woman in black did not take part in the scramble. Instead she withdrew and turned to the street.

Mollie stared at her from a distance of perhaps six feet. The woman stared back. Her face was red and puffy and one eye was still swollen shut. "You," the woman said. "I kill you." She lunged for Mollie and two of Frankie Miller's men materialized as if from nowhere and flanked her. Mollie saw Miller's hands emerge from his pockets. There was a pistol in each fist.

"There was no one anywhere in the house," Miller said. "And no bees on the roof, but there was ten jars of honey in the kitchen."

"That's a considerable amount of honey," Josh said.

"Yeah, that's what I thought too. And the whole tenement's fixed up like one house. Those places, usually they're jammed full of people. You know how it is. But not number thirty-two," Miller shook his head, "no sir. Only two people live in thirty-two. The woman and her son. He's the one keeps the bees. Looked like he'd cleared out recently."

"Where to?" Josh asked.

"I couldn't get her to say. You and Mrs. Turner, no rough stuff you said."

"And the money wasn't effective?" He'd given Miller two hundred dollars. Said he was to buy the information they needed.

"It worked for everything except where her son was. Guy driving the wagon was Tony Lupo, just like we thought. We even found the DeAngelo Brothers sign down in the cellar. Just a board with the words painted on. Two hooks, so you could hang it anywhere you wanted. Story is, Lupo uses the house for when he wants to have meetings and such like. The woman cooks for him when he's there. So maybe it's Lupo as likes honey."

"The voices my wife heard the day she escaped—"

"According to the woman, Lupo was in that room off the hall, like we thought. And the man with him sounds like it has to have been Sol Ganz the pawnbroker. She described him real exact. Ganz for sure. Thing is, Mr. Turner, the woman says she only ever seen Ganz that one time. Says she went in to bring 'em coffee—that black, bitter stuff the Eye-ties drink—and there was a big pile of money on the table. Stacks of greenbacks. She ain't got no idea how many. Says there was an empty satchel as well. Said it seemed to her like the man, Ganz like I say, he brung the money to buy something."

Close to sunset by the time Josh got to Avenue A. He'd been thinking of what he'd do if the pawnshop was closed, but the door opened as soon as he pushed it, and the customary bell tinkled over his head.

"So, Mr. Turner, I have been expecting you."

"According to Mrs. Brannigan," Josh said, "that's what you said to her when she showed up here soon after my wife was abducted."

Solomon Ganz shrugged. "That is probably correct. I don't recall exactly, but certainly I did expect her."

"Because," Josh said, "Tess had already told you Mollie had disappeared."

"That is definitely correct."

"How long has Tess been spying on my household and reporting to you?"

"A long time, Mr. Turner. And before you tell me how angry that makes you, perhaps we should insure that we are not interrupted and go in the back where we will be more comfortable. I believe we have a good deal to discuss."

Joshua nodded agreement. Ganz locked the door of the pawnshop, then turned and drew aside the curtain that shielded his small back room. "After you, sir."

Nothing had changed since years before when Josh had come to reclaim Eileen Brannigan's jewelry. The back room boasted the same two chairs, and what appeared to be the same oil lamp. A piece of velvet cloth and a jeweler's loupe all sat atop the same ancient table. Nothing else. "Please, sit down," Ganz said. Then, "Listening is my livelihood, Mr. Turner. It is foolish for you to reproach me for it."

"It's called spying," Josh repeated. "And it's detestable. And according to the three balls outside your place of business, you're a licensed pawnbroker. I don't see what that has to do with what you call listening."

"A man can have more than one source of income, Mr. Ganz. You are a builder, a landlord, and sometimes a property seller and a mortgage broker. Why should I be any different?"

Josh gestured to the small dark and incommodious room. "What does it all get you? Mrs. Brannigan tells me she's been paying you half of what she earns from my corporation. And like your arrangement with Tess, she's been doing it for years. But look at this place. What are you doing with your money?"

Ganz shrugged. "I have grandchildren."

"And will they someday be proud to see their grandfather in a court of law accused of gangland activity?"

"Gangland . . . Mr. Turner, I believe you know it was Tony Lupo who abducted your wife. Do you imagine he did so on my orders?"

"What else am I to think? Mollie saw you the day she escaped. Coming out of the house where she'd been held."

"Of course. I remember it well. I had to walk for some blocks before I found another cab. And in that neighborhood." Ganz produced an exaggerated shiver. "It was not pleasant I assure you. But I was glad the hansom I brought to Bayard Street, however unwittingly, helped Mrs. Mollie get away. I hope she is fully recovered from her ordeal."

"How did you know who took her if Lupo doesn't work for you?"

"New York City, Mr. Turner, is a strumpet who whispers her tales in the ears of whoever will listen. I have many sources. I have no intention of telling you who or what they are."

"As it happens, Mr. Ganz, I have heard that before." It's what Trenton Clifford had said when Josh sat with him in the bar of the Grand Union Hotel, that first time he'd seen the bastard since Belle Isle. "Years ago," he said.

"Yes. I know that as well. Captain Clifford gave you a useful tip on that occasion, no? Without him you'd never have found the dwarf, or been able to make steel to get you started on what has become the mighty St. Nicholas Corporation. It was all quite marvelous, wouldn't you say?"

"Who in hell's name are you? A magician with a crystal ball? How do you know about Clifford?"

Ganz shook his head. "If we keep going over the same thing we will still be sitting here tomorrow and nothing will be changed. You and yours will still be in danger. But not, I assure you, from me. I wish you no ill, Mr. Turner. I am quite satisfied with my share of your endeavors, and even without a crystal ball I will predict that as long as you act wisely now, you will be even more successful in the future."

Josh forced down his frustration and tried a different approach. "If it's true that Lupo does not work for you, what were you doing on Bayard Street?"

"That's easy to answer. I went there to pay a ransom. Three hundred thousand dollars. It was all I could come up with on such relatively short notice. I hoped it would be enough to get Lupo to back off his demand for your Fourth Avenue property. And before you ask, I knew about that demand because Mrs. Brannigan told me. Everything I know, Mr. Turner, eventually it turns out to be because someone told me. That's not so mysterious, is it?"

"I'm not sure. But that aside, you're asking me to believe you were going to pay such an extraordinary sum to secure my wife's freedom?"

Ganz nodded. "I am because it's true. After that, Mr. Turner, after I brought her back to you, I intended to produce a note of indebtedness. Half your profits every year until the sum was repaid. With interest, of course."

"And you thought I would sign such a note?"

"I knew you would sign it, Mr. Turner."

"How could you know that?"

"Because you are a man of honor. And despite how bad things have been between you and Mrs. Mollie since she had the misfortune of losing her child—don't look so astonished, remember Tess o' the Roses—you were devastated after her abduction. You are devoted to your wife, Mr. Turner, why else have you not taken what might be called a lover, simply allowed yourself the occasional company of a not-so-young lady on Bowling Green? For a man of means like yourself, a man in your prime notwithstanding your missing appendage, there are many more enticing prospects in this city. You, however, avoid them in favor of a . . . I mean no disrespect to the lady when I say a mere convenience." Ganz stood up. "Now, you will sit here and I will excuse myself for a moment and go upstairs and get us some refreshment. Don't leave, Mr. Turner. We have much more to discuss."

Ten minutes later he returned, carrying a tray with two glasses of steaming tea and a pot of cherry jam. Ganz stirred a spoonful of the jam into both glasses and handed one to Josh. "Despite the incongruity, hot tea is cooling on a hot day, Mr. Turner. The natives of India and other tropical climes have known that for many years."

"Have you been to such exotic places, Mr. Ganz? Or did someone tell you about them?"

Ganz chuckled. "You are being humorous, and even though it's at my expense, I take it as a good sign, Mr. Turner. I believe it means we will be able to conclude our business without acrimony. As to your question, I have never been to India, but I read many books and journals and newspapers. They too provide some of my information. Some comforts, however, are better experienced than read about." He opened a drawer and produced a small silver flask. "Schnapps, Mr. Turner. I have been in New York since I was five years old and I consider myself a proud American, but I learned about schnapps from my Austrian father and grandfather. I have found nothing better." Ganz leaned forward and poured a generous splash of the potent spirit into Josh's tea. "Your health, sir. And that of Mrs. Mollie."

Josh hesitated.

"So," Ganz said softly, "you still don't wish to drink with me. Why is that?"

"Half my profit," Josh said. "In return for your having righted a terrible and cruel injustice. Once you knew where Mollie could be found you didn't come to me with the information, help me free her. You left her where she was and tried to make money out of her suffering. Is that supposed to make me admire you?"

"Admire is not the word I would choose." Ganz produced another shrug and sipped his tea. "Will it change your opinion," he asked, "if I tell you that after you signed the note I was going to tell you how you could pay me back in two years, perhaps less?"

"Two years. Three hundred thousand dollars plus whatever extortionate interest you assigned. I don't believe that's possible, Mr. Ganz."

"Ah, but I do. And in this instance I am right and you are wrong. Fourth Avenue, Mr. Turner. Exactly what Lupo wanted. Though I don't believe he would have had any idea of how to best capitalize that asset. Much less the means to do so. You, however, have both. Drink your tea, Mr. Turner. Then I will explain."

Josh hesitated a moment more. Finally, he lifted the glass and took a long swallow. The mixture of fiery alcohol and sweet, cherry-flavored tea went down easily, then hit his stomach with a powerful jolt. "Schnapps," he said. "I don't believe I've ever had it before."

"It is made with cherries. The French, I believe, make a similar drink they call *eau-de-vie*. But we are not considering the art of distilling, Mr. Turner. Rather the art of making large sums of money from land that is at present mostly a dumping ground for rubbish. Both material and human." Ganz leaned forward. "Develop each of the eight Fourth Avenue blocks you own, young man. Put up more of your tall buildings in which people are stacked one on top of the other. What are they calling them these days? Apartment houses?" And when Josh nodded, "But do not make the mistake of thinking you will lease these particular apartments to the same sort of men who rent units in the other of your buildings. Indeed, you finally have competition for that segment of the market."

"The Manhattan," Josh said. "The Rhinelanders' new building on Eighty-Sixth Street and Third Avenue."

"Precisely. Six stories containing thirty-one small units meant for the common man. The Rhinelanders have a nose for making money," Ganz added. "When Mr. William Rhinelander died a few years back his estate was worth fifty million dollars." Then, seeing Josh's expression, the pawnbroker leaned forward. "It took them nearly two centuries to become so wealthy. You, Mr. Turner are fortunate to have been born into our golden age. You can do the same and much more quickly. I assure you, upper Fourth Avenue is going to become one of the most sought after areas in the city. And thanks to your dear mother's foresight, you own a good-sized piece of it."

"It will be Park Avenue," Josh said quietly. "As it's called down in Murray Hill."

Ganz nodded. "So you too have been listening to what the city tells us. Park Avenue. I agree. Just now, however, that avenue is poised to go in the same direction as Fifth and perhaps Madison, become a street where rich men build mansions and occupy them. Grander than your own house, perhaps, but essentially the same, a residence for a single family. If, however, you put up your apartment houses, only this time designed to appeal to a clientele who can afford a luxurious home if perhaps not a millionaire's mansion, I believe—no, I know—you will shape the character of the neighborhood. And become astonishingly rich by doing so. You will not sell eighty lots, Mr. Turner, as Lupo would have done, and walk away having pocketed an excellent one-time windfall. You will, in effect, lease eight hundred lots over that very same stretch of land, and continue to profit from them month after month, year after year. And you will, Mr. Turner, become as rich as Croesus as a result. May I offer you more schnapps?"

Joshua's heart was thudding. Ganz had described exactly the idea that had been percolating in the back of his own mind; set aside after Mollie's abduction, but not forgotten. He held out his glass and the pawnbroker dolloped in a splash of spirit, doctoring his own glass in the same fashion. "I have been thinking," Josh said, "of something of the sort. But it will take more than two years, I assure you. Each building will finance the next. The real profits won't come until after they are all completed."

"That is a sensible way to do business," Ganz said. "On this occasion it will not be necessary."

The schnapps was spreading warmth and a kind of calm. He had a glimmer of where the conversation was going, but his voice showed none of his excitement. "Why is that, Mr. Ganz?"

"Because," Ganz said softly, "I will finance the cost of initial construction with a loan of a million dollars." He waited for the space of perhaps two heartbeats, just long enough for the incredible number to sink in. Then, "At nine percent interest, compounded quarterly. Plus a modest share in the ownership of these remarkable new apartment houses on Park Avenue. Say fifteen percent. In addition, of course, to my share of Mrs. Brannigan's profits. I intended to make this suggestion before Mrs. Mollie was taken away. When she was, I simply altered my plan in what I believed to be the best interest of all of us."

Josh sat quite still for a few moments. Nine percent. He might be able to get a better rate if he trolled among the moneymen. But as it stood he'd be dealing with the devil he knew, and that devil apparently shared his belief in the future of the upper East Side. "Interest-only payments," he said, "until construction is complete. And I can assure you that will take three years, not two."

Ganz nodded. "A fair proposal, Mr. Turner. I accept."

Josh raised his glass of tea with cherry jam and schnapps. "Your good health, Mr. Ganz."

"Thank you, Mr. Turner. And yours."

The men finished their drinks. Josh rose to go, then paused. "One thing more if I may." The old man waited. "That three hundred thousand in cash money you brought to Tony Lupo's lair, am I to believe he just let you walk out the door with it?"

"You are, Mr. Turner. Because that is what happened. Mr. Lupo, as you may have guessed, is not your ordinary criminal. He too listens. We have learned to respect each other's areas of expertise."

"You work with him, that's what you're telling me."

"Sometimes. Not on this occasion. I was very disturbed when I learned he was behind taking Mrs. Mollie. I told him so."

"And after that, and after he'd lost his captive, he still allowed you to leave with your satchel full of money?"

"He did," Ganz said. "There will be other occasions for mutual profit. Mr. Lupo knows that and so do I."

"Will you tell me where Lupo is now?"

"Of course not. You didn't really expect me to, did you?"

"No, I suppose not. What about Tess? Do you mean to go on paying her to spy on us?"

Ganz smiled.

They were in the second-floor living room. Mollie sat beside Josh, head bent over a pad on her lap, her pencil flying over the page. "Nine percent compounded quarterly on such an enormous debt is an astonishing amount of interest," she said.

"I know. And if I did not, the fact that you felt you had to check your calculations on paper would have convinced me. And remember, it's thanks to you and your bees I'm not in hock to Mr. Ganz for an additional three hundred thousand plus half my profits." He clapped a dramatic hand to his brow in imitation of a music-hall performer. "Ruined! And all for love!"

Mollie's head shot up. The last word hung in the air between them. He had gone to great lengths to rescue her, but she was his wife and he was a man with a keen sense of doing what was right. Might he still love her? She could not find the courage to probe the question. "Don't tease," she said gravely. "You are putting an enormous amount at risk if you agree to Mr. Ganz's plan."

"I know that as well. But the gains will be phenomenal."

"If you succeed."

"I intend to succeed. I'm not breaking new ground remember. There are already at least ten buildings offering luxury flats of twelve rooms or more." He began ticking them off on his fingers. "The Gramercy across from Gramercy Park, the Rembrandt on West Fifty-Seventh, the Central Park Apartments on Seventh Avenue."

"Yes. And I read there's to be something called the Chelsea on Twenty-Third Street. But they're all in the fashionable parts of the town," Mollie said. "Not up here in the wilderness." She got up and went to the window. There was no view of her garden from where she stood, only of the street. "Park Avenue in the Eighties and Nineties," she said. "A grand thoroughfare lined with elaborate buildings of flats meant for the upper, upper classes. It's hard to imagine."

"Not the upper, upper. Not the Belmonts and Vanderbilts and Morgans. They will continue to build their Fifth Avenue mansions with solid gold banisters. Do you remember? We talked about them the day I took you coaching."

"I remember. Will you have Mr. McKim design these new buildings?"

"Perhaps. He's just taken a new partner. A Mr. Stanford White.

Charles tells me they are occupied with country houses at present, but I think I might intrigue him."

Mollie didn't say anything more. Josh reached for her pad and pencil. "May I?" And when she nodded. "Here's what I have in mind. Say I begin with Eighty-Eighth Street and work north." He made a rough sketch showing eight and ten story buildings as far as Ninety-Fourth Street. "I'm thinking four buildings per block. Perhaps on average thirty apartments in each—they have to be much larger than what I've built before remember. Some might be two floors. Even three. Nonetheless, this scheme should yield some seven hundred units."

"Didn't Mr. Ganz say eight hundred?"

He'd repeated much of what the pawnbroker had said word for word, a way to convince himself the extraordinary conversation had actually taken place. Not everything certainly. No mention of Tess, or what she said when Joshua confronted her. *I thought I was doing you good, Mr. Turner. Mr. Ganz said he was sort of watching over the pair of you.* Doing good and getting paid for it. Hell, much of the world operated on worse delusions. *Will you tell Mrs. Turner? I wouldn't want her to think what she went through was my fault.* Accompanied by floods of tears. He'd promised to say nothing. And he had not dismissed her. Because in fact nothing Tess had done had brought any harm upon them, and Mollie had been through quite enough on his behalf. "Ganz," he said now, "is to be an investor. He shan't dictate what I build or how."

She was looking at his drawing. Josh was no artist, much less an architect, and the lines were crooked and the rows of different size squares that indicated doors and windows uneven. It was nonetheless quite clear what he intended. "You haven't shown anything on our block."

"I won't put up anything right next to your garden, Mollie. It would steal the sun and light. I'm thinking perhaps we could eventually put a small park between the garden and the corner."

"No," she said. "That's foolish and impractical."

"Mollie, I—"

"Let me finish. I had a good deal of time to think in that cage on the roof, Josh. I spent some of it considering what is important and what is not. I love my garden, but it is not the most important thing in my life. I was very foolish to allow it to become so. Since you will be assuming such an enormous indebtedness, you must plan to incorporate our block into your new Park Avenue. It makes good economic sense. Now, if you will excuse me, I am suddenly very tired."

She was nonetheless awake when he tapped on the door.

"May I come in, Mollie?"

She understood the nature of the question. "I have," she said quietly, "been hoping you would wish to do so."

The bedside lamp was turned low and he could see her dark hair and her neck, and the slope of her pale, cream-colored shoulders above the coverlet. It was obvious she was not wearing a nightdress.

Josh had already taken off his clothes and unhitched his peg. He took off his dressing gown and slid in beside her. "Put out the lamp," Mollie whispered.

"Must I? I have always loved to look at you."

"I'm older now," she said. "Not the way I was."

He chuckled. "You don't seem old to me." Nonetheless, he did as she asked. The curtains, however, were not drawn and the room was flooded with the light of a full moon. That had been true that first night on Grand Street as well.

He touched her tentatively at first, exploring the angle of her hip and the sweep of her rib cage and the gentle roundness of her breast as if the shape of her were unfamiliar to him. She was thinner than he remembered. Harder somehow.

"I'm afraid the outdoor work has toughened me," Mollie whispered. "Are you disappointed?" She had lavished herself head to toe with unguents since the night Auntie Eileen told her about Francie

Wildwood. At least with the lamp out he could not see how brown her hands and even her forearms had become during the spring planting season.

"Not a bit disappointed," he said. And he was not.

Her flesh was supple to his touch, and when he bent to kiss her she opened her lips and when he caressed her she sighed with pleasure. And when finally he took her she rose to meet him, and her shudders of delight were proof she had allowed him total possession of not just her body but her spirit. "We are new made," he whispered.

22

JOSH WAS FINDING the stiff white bow tie particularly awkward. The light perhaps. It was dimmer than usual, and provided only by lamps. Even with their wicks turned up, large portions of the expansive master suite were dark. The wall sconces nonetheless remained unlit.

Mollie stepped up and tied the tie, patting it into place with satisfaction. "There, you look splendid, quite regal in your tailcoat. As well you should. It's your night of triumph."

He took her hands and spread them in that way he had when he wished to get a good look at what she was wearing. Her gown of what he'd been told to call magnolia-colored satin—ivory with a hint of rose—had a deep décolletage and a slim skirt embroidered with seed pearls. A long train descended from two bouffant puffs that were the latest iteration of the bustle. The oil lamps caused creamy pink shadows to play across her bare shoulders, and he loved the way she had drawn her hair back and allowed the curls to fall free behind. The diamond earrings she wore had been his gift the previous December, presented not at Christmas but on the eve of the new year. *This is to be our year, my love. You shall wear these to a great celebration, I promise.*

May of 1883 now, and the occasion he promised had arrived and she was wearing the diamond earrings for the first time.

"Exquisite," Josh said, completing his examination of her outfit and releasing her hands. "As for it being my night, no one will notice me. They shall all be looking at you."

Mollie drew on long white kid gloves that reached almost to the ruched cap sleeves of her gown, then added the final touch, a wide gold-and-diamond bracelet Josh had given her to mark the day they moved into the twelve-room apartment on the sixth and seventh floors of 1160 Park Avenue. There was a three-story twenty-four room flat above their heads, the "penthouse," as modern usage had it. Josh had intended it for them, but Mollie had been miserable at the thought, insisting they should rattle around with no purpose. Eventually he realized the amount of space simply reminded her of the family she did not have and gave in. The penthouse, offered for three hundred and seventy-five dollars a month, remained empty. Perhaps after tonight that would no longer be the case.

"Ready?" he asked.

"Ready."

"You go ahead then. I'll join you after I put out the lamps."

"Jane and Tess will see to the lamps, Josh."

"Not tonight," he said. "Tonight I shall do it myself. Besides, I've already sent them outside." Still she hesitated. "What?" he asked.

"I shall miss this gentle play of light and shadow," she admitted. Then, seeing his face, "But I know it will be wonderful to uniformly glow in the dark as we shall."

"And," he said, "gas lighting is impure, dirty, and unhygienic, and gas jets take all the oxygen from a room and give ladies headaches."

Mollie smiled. "How odd. I would have sworn I read that in *The Times*. I believe the reporter said he'd been given the information by a

Mr. Joshua Turner of the St. Nicholas Corporation. Which gentleman was building a remarkable series of apartment buildings on the upper reach of Fourth . . . no, Park Avenue, all of which were to be electrified."

Josh's laugh trailed after her as she made her way downstairs to the front door, the apartment darkening behind her.

There had been electric light on a number of New York streets and avenues for a few years. Ornamental, twenty-foot-tall cast-iron posts topped with arc lights that lay down a broad carpet of brilliance were distributed one per block and fed current passed along overhead wires. The lighting was a great success, credited with reducing crime and contributing to the population's general health and well-being, but such an arrangement could not be used inside a man's home. Josh hadn't considered electrifying his new buildings until in the autumn of 1880, soon after construction began, Thomas Edison gave a banquet, at which he demonstrated his latest invention, the incandescent bulb.

Josh was at the banquet—he and Mollie were seated across from Sarah Bernhardt—and certainly he was impressed. So were the politicians. The city gave Edison permission to install underground wires in the square mile from Wall Street to Canal. "He's bought two old ramshackle buildings on Pearl Street near the fish market," Josh told Hamish Fraser a few weeks later. "They're to house the steam generators that will produce his power."

"Och, I heard as much, Mr. Turner. I'm told the asking price for the pair was a hundred and fifty-five thousand. It's a fearful amount o' dollars to light the inside o' a man's wee house when gaslights do the job."

Josh thought the same. Until he saw Edison's own four-story brownstone illumined by a hundred of the small and softly glowing globes. Two nights later he brought Mollie to see it as well. They arrived on the corner of Fourteenth Street and Fifth Avenue in deep dusk and stood waiting with all the others who came every night to exclaim at the sight. When at last the dark descended and—as if a fairy had waved a wand—the house came instantly alight, there was a universal gasp of wonder. "Convinced?" Josh asked. "Despite the expense?"

"I didn't think it would be so different from gas lighting," she admitted. "But it's steadier and infinitely brighter. With a whiter light. Undoubtedly an amenity the rich will soon expect. You must do it, Josh. Regardless of the cost. If an ordinary brownstone can look like this, your stretch of buildings will be . . . magical. That's the correct word, I'm sure."

Magic came at a price.

Josh's crew dug the necessary trenches the length of his eight blocks. Edison's men came after them and laid massive copper power mains and insulated them with a mix of asphalt, linseed oil, paraffin, and—Mollie shuddered when she heard—beeswax. Wires were fed from the mains to the buildings, buried in the walls, and connected to the lighting sconces originally intended for gas. Finally, a steam generator was installed in the basement of one building on each block. It raised the rent on every apartment something close to fifteen percent. They were snapped up despite that. Wall Street bankers and doctors—not the ordinary sort but the specialists who these days earned fortunes—and lawyers with partnerships in the town's most prestigious firms, even a few foreign dignitaries all showed themselves willing to break new ground and live in this isolated stretch of glory. After all, whatever else they were New Yorkers, convinced that wherever they went, the rest of the world would soon follow. The first tenants took occupancy in early '81. Josh supplied an abundance of oil lamps at his expense and guaranteed electric light by Thanksgiving of '83.

He was six months ahead of schedule.

Something to celebrate indeed. And by God, the hordes come to marvel were themselves a sight.

Here as downtown in Murray Hill, the median that ran the length of the avenue had been planted with trees and greenery to mask the vents of the train-tunnel underground. Josh had arranged for a podium—potted greenery and flowers and velvet ropes—as well as chairs on the grass along his entire eight-block stretch, but the crowd had swelled so there was only standing room.

Mollie was waiting for him in the magnificent marble lobby. The liveried doorman as well. That rendition of the old-fashioned concierge—the nosy old biddy guarding the front door—had become one of the things that persuaded the elite to live in apartments rather than private homes. It was like having a butler without having to pay his wage.

"Go on," Josh told the doorman. "You'll have a better view of things outside. Mrs. Turner and I will be along straightaway." The man touched his peaked cap and left. Josh drew Mollie to the tall window beside the mahogany double doors. A sea of people waited. The men's ties and boiled shirtfronts gleamed white in the encroaching dark and the ladies' jewels sparkled. "Well," he murmured, "what do you think?"

"You know what I think. It's quite wonderful, and no more than you deserve, and—oh, Josh, look! The Tickles and the others. In the front row about half a block south. They look quite splendid."

Indeed they did. Maude Pattycake wore a blue gown and a tiara. Both Ebenezer and Israel McCoy were in evening dress, as were Obadiah and Henry and Washington and Sampson who stood just behind them. The finery had been made to measure and cost him a fair bit, but looking at them now Josh smiled. "Quite splendid," he echoed.

He felt suspended in time, as if he could stand where he was indefinitely, but after a few seconds Mollie nudged him forward. "Everyone's waiting, dearest."

He drew a deep breath, tucked his cane under one arm—he would cross the damned street under his own power, by God—and swung open the door. Mollie stepped outside. He took his place beside her and she linked her arm in his.

The dais had been erected directly in front of 1160 for the same reason Josh and Mollie lived there. The building was on the south-west corner of Ninety-Second Street, and as such pretty much in the middle of the St. Nicholas stretch. Josh and Mollie didn't have far to go, but they walked to the platform on a wave of thunderous applause, and thanks to having Mollie on his arm Josh didn't need his cane to climb the steps. Instead he could stretch out his right hand to greet the visiting dignitaries.

Mollie had questioned the wisdom of planning the occasion for the day after the formal opening of the Brooklyn Bridge. Josh thought they could profit from some of the grandeur of that occasion. "From what I hear," she'd said, still resisting, "most of the carry-on will be in Brooklyn. New Yorkers are predicted to be largely unfazed."

"Only according to the business community. They prefer not to acknowledge what they see as a great siphon that will suck their cus-tom across the river. The press will nonetheless use barrels of ink to describe it. The president is coming after all, and Governor Cleveland of course. I'll invite both to our electrification ceremony. You never know, they might come."

Chester Arthur had sent congratulations and regrets—they ar-rived on very impressive Executive Mansion stationery—but Grover Cleveland had turned up. And Thomas Edison, of course. Josh sus-pected him to be the real reason for the crowd. Two-thirds of the units were sold; nonetheless the number of people was far too great to be only the owners and their guests and staffs. Such a turnout had to be down to Edison. In money-crazed, kick-up-your-heels New York an inventor and entrepreneur of his stature figured to be a much greater draw than any politician.

He delivered Mollie to her seat. The applause died away. Time for the speeches. Josh went first, offered his few words of welcome, and presented the mayor. He rambled on for a while, then introduced the governor. Cleveland's speech was bound to go on for a time; word was he had a run at the presidency in mind. That gave Josh an opportunity to examine that part of the assembly he could see. Eileen was seated

to the left of the dais, with Zac and Simon and the rest of the family.
She was nodding off. At sixty-one, that was to be expected. Solomon
Ganz was also in that section of the audience. Josh had invited him to
a place on the dais, but Ganz had refused. "Thank you, Mr. Turner, but
I prefer a less obvious position." Josh had no idea how old the pawn-
broker was, but he seemed wide awake and listening to every word.
Everything I know, Mr. Turner, is usually because someone has told me.
He wondered what the governor might be saying that he was missing,
and how Sol Ganz might turn whatever it was to profit.

More applause. Cleveland was finished. It was time for Josh to introduce Edison. He started to get to his feet. A hand touched his arm
from behind. "Gentleman gave me this," Ollie Crump said quietly.
"Claims he lives in one of your other buildings."

Josh palmed the note and slipped it into his pocket. Ollie was a
likely messenger. Josh had set him up as manager of a public stable
on Third and Ninety-second. *A lot of our residents will own carriages,
Ollie. It's ready-made custom. Do a good job and I'll sell you the place
in a few years.*

"He said to tell you it was urgent, Mr. Turner."

Josh nodded, but still did not read the note. Whatever the urgency
might be, it would have to wait. Everything about this event had been
meticulously planned, and timing was the key to all else. He took his
watch from his vest pocket. Three minutes to eight. They'd guessed
correctly about how long the governor would speak. He didn't need
to draw things out and neither would Edison. He rose and stepped to
the podium.

"Distinguished guests, ladies and gentlemen, as those of you who
live in the St. Nicholas buildings know, we have been planning for
this night since our great upper Park Avenue adventure began. And
let me explain for any who don't already know, the reason you see no
flicker of light in the windows across the way is because the oil lamps
in every apartment have been deliberately extinguished, and by design every sconce connected to electric power and provided with that

miracle of our time, an incandescent bulb. Tonight, also by design, those sconces have been switched on and every curtain left undrawn. We await only the golden touch of the remarkable wizard we all know as Mr. Thomas Edison." He turned to where Edison waited, hand on a large brass lever.

It was, Joshua knew, an utter fake.

The power would be switched on in the basements of the buildings containing the generators at precisely eight o'clock. Another glance at his watch. Josh raised his hand. "Count with me, ladies and gentlemen, and Mr. Edison will light up our world when, in ten seconds' time, the clocks of New York strike the hour. Ten, nine, eight, seven, six . . ."

"One!" the crowd at last shouted in a roar of anticipation. Edison threw his sham switch.

The St. Nicholas apartments on Park Avenue came to life in a blaze of shining light that must, Josh thought, resemble the first day of creation.

They had tested the systems repeatedly in each building and on every floor, but until this moment no one could have predicted with certainty that what Mollie called his P. T. Barnum imitation would work.

It had. Josh achieved his moment of triumph. But what he saw in the dazzling illumination of the world he had brought into being was the face of DuVal Jones, standing at the foot of the dais with his back to the newly lighted buildings. He was staring up at Josh with a look of concentration stunning in its intensity.

"You're absolutely certain the house is occupied by Trenton Clifford?" Josh asked. "I heard he'd returned to the South years ago."

"He did," DuVal Jones said. "Now he's come back."

"How do you know?"

"I know."

Even if it were true, it was hard to see why Jones had come to him with the information. "Your glass is empty, Mr. Jones. I'll get you another brandy, shall I?"

They'd not come upstairs to his study until after the electrification celebration finally ended, and that had taken a number of hours. Delmonico's had catered a full banquet served in the lobby of each building, then swept it all away to make room for six-piece orchestras that provided music for dancing. He and Mollie had shown up at every party. Nearly two in the morning now. Josh's household had retired, Mollie included. He took Jones's snifter as well as his own and made his way to the decanter on the table across the room. The task gave him a few moments to think.

Jones meanwhile was staring up at the elaborate rococo-style plaster ceiling, all swirls and seashells. "Outdid yourself here, didn't you, Mr. Turner? Nothing like this down on Sixty-Third Street."

"Meant for a different market, Mr. Jones. What about this house in Brooklyn where you say Clifford's living. Is it luxurious? I'm told there are some fine homes on what they call the heights."

Jones took the brandy and murmured his thanks. Josh sat down across from him. "Clifford's place," Jones said, "is at the foot of Water Street. Closer to the docks than to the respectable folk of the Heights. Tucked away you might say. Hard to find. And it's in the bridge's shadow these days. On the other hand, luxury's a matter of debate, isn't it? Take my flat, for instance. Stack it against a rooming house on Bowling Green and that's one thing. Compare it to what you've done up here . . ." He shrugged and tossed back his drink. The clock on Josh's desk chimed twice and cherubs spun around under a glass dome. "Like you say, Mr. Turner, it's late. I'd best be going."

"I'm sorry I couldn't speak with you earlier. But—"

"You had important guests to attend to. I understand." Jones stood up.

Josh did the same, but paused before showing the other man out. "Look, do you want to tell me why you've come to report this? And why tonight of all times?"

"I thought you should know. Because of Lupo and your interest in him a few years ago. You mentioned Trenton Clifford's name back then as well."

"And you said you knew nothing about him."

"Did I, Mr. Turner? Well, as I said, all that was three years past. I know enough now to know that Lupo and Clifford have some . . . mutual concerns you might call them. They tend to impinge on yours."

"What the hell does that mean?"

Jones appeared to hesitate, then he shrugged. Josh was hard put to decide if it was genuine reluctance or an instance of Thomas Edison's brass lever.

"The dwarf who got killed in your house," Jones said, "back when you were living on Grand Street . . . No reason not to tell you now. Lupo's the one did the big job. The one-eyed bastard himself, not anyone he sent. The way I hear it, that was a personal favor for Clifford. Because Captain Clifford, he wasn't too happy with the thought the little fellow might tell you things."

"About what had happened in Kentucky years before," Josh said, speaking his thoughts aloud as they occurred. "About Clifford being the one who told Bessemer how to make steel with a converter. Kelly's process. Which mattered because that was back when Clifford thought I was violating Bessemer's patent, and he could use that to shut me down."

Jones shrugged. "You'd know more about the details than I, Mr. Turner. But as I said, things that impinge on your interest."

Josh couldn't let it go, even though the Park Avenue project was a reality and it was hard to see how Clifford and Lupo could hurt him. But given the attempts made in the past, and the way they'd both caused Mollie so much grief, he was more than wary. He summoned Frankie Miller on Saturday afternoon. "Put your ear to the ground, Mr. Miller. And listen very closely. There's no reason I know of for DuVal Jones to give me false information. I want to know whatever you hear about Lupo and whether it's true that Clifford is back in town."

Miller was back in two days. Josh led the way to the library. "Clifford?" he asked as soon as he closed the door.

"A sniff here and there," Miller said. "Someone mentioned he'd been at Kate Meacham's whorehouse. Someone else said they saw him at Delmonico's. But so far no talk of what business brought him back to the city."

"After an absence of what . . . three years?"

"Something like that," Miller agreed. "But that's not your biggest worry at the moment, Mr. Turner. Leastwise I don't think so."

Josh was startled. Frankie Miller didn't normally volunteer that sort of opinion. "What then, Mr. Miller, is my biggest worry?"

"Lupo," the gunman said. "He's taking over the business of collecting garbage from buildings like yours. Claims to be organizing the workers."

"On behalf of the labor movement? Tony Lupo?" Josh couldn't conceal his astonishment.

"That's what he says. What it comes down to . . . he's going from building to building, and each time he winds up with a contract to be the one as takes away their swill. Way I see it, the union organizing's just an excuse. Gets his foot in the door. You ask me, he's planning to put all the other garbagemen out of business, then he'll put the squeeze on the owners of the buildings. Men like yourself. He gets paid extra or the swill won't be collected. How many weeks you think it'll be before the stink will attract every rat in the city? Drive all the tenants out."

"Not many. So, how come I haven't been approached by Mr. Lupo? I own a fair number of buildings in this city, Mr. Miller. How come he's ignoring me."

"That's the thing, Mr. Turner. I don't think he is, I think Lupo left you for last because he knew you'd be the toughest nut to crack."

Josh took a day to think it over, then called Miller back. "There's a piece of the puzzle still doesn't fit. What's the interest of DuVal Jones?"

Miller looked thoughtful. "I can't say for sure, Mr. Turner."

"Try this," Josh said. "What if Lupo is trying to take business from Mr. Jones's employer."

"The mayor of Brooklyn?"

"The man who extorts protection money from the lottery offices, yes," Josh said. "Maybe Lupo is trying to—what do you call it?— muscle in."

"That's very unusual, Mr. Turner. Men like Lupo and the mayor, they usually respect each other's territory. Besides, if DuVal Jones was looking out for his boss's business, he wouldn't come to you for help. I mean no disrespect, sir, but what can you do for him that the mayor's own men can't do better?"

It was a question for which Josh had no answer. "I still think Clifford's the key," he said. "What about the house in Brooklyn supposed to be his?"

"It's nothing much. Right under the bridge these days. And it's empty. I put a man out there right away, but so far he ain't seen Clifford or nobody else."

"Keep watching," Josh said. "My guess is he'll show up." It struck him that the house Frankie Miller described was unlikely to be where Clifford lived. Rather, he suspected, a trysting place.

Monday morning he sent Hamish to the Brooklyn City Hall. "I expect it may take a bit of time, Hamish, given that it's over in Brooklyn, but I need to know whose name is on the deed."

"Och, not so much time as all that, Mr. Turner. Not the way it might have done in the past."

"Before the bridge, you mean? I suppose it will get you across the water faster than the ferry once the novelty wears off, but just now it's so crowded you can't—"

Hamish smiled. "I dinna' mean exactly that, sir."

Josh took a moment, then caught on. "You've got the Brooklyn clerk on our payroll as well?"

"It was Mrs. Turner's idea, sir. A wee notion she had when it began to appear the bridge might after all be finished."

"Thank you, Tess. That's beautifully pressed. Now hang it away. I don't know when I shall wear it next."

"What about that Metropolitan Opera I read about?" Tess carried the magnolia-colored evening dress to the clothes closet Mr. Turner had built right in to each of the bedrooms so no wardrobe was necessary. It was to her one of the most marvelous of the wonders of Park Avenue. "They sing songs where no one understands the words and no one can sing along. But folks get all dressed up to go and listen."

"Yes, they've a new building on Thirty-Ninth and Broadway. It's meant to be quite grand. But I don't think I could convince Mr. Turner to take me to the opera. Perhaps I shall ask Mr. Ganz to be my escort. He's from Germany, isn't he? I believe they enjoy opera in Germany."

"Not Germany, Austria. It's different. Like my third husband, the MacLachlan. He got devilish upset when anyone said England and meant Scotland. That's how Sol Ganz is about mixing up Austria and Germany."

"My word, Tess, I'd no idea you knew so much about Mr. Ganz. And you're as red as Mrs. Hannity's raspberry jam. Here, sit down."

"No need for that." Tess used her apron to fan her flushed face. "It's warm in here, that's all."

"Well, sit down anyway. Tell me how you know Mr. Ganz is from Austria."

"It was his wife, Mrs. Turner. Esther Cohen when I knew her first. She was a milliner ahead of she married Sol Ganz. Made me my hat."

"Did she! Mr. Ganz's wife. He speaks of her with great fondness. How did she die?"

"Consumption. Took her when she was still just a girl. Such a pity. And them never having no children or nothing. I always thought he'd marry again but— What is it, Mrs. Turner? You've gone all over pale. Oh dear, I shouldn't have said . . . I didn't mean to . . ."

"I'm fine, Tess. And thank you for pressing the gown and telling

me about Mrs. Ganz. Now you'd best go back to the kitchen. I'm sure
Mrs. Hannity wants you for something."

Josh's office continued to be a movable feast. For the past month it
had been located in the first of his buildings, in flat Two B in the
St. Nicholas on East Sixty-Third Street. At just before lunchtime Mollie knew there was no guarantee she'd find him there, but it was the
best chance and she took it.

She didn't bother with the elevator, instead climbed the stairs,
knocked on the door, and opened it without waiting for a reply.
"Hamish, is Mr. Turner here. I need—"

"Right here, my dear." Josh appeared in the doorway of one of the
bedrooms. "What is it?" Then, seeing the look of her, "Hamish, perhaps you'd like to go off to lunch."

"Och, I'm away just now, Mr. Turner," tipping his hat to Mollie as
he left.

"Now," Josh said, "sit down and tell me what it is that couldn't wait
until I came home."

"It's about Sol Ganz," she said. "I've discovered the most remarkable thing."

"If it's about Tess, I'm afraid I know."

"You know that Mr. Ganz's wife was the milliner who made Tess's
hat?"

Josh shook his head and cursed himself for jumping to conclusions. "I'm sorry. I'm apparently on the wrong trail. But surely you've
not come here to talk about Tess's hat?"

"Not exactly. But it does have a bearing on the matter. Tess just told
me that Esther Cohen the milliner was her friend, and Esther married
Sol Ganz. But when Mrs. Ganz was still very young the poor thing got
consumption and died. The remarkable part of Tess's story, however, is
that the Ganzes never had any children. And Mr. Ganz never remar-
ried. Do you see?"

"No, forgive me, I do not." Perhaps, Josh thought, because he was concentrating so hard on Clifford and Lupo. "Look, can you just say exactly what it is that's troubling you? I'm not doing well with guessing."

"I don't mean for you to guess. I'm referring to what happened after I was abducted, when you confronted Mr. Ganz. You told me you asked him why he was mixed up with such sordid people as Tony Lupo. Do you remember?"

"I suppose I do. Words to that effect at any rate. As I recall, I pointed out he didn't live in luxury and he said—" Josh broke off, then spoke with conviction. "Ganz said, 'I've got grandchildren.' With one of those dismissive shrugs to which he's prone."

"Exactly. But he has none, Josh. Mrs. Ganz died never having given her husband a child. Tess told me so. Then she got all flustered because I looked shocked. I imagine she thought it was down to her having spoken of childlessness. Of course, that wasn't it. I just realized quite suddenly that Mr. Ganz had lied. Perhaps it isn't important, but it doesn't seem logical, Josh. Why tell an untruth then, at the same moment he was offering you a million-dollar loan and trying to convince you he was a worthy business associate? And why a lie that has so little actual bearing on business?"

"I don't know. About Tess, did you tell her what was in your mind?"

"No, of course not. It's none of her affair. Why would you think—"

He was wondering if Tess would have thought it necessary to immediately run downtown and report the morning's conversation to Ganz, but this didn't seem the time to say so. Josh waved a dismissive hand. "I'll explain later." He would too. Should have told Mollie about Tess and Mr. Ganz years ago, he realized. But it wasn't his first priority now. "I've just remembered your Aunt Eileen telling me Ganz told her the same thing. Something about sometimes bending the law for the sake of his grandchildren."

Josh got up, motioning her to stay where she was, and went into his private office, returning moments later with a paper Mollie at once recognized as a deed. "Hamish got this a couple of days ago. From the Brooklyn City Hall property clerk. Whom you've apparently been bribing for the past year, so he's inclined to give Hamish whatever he asks for without making him wait weeks or months or plow through tons of illegible records."

Mollie showed no remorse. "It's not bribery. Just good business. Auntie Eileen taught me the importance of looking after those who can look after you." He'd handed her the deed, meanwhile, and she was quickly scanning it. "A house on Water Street in Brooklyn. Owned by—"

"Trenton Clifford," Josh finished for her.

"I thought he disappeared years ago. Probably went back to the South you said."

"Yes, around the time you were kidnapped. Frankie Miller couldn't find him anywhere and Zac and I presumed he'd gone back to Virginia since Reconstruction had just ended and there were business opportunities. But the other night, after the electrification ceremony, DuVal Jones came to see me. He lives in this building you may recall."

"One D. Yes, of course. Why did he bother coming all the way uptown to Ninety-Second if he could see you here?"

"I don't know. I'm unsure of any of his motives. But according to Mr. Jones, Clifford and Lupo are a team—which I suspected from the first—and right now they again present some sort of danger to me. And there," he pointed to the deed she still held, "Jones said, is where Clifford can be found."

"Josh, you won't do anything foolish. You can't pit yourself against—" Mollie broke off. She knew her glance had dropped to his peg. She wanted to bite off her tongue, but it was too late.

"I can't take on the likes of Clifford and Lupo with one leg," he said grimly. "You needn't remind me. I know."

"Josh, I did not mean—"

He put both hands on her shoulders and leaned in and kissed her forehead. "I know you didn't. And you mustn't worry. I've no intention of being foolish. That's what Frankie Miller and his men are for. Now go back home and leave this all to me. And thank you for the very useful information."

She was on her way out of the building just as a small and very pretty woman was on her way in. Blonde and pink and dimpled, Mollie noted, dressed in ice-blue silk and feathers and ribbons. The sort Auntie Eileen always called a mantrap. And somehow familiar.

The woman seemed to share that impression. She paused. Mollie offered a polite nod. The blonde returned the courtesy. Neither spoke, but both wore looks that said, *I think I know you.* And the blonde— natural, Mollie decided, or at least only a touch of help from the per- oxide bottle—seemed somehow agitated.

Mollie's first thought was that perhaps, once upon a long ago, the woman had worked at Brannigan's. Some of the prettiest had become respectable despite that. If so, running into someone who knew about one's past would certainly be unnerving.

The woman turned away, walked down the hall as far as the door to One D, then produced a key. Mollie clapped a hand to her cheek. Of course! Amanda Jones, wife of DuVal Jones. They met the day Mollie went to Bowling Green to tell the wives about the St. Nicholas flats. *That's what a wife and mother's supposed to be. The angel of the hearth.* How could she have forgotten?

The woman turned the key, then paused before opening her door and looked back at Mollie, who guiltily dropped her hand to her side. A moment more, then the angel disappeared.

It was like a jigsaw puzzle. Josh had all the pieces, but he could not put them together. He sat for a time in the inner office he'd made from Two D's larger bedroom, writing the names on a series of pieces of paper: Jones, Lupo, Clifford, and Ganz. He kept pushing them into different configurations, but the pattern did not become clear.

Lupo and Clifford he could dismiss as men with no honor and

their eye always on the main chance. It was obvious now that Clifford
had sent him into the world of Manhattan real estate as a stalking
horse. When he'd come up a winner Clifford wanted his reward and
used his cohort Lupo to try and get it. They shared other schemes
as well. Witness the attempt to involve Zac in the building of an underground railway. So it was logical they would work together on the
business of undermining Joshua Turner. Ganz had also confessed to
working with Tony Lupo on occasion. But his motives were a good
deal murkier, and made more so by what Mollie had just reported.

All the pawnbroker's talk of making money for his "grandchildren" was rubbish. He had none. Moreover, for the last three years
Sol Ganz had shown himself a totally reliable business associate, and
seen exceptional profits as a result. There were, Josh knew, men for
whom nothing was ever enough, but somehow he could not assign Sol
Ganz to their ranks. So what in God's name was he really after? As for
DuVal Jones, he was a small-time crook who operated across the river
in Brooklyn; the strong-arm man for a more important criminal, who
nonetheless had, as far as Josh knew, no connections or concerns in
New York City and . . .

And Clifford was the key. He had to tell Miller that. Emphasize the
point. Lupo was one of the puppets, important, yes, but Trenton Clifford pulled the strings.

He'd brought his telephone here from his previous office. It lay on
the floor, a useless wooden box since the company hadn't sent anyone to connect it. And it made no difference since, like most people,
Frankie Miller wasn't on the exchange. Josh reached for his hat and
his gloves.

The hansom slowed. Josh lowered the window of the carriage and
peered at the colossus looming in front of him. The Brooklyn Bridge
had changed the world. Six thousand feet long, it stood a hundred and
thirty-five feet above the East River and was eighty-five feet wide at

its base, the expanse divided by a sixteen-foot pedestrian promenade raised a bit above the vehicular traffic flowing east and west either side. It had cost seventeen million to build—more than three times the original budget—and was said to weigh some fifteen thousand tons and to be the longest suspension bridge in the world. Certainly, in the matter of New York City, it cast a real and figurative shadow unlike any the island city had previously known. A marvel of civil engineering that some called the eighth wonder of the world, the Brooklyn Bridge had created a swathe of Manhattan that would never again see the sun.

The driver got down and came around to open the carriage door. "This is the place, isn't it, sir? Roach's Tavern."

"Yes, this is it." The shadows were so deep he could barely see the mangy old bull beside the door. "I shan't be long. Please wait."

Not long at all. Miller wasn't at the tavern and no one could say when he'd return.

Josh climbed back into the carriage, looking again at the bridge meanwhile. It was clotted with people on foot and in slow-moving carriages. All of them shouting and waving and enjoying an adventure, not minding that it would take them hours to get across. Not an adventure he wished to share just now.

The driver lowered the window and leaned in, waiting for instructions. "The Brooklyn ferry," Josh said.

Take the bull by the horns. Maybe, like Mr. Roach's effigy, it would turn out to be blind and deballed.

23

THERE WAS A small glove maker's shop on Sixty-Ninth Street in the shadow of the Third Avenue El where Mollie was a frequent customer. Since she was so close she stopped there on her way home from Josh's office and spent twenty minutes with her elbow on a cushion and her hand up in the air, while the craftsman fitted different models. She could have either smooth leather or sueded, she was told. And any number of shades were available. Eventually she selected particularly supple gray kid, and requested the same style be made for her in pale blue and in beige. It was nearly one when she got back into the waiting hansom, and close to half past the hour when she arrived at 1160.

"Good afternoon, Mrs. Turner. There's a lady waiting for you just over there." The doorman nodded toward one of the velvet-covered banquettes that ran along the wall of the lobby.

Molly turned her head. Amanda Jones rose to greet her.

❧

"I knew you recognized me as I did you."

"Indeed," Mollie admitted. "Not immediately, but when I saw which flat was yours I remembered meeting you years ago on Bowling Green. Please sit down, Mrs. Jones."

They had ridden to the sixth floor in silence. Jane was waiting by the door—one of the wonders of the new electrification was a means for the elevator operator to notify the servants in each apartment when their master or mistress was on the way up—but Mollie had immediately dismissed the maid and herself showed her caller to the library. Now she glanced at the bell rope. "Will you take tea?"

"Thanks, no. But I wouldn't mind a glass of that." The blonde indicated a decanter of sherry.

Mollie poured a generous portion for each of them, then took the chair across from that of Amanda Jones. It seemed absurd to inquire after her visitor's health or compliment her on her hat. None of the usual social norms felt appropriate. Mollie simply waited.

"It's about me and DuVal," the other woman said. "And someone else. I suppose you've already guessed that."

"Not exactly. I have no idea why you would wish to speak to me about anything to do with your husband."

"I think he came to see you recently."

"Not me," Mollie corrected. "I am aware that he called on my husband. But only because I was told."

Amanda Jones turned her head, taking in the size and decor of the room. "Place like this," she said. "I guess it's possible for your husband to see somebody and you'd never even know. Nothing like that can happen at the St. Nicholas. How many rooms have you got here anyway?"

"Twelve," Mollie said.

"Like it was a whole house."

"Yes, rather."

"I want a house. A whole one of my own." Amanda Jones spoke with sudden urgency. "And a maid. DuVal could buy me those things.

He handles thousands and thousands of dollars for the mayor of Brooklyn. Every week. Do you know about that?"

Mollie shook her head. According to Josh, Jones worked for a small-time hoodlum, which was what Mollie had suspected ten years ago, but they'd not spent any time on details. "I know very little about your husband's affairs," she said.

"No reason you should, I suppose. You're a grand lady now. Don't involve yourself in your husband's business like when he was just getting started and you came to talk to us down on Bowling Green. Doesn't matter. I can tell you for sure, DuVal always pays the rent on time. Otherwise he might have to find some other place to put us. Me and my daughter. She's ten and I keep telling her we're going to move to someplace really nice pretty soon, but I don't think she believes me anymore. It's all like a fairy tale far as she's concerned." She raised her glass and finished her sherry.

Mollie did not bother to defend the niceness of the St. Nicholas. It was a relative matter, as she knew well. "Would you like another, Mrs. Jones?"

"Don't mind if I do."

Mollie got up and brought the decanter to where they were sitting, then filled the other woman's glass. "Do I take it you have only the one child, Mrs. Jones?"

"Absolutely. I made it very clear to DuVal I wouldn't have another until he bought us a house." She smiled but it did not seem to Mollie to be an indication of pleasure. "Couple of times he thought he'd gotten me in the family way despite that, but it always turned out he was wrong. We ladies know how to take care of that when it's necessary, don't we, Mrs. Turner? And don't look so disapproving. I know all about who you was before you married your one-legged millionaire."

"I'm not disapproving, Mrs. Jones. Everyone has to decide such matters for themselves."

Amanda Jones got up and carried her sherry to the window. "You can see the Central Park from here. I didn't realize that."

"Yes, we can." Even if Fifth Avenue and Madison were to be developed this far uptown, Josh was convinced both streets would be given over to private mansions and the upper floors of Park Avenue wouldn't lose their serene outlook.

"So what good's all this to you? The fancy apartment and the gorgeous view. The way I hear it, you never could have children and that ruined your life. People say it's God's punishment for your having lived all those years in a house of ill repute."

Mollie refused to let the direct attack disarm her. "As I recall, Mrs. Jones, back when we met on Bowling Green you insisted the role of a wife and mother was to be the angel of the hearth. Now you tell me you have defied your husband in the matter of a family."

Amanda Jones turned her back on the view and looked at her hostess. "Back on Bowling Green I was a girl of barely sixteen. I've learned a few things since then. Had them shoved down my throat, you might say."

"Exactly what do you want from me, Mrs. Jones?"

"My chance, Mrs. Turner. Mine and my daughter's."

"I don't understand."

"Captain Trenton Clifford's going to buy me a house of my own. He's promised. Only DuVal found out about me and the captain. He doesn't dare do anything about it. The mayor doesn't want that kind of trouble and he would do something terrible to DuVal if he caused it."

"I don't see that this has anything to do with Mr. Turner and myself, Mrs. Jones." Mollie's heart was pounding, but she knew she mustn't allow her feelings to show. She'd lose whatever advantage she might have if she did that.

"Course it has. I wouldn't have come here otherwise. DuVal's trying to make your husband do his dirty work for him. But if Mr. Turner does what DuVal wants, he'll be in terrible trouble. Maybe lose everything. Go to jail even. Where will you be then, Mrs. Turner?"

❦

Coming across on the ferry the sunlight on the river had been almost blindingly bright. Now, on the Brooklyn side, Josh was once more in the shadow of the bridge and deafened by the ceaseless rumble of its traffic.

According to Miller, he had a man observing the Water Street house day and night. Josh could see no evidence of him; that after all was Miller's stock-in-trade. Josh didn't fool himself he had the same ability to be unseen, but he stood in the deepest shadows and studied Clifford's house.

It was small and old-fashioned, a one-story cottage with a ramshackle addition tacked onto one end. Most likely an outhouse. Best guess: the place had once belonged to a fisherman, perhaps an oysterman working the beds on the Brooklyn side of the Narrows. Doubtless he'd have sold his day's catch by going around the grand houses on the hills of the nearby Heights.

Fair enough. What difference did it make to him? What in hell was he doing here? Miller said the house had been empty for forty-eight hours and he and his men knew their job. So what did Josh expect to find? And what might he do about it when he did? If he—

A shadow passed across the window of the front room.

The curtains were drawn so he couldn't be sure, but he'd wager a fair bit he was looking at Trenton Clifford. The silhouette clearly showed a man with a full head of hair that curled around his coat collar. The shadow paused, as if he were deliberately announcing his presence to anyone watching outside, then moved on. Josh wondered how he could signal Miller's man to show himself. He couldn't tackle Clifford alone. It was entirely possible the bastard was armed and—

He felt something pressing into the base of his spine.

"Good afternoon, Mr. Turner. Name's Tony Lupo, though I stretched that to Anthony Wolfe when we met last. Up at the St. Nicholas, if you recall. You've come a long way since then, haven't you? And I'm delighted to see you here. Saves no end of trouble. Now walk across the road, please. And don't get any stupid ideas about running. Not with that peg of yours. The Colt fires six shots one after another, but I wager I'd get you with the first one."

"I doubt you believe me, son, but I'm disappointed it's come to this." Clifford held a drink, but he had not offered one to Josh. Lupo had helped himself from a bottle of bourbon standing on a ledge beneath the window.

"I doubt," Josh said, "you're as disappointed as I am."

"Probably true." Clifford chuckled softly. "Now, Antonio my friend, how do you think we'd best proceed?"

"Simple," Lupo said. "I go and speak with Mrs. Turner. I'm sure once she knows we have her husband in our care she'll be willing to provide us with the deeds to the Park Avenue buildings. Soon as I have them I bring her and Duggan back here and Mr. Turner signs over the deeds to us." A brief pause, "After that we'll have what we want, so no reason Mr. and Mrs. Turner shouldn't return home, is there?"

"None," Clifford agreed, "but I would make a slight alteration in the plan. We leave Turner here and go together to see Mrs. Turner and the attorney. I wouldn't want you to think I didn't trust you, Antonio, but I'm a man who has learned caution over a long and eventful life."

Lupo hesitated, then nodded his head. "Since it's never been in my mind to cheat you, I have no objection. But we have to be very certain this resourceful gentleman doesn't get away once we leave."

"In that we're in complete accord, Antonio." And turning to Josh, "Give me your cane, son. Come, don't be foolish. There's nothing you can do, so we may as well accomplish this the easy way."

Josh gritted his teeth, but knew he had little choice. The revolver was on a table near the door to what he imagined was the kitchen, but both Lupo and Clifford were between it and himself. There was a rifle propped beside the fireplace. Josh assumed it was loaded, no other reason for it to be here, but he dared not lunge for it. Clifford was closer to the weapon than he was. The bastard would bring him down as soon as he moved.

Josh turned his stick around and offered it horse's head first.

Clifford took it. "Thank you. Now the peg."

"I can't—"

"You can't walk without it and the cane. Now don't you think I know that, son? Take off the peg, Joshua. We're waiting."

He thought of diving and shouting for Miller's man. The fellow had to be out there somewhere. At least that would improve the odds. Thing was, he couldn't see how he'd be heard, whatever kind of commotion he managed to make. The rumble of the bridge traffic was almost as loud in here as it was outside. "I need to sit down to do it," he said.

"So you do, son. I apologize." Clifford dragged a small chair over to where Josh stood. "Please, be my guest."

He'd take off only the peg. Could be the harness would eventually be useful, and neither of his captors were likely to have any idea how the assembly worked. It was easy enough to pull up his right trouser leg, the one stiffened with Mollie's buckram, and he left it in a position that obscured the straps leading to his waist. The wooden leg was anchored to the frame with metal clamps that locked into position. There were five of them and he unlatched them as slowly as he could.

Lupo's glass was empty and he walked over to the ledge that held the bottle of bourbon.

Josh now had a clear path to the Colt on the table.

"Come along, son. I'm getting a tad impatient. You might recall I'm not at my best when that happens."

The peg was free in his hand, but Josh didn't pull it away from the frame. A number of things were obvious to him. They would tie him up when they left, not simply leave him to hobble about on one leg. When they returned, Mollie would be with them, and there was no doubt in his mind they would use threats against her to force him to sign the deeds. Once that was done they would kill them both. But until he signed those deeds they wanted him alive. The conclusion was obvious. Now or never.

He shouted at the top of his lungs and hurled himself at Clifford, using the peg as a battering ram. It caught the other man in the stomach and flung him against the fireplace. The rifle clattered to the floor and skidded away. Out of the corner of his eye Josh saw Lupo hurl himself toward it, but he concentrated on forcing the peg deeper into Clifford's gut. He heard the wood snap just as he lost his balance and fell. Josh let go of the peg and dug his elbows into the floor, using the strength of his arms to thrust him toward the table and the revolver.

He reached up. The gun was inches from his hand. A shot rang out.

Josh waited for pain to tell him where he'd been hit. He felt nothing. Only the handle of the Colt in his palm. He clicked off the safety as he rolled over. He expected to see Lupo with the rifle, but all he saw was a stranger standing by the door to the kitchen. The man's trousers and the bottoms of a two-piece undersuit were down around his ankles, and he held a smoking revolver in his right hand. "Don't shoot, Mr. Turner! I'm one o' Frankie's boys."

Josh caught a movement out of the corner of his eye. Clifford was on his knees, the rifle at his shoulder. Josh swung the Colt in his direction and fired.

The peg was covered in blood, but it was useless in any case; snapped in two from the force of his thrust into Clifford's belly. The hole he'd put in the Southerner's forehead seemed as if it might have been superfluous.

"This one's dead as well," the gunman said. "And I'm thinking it's Tony Lupo." He was standing over Lupo's corpse, struggling to pull up his clothes, and he sounded morose.

"That's who he is," Josh agreed.

"Sweet Jesus. And I did it over here in the mayor's territory. There's going to be hell to pay."

"Personally, I rather prefer this outcome to the alternative. What in God's name took you so long?"

"I was in the crapper— Begging your pardon, Mr. Turner, in the outhouse. There's a door from the outside as well as this one here and I broke in earlier. Truth is, I've been spending most of my day in there squirting out of both ends. Must have been the oysters I had for lunch. Should have known better. June . . . Like they say, never eat oysters in a month without an *R*. And there's all the noise from that damned bridge overhead. I didn't hear anything until one almighty shout from in here."

"That was me."

"Yeah, I figured that out now. But when I came through the door I didn't know what to expect. Only thing I saw was Lupo going for the rifle, so I shot him. Couldn't do nothing else, could I?"

"No, I don't imagine you could. I've seen you before, haven't I? What's your name?"

"Donovan, Mr. Turner. I been with Frankie up at your place a few times."

"Right. Hand me that cane, would you, Donovan."

The gunman went on speaking while he did as he was bid. "I think you better get out of here, Mr. Turner. I don't expect no coppers, but you never know. Best thing is, I wait until somebody comes to relieve me. Once it's dark and there's two of us, we can get the bodies to the river." Then, looking at the shattered peg, "There ain't any hansoms come by here regular, but I could go get you one, Mr. Turner. Bring it back."

"No, that's not wise. As you point out, it will attract attention in this neighborhood. I can manage with just the cane for a few blocks."

Fully four as it turned out, and they seemed particularly long. Josh was trembling with fatigue and covered in sweat by the time he saw a cab stand on Front Street. He made sure he was safely inside before he said, "Eleven-sixty Park Avenue over in New York." The thought of getting out of the hansom and onto the ferry, then repeating the exercise on the other side was daunting. "You can do that, can't you? Now that you can take the bridge."

"I can do it. Take a bit of time, though. And there's a five-penny toll for carriages. Only a penny if you walk, but that's not going to suit you, is it, sir?" Making it apparent he had observed the empty right trouser leg and the effort required to get into the cab.

"No, it doesn't suit me," Josh said. "I'll pay the toll and I don't care how long the journey takes." Then, promising to make it worth the cabby's while, he leaned back and closed his eyes.

Mollie had looked for him everywhere she could think of. Everywhere Ollie could think of as well. This was her second trip back to the St. Nicholas and Hamish still reported no sign of Joshua. "I've run out of ideas," she said. "And I should let you go back to the stable, Ollie. It was good of you to drop everything to drive me about."

"It's no bother, Mrs. Turner. Mr. Turner's always telling me a good manager knows how to delegate responsibility. The boy I left in charge will manage for a few hours."

"Well, if you're sure . . . Take me to Fifth Street and Avenue A, Ollie."

It remained unclear if Mr. Ganz was her ally or her enemy, but Mollie was certain he was somehow in the middle of all that had happened.

He was not, however, in his shop. The door was locked and the curtain pulled across the window. Mollie tugged firmly on the bell, waited a few seconds, and rang it again. This time with obvious impatience. A second-story window opened and a woman leaned out. "He ain't here. You can come back tomorrow."

Mollie tipped back her head. The woman must be Mr. Ganz's housekeeper. She wore an old-fashioned mobcap and had a duster in her hand. That the pawnbroker lived above his shop despite having access to apparently unlimited sums of money was at the heart of the mystery surrounding him. "I'm Mrs. Joshua Turner," she called up. "I've not come to pawn anything. Mr. Ganz is a business associate of my husband and it's urgent that I speak with him. Can you tell where he might be found?"

"Not so's it'll do you any good. Only thing I know is he went to Brooklyn. Said he was going to take the new bridge and left a few hours ago. Didn't say when he'd be back."

Josh pulled out his pocket watch. It was approaching six. He'd so far spent two hours in the back of the hansom, traveling at a snail's pace across the bridge. Plenty of time to contemplate the fact that he had killed a man.

He did not, he decided, feel remorse. Regret perhaps. But he could see no way he could have acted differently. And he could tick off a long line of men who had died at Clifford's hands, starting with the prisoners he shot for sport and continuing to poor little George Higgins, whose death Clifford doubtless ordered, even if Jones was correct and the murder was actually done by Lupo. Not to forget Ebenezer Tickle's story of the deadly chariot races in Kentucky. Good riddance then. If the preachers were correct, Clifford had to answer for his actions to a higher authority. In which case so would he someday. Shooting Trenton Clifford in what was, at the minimum, self-defense was unlikely to be his greatest sin. As for the death of Tony Lupo, he was the immediate cause of Mollie's suffering and grief, and that of God knows how many others. He had no tears to waste on Lupo.

The cab was making progress but it was incredibly slow. Josh could hear the rumble of the trains on the tracks that connected the elevated railways of the two cities, and the tramping of the pedestrians on the wooden walkway raised a short distance over his head. All he could see of them from the cab's window were their feet and legs, but it was obvious they moved with greater speed than anyone in the crush of private vehicles, his hansom included. Nonetheless, New York was getting closer.

The buildings of the great city were spread in front of him like a swathe of inky black against the brilliant blue of the sky.

Josh lowered the side window and leaned out for a better view. The spire of Trinity Church was immediately identifiable; on the Manhattan side it was the only thing higher than the bridge tower itself. If he moved to the other side of the cab he could distinguish as well the elaborate top of the ten-story Western Union Building. Apart from those two landmarks, the skyline of Manhattan was a solid phalanx of thrusting iron and stone. Some steel as well these days. And surely more of it to come. If it did nothing else this bridge would enhance the reputation of the strongest metal in the world, and . . . Jesus, God Almighty. What was happening?

It began as a thrumming, a kind of syncopated chant of terror. Josh heard it first from the pedestrians above his head. Then it echoed from carriages in front and behind.

The bridge is collapsing. Collapsing. Collapsing. Collapsing.

The panic descended in the blink of an eye. One moment Mollie was sitting up next to Ollie in the brougham—she'd left the interior of the carriage in favor of the view from the higher driver's perch—scanning the crowd streaming off the bridge, looking for a glimpse of Sol Ganz. The next there were piercing screams and a terrified horde of men and women shoving and pushing and thrusting as they tried to get to the street. "What is it, Ollie? What's happened?"

"I'm not sure, Mrs. Turner. Looks like a sort of stampede. I'd better get you out of harm's—"

"Out of the way! Give 'em room!"

A couple of policemen were shouting, trying to turn the horses by yanking at their bridles, and screaming that all the nearby carriages on Chatham Street had to move off.

"Give 'em room. For the love of God, room's what's needed."

Ollie concentrated on getting the carriage out of the traffic and controlling the chestnut, who was picking up the surrounding panic

and threatening to bolt. Mollie paid no attention to the horse or where
they were going. She was twisted around, staring in horrified fascina-
tion at what was happening behind them. The crush appeared to have
started on the stairway. It was a short double flight, no more than eight
feet wide, with a landing between that was equally constricted. This
was the only pathway for both ascending and descending foot traffic,
and quite suddenly what had been an orderly if slow procession of
people in both directions had become a pile of bodies collapsing one
upon the other, piling up so there could be no question of those underneath surviving. While she watched, the deadly snarl on the stairs
spread to the bridge itself in what seemed an inexorable wave.

Mollie saw a hand thrust out from a pile of bodies and knew that
whoever was on the bottom must be pressed to death. Then someone
kicked at the hand and it skidded away on its own. There was an iron
fence either side of the stairs. The top was meant to be used as a hand-
rail, but the whole thing served instead to make the horror worse and
prevent escape. Meanwhile, the crowd on the bridge kept surging forward, screaming and crying that they must get off, while every thrust
made that more of an impossibility.

Some people did manage to get away. Mollie saw a woman pull
herself free of the melee and wander off. She still wore her hat and her
gloves and the top of her frock, but she was totally naked from the
waist down, her skirt and her petticoats and pantaloons apparently
torn away in the crush. One man leaped onto the back of another and
literally walked across the heads of those in front of him until finally
he jumped off into the street and ran away. There was a shower of
hats tumbling from the upper reaches of the bridge approach, falling
onto the rooftops and railroad tracks below. While she watched, an
infant was torn from its mother's arms just as the woman was nearing
ground level. The infant landed in the street and the woman somehow
managed to clamber off the side of the bridge and climb down the
framework using the struts for handholds. Mollie hurled herself out
of the brougham and ran forward, ignoring Ollie's shouts behind her.

She and the woman reached the baby at the same moment. "He's mine!" the woman shouted, as if she thought Mollie meant to steal the child, and reached down and snatched up the tiny figure and ran off. Through it all the infant remained so still that Mollie feared the worst.

When she looked back to the bridge she saw that others had followed the woman's lead and were climbing down by means of the supporting structure. Soon that escape route was also hideously overcrowded and she watched at least two people fall off and land on the road below. Another she was quite certain simply jumped to his death. "Oh, God! Oh, dear God," she whispered.

The words were as much a prayer for those in the terrible situation unfolding before her eyes as an exclamation of shock. Indeed, they were the first sound she'd managed to make since the stampede started, and a way of shaking herself free of the sheer weight of the horror.

A copper shoved her with no apology for his rudeness. "Out of the way, miss. Out of the way!"

Mollie ducked away from his grasp, meanwhile seeing that police and soldiers had arrived seemingly from nowhere and were converging on Chatham Street. One man had a hammer and a chisel and immediately started hacking at the bolts that held the iron stair rails in place. Others soon joined him, using whatever makeshift tools they could find, and in moments they had torn away first one section of the fence and then another.

The mortal snarl was relieved as suddenly as it had formed.

Done and over. Except for those for whom it was not.

Men piled the bodies of the dead on one side of the road to await hearses. Most showed by the blood that had oozed from their noses and ears that they had been pressed to death. Others had been torn apart and were missing body parts and apparently had bled away their lives. As for the wounded, they were laid out on the other side of the road to wait for ambulances.

There was a constant hum made up of groans of pain, and sobs, and here and there the sound of praying. Mollie found a horse trough that had some water at the bottom and ripped off a piece of her petticoat and soaked it and went among the injured, wiping faces and hands and promising that help was on the way, unable to think of anything else she could do. She spied a child kneeling on the pavement next to another and hurried over. A little boy—five or perhaps six she guessed—dark-haired and with enormous brown eyes, looked up at her. "My little sister's hurt her leg. She can't walk." He was holding the hand of a small girl lying on the ground. Her hair was as dark as his, though her eyes were an improbable blue.

Mollie reached down and stroked the girl's hair back from her forehead and sponged her face. The child didn't respond, though she was clearly alive. Just, Mollie realized, made silent by terror. "What's her name?"

"Essie."

Mollie turned back to the girl. "There are doctors coming, Essie. They'll get you well soon. You must be brave, and I know you will be." The girl's brother meanwhile had not let go her hand. "My name is Mollie Turner," she told him. "What's yours?"

"I'm Michael," the boy said. "And her real name is Esther. She was named for Grandfather Sol's wife who went to heaven."

Mollie caught her breath. It seemed so far-fetched, but she had after all been told that Sol Ganz had gone to Brooklyn over the new bridge and she had come here precisely because she hoped he'd come back the same way. "Esther and Michael," she said. "Those are nice names. Do you know where your grandfather is now?"

"Over there." Michael gestured to the people stretched out on the pavement waiting for the ambulances.

"Stay here," Mollie said. "Don't move. I promise I'll come back for you. Do you understand, Michael? If anyone asks, remember my name. Mollie Turner. Say it now."

"Mollie Turner," the boy repeated dutifully.

"Yes, that's very good. Mrs. Joshua Turner. If someone asks or tries to get you to go anywhere say I'm returning for you. I shall, Michael.

I promise. I'll come back for you and Essie." She waited until the boy nodded, then moved to the ranks of the wounded.

It took only a few minutes. Sol Ganz was lying some twenty feet beyond the spot where she'd found the two children, close to the railing that surrounded City Hall Park. Mollie got down on her knees beside him. "Hello, Mr. Ganz."

His eyes were open and he smiled up at her. "So, Mrs. Mollie, I was thinking of you," he said. "Now here you are."

The words were spoken quietly. She had to bend close to hear. She could see no obvious wounds, but when she took his hand it was chilled and his pulse was so rapid it could be seen fluttering beneath the skin of his wrist. "There are ambulances on the way, Mr. Ganz. I'll wait here with you until they come. Don't try and speak. Save your strength."

"The children . . . ," he muttered.

"They are not far. I'm watching them. Michael told me where to find you. He said he's your grandchild."

"I have many grandchildren. All over. In the city and in Brooklyn. Now . . ."

"You mustn't use your strength like this, Mr. Ganz. You can tell me later. I promise."

"No. I don't think so. Now I must tell you. I was considering you, Mrs. Mollie. For a long time I have considered. Some of the children have not even one parent . . . You and your husband, you have no . . ."

His voice trailed away and he closed his eyes and Mollie thought he was gone. But when she pressed her ear to his chest she could hear his heart. Faint, and very rapid. When she lifted her head he was again looking at her. "All day I thought, I can bring these two to Mrs. Mollie and Joshua. With the others, the ones who are Jewish, it would be a sin. But these two . . ."

"Mr. Ganz, you must save your strength."

"No. Listen to me. Michael and Esther, their father was Jewish. Not their mother. So it's not such an *averah*, a sin, to give them to *ger toshav*, good people who do not worship idols. Not even money.

Michael and Esther, since they have no one—" His words were interrupted by a fit of coughing.

Mollie looked back over her shoulder. She could see the children, still alone, still where they had been. "Mr. Ganz, are you telling me these children are orphans?"

"Yes. The parents, both dead. Only me they have. So you—" More coughing. Mollie tried to support his shoulders and raise him up. "No," he muttered. "Listen, all my grandchildren. You must . . ." He stopped, and his next words were not, she realized, meant for her. He was saying a prayer she thought, but in a language she did not know.

After that there was a trickle of blood from the left side of his mouth and he stared sightless at the sky.

Mollie heard her name being called as she brushed closed Sol Ganz's sightless eyes.

She looked up to see Josh coming toward her. He was leaning on Ollie and his clothes were in shreds, and he seemed to have neither his cane nor his peg. Mollie sprang up and rushed to him. "Dear God, Josh, what happened? Were you in that terrible crush? Are you injured?"

"Absolutely fine," he said, and repeated it as if to convince himself. "I'm fine." Then, "Ollie, can we get to the fence do you think, so I can lean on that. And perhaps you can find me a cane in all the abandoned things that are lying about. Anything will do."

Mollie glanced again at the children. Michael was watching her intently, following her every movement with his eyes. "This way, Ollie," she said, maneuvering them to a portion of the fence nearest the youngsters.

Josh's arm around her waist was for more than support, she realized. He was hugging her close. "What happened, dearest? How did you lose your peg?"

He shook his head. "I'll tell you that part later. The worst of all this ▸rror was apparently here at the stairs. I was some further back. It wasn't bad once we got the crowd to stop trying to move, just stand and wait."

He'd seen some soldiers trying to quell the panic by swinging from the rafters above the heads of the crowd, carrying the message that the bridge wasn't falling, that there was a crush at the stairs, nothing more. That was something he could do as well, Josh had realized. After that he'd spent many minutes swinging from the upper beams of the bridge, carrying the message that the only thing needed was patience and everyone would get off without harm. When it was over a couple of the troops propped him up on either side and helped him return to the Manhattan exit on Chatham Street. He might not have found Ollie given the chaos, but the chestnut apparently spotted him and neighed loudly in greeting.

Now it was growing dark. The horizon was a streak of orange and the arc lights that had been installed at intervals along the bridge went on one after the other, a string of jewels connecting the two cities above the silver stream of the water. Here and there electrified buildings around City Hall came alight as well. Ollie was illumined by their glow when he returned with a sturdy shillelagh. Josh grasped it, grateful that it kept him from feeling so helpless, but exhaustion was returning as the adrenaline ebbed. "I don't have the strength," he said, "to ask what you're doing here, my love. But do you think we might go home now?"

Mollie shook her head. "Yes, of course. But just one moment more, please."

She ran over to where the two children waited. "That's my husband over there, Michael. He is very tired because he has been helping the people trapped on the bridge. He would like to go home now and so would I. Would you and Essie like to come with us? Your grandfather seemed to think it would be a good idea."

The child hesitated, "I guess so. Seems like it would be all right if Grandfather Sol said so."

"Yes"—the voice came from the child still lying on the pavemen

"I'm sure it's a good idea." They were the first words the little girl had spoken and Mollie instinctively reached down and kissed her cheek.

"Indeed it is. May I pick you up, Essie?"

The girl said she could, and Mollie did, and took Michael's hand and brought both children to where Josh stood watching her.

"These two were being brought to us by Mr. Ganz," she said. "I'm afraid he has passed on." She nodded her head in the direction of the ranks of dead and injured. "Their names are Michael and Esther, and they're orphans now, but I believe he was supporting the family before the parents died. There are, I suspect, many others. That's what he meant about having grandchildren, Josh. They're here in the city and in Brooklyn as well. He said so before he died. I'm sure you will find some sort of record at his shop. If you look."

He reached over and touched her cheek. "Of course I will look. And I'll see to it that what needs to be done is done. You have my word." If in some grand scheme payment was required for the life he'd taken, perhaps this would qualify.

"Thank you," she said. "And Essie and Michael?"

He smiled. At her first, then at the children. "I'm thinking," he said, "that it's a good thing I still haven't rented the penthouse at 1160. A family of four can use the space." Then, to the stableman, "See if you can get the carriage any closer, Ollie."

Moments later the brougham was a few feet away. Mollie carried Essie toward it. Josh took a tentative step using the unfamiliar shillelagh to provide balance.

The little boy, Michael by name, Josh remembered, stepped close to his side. "Here, sir, I can help if you'll just put your hand on my shoulder."

Author's Afterword

THE NEW YORK subway system, so often discussed—indeed longed for—in this novel, ultimately evolved as extensions of the elevated railways. The first underground tunnel was opened in October of 1904. It belonged to the Interborough Rapid Transit Company, the IRT, which owned the Ninth Avenue El, and the Brooklyn Rapid Transit Company, later the Brooklyn and Manhattan Transit Company, which became known as the BMT. The independent Eighth Avenue line, the only one originally owned and operated by the city, was the IND. These separate subway systems were for nearly a century the form in which New Yorkers knew, loved, and sometimes hated their subway system. Today's unified, color-coded routes are a considerably later development.

The construction method adopted for much of the early underground portions of the subway system (some forty percent of it is, ✦ this day, run above ground on elevated railways), was "cut and cov✦ The street was first torn up, the tunnel built, then covered over an✦ graded, newly surfaced, etc. Such was the origin of what many ✦

tions of New Yorkers would call the Lexington Avenue Line. Bringing me to a small puzzle.

Lexington Avenue was not on the original grid as laid down in 1811. It came into being in the early 1840s at the behest of Samuel Ruggles, when he created Gramercy Square Park and surrounded it with new and expensive (and taxable) luxury houses. Most sources agree that in this original incarnation the thoroughfare went only as far as Forty-Second Street. Indeed, for much of the nineteenth century everything above Forty-Second was pretty much no-man's-land. As happens in the story, things began to change with the opening of the Grand Central Depot in 1871. In this novel, however, as in some reference sources, Lexington is among the avenues that in the early 1880s still had not pushed north. Evidence to the contrary can be found on the Galt & Hoy map, but Josh deals with that in chapter 18, and it seems to me other evidence supports him. Beyond question, however, the avenue became a major north-south artery in the late 1880s. That's when the old dirt road was torn up and built anew to accommodate the building of the IRT's Lexington Avenue subway.

As a result, readers looking for any trace of the Carolina or St. Nicholas apartment buildings in today's ultra-fashionable East Sixties will not find them. In the parallel universe of this novel's truth, they were torn down to make way for the subway. Trenton Clifford's ghost no doubt looked on from hell and laughed.

And as additional evidence for this version of history, in this neighborhood the beautiful single family townhouses date from after 1900. Park Avenue, not Third, smiled on the East Sixties and carried the day.

Acknowledgments

ALL BOOKS STAND on the shoulders of other books—in no instance is that more true than in the matter of historical fiction. This one, like the others in the series, owes an enormous debt to the writers and editors who over two centuries created the books that chronicle New York City and now fill two entire shelves in my office. They are too many to mention, but my gratitude to them is boundless. With regard to the quintessential New York quest, still a source of angst and ecstasy—finding a place to live—I relied on Charles Lockwood's *Manhattan Moves Uptown* (Houghton Mifflin, 1976), and *New York, New York: How the Apartment House Transformed the Life of the City*, by Elizabeth Hawes (Knopf, 1993).

The great Sydny Miner, editor extraordinaire, midwifed this book into existence as she had the others, but moved on before I finished it. Her impossibly large shoes were filled by a trio I have come to think of as my "rose-lipt maidens": Michelle Rorke, Kate Ankofski, and most particularly Michele Bové, who was tireless in shepherding the manuscript through the quirks and quandaries of the production proce
The final story owes much to the youthful energy and assorted po

of view of all three. Mollie especially benefited from their attentions. They have my thanks.

As to making possible the book you actually hold in your hands—in whatever format—it would be considerably less than it is were it not for Loretta Denner, a senior production editor at Simon & Schuster. In terms of knowing what to ask, whom to ask, and how to get it done, she is, quite simply, in a class of her own. Thank you. Henry Morrison brought his customary quite special skill to the origins of the project, and Marly Rusoff graciously—and effectively—became its supporter and chief cheerleader. I could not have done without either.

And finally, as always, I thank my husband, the wind beneath my wings.

READING GROUP GUIDE

City of Promise

Beverly Swerling

INTRODUCTION

City of Promise, the fourth novel in Beverly Swerling's *City* series, brings to life a New York City humming with potential: opulent buildings are transforming the city's skyline; elevated trains are sparking the city's movement uptown; immigrant laborers are pouring into Five Points and powering the industrial boom; and the Brooklyn Bridge, a symbol of astounding innovation, is rising steadily in the background. In *City of Promise,* Joshua Turner, a young man who has lost a leg in the Civil War, capitalizes on this cacophony of late-nineteenth-century industry and becomes one of the city's first real estate tycoons. Early on, Josh marries Mollie Brannigan, raised by her remarkable Auntie Eileen in the finest brothel in New York. Mollie uses her cleverness and her understanding of how things work in the city to support and expand her husband's growing empire. Then tragedy strikes and Mollie retreats into silent pain, shutting out Josh and all else except the garden she builds in the wilderness of the Upper East Side, while Josh goes on to still greater accomplishments without her—until the moment when both Mollie's life and Joshua's fortune are threatened by ⸱ enemy they can only defeat together, and in a few hectic hours all N York makes choices that will determine the future.

Topics and Questions for Discussion

1. Which plot twists in *City of Promise* did you predict, if any, and which twists took you by surprise? Of the following characters, whom did you like better at the end of the story: Zachary Devrey, Tess o' the Roses, Solomon Ganz, Eileen, Trenton Clifford, Ebenezer Tickle?

2. Did you feel that the characters grew and changed as the novel progressed? Do you like a story more when there is such change, or do you prefer to stay with the characters as you first get to know them?

3. Did Swerling's description of how easy it was for a family like that of Ollie Crump to become destitute and wind up in a rookery shock you? Do you imagine that that kind of abrupt change of fortune can happen today? If you do, what do you think of what progress we have made as a society?

4. Did the novel make you feel differently about P. T. Barnum and his famous circus? Do you think Tom Thumb or Ebenezer Tickle to be better off?

5. In *City of Promise* Mama Jack's Cave is an important venue; do you think there are any parallels in modern society?

6. Swerling wrote that Eileen had "spared [Mollie] the horror of growing up in some depraved Five Points rat-infested hovel with the rest of the drunken, brawling, dirt-poor Irish who poured into the city looking for a dream and finding a nightmare" (page 15), while mere blocks away, and further uptown, wealthy New

Yorkers lounged in mansions of unprecedented lavishness and expense. Do you think such shocking levels of inequality still exist in America today? Why or why not?

7. *City of Promise* is, in many ways, a history of the industrial development of New York City. Which aspects of the industrial growth did you find most impressive in scope, creativity, or plain ambitiousness? Which aspects struck you as fairly obvious in retrospect? Were you surprised to learn of the advent of telephones and elevators and electricity during the period 1864–1883? Did you think any of those things to have come about earlier or later?

8. *City of Promise* depicts a New York City run almost exclusively by wealthy white men. Bribery regularly greased the wheels of governments both official and informal, women couldn't vote, upward mobility largely eluded the immigrant tenements and slums, and closed-door meetings of a select few often determined the fates of many. In what ways are America's cities and governments different now—and in what ways are they still the same?

9. Eileen Brannigan and Mollie Turner both gave "little donations" to various officials in exchange for information and protection. As Eileen explained to Mollie, "Never forget . . . the authorities must be dealt with. . . . I believe in looking after those who can look after you." (page 29) Given the historical context, do you think these small bribes were ethically sound? At what point, if ever, does the prevalence of an action justify its being taken?

10. Discuss the societal constraints placed on women in *City of Promise*. How did they exert influence in their daily lives despite these expectations?

11. According to Eileen, women had three options in life: as she said to a young Mollie, "[S]ince I am opposed to your being a spinster and you're too lean and too clever to be a whore, you must be a

wife." (page 32) Why were the options for women so limited at the time? At what point in the past century do you think women started breaking out of these prescribed roles? Do you think women are entirely free of these expectations today?

12. In what ways did the women in *City of Promise* subtly control and influence the industrial growth of the city?

13. Eileen described the male fantasy that she catered to in her whorehouse as "the one in a man's most hidden heart: That a woman who looked and sounded and acted like the demure and chaste creature he thought he'd married would, once they were in the bedroom, behave as the willing, even lusty, companion of his most secret imagining." (page 17) Given the societal expectations of the time that women remain completely pure until marriage, do you see this fantasy as more of a fleeting hope, a realistic goal, or a hypocritical demand? Do you think this kind of expectation still exists?

14. Mollie considered herself firmly ensconced in spinsterhood at twenty, while today's median age of marriage is twenty-six for women without a high school diploma, and thirty for women with a college degree (per the U.S. Census). In addition, Ollie Crump began working full-time for Mollie and Josh as a child, an arrangement that would be illegal in America today. Given these two examples, how—and why—do you think our society's views on adolescence and growing up have changed since the late 1800s?

15. How did Mollie's upbringing in Aunt Eileen's whorehouse, and Eileen's advice to her niece, influence Mollie's marriage and her views on sexuality?

16. When Mollie showed up at the wedding of Ebenezer Tickle and Maude Pattycake in her daring dress that flaunted her pregnant

figure, Josh immediately recognized the message she intended to send: her husband, despite his peg leg, was a real man. In what other ways did men prove their masculinity, and women their femininity, in *City of Promise*?

17. After Mollie lost her baby, she grew very quiet and reserved. Only after she started gardening did life come back to her: "She stretched out both arms and held them open, as if she were welcoming someone. A child. No, never. But her embrace was not quite as empty as it had been before." (page 301) Why do you think Mollie felt so comforted by her garden?

18. Swerling wrote that after the financial crash of 1874, "the streets were full of newly made beggars and tramps and half-naked children become urchins overnight. Work or bread was the cry. The response was a demand for patience, and the customary diatribes about the evils of overmuch charity." (page 296) Compare this financial crash to the recent Great Recession. Allowing for changes in technology and government support systems, do you think history is bound to repeat itself?

19. If you've read Swerling's other *City* books, or any other historical novels that take place in a big city during the Gilded Age, how does this book measure up in terms of historical detail and richness? If you haven't read any similar novels, do you feel you have a solid grasp of Gilded Age New York after reading this book?

20. Swerling wrote, "All prayers are answered. Sometimes, however, the answer is no." (page 152) What do you think the men and women in *City of Promise* prayed for? Whose prayers were granted, and whose were denied?

21. Consider the book's title: *City of Promise*. What was promised, and to whom, in this story? Which promises are broken, and which are kept?

Enhance Your Book Club

1. Do a bit of research on the New York City brought to life in *City of Promise*, and bring your findings to a book club. Perhaps divide up topics amongst yourselves, and present your research to one another. Possible areas of research include, but certainly aren't limited to: Boss Tweed and Tammany Hall; women's rights in the late 1800s; the financial crash of 1874; the creation of subways in New York; Belle Isle prison camp; the construction of the Brooklyn Bridge; P. T. Barnum and his traveling shows; Five Points and the tenements in New York; and the northern expansion of New York real estate in the late 1800s.

2. Pick a movie to watch after your book club meeting that dovetails with some of the many themes in *City of Promise*. Consider the following films:

   a. **Holiday** (1938)

   Dir. George Cukor; with Katharine Hepburn and Cary Grant. The free-spirited Johnny Case finds himself engaged to the daughter of a wealthy New York industrialist who expects Johnny to buckle down and work in big business.

   b. **Life with Father** (1947)

   Dir. Michael Curtiz; with William Powell, Irene Dunne, and Elizabeth Taylor. A comedy, set in 1880s New York, about a wealthy businessman who tries—and often fails— to run his large family as strictly and efficiently as his business.

c. The Heiress (1949)

Dir. William Wyler; with Olivia de Havilland, Montgomery Clift, and Ralph Richardson. A romance, set in mid-1800s New York, that follows a plain yet wealthy woman as she falls for a handsome yet poor man, to her father's deep disapproval.

d. The Age of Innocence (1993)

Dir. Martin Scorsese; with Daniel Day-Lewis, Michelle Pfeiffer, and Winona Ryder. A tale of nineteenth-century New York high society in which a young lawyer falls for a married woman while he is engaged to the woman's cousin.

e. The House of Mirth (2000)

Dir. Terence Davies; with Dan Aykroyd, Gillian Anderson, and Laura Linney. A romantic drama, set in 1890s New York, that tells the heartbreaking story of Lily Bart, a renowned beauty whose search for a wealthy husband ends in tragedy.

f. Gangs of New York (2002)

Dir. Martin Scorsese; with Leonardo DiCaprio, Cameron Diaz, and Daniel Day-Lewis. A saga set in the mid-1800s in the Five Points neighborhood of New York that follows a gang leader in his roles as a crime boss and political kingmaker under Boss Tweed.

3. Research and visit a teahouse nearby—or, if you're up to the challenge, prepare and enjoy your own Gilded Age–themed afternoon tea! You can draw inspiration from the following resources:

a. Afternoon tea menu for the Flagler Museum, a Gilded Age mansion in Palm Beach, FL: *www.flaglermuseum .com/visiting/cafe-des-beaux-arts*

b. Afternoon tea menu for the Driehaus Museum, a Gilded Age mansion in Chicago, IL: *driehausmuseum.org/visit /program-list.php?group_id=8*

c. Site with excerpts from the 1889 book *The Home Manual*: *www.thecompletevictorian.com/PlanningATea.html*

d. Site with food and tea tray suggestions: *www.planners guide.com/tea_party.htm*

e. Site with many links to other tea-related resources: *www .mostly-victorian.com/links/food.shtml*

4. Indulge in the lifestyle of Gilded Age business tycoons with your book club:

a. Plan a visit to a garden like Mollie's near you. Visit www .gardenvisit.com and search for local gardens and nurseries, or visit a local arboretum.

b. Take a carriage ride, if you have access to a stable that offers them. Or, if you're feeling adventurous, take a horseback riding lesson with your book club! Visit www .equinenow.com/lessons.htm to search for stables that give lessons, including beginner lessons, near you.

c. Research historic mansions near you and plan a group tour.

d. Try living like Josh and Mollie at the beginning of *City of Promise* and go without electricity for the first thirty minutes of book club. Turn off your cell phones, swap lights for candles, and light a fire in your fireplace, if you'd like.

e. Sip on sherry, bourbon, whiskey, or scotch (or tea as a nonalcoholic option) during your book club.

f. Use lengths of fabric to create skirts that are fitted in front and bustled behind.

A Conversation with Beverly Swerling

On your website (www.beverlyswerling.com), you describe the plot matrix that you write out for each *City* book. How did you develop your matrix technique?

Because I don't outline I need a way to let my editor and publisher understand the novel I hope to write. The so-called matrix allows me to give them enough information to feel comfortable, and gives me the freedom to let a story develop on the page.

Did you intend to write a series of four *City* novels before you started in on the first one, or did you find yourself wanting to continue the story after each book came to a close?

The latter definitely. I never intended *City of Dreams* to be the first in a series. I'd have done it differently if I had. But I heard from numerous readers asking me to take the story "one generation further," so ultimately I did.

Which comes first for you—the story or the research?

The story. I begin with characters who are born in my head and linger there, sometimes for many weeks, and a story starts to grow around them. Then I go looking for the facts that will shore up my ideas.

What (if any) particularly bizarre or surprising historical tidbits about Gilded Age New York surprised you?

I was astonished to discover how bad the traffic was, and how congested the streets. From the beginning of the nineteenth century, New Yorkers were overwhelmed by the difficulty of simply getting around in the city, and how long it took to get from one place to another. I had no idea that it was such a struggle back then. I thought it must be a modern problem.

What is your favorite scene in *City of Promise*?

I have many, but I love Maude and Ebenezer's wedding, and the way Mollie gets away from her captors later in the novel.

Mama Jack's Tavern is an incredibly vivid, peculiar, oddly joyful place. What inspired you to create Mama Jack's? Which details of Mama Jack's are drawn from your historical research, and which came straight from your imagination?

I first encountered the "Bawdy Houses" that were special kinds of bars and taprooms when researching *City of Dreams*, and I used that information in that book. Such places play a part in the later books as well, and in my mind I sort of thought of Mama Jack's as being an evolution of Martha's bawdy house in *City of Dreams*. Readers who have read both books will find the echo of that earlier place in this one that is posited to exist over two centuries later.

Did you have any specific promises in mind when you titled this book *City of Promise,* or do you see the title as more of a metaphor for life in New York?

The book was originally to be called *City of Gold,* but the marketing folk at Simon & Schuster thought we were making their lives more difficult by using another 'g' in the title (after *City of Glory* and *City of God*). I don't remember who first suggested the title *City of Promise,* but it was such an obvious and good choice that we adopted it almost immediately. Certainly to this day New York is the nation's City of Promise.

Your bio on your website mentions that you started writing non-fiction at first, and branched out into fiction much later. Why did

you initially gravitate toward nonfiction, and what caused the eventual shift?

That's easy. Nonfiction is a great deal easier to write than fiction. I had to muster my courage.

Where did you live in Europe? Did your time abroad enhance your interest in history and historical fiction?

We have lived extensively in England, France, and Lanzarote in the Canary Islands (belongs to Spain). I have always been a history buff, but Europe certainly whets that appetite to understand.

Your bio on Simon & Schuster's website describes you as an "amateur historian." Did you study history in college? If not, what motivated your foray into history?

I have no professional training in history (I was—no surprise—an English major). But I learned that if you are rigorous in your pursuit of the facts and rely as much as possible on prime sources, you can come up with credible information. That is particularly true in a series based on the growth of New York City. The sources are dizzying in their variety and availability. As I have said before, in the matter of research New York on New York is as good as it gets.

How did you get into the consulting and mentoring side of book publishing? Do you find that working with new writers helps your own craft?

My husband runs Agent Research & Evaluation, Inc., an online business that for fifteen years has been helping writers find the right agent. I sometimes act as a consultant to that business—bringing the writer's point of view—and over the years I've become more and more involved with many of the clients. It's enormously gratifying, particularly when they go on to publication and success. I'm as thrilled as they are.

If you could time-travel to any single historical period in New York City, which era would you visit and why?

Probably the gilded age of *City of Promise*—enough comforts not to be too daunting, and all that wonderful glitz and glamour. I'd like to be at the dinner Thomas Edison gave to introduce the incandescent light bulb, or see President Arthur cut the ribbon to open the Brooklyn Bridge.

"Riotously entertaining...
These private and national escapades play out in a great swirl of plots and counter-plots. . . . Clearly, if Swerling had been my history teacher, I would have paid closer attention."

—Ron Charles, *The Washington Post*

Read more books in Beverly Swerling's critically acclaimed epic saga of New York!

City of Dreams

"A whopping saga . . .
a near perfect historical novel."

—*Los Angeles Times*

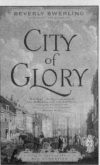

Shadowbrook

"Vividly drawn . . .
A fine and warm-blooded book."

—*San Jose Mercury News*

City of Glory

"Swerling's swashbuckling tale
brings old Manhattan vividly to life."

—*Publishers Weekly*

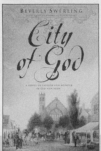

City of God

"Remarkable . . .
characters who seem tangibly real."

—*Pittsburgh Tribune-Review*